THE VICTORIAN MYSTERY SERIES BY ROBIN PAIGE

DEATH AT BISHOP'S KEEP

. . . in which our detectives Kate Ardleigh and Sir Charles Sheridan meet for the first time as they are drawn into a lurid conspiracy . . .

DEATH AT GALLOWS GREEN

. . . in which two mysterious deaths bring Kate and Sir Charles together once more to solve the secrets of Gallows Green . . .

DEATH AT DAISY'S FOLLY

. . . in which Charles and Kate discover that even the highest levels of society are no refuge from the lowest of deeds—such as murder . . .

DEATH AT DEVIL'S BRIDGE

. . . in which newlyweds Charles and Kate Sheridan begin their lives at Bishop's Keep—only to find a new mystery right in their own backyard . . .

MORE PRAISE FOR ROBIN PAIGE'S VICTORIAN MYSTERIES . . .

"I read it with enjoyment . . . I found myself burning for the injustices of it, and caring what happened to the people."

—Anne Perry

"I couldn't put it down."

—*Murder & Mayhem*

"An intriguing mystery . . . Skillfully unraveled."
—Jean Hage, author of *Blooming Murder*

"Absolutely riveting . . . An extremely articulate, genuine mystery, with well-drawn, compelling characters."

—*Meritorious Mysteries*

"An absolutely charming book . . . An adventure worth reading . . . You're sure to enjoy it."

—*Romantic Times*

DEATH
AT
GALLOWS
GREEN

Robin Paige

BERKLEY PRIME CRIME, NEW YORK

THE BERKLEY PUBLISHING GROUP
Published by the Penguin Group
Penguin Group (USA) Inc.
375 Hudson Street, New York, New York 10014, USA
Penguin Group (Canada), 90 Eglinton Avenue East, Suite 700, Toronto, Ontario M4P 2Y3, Canada
(a division of Pearson Penguin Canada Inc.)
Penguin Books Ltd., 80 Strand, London WC2R 0RL, England
Penguin Group Ireland, 25 St. Stephen's Green, Dublin 2, Ireland (a division of Penguin Books Ltd.)
Penguin Group (Australia), 250 Camberwell Road, Camberwell, Victoria 3124, Australia
(a division of Pearson Australia Group Pty. Ltd.)
Penguin Books India Pvt. Ltd., 11 Community Centre, Panchsheel Park, New Delhi—110 017, India
Penguin Group (NZ), 67 Apollo Drive, Rosedale, North Shore 0632, New Zealand
(a division of Pearson New Zealand Ltd.)
Penguin Books (South Africa) (Pty.) Ltd., 24 Sturdee Avenue, Rosebank, Johannesburg 2196,
South Africa

Penguin Books Ltd., Registered Offices: 80 Strand, London WC2R 0RL, England

This is a work of fiction. Names, characters, places, and incidents either are the product of the author's imagination or are used fictitiously, and any resemblance to actual persons, living or dead, business establishments, events, or locales is entirely coincidental. The publisher does not have any control over and does not assume any responsibility for author or third-party websites or their content.

DEATH AT GALLOWS GREEN

A Berkley Prime Crime Book / published by arrangement with the authors

PRINTING HISTORY
Avon Books edition / 1995
Berkley Prime Crime edition / December 1998

Copyright © 1995 by Susan Wittig Albert and William J. Albert.

ISBN: 978-0-425-16399-3

BERKLEY ® PRIME CRIME
PRIME CRIME Books are published by The Berkley Publishing Group,
a division of Penguin Group (USA) Inc.,
375 Hudson Street, New York, New York 10014.
The name BERKLEY PRIME CRIME and the BERKLEY PRIME CRIME design
are trademarks belonging to Penguin Group (USA) Inc.

PRINTED IN THE UNITED STATES OF AMERICA

19   18   17   16   15   14

For Ruby Hild, with our grateful thanks

Susan and Bill

1

"Where shall I begin, please your Majesty?" he asked.

"Begin at the beginning," the King said gravely, "and go on till you come to the end; then stop."
—LEWIS CARROLL
Alice's Adventures in Wonderland

The gentle southern breeze that riffled the fresh green grass of the Essex meadows was mild and fragrant. Both sides of Lamb's Lane were strewn with lacework of celandine and angel eyes and stichwort, and a glossy blackbird showered the hawthorn hedge with his courtship song. Amelia walked with a watchful trepidation, her heart beating as she scanned the hedgerows for a sign of Lawrence. Once or twice, she glanced back in the direction of Mrs. Windell's garden to make sure that none of the members of the Girls' Friendly Society had seen her steal away. It was unlikely that they had, for the group was large and celebratory and Mrs. Windell and the parish ladies were greatly harried by the exigencies of teapot and tea tray.

But the cucumber sandwiches and fresh strawberry tarts on the tables in Mrs. Windell's garden would shortly be eaten and the program would begin. It was to consist of a dramatic reading of "Napoleon at Waterloo" by Mr. Windell, a recitation by the Infants of the National School (dressed for the occasion as fairies, barefoot and with tulle wings stiffened with wire), and several songs by the school's monitress, Miss Flora Watson, among them "Home, Dearie, Home" and "Because," which always made Amelia's sentimental heart melt within her. Sadly, Amelia's errand required her to forgo these delightful entertainments, but the afternoon was short, and she had to be back at Bishop's Keep to help Mrs. Pratt with tea. It was true that her mistress, Miss Ardleigh, was away at a house party near Long Melford, but all the other servants would be there, and Amelia would be missed if she were absent. Mrs. Pratt had allowed her an extra half day to attend the annual garden party given for the young women in service in the parish, and she would be livid if she suspected Amelia of exploiting the occasion for a hole-and-corner rendezvous. So if Amelia were to see Lawrence at all, it would have to be during the program.

Amelia's chestnut hair was thick and shiny, her eyes were cornflower blue, and she was wearing her best dress, a white lawn with a frill of knitted lace pinned at the throat and a narrow flounce at the hem. Lawrence, the handsome, dark-haired footman at neighbouring Marsden Manor, would not be her last lover, but he was her first, and the anticipation of their meeting brought a deeper blush to her already pink cheeks.

"Oh!" she exclaimed, as if surprised and even frightened by the sudden large hands that spanned her slim waist. And then "Oh" again, as the hands whirled her around, and "oh," quite muffled, as Lawrence boldly kissed her, her small hands beating in a pretense of resistance against his broad shoulders.

"Lawrence, you naughty!" she exclaimed, when she was released and could breathe again. "Not in the lane! We'll be spied!"

"We cud go through th' 'edgerow, then," Lawrence suggested with a sly grin, possessing himself of her hand. He pointed. "That's th' back o' Mr. McGregor's garden, below 'is apple trees. Wudn't be spied on there, now wud we?"

Amelia's answer was a rosy giggle, and in another minute the two had slipped through a twiggy gap in the hedge and into the green and silent garden beyond, where after a moment's warm embrace, a flurry of kisses, and more stifled giggles, Lawrence tugged his pretty charmer in the direction of a thickly wooded copse.

"I can't," Amelia said, resisting. "I have t' get back."

"Wot's yer 'urry?" Lawrence asked, teasing her forward a step. "There'll be songs fer an hour." His smile was guileless. "Anyway, we're jes goin' t' sit a minnit er two. Won't 'urt t' bide a bit, will it?"

"We-e-ll," Amelia said slowly, allowing herself to be persuaded in the direction of the copse. Who knows what improprieties Lawrence might have tempted her to, had they not come upon an unexpected huddle of navy serge, deep in a thorny blackberry tangle.

Amelia stepped back, startled. "Who's that?" she exclaimed.

"Dunno," Lawrence said, pushing the burgeoning undergrowth aside and bending over for a better look. "A gypsy, I reckon. Sleepin'. There's a flock of 'em camped in th' field at Bailey's Farm."

"That's no gypsy," Amelia hissed to Lawrence's bent back. "Not in that getup. An' he's not asleep, 'cause his eyes is open. He's drunk." She wrinkled her nose in distaste. "Come away, Lawrence, an' leave th' man be. I don' want him to see us."

Lawrence straightened and turned, grim. " 'Ee's not goin' t' see us," he said. "Not nobody else, neither."

Amelia took a step backward, wondering at the look on Lawrence's face. "Why not?"

" 'Cause 'ee's dead," Lawrence said. "Poor bugger," he added with feeling.

The poor bugger was Sergeant Arthur Oliver of the Essex constabulary, late constable of the hamlet of Gallows Green. He had been shot in the chest at very close range.

2

The house party at a large country estate was one of the most important, if complicated, social rituals of Victorian England. It allowed the guests to participate in gossip, sport, romance, political intrigue, and to display their wealth and power. It was, in short, an essential part of British upper-class life.

—ANNE RILEY RICHARDSON
Social Life in Victorian England

"Bother."

Kate Ardleigh was annoyed. She had wetted her last pair of dry shoes. She paused beside a tall hedgehog holly and glanced through its variegated leaves at the puddled path around the fish pond, up at the gloomy, pewter-coloured sky, and across the park at several lavishly costumed women playing a desultory game of croquet on the lawn before Melford Hall. Sighing, Kate elected to walk round the pond, however muddy the path or drizzly the afternoon. Her shoes were already soaked through, and walking was preferable to the trivial pursuit of a croquet ball or the even more trivial conversation of the players. She started off down the path.

Her walk was interrupted, however, by a rustling scramble in the underbrush, the crackle of twigs, and a duet of shrill squeals and cross mutters. Kate turned, startled.

"Who's there?" she called.

A short, round young woman in a plain green merino dress and sensible boots backed out of the shrubbery, her straw hat knocked askew. An instant later, she was followed by a fat white rabbit, which darted around her skirt and down the path. Quick as thought, Kate reached down and scooped it up. It struggled briefly, scratching and squealing, but she held it, firm, in both hands.

"Is this . . . yours?" Kate asked.

"Indeed he is," said the young woman. She came forward and took the rabbit. Her round face was flushed with exertion, and her brown hair escaped untidily from under her hat. "Peter, you wretched thing," she scolded. "You have disgraced both of us." She tucked the rabbit under one arm with a practiced gesture.

"I'm glad he's been recovered," Kate said, and then wasn't sure what else to say. It was a bit disconcerting to encounter a woman with a rabbit.

"He wanted a walk out, you see," the young woman said. "Only when I put him down, he fancied a bit of fresh cress by the lake. And then he insisted on having it in the very densest part of the shrubbery." She stroked the pink ears. "Rabbits are creatures of very warm temperament," she added. "At one instant Peter is quite amiable, and the next he's a regular demon, kicking and scratching and spluttering. But if I can lay hold of him without being bitten, in half a minute he's licking my hands, utterly contented to be held."

"He seems quite contented now," Kate said, eyeing the rabbit for signs of his becoming demonic. She was intrigued by this plainly dressed, shy-looking woman with soft brown hair and prominent brows, curving like parentheses over the corners of her deep blue eyes. On closer inspection, though, she seemed not as young as Kate had thought, close to Kate's twenty-seven, probably, and also unmarried, for she wore no ring. At that age, and with her demeanour, she was probably the nanny of young William, Lady Hyde-Parker's little boy, and the rabbit belonged to her young charge. But nanny or governess, she was by far the most interesting person Kate had met on this visit.

The house party was Kate's first since arriving in England from America the year before. Her first ever, actually. Before she came to live with her Aunt Sabrina Ardleigh and Aunt Beatrice Jaggers at Bishop's Keep, she had lived in New York, where she had supported herself as a writer of sensational fiction. Under the pseudonym of Beryl Bardwell, her penny dreadfuls (with such titles as *Missing Pearl* and *The Rosicrucian's Ruby*) had attracted quite a following of loyal readers in *Frank Leslie's Popular Monthly*.

But since coming to England as her aunt's secretary seven months ago, Kate had finished only one story, *The Conspiracy of the Golden Scarab*. It was in part a record of the tragic poisonings of both her aunts. Upon their deaths, Kate had inherited Bishop's Keep, which included a holding of several hundred acres, a substantial Georgian house, and a coterie of servants. Since then, her new role as mistress of the manor had left her little time for writing and less time for house parties, even if she had not been in mourning.

But six months had passed since the deaths of Kate's aunts and she was beginning to feel comfortable in her new duties. Her friend and neighbour Eleanor Marsden, recently married to Mr. Ernest Fairley, had insisted that she be out and about and see something of England. At Eleanor's suggestion, Lady Hyde-Parker of Melford Hall had invited Kate to spend a week at the Hyde-Parker estate near Sudbury, in Suffolk. Kate had accepted the invitation gladly, not only because she looked forward to a week's refreshing respite in a lovely English country house, but also because she wanted to be writing again. ("Please, dear lady," the editor of *Frank Leslie's Popular Monthly* had pleaded in his last letter, "do, *do* oblige your readers with another tale of Death and Passion.") Kate had hoped that Melford Hall might be the place to collect ideas for Beryl Bardwell's next thrilling narrative.

But sadly, Kate had discovered that the most sensational events at Medford Hall had taken place several hundred years before. The mid-Tudor residence was grandly constructed of two wings of mellow red brick enclosing a grassy courtyard, with matching octagonal turrets fore and aft. Melford's builder had been William Cordell, Speaker of the House of Commons and Master of the Rolls under Elizabeth I, and in 1578, Cordell entertained his queen and two thousand of her retainers in the Great Hall. From the Cordells the estate passed to the family of Lord Rivers, a Catholic Royalist. In 1642 the rabble sacked the house, destroyed its furnishings, and made off with all the deer in the park. Lady Rivers was remanded to debtors' prison and died within the month.

Contemporary Melford bore little visible trace of its dramatic history. There was the stained glass portrait of Elizabeth, dressed in blue and gold for the Service of Thanksgiving that commemorated her victory over the Spanish Armada, and a rather nondescript oil of the ill-fated Lady Rivers, both located in the East Gallery. But Melford's present owners, the Hyde-Parkers, seemed serenely unconnected to the cataclysms of past centuries. The grand old house, impressive as it was, did not even harbour a ghost, although Kate had heard rumours of a medieval vaulted chamber beneath the Banquet Hall, which she had hoped to visit until she learned that it was walled up after the house was built.

There was very little of the sensational about the guest list, either, since the socially ambitious still lingered in London, taking advantage of the last month of the season. The Hyde-Parkers, however, were secure enough in the social elite not to care about missing a few last parties, and Lady Hyde-Parker, who loved to garden, always indulged herself with long stays in the country even at the height of the season. Her guests for the week included several Hyde-Parker relatives and their children, mostly kept out of sight on the nursery floor or in the back garden; two young women who had not gotten husbands in the requisite three seasons since being "out" and were hence considered failures; one dour dowager swathed in black shawls; and a white-haired military gentleman who kept putting snuff up his nose. Kate's days had been spent in dressing for and then sitting down to breakfast, lunch, and tea, with croquet and a ramble around the pond as a respite. Her evenings were filled with dressing for dinner, then dining and playing whist as the conversation revolved around people and events of which Kate knew nothing. She was unutterably bored.

But the weekend promised improvement. Eleanor Marsden Fairley and her husband were due to arrive shortly from London. And here was this odd little governess or nanny, or whatever she was, pressing a white rabbit to her neat green bosom and offering a lecture on the creature's life-habits.

"Thank you for snatching him up so quickly," the odd person said. "Most wouldn't, you know. They don't much care for rabbits, except in rabbit pie." She shuddered.

Kate smiled. "But you do care?"

"Oh, yes, particularly about Peter, and Benjamin too, of course." She gathered her skirts with her free hand. "Well, now that I've got him again, I expect I'd better go. Mrs. Tiggy-Winkle has to be let out, and there's no end of unpacking."

Kate wondered who Mrs. Tiggy-Winkle was and why she might be confined. Was she some incompetent relative, some *mad* person, perhaps? Kate had read of many such tragic women, who upon exhibiting symptoms of madness (or perhaps merely the wish to choose the course of their lives for themselves) were kept close confined for years upon end, able to see no one. Kate's human sympathy—and Beryl Bardwell's authorial interest—suddenly were invoked. But there was a limit to what one might decently ask. The standards of politeness did not permit her to probe the state of Mrs. Tiggy-Winkle's mental health.

"You have recently arrived, then?" Kate inquired.

"Oh, yes, just," the woman said eagerly. "On the railroad. I came alone." In her voice Kate heard an unmistakable note of triumphant delight. Why should anyone take such satisfaction in traveling on the railway, which to Kate seemed a noisy, dirty business? That she had traveled alone seemed to suggest that Mrs. Tiggy-Winkle was already here, perhaps *lived* here, was perhaps some mad relation of Kate's host and hostess. Beryl Bardwell immediately imagined the poor lady in the garret, let out only when someone was available for close supervision. Perhaps the rabbit belonged to the mad woman.

"I'm sorry," Kate said. "I don't believe I quite got your name. Mine is Kate Ardleigh."

"You're an American, aren't you?"

Kate smiled. "I suppose my speech gives it away."

"How interesting you Americans are," the other woman remarked, "announcing your given name straight away, without bothering with misses and misters and all that stuff and nonsense."

"I suppose we do," Kate said, warming to the woman's candour. "It seems easier that way, and friendlier. What's your name?"

"Bea," the woman said shyly, almost as if she were experimenting with it.

"Will I see you at tea?" Kate asked, and then regretted her thoughtless question. Bea would no doubt be busy with her ward. Anyway, staff did not come to tea. "Or perhaps we could walk together," she added hurriedly. "At your convenience, of course."

"I'd like that," Bea said happily.

"Tomorrow afternoon at this same time, then?" And as Bea nodded, Beryl Bardwell felt a surge of anticipation. The mysterious Bea was an interesting character in her own right. And perhaps through her, Beryl could meet the madwoman in the attic!

3

... To die, to sleep;
To sleep: perchance to dream: aye, there's the
    rub;
For in that sleep of death what dreams may
    come
When we have shuffled off this mortal coil,
Must give us pause.
                    —WILLIAM SHAKESPEARE
                    Hamlet, III, i

Police Constable Edward Laken stood at the foot of McGregor's garden, his hands in his pockets, staring bleakly down at the cold, still form of his friend and colleague, Sergeant Arthur Oliver.

"Dead," said Lawrence, the footman at Marsden Manor, who had discovered the body and summoned Edward. "Shot, it happears," he added unnecessarily.

It did indeed appear that Arthur Oliver had been shot, and a great grief welled up in Edward Laken. He and Artie had been boys together, fishing in the River Stour, padding the dusty lanes in search of birds' nests and berry bushes, skating on the thin ice of Bailey's Pond and once, even, falling through. He might have drowned that winter afternoon if Artie had not crawled out and pulled him to safety with a willow branch. A passage from *Hamlet* came into his mind, a passage he had once got by heart, playing Hamlet to Artie's Laertes in a parish theatrical. And now Artie lay on his side in a bramble thicket, eyes open, staring upward in the sleep of death, dreaming who knew what dreams, the navy serge of his uniform jacket thickly matted with cold dark blood.

With an effort, Edward pulled his gaze from the dead eyes and looked up. McGregor, whose garden this was, served as an assistant gamekeeper on the Marsden estate. His cottage was some distance away, beyond the apple trees. The garden was deep, and backed up to Lamb's Lane. He looked back at the footman. "How was it that you happened to come here?"

Lawrence spoke carelessly, but avoided Edward's eyes. "T'were a young lady, sir. We come 'ere fer a bit o' privacy, you might say. Through th' gap in th' 'edge." He became defiant. "I'll take my affidavy it's th' truth."

Edward pulled out his notebook. "The young lady's name?"

Lawrence looked up, eyes wide, and his tone suddenly changed. "Oh, no, sir, please, sir. I promised. Mrs. Pratt 'ud be most ferocious to 'er." He stopped, conscious that he had said too much.

Edward knew the servants at Bishop's Keep, for he had interviewed them all six months before, upon the deaths of the elder Miss Ardleigh and her sister Mrs. Jaggers. He had been there several times since, and he knew Mrs. Pratt. He did not need to wonder which of the servants had been the object of Lawrence's attention and his accessory in this discovery.

"Amelia, I suppose," he said.

Lawrence sighed, resigned.

"I'll be as circumspect as possible in my inquiry," Edward said. He looked once more at the huddled figure of his friend. "You saw no one?"

"No one but 'im," Lawrence said. He too turned away from the dead gaze. "D'you suppose it's true?"

"What's true?" Edward asked.

"That th' dead takes a pitchur o' th' last thing they see wit' their open eyes. If 'tis, mayhap 'ee's took a pitchur o' th' one 'oo kilt 'im.''

"Mayhap," Edward said. Gently, he bent down and closed the eyelids of Sergeant Arthur Oliver. Let him dream in peace.

4

Although the camera was used from the mid-1880s to record the features of known criminals for the purpose of identification, it was not systematically employed to document a criminal investigation until much later. In the late nineteenth century, a crime scene was photographed only when an amateur photographer happened upon some criminal event, or when one was summoned by an astute constable who recognized the great utility of such permanent evidence. Few police forces officially possessed a camera.

—DANIEL TRIMBLE
Early Forensic Photography

Sir Charles Sheridan, a leather case in one hand and a wooden tripod over his shoulder, strode down the path in the anxious wake of Mrs. McGregor, who churned like a fervent little tugboat against a surging current. She stopped when they reached the foot of the garden, so unexpectedly that Charles bumped into her.

"Oh dear oh dear oh dear," Mrs. McGregor said, twisting one corner of her white apron. "I'm sure I don't know wot Mr. McGregor'll say when he finds that murder's been done in th' back garden. He'll be that put out, he will. That's where he allus sets his rabbit snares."

"I doubt," Charles said, "that this event is likely to affect the rabbit population." He set the case down and extended a hand to Laken, while Mrs. McGregor stood behind, her eyes averted from the body. "I came as soon as I got your message, Ned. I'm very sorry. Artie was more your friend than mine, but I remember him with great affection."

It had been over twenty years since those halcyon days when Charles had spent summers in East Bergholt, just on the other side of the River Stour, visiting his mother's family, the Constables. But he had forgotten neither Artie nor Ned. They had been comrades in grand misadventure from the mill at Dedham to the tidal flats at Mistley and beyond.

"He was a good friend to both of us," Edward said. The grief was written on his narrow face. "Thank you for coming, Charlie. I thought two pairs of eyes would be better than one."

Charles positioned the tripod. "And here's another eye, which won't forget anything it sees." He opened the leather case, unfolded a camera, and fastened it onto the tripod. He had acquired the compact, portable bellows camera in France just a month before. It was the most recent addition to the growing collection of cameras he kept in his London house.

"You'll be at Marsden Manor for a few days?" Edward asked, as Charles draped a black camera cloth over his head.

"For an indefinite period," Charles said. He peered into the ground glass viewing screen at the back of the camera, adjusting the rack and pinion that operated the helical lens to focus the inverted image of Artie's body, lying on its left side, the neat round hole and matted blood quite evident on the uniform jacket.

" 'xcuse me, Sir Charles."

Charles pulled his head out and whirled around, noticing for the first time that Edward was not alone. "Lawrence? What the devil are *you* doing here?"

Lawrence ducked his head. "Well, sir," he began, "y'see, sir—"

"He and a young lady companion discovered the body," Edward put in.

"A young lady?" Mrs. McGregor cried shrilly. She stamped her foot. "F'r shame! Wot Mr. McGregor'll say t' such wild gooin's-on in the garden, I don't know."

Lawrence fairly bristled with indignation. "There warn't no wild goin's-on." He turned to Charles. " 'Pon my life, sir! 'Twas innocent. I swear!"

"You're acquainted with Lawrence?" Edward asked, frowning. Then, "Of course. He's employed at Marsden Manor."

"He is my valet," Charles said. "My acting valet, that is." His man had given him notice only a fortnight before, and when he arrived for an extended visit at the manor Lady Marsden had insisted upon supplying him with Lawrence. Charles turned back to the body. "I suppose the primary question is whether Artie was shot here or someplace else."

"Just so," Edward agreed. "The ground is dry here, and there's a great deal of bramble. No chance of footprints." He turned to Mrs. McGregor. "Did you hear a gunshot in the last twenty-four hours?"

"Gunshot?" Mrs. McGregor was wry. "Ooh, aye, there be many a gunshot 'round here. Mr. McGregor's one o' th' gamekeepers at Marsden Manor, y'see. He's allus about wi' his gun, day an' night, he is. I say t' him, 'Mr. McGregor,' says I, 'd'you niver think t' lay doon yer gun an' hang up y'r billycock an' be done wi' gamekeepin'?' An' he says to me, 'Niver,' Mrs. McGregor,' he says, 'as long as I has me two gud eyes.' There be that many weasels and other varmints hereabouts, y'see. Th' gamekeeper must keep th' game safe."

Charles smiled a little. He himself had never been a hunter, and felt it a deep irony that the game was preserved from its natural predators at great effort and expense, only to be slaughtered by the thousands during a hunt. He and Edward exchanged glances.

"When can we see Mr. McGregor?" Edward asked.

"When he's t'home," Mrs. McGregor said.

"This evening?" Edward inquired.

"Cert'nly. The pore man's got t' have his tea, now, don't he?" She shook her head mournfully, still twisting her apron.

"Although how I'm to make it f'r him, I don't know, be-twattled as I am 'bout dead men an' young ladies an' wild gooin's-on in th' garden."

"Tell your husband we'll stop 'round at teatime," Edward said. "Thank you, Mrs. McGregor. You may go." He turned to Lawrence. "You, too, Lawrence."

"You'll remember?" Lawrence asked. He looked warily at Charles. " 'Bout Mrs. Pratt, I mean."

"I'll remember," Edward promised. Lawrence sketched a bow to Charles and made swiftly for the gap in the hedge.

About to return to his camera, Charles stopped. "Mrs. Pratt? The housekeeper at Bishop's Keep?"

Bishop's Keep was familiar to Charles as the home of Kate Ardleigh. He had met the young woman upon her arrival in England and had been quite taken by her, especially by the way she had dealt with her aunts' deaths. She had, in fact, quite surprised him with her courage and common sense. They had seen one another several times since, and he had begun to think that something might come of their acquaintance.

"Yes," Edward said. "When Lawrence discovered the body, a maid from Bishop's Keep was with him. Can you make a close shot of the chest, Charlie?"

Charles pulled the hood over his head and set to work again. When the camera's focus satisfied him, he inserted the plate-holder and snapped the shutter. "From the look of things, I don't believe he was shot here," he said, emerging from under the cloth. "What do you think?"

"Doesn't seem so to me, either," Edward said, bending down and putting a finger to the bloodstain on the dead man's chest. "There's grassy debris in the congealed blood, as if he died face down. And yet he was found in this position, lying on his side. There's no blood on the ground beneath or around him, either, although there should have been, if he died here."

"Are those grass seeds in the blood?" Charles asked.

Edward straightened up. "See for yourself."

Charles took a folding lens out of one of the pockets of his bulky coat and knelt beside the body. After a moment's close inspection of the wound, he took out a penknife and a small square of oiled paper and scraped a sample of debris from the bloody jacket onto the paper. He folded it carefully and put it into another pocket.

"From the size of the entry wound," he said, "the weapon appears to have been of rather large calibre. Not likely a rifle, though, since there's no exit wound. Most probably a pistol." He stood up. "Shot in the heart, it seems."

"If he wasn't killed here," Edward said, "he must have been dragged through that gap in the hedge. That's Lamb's Lane on the other side."

Charles pocketed his penknife, followed Edward to the hedge, and studied the ground carefully. The soil was packed and hard and there were no footprints. But there were indications that something had been dragged through the gap. And on a twig at the height of his elbow, he found something interesting: a triangular flag of faded red cloth about the size of his thumbnail. He repositioned the camera, photographed the cloth, then retrieved it carefully. It went into another piece of oiled paper. "May I take this and the scrapings?" he asked. "You'll get them back."

Edward nodded. "You're thinking the killer left this scrap behind?"

"Lawrence was wearing a blue jacket," Charles remarked thoughtfully. "What colour dress was his companion wearing?"

"I'll find out." Edward jotted something in his notebook. He looked up as a cart, pulled by a brown horse and driven by two uniformed policemen, came to a stop in the lane. "The chaps from Colchester," he said bleakly, "are here for the body." Charles began to repack his gear. "I'd appreciate a copy of the surgeon's notes," he said.

"I'll see what I can do." Edward put away his notebook. "Would you mind coming with me?"

"To Bishop's Keep?"

Edward's face was grim. "To Gallows Green. Artie's widow has yet to be told."

5

Once upon a time there was a very beautiful doll's house; it was red brick with white windows, and it had real muslin curtains and a front door and a chimney.

—BEATRIX POTTER
The Tale of Two Bad Mice

Betsy sat in the corner between the coal box and the fire, her back turned toward the room, her collie dog, Kep, asleep on the floor beside her. In front of her was the doll house. It was two stories and its wooden front and sides were painted to look like red brick, with windows painted on and two clever balconies, a front door that really opened, and a chimney. It had been made for her by her father, and her mother had made the curtains out of scraps from her sewing box and had knitted the parlour rug of the wool left from Betsy's Christmas mittens. Auntie Mabel, who was in service to a great lady in Brighton and earned pots of money and got a new dress every Boxing Day, had sent her a table and chairs, a bed and a sofa, and a little wooden box full of shavings that also contained two red lobsters, a ham, a fish, a pudding, and some pears and oranges that would not come off the plates but made the dining table look utterly splendid. Taken all in all, the dollhouse was much grander than any real home in the entire hamlet of Gallows Green. Betsy, who was not a domestic child nor given to dolls, loved it, not least because she had watched her father make it, and he had permitted her to paint the tiny bricks, as well as the white roses that twined over the front door.

Into this admiring reverie, her mother's voice intruded. "Betsy, Betsy, where are you?"

Kep raised his head. Betsy gravely considered the question. She was probably wanted to run an errand, perhaps to the grocer, to get some starch for Father's shirts. Last time, her mother had given her threepence for a pack of Robin's Starch, and an extra ha'penny for an ounce of Fairley's chocolate drops to be shared with her dolls, Lucinda and Jane. Of course, Lucinda and Jane had the lobsters, a fish, and a ham, not to mention fruit and a pudding. So Betsy had eaten the chocolate drops, all except one, which she shared with Kep. She thought of offering one to Jemima, her pet duck, but did not, for fear that chocolate might not be good for Jemima's digestion.

"Betsy?" her mother called again, louder now. There was an odd note of urgency in her summons.

Betsy shoved Lucinda and Jane into their bedroom, although it was much too late in the day for naps, and pushed the doll house against the wall. Perhaps she would not get chocolate drops, after all, but humbugs, striped, and flavoured with peppermint. She mentally counted the pence knotted in a bit of cloth behind the loose skirting board in her corner of the loft. Or perhaps she would forgo the humbugs and apply the ha'penny to the hoop she coveted, an iron one with a proper stick with a nail in it, like her friend Baxter's. Girls had wooden hoops, and bowled them with hedgesticks or their hands. Betsy coveted an iron one with a *real* stick.

"Betsy!"

Betsy got up and went into the kitchen, Kep trailing behind her. The kitchen was her favourite place to be, if you didn't count the shed, where her father made things of wood and mended broken crockery and whistled while he sharpened his gardening tools. There were such wonderful things hung on the shed's walls—rakes and hoes and shovels and saws and ropes and pulleys and even a shiny galvanized watering can. It was also where Jemima Puddleduck spent the night with

Mr. Browne, whom Betsy had rescued as a tiny owlet from Mrs. Wilkins's fierce gray tabby.

But the kitchen was where her mother reigned, like the Queen (but ever so much younger and prettier, of course) over her empire. With its fresh-painted walls and bright hearth rug, the cheerful coal fire in the stove that had been set into the old fireplace, and the even more cheerful-scented pelargoniums blooming at the casement window, flung open now to catch the May breeze—the kitchen was a palace to Betsy. She scarcely noticed that the ceiling was so low her father had to stoop, or the table so tiny that the three of them sat elbow-to-elbow at their meals. For always at one end of the table was her mother, cheeks shining, and at the other end her father, beard combed and eyes twinkling, and she in the middle, with Kep under her bare feet, and Jemima making small quacks outside the door, and sleepy Mr. Browne nodding on his perch in the shed. No matter that the flagstone floor was cold and damp, or that the eaves were low or the roof merely thatched. To Betsy it was better than Buckingham Palace.

Her mother was in the kitchen now, sitting beside the scrubbed wooden table. To Betsy's surprise, two men were with her, both standing. One, whom she didn't recognize, was very tall and lean, as tall as her father, with brown eyes like Fairley's chocolate drops and hair and beard the exact colour of her father's tobacco. He was wearing a heavy khaki coat with dozens of pockets, and every one of them filled, to judge from the interesting lumps and bulges. The other man was short and slender, with sandy hair and a round, ruddy face and a uniform like her father's, its navy serge brushed and its buttons polished like the lucky gold sovereign her father wore on his watch chain, which he sometimes let her hold when she had a stomachache.

"Hello, Uncle Ned," she said. She frowned a little. His gray eyes were not smiling, as they usually did. His brows were pulled together and his face troubled. Her mother's mouth, too, was set. She was pinching her lips together, and her eyes had a queer look.

Uncle Ned squatted down in front of her. "I find, Betsy,

that I am in need of tobacco for my pipe.'' He opened his palm and held out three threepenny bits. "Would you be so kind as to run to the green grocer and get me fourpence worth? You may use what is left to buy a sweet for yourself.''

Betsy did a quick bit of mental arithmetic. She would have fivepence left! With that and the coins in the bit of cloth, she could buy the hoop! Betsy looked to her mother for confirmation and got a quick, hard nod of the head. Still, she did not move. Something was wrong, she knew it. Kep knew it too, with the unerring sense that dogs have for things gone wrong. She could feel him crowding close against her, quivering. She swallowed.

"Must I go just now?" she asked her mother. "I want to stay and—''

"Betsy," her mother said, in a strange, tight voice. "Betsy, your father—''

The very tall man stepped forward. "Let me introduce myself, Miss Oliver," he said with great courtesy. "My name is Sir Charles Sheridan.''

Betsy narrowed her eyes, forgetting for the moment her uneasiness. She had never before been personally introduced to a "sir," although she saw the Gentry every week, riding helter-skelter down the High Street on skittish horses, brandishing riding crops, and shouting arrogantly at the villagers who got in their way. She herself had often been pinned against the churchyard wall by the horses. She had no admiration for gentry.

"How fortunate that you are going to the green grocer's," Sir Charles remarked. "Your errand reminds me that I meant to buy a button for my coat." He bent over and showed her his sleeve, from which indeed a button was missing. "If you will permit me, Miss Oliver, I will accompany you to the grocer's. There, perhaps you would be so kind as to inquire after a proper button for me.''

Betsy sighed. Really, these Gentry. Why they couldn't take care of themselves instead of always depending on other people to do it for them—

She looked up just in time to glimpse the unmistakably

grateful look Uncle Ned gave to Sir Charles, and the naked loss in her mother's tear-filled eyes. Her heart stopped, and she forgot all about her hoop and the proper button for Sir Charles's coat.

6

Riddle me, riddle me, rot-tot-tote!
   A little wee man, in a red red coat!
A staff in his hand, and a stone in his throat;
   If you'll tell me this riddle, I'll give you a
groat.

—BEATRIX POTTER
The Tale of Squirrel Nutkin

The McGregors' cottage was painted a faded pink and heavily thatched, with yarrow growing against the wall, and lavender and rosemary blooming, and roses climbing in great masses over the brick wall. On the stoop in front of the door sat a pair of muddy boots, heavily hobnailed and with a patch on one instep, and beside the door, leaning against the plaster wall, was a stout staff. McGregor, Charles deduced, was at home.

The door stood ajar, as most cottage doors did when the weather was fine, and Edward Laken raised his hand to it. When he had knocked twice, Mrs. McGregor opened it wide.

"I tol' ye," she said with asperity, as if the affair in the back garden had been their fault. "He's that put out." She lowered her voice. "An' mind wot ye say t'him. He's a ogre when he's crossed." She stepped back and allowed them to enter the flagstoned passage, at one side of which ascended an uncarpeted stair. On the other was a small, neat sitting room with a woven rush mat on the stone floor. Behind that was the kitchen, where the redoubtable McGregor, an undersized, ferret-faced man with thick eyebrows and a surly mouth half-hidden in wire whiskers, sat with both elbows on the table, devouring a thick slice of crusty bread and cheese.

"Good even' to you, sir," Edward said.

McGregor grunted, reached for a china mug, and swallowed a mouthful of tea.

"About this business in the garden," Edward began.

"Don't know nothin' 'bout it." McGregor's voice was rough and gravelly. He wiped his mouth with his sleeve. "Cheese, Tildy."

Mrs. McGregor fetched cheese from a shelf and sliced it. Edward said, "We're curious about your gun."

"Shu'n't wonder," McGregor said shortly. "There 'tis." He gestured with his head. Charles turned to look. A shotgun was leaning against the wall beside the window.

"Is that your only gun?" Edward asked.

McGregor's "Sart'nly" was emphatic. " 'Tis all I need f'r varmints 'n' such-like."

Mrs. McGregor paused in her slicing. "Don't fergit Tommy's pistols," she offered. "Tommy's me brother," she added helpfully to Edward. "We bin keepin' 'em f'r him."

Mr. McGregor said nothing, but his look was thunderous. Mrs. McGregor flinched and bit her lip, and fumbled the cheese hurriedly onto her husband's plate.

"Where are the pistols?" Edward asked. When Mr. Mc-Gregor did not speak, his face hardened. "I warn you, McGregor. This is a very serious matter. A constable was found dead at the foot of your garden. I have every right to assume that you know something about his murder." His tone became flint. "Fetch those pistols."

With a venomous look at his wife, McGregor pushed back his chair and got up. Standing, he proved dwarfish, shorter by half a head than Mrs. McGregor, and stooped. He went to a corner cupboard that housed dishes and crockery, a mortar and pestle and several tarnished brass candlesticks, and took from the top shelf a worn leather case, brass-trimmed, with a brass lock. He slapped the case on the table, fished a key out of a cup, and unlocked it.

"Yer so cunnin'-like," he said sourly, sitting down again to his tea, "ye c'n look f'r yerself."

Charles watched as Edward opened the case. It was lined with threadbare blue velvet and contained space for two large pistols. Only one—a silver-plated dueling pistol, a muzzle-loader—was in the case. Charles glanced at Mrs. McGregor, whose wrinkled face was deeply perplexed.

"Where's the other pistol?" Edward asked.

"Gone," said McGregor. "Sold."

The perplexity on Mrs. McGregor's face changed to indignation and her cheeks grew red.

Edward closed the case. "When?"

"Afore Easter." McGregor's eyes slid to his wife. Some of the surliness went out of his mouth, and was replaced by defiance. "Well, I needed the money, din't I, Tildy?"

"T'wern't yourn t'sell, Mr. McGregor," she said stonily. "T'were Tommy's. Wot am I t' tell him when he comes fer his guns? Tell him you sold one o'em? An' wot's he gooin' t' say t' that?"

"To whom did you sell it?" Edward asked.

The woolly eyebrows made a deep *V*, and the mouth went surly again. "T' a navvy," McGregor growled. "Passin' through. Give me a gold suv'rin, he did."

"A suv'rin!" Mrs. McGregor gasped. "Why, I niver thought 'twere worth—"

"If you sold it for a sovereign, you were cheated," Charles remarked. "One of these guns is worth twice that." He pointed to a pile of red cloth heaped on a workbasket beside the fire. "Is that your coat?"

McGregor's scowl deepened. "Wot if it be?"

Charles picked it up. The coat was old and heavily worn, the red colour faded. On the right sleeve, near the shoulder, a thumbnail-size triangular piece was missing. It was this fresh-looking rip that Mrs. McGregor was apparently patching, for a small piece of cloth, of a different weight and shade of red, was being appliqued over it, like a triangular badge.

"How did you come to rip your coat?" he asked.

"How should I know?" McGregor growled. "One day 'twas whole, next 'twas ripped."

Edward put the pistol case under his arm. "I'm taking this with me," he said. He looked at Mrs. McGregor. "You will have it again in due course," he added, not unkindly.

"And the coat," Charles said, picking it up.

"Wot's a man t'wear?" McGregor was stormy. "How's a man t' keep th' rain off while th' bloody coppers has got his coat, is wot I wants t' know."

"What I want to know," Edward said sternly, "is whether you've seen anything unusual going on in the neighbourhood. Have there been any suspicious goings-on?"

McGregor shrugged. "Allus somethin' gooin' on, suspicious-like. Allus sheep goin' missin'—"

"Sheep?" Charles asked. "Whose sheep?"

"Just sheep," McGregor said vaguely. "An' harses. Jarge Styles lost his grey, din't he?"

"That was two years ago," Edward said.

"Happen Jarge Styles still's lookin' f'r it, i'n't he?" McGregor retorted with a snaggle-toothed grin. "Allus somethin' gooin' on, I say. If ye don't wanter know, don't ask."

Edward took the coat from Charles. "We may have occasion to ask you for additional information."

McGregor sat down and applied himself once more to his tea. "No mind o' me," he said with a careless shrug. "Ye'll git a groatsworth an' no more."

7

The housekeeper must consider herself as the immediate representative of her mistress, and bring, to the management of the household, all those qualities of honesty, industry, and vigilance, in the same degree as if she were at the head of *her own* family. Constantly on the watch to detect any wrong-doing on the part of any of the domestics, she will oversee all that goes on in the house.

—*Mrs. Beeton's Book of*
Household Management, 1888

"Hurry along, now, Harriet," Sarah Pratt said firmly, "an' don't dawdle. Time's a-wastin'." Tea was over, and there was the washing up to do and the kitchen to tidy and ready for breakfast. While Miss Ardleigh was gone to Melford Hall to her house-party, breakfast at Bishop's Keep was not the formal affair it was when she was at home. But it would not do to let things slide.

Mrs. Pratt surveyed the newly appointed hall where the servants took their meals. While she still mourned the death of the elder Miss Ardleigh, she could say without fear of contradiction that the demise of Jaggers (the younger of the two Ardleigh sisters) had occasioned a great change in the management of the household. Now that the young miss was in command, with herself, Sarah Pratt, at the helm, so to speak, the ship sailed along ever so smoothly. Her gaze lingered on the sofa that had been brought down from the attic. And ever so comfortably, too. No more sugarless tea for the servants, and that made from sweepings, the poorest to be had. No more stale buns, either, but fresh buns with raisins, and she'd been given back the drippings to sell for her profit, as was her right. No penny-pincher, was the young miss! She had begun on good bottom, as the unfortunate Mr. Pratt would have said, and she was carrying on that way.

There was in Mrs. Pratt's otherwise quite high esteem of her employer, however, one niggling apprehension. It was not that she was actually doing anything wrong, of course. The difficulty was that she held certain unconventional views as to the propriety of certain behaviours. She undoubtedly held these views because she was an American and not properly brought up, no disrespect intended. However the habit had arisen, Mrs. Pratt had to say that the young miss did not sufficiently concern herself with what other people thought. In particular, she did not worry about setting an example for the servants.

And that was the pickle in which Mrs. Pratt found herself. Among other things, Miss Ardleigh was in the habit of riding a bicycle in the evening. On a *Sunday* evening, while everyone else was at Evensong, and with Constable Laken, alone! In the minds of villagers, (Mrs. Pratt heard this regularly from her sister Rose), Miss Ardleigh and the constable were a "friendly" couple. If Miss Ardleigh did not intend to marry the man, she was running the risk, the very *definite* risk, of appearing fast. And if she *did* intend to marry him . . . Well, while Mrs. Pratt had every respect for the constable, the match was not appropriate to Miss Ardleigh's station. In her opinion, the young Marsden heir—Bradford Marsden—was a far better choice. Not necessarily a better man, mind you, for the constable had a kind nature and was liked by all, while the future Baron Marsden was something of a rake. But still, one was aware of the social realities, even from the kitchen. And it would present no end of difficulty if Miss Ardleigh were really to prefer the constable.

Not that any of this was Mrs. Pratt's business, of course; she was not a dragon of propriety. But what *was* her business was the discipline of the servants. And how was she to maintain a proper discipline, she'd like to know, if the mistress went riding with the constable, alone and unchaperoned, until nearly dark? The servants, who knew as well as Mrs. Pratt what was going on, wouldn't stick at using such behaviour to excuse their own misdemeanours. If they used the mistress as a model of behaviour, who knew what kinds of cutting-up they might get into?

Mrs. Pratt's concern might not have been so acute if it were not for the fact that two of the servants—the coachman Pocket and Amelia, lady's maid to Miss Ardleigh—were at a vulnerable age. To complicate matters, Amelia was Mrs. Pratt's niece, her only sister's second daughter. And Mrs. Pratt's worry was not without foundation. Amelia had come in that afternoon, her face flushed, the flounce on her skirt torn, her shoes dirty. She had washed up, helped with tea, and said scarce a word, keeping her eyes on her work the whole while.

By itself, this behaviour might not seem of great consequence. But Amelia was not the first of Mrs. Pratt's nieces to have been in service at Bishop's Keep, and therein was the genesis of Mrs. Pratt's uneasiness. Amelia's sister, Jenny, had been a parlour maid. Remembering Jenny, Mrs. Pratt's lips pinched together and she shivered. Jenny had been a foolish girl, and pretty, but not half so pretty as her younger sister. Her foolishness was in the way of bearing sad fruit when the situation came to the notice of Jaggers, who turned her out. Six months later, the Chelmsford constable had come bearing a little bundle of clothes. Jenny had died in the workhouse there, she and the babe with her. It had been a bitter, bitter thing, for Mrs. Pratt had felt in her soul that she was responsible for Jenny's misconduct. And now there was Amelia, who seemed to be following along the dangerous path of her sister, slipping and sliding to certain ruin.

It was in this preoccupied state of mind that Mrs. Pratt finished clearing the dishes onto a large tray, including the pink-and-white pie dish from which the household staff had eaten every crumb of a fine steak-and-kidney pie, and carried the

tray to the kitchen, where she poured hot water from the kettle
into the basin and began the washing-up. While she did so,
Harriet the scullery tidied the table, swept the floor, mended
the fire, and brought in a scuttle of coal, pausing at the last to
fill the large china teapot with boiling water for Mrs. Pratt's
after-dinner cup.

Mrs. Pratt was polishing the last dish when Mudd came in
and poured himself a cup of tea. "Shall ye 'ave a cup too,
Mrs. P?" he inquired. There was a more-than-usually-thought-
ful look on his thin face. Mudd was only twenty-six, too young
to be a proper butler, and had been until year before last a
London footman. Mrs. Pratt would have given a good deal to
know why he had taken a place in the country, away from the
enticements of city living, but so he had, and he had done
modestly well. He was uncommonly intelligent, able to speak
both the upstairs and downstairs dialects (an unusual ability
that he used to clear advantage with both servants and masters), and rather more conscientious than most servants. Mrs.
Pratt saw in him a clear promise, if he could keep his mind
on learning to butler and cease fancying himself quite the
dandy.

"I b'lieve so, Mudd, thank ye." Mrs. Pratt took off her
apron and shook it, then put it back on again, clean side out.

As she took her mug of tea and sat down by the fire, Mudd
caught her eye and nodded significantly at Harriet, who was
hanging up the pots. Mrs. Pratt took his meaning and nodded
back.

"That'll be all fer t'night, lass," she said. "Tomorrow'll be
fish, if Willie Hogglestock has a decent plaice in his cart, an'
you shall cook it." Upon Jaggers's demise, Mrs. Pratt had
been promoted from cook to housekeeper. She still carried out
most of the cooking duties, but Harriet (although young) was
in training for the place. Whenever possible, Mrs. Pratt gave
the girl the opportunity to exercise responsibility.

Harriet's face glowed. "Thank you, Mrs. Pratt." She swallowed, then emboldened herself. "May I . . . may I take a candle? I 'ud like t' read."

Mrs. Pratt's hesitation had more to do with the reading than
the candle, for Jaggers's passionate injunctions against novels

still echoed in her ears as loudly as did the injunction against an open flame in the servants's sleeping quarters. It did seem to Mrs. Pratt that what was printed these days was mostly trash, full of murders and thieving and illicit affairs, not morally fit for a young girl.

But Miss Ardleigh had quite a different attitude. She had instituted daily periods of reading aloud for Harriet and the tweeny, Nettie. They had begun with the newspaper, but the young miss, for Christmas, had given each of them a book: to Nettie a copy of *Little Women*, and to Harriet *Jo's Boys*, both by an American woman named Alcott. Nettie had little interest in her book and soon laid it down. But Harriet (Mrs. Pratt knew) stole a few minutes daily to pursue hers. She had finished it some weeks ago and was now reading Nettie's.

Mudd settled himself by the fire. "Let 'er take hit," he said, in the strong native Cockney he used on the servants' side of the green baize door. "Won't 'urt 'er, I warrant." He twinkled up at Harriet, for whom he was known to have a brotherly softness. "So long's ye don't burn th' bloody 'ouse down," he added.

Mrs. Pratt nodded, although with reluctance. The matter of novel reading had become quite vexed since Amelia's discovery, in the young miss's room, of a sheaf of typed pages. It appeared to be a story that Miss Ardleigh was in the process of *writing*. Amelia had spoken of her find to Clara, the new parlour maid, who had told Mrs. Pratt, and well she might, since it was Mrs. Pratt's responsibility to know what went on in the house. The story was entitled *The Conspiracy of the Golden Scarab* and appeared written under the name of one Beryl Bardwell—and a very sensational story, at that. What's more, under the bed they found several other stories under that same name, all published in an American magazine. It was an unsettling discovery.

"Imagine!" Clara had breathed excitedly as she flipped the pages in one of the magazines. "Our young miss is famous! I wonder why she don't let her light shine i' th' world, 'stead o' hidin' it under a bushel."

"She has her reasons, I'm sure," Mrs. Pratt said evasively, although she did not think that the Biblical quotation could be applied to what her mistress was about. And she could not for the life of her imagine why Miss Ardleigh, with the fortune she had inherited, would spend her time hunched over a typewriter, pecking out scandalous stories. But the young miss had stood for her when she needed a friend, and she'd stand for the young miss, as long as need be—although she had to admit to reservations about novel writing and bicycle riding during Evensong.

She pushed the magazines back under the bed. "Stop gabblin' and get t' yer dustin'," she'd told Clara sternly. "An' not a word o' this bus'ness outside th' house, if ye value yer place." The next morning, all the servants had been warned to hold their tongues, and all had pledged their solemn promise to keep Miss Ardleigh's secret. The fact that Mrs. Pratt had not heard a whisper of it in the village proved that they had been true to their word.

"Well, now," Mrs. Pratt said, when Harriet had scurried away with her candle, "what's in yer mind, Mudd? Ye look that vexed, ye do." For with Harriet's departure, Mudd's face had gone dark.

"It's Amelia," said Mudd.

"What about Amelia?" Mrs. Pratt asked.

"Lawrence," Mudd said, cupping his mug. "The Marsden's footman."

Mrs. Pratt felt the stirrings of a deep foreboding. "How d'ye know this?"

"She told me." He gave her a direct look, and softened his tone. "Steel yerself, Mrs. P. There's been a killin'."

Mrs. Pratt felt her heart lurch in her chest. "A killin'!" she whispered, scarcely able to comprehend. "A *killin'*?"

But before Mudd could elaborate, there came a loud knock at the kitchen door. Mrs. Pratt, still in a state of stunned shock, got to her feet, groped her way to the door, and opened it. On the doorstep before her, as if summoned by Mudd's awful revelation, stood none other than Constable Laken. Mrs. Pratt felt she knew the constable quite well, for she had once spent a night in his gaol and a good part of the next morning answering his impertinent questions pertaining to the deaths of the elder Miss Ardleigh and her sister Mrs. Jaggers. But she had long since excused that impertinence. The constable had only been doing his duty then, as he clearly was now.

"Yer've come fer Amelia," Mrs. Pratt said, low.

"Yes," the constable said. He stepped inside. "You know, then?"

Mrs. Pratt closed the door. "The worst," she replied. Automatically, she went to the teapot, filled a mug, and handed it to the constable. He pulled a chair forward to the fire, warming his hands.

"Pore Lawrence," Mrs. Pratt said, shaking her head. She had only seen the man a time or two—handsome, he was, with a quick tongue. Little good his looks or his tongue would do him now.

"Yes," the constable said. "It's very difficult for him, too, you understand."

Mrs. Pratt sat down. "I'd *say*," she said. She knew the constable to be a man of understatement, but this was remarkable even for him. "What'll happen now?"

"I'll need to talk to Amelia, of course," the constable said. "Is she here?"

"I'll fetch her," Mudd volunteered, and left the room.

"Will ye 'rrest her tonight?" Mrs. Pratt asked fearfully, thinking of the cold, dark gaol, and wondering how she was ever going to break the news to her dear sister Rose, who had not yet recovered from sweet Jenny's death. And to Miss Ardleigh. That such a thing should happen when she, Sarah Pratt, was alone with the household, in charge of the staff, and responsible for her niece's behaviour! Mrs. Pratt felt as if she herself had done the unspeakable deed.

"No," the constable said. "I won't arrest her at all."

Mrs. Pratt's moral indignation flared. "Not at all!" she cried, her heart swelling for the victim. "Why, man, a murder's been done! Where's yer sense o' justice? If 'twere my own daughter killed Lawrence, I'd have ye 'rrest her!"

"It wasn't Lawrence who was killed," the constable said. "Where'd you get that idea?" He looked into his cup. "It was Sergeant Oliver, the constable from Gallows Green."

"Sergeant Oliver!" Mrs. Pratt threw her apron over her

head, her dismay unbounded. "Dear Gawd, an' him with wife an' babe! How could she? How *could* she?"

"I hardly think that Amelia is all that much to blame," the constable said mildly. "All she did was go larkin' with Lawrence. They stumbled on Oliver's body when they went through a hedge on Lamb's Lane."

Mrs. Pratt dropped her apron and stared at him. "She didn't—?"

But her question was interrupted by the appearance of Mudd and the ashen Amelia, a fact for which Mrs. Pratt would be forever after grateful. She would hate to admit to the constable, or Mudd, or most especially to Amelia, that she had for even one instant considered her niece capable of murder.

By the time the constable had finished questioning Amelia, Mrs. Pratt had fully recovered herself. After showing the constable out, she closed the door and whirled on the girl in full fury.

"The lane!" she cried. "An' wot were ye doing, my fine girl, skulkin' in the lane with a footman?"

Ten minutes later, a contrite Amelia crept out of the kitchen, and Mrs. Pratt, feeling that her duty to her sister, to her mistress, and to God had been fully discharged, went to the cupboard and uncorked the cooking wine.

8

"Lady Stanhope's man servant proved to be the thief, I am sorry to say. A great pity, too, for he had fine manners and was quite handsome."

"Ah, well, but it often turns out so does it not? The greater the servant's apparent trustworthiness, the greater the cause to distrust him. Always keep the silver under lock and key, I say. And always secure the jewels."

—BERYL BARDWELL
The Rosicrucian's Ruby

"Oh, Kate, *DEAR* Kate! I *AM* so very glad to see you!"
"Marriage hasn't changed you one bit, Ellie," Kate said, returning her friend's warm embrace as they stood in a corner of the Melford drawing room.

"Not at all?" Eleanor Marsden Farley asked with a little pout, displaying a dainty white arm decked with diamonds. Beside her stood a short, stout, wary-looking man of forty or so, wearing a pince-nez on his too-short nose and garbed in a double-breasted frock coat and a white satin waistcoat strained across the buttons. Eleanor took his left hand and pulled him forward, smiling winsomely as she made introductions. "Miss Ardleigh lives very near Marsden Manor, Mr. Fairley. She was a guest at our wedding, you will recall."

Mr. Fairley might well not recall meeting her, Kate thought, especially since the guests had numbered nearly five hundred. But she could not forget the wedding. The Marsden-Fairley nuptials had been celebrated at fashionable St. Paul's in Knightsbridge, whose wedding register was a roster of social luminaries. It was a glittering event, for which Lord Marsden was said to have laid out the equivalent of a year's rents.

Mr. Fairley peered at Kate over his pince-nez. "Miss Ardleigh, to be sure." He coughed slightly. "Mrs. Fairley has spoken of you."

"I'm glad," Kate said, looking at Eleanor. "I think of her often." It was true. Life at Bishop's Keep was always interesting but often lonely, for although Kate was surrounded by servants, there was no one to whom she could talk openly. Ellie had not yet proved to be that kind of friend, but she might have been, had they more time together.

"Mrs. Fairley might perhaps enjoy a renewal of her acquaintance with you," Mr. Fairley remarked speculatively, as if Eleanor were not standing at his elbow. "Perhaps if you came up to London, something might be arranged."

If the thought of Kate's visit gave Mr. Fairley any pleasure, he did not reveal it. Kate knew from Eleanor's premarital confidences that he was a widower, his first wife having been a woman of no particular family, who had borne him only one child, a son. Mr. Fairley's fortune had been established in the 1850s by his grandfather Franklin Fairley, the esteemed founder of Fairley's Finest Fancy Candies, and on this account he was a man of some considerable consequence. However, he was in trade and went daily to an office in the Fairley Building in Lombard Street, and hence could not aspire to any particular social recognition beyond that accorded to a newly rich man who could keep a fine house, three carriages, and two footmen with crested buttons and gold lace. But he could use his wealth to marry the social distinction he lacked, and so he had. His father, like his grandfather, had been a chocolatier. Eleanor's was a baron. It was exactly the kind of marriage any man in business must have longed to make.

Poor Eleanor, Kate thought. But then Eleanor's diamonds caught her eye, and she thought again. She felt it was wrong to marry for anything other than love, and she wouldn't do it. But society marriages were made for society's reasons and had very little to do with the heart's deeper motives. If Eleanor were dissatisfied with the choice she had made (mostly, Kate knew, at the urging of her mother), she did not show it. Indeed, she looked exceedingly well, in a rich turquoise silk with tight-fitting bodice and diamonds at her wrist, her ears, her throat. She was obviously using her husband's fortune to suit herself.

Eleanor smiled at Mr. Fairley and fluttered the ivory fan fastened to her wrist with a gold cord. "Would you allow us a few moments?" she asked. When he inclined his head and moved away, Eleanor's pretty mouth tightened slightly, and the lightness vanished from her voice. "I must talk to you, Kate. I have just discovered something terribly unsettling, and I am hoping that you will be able to help me."

"I trust all is well with you, Ellie," Kate said, allowing herself to be pulled a little apart from the crowd.

Eleanor's mouth tightened imperceptibly. "It is not about myself that I am concerned, Kate. It is about Mama."

Kate was surprised. Lady Henrietta Marsden was a strong woman, a law unto herself. Even Lord Marsden acquiesced to her wishes. "I hope your mother is not ill."

"Not ill," Eleanor said. She leaned closer and lowered her voice. "There has been a theft, Kate. One of the servants has stolen my mother's antique emeralds."

"How terrible for her!" Kate said. Everyone in England who could possibly afford it used domestic help, even if only a young girl to help with the cooking and cleaning. And many who had servants suffered from moments of doubt and fear, and even terror. There were frequent reports in the newspapers of servants making off with the silver and even, quite recently, of a lady's maid who murdered her mistress and fled to France with that lady's jewels and best dresses.

The dour, black-shawled dowager walked past and said a word of acerbic greeting to Eleanor. She smiled and bowed, replied, and then turned back to Kate. "Fortunately," she said behind her fan, "Mama does not yet know of the theft."

Kate raised her eyebrows.

"She does not yet know of it," Eleanor went on, "because

I myself had a loan of the emeralds—a necklace, earrings, bracelet, and two rings. They are quite lovely, but several of the stones are flawed so that while they are valuable, they are not priceless. I wore them at a ball given in my honour several weeks ago. Shortly after the ball, I returned the jewels to their box in the safe in Mama's sitting room, with the exception of the small tea ring, which I had forgotten. Yesterday, when I went to return the ring, the box was gone.''

''Perhaps your mother took them,'' Kate said.

''My mother does not *know* that they are gone,'' Eleanor replied with some agitation. ''When I mentioned the tea ring, she asked me to give it to her so that she could put it with the others.''

''What did you do?''

Eleanor coloured. ''I told her a lie,'' she said with the discomfort of one who has been raised to tell her mother the truth. ''I said that I had forgotten the ring and left it in London.''

''And you deduce from this that—''

''That Mama does not yet know that her jewels are missing. The safe is quite crowded with other things and this particular box is small. She wears the jewels only on special occasions, and sets a great sentimental store by them. Oh, Kate, she will be *livid* when she discovers that they have been stolen! And I myself feel an appalling responsibility.''

''You?'' Kate asked in some surprise. ''Why should you hold yourself responsible?''

Eleanor bit her lip. ''Because I fear that when I returned the jewels I failed to lock the safe. I was in a great hurry to dress for dinner, and Mama's footman came in with a message just as I was putting the emeralds back. He distracted me with a question and I left the room without assuring myself that the safe was locked.''

Kate frowned. ''Do you then suspect the footman?''

''Lawrence?'' Eleanor's lavender eyes clouded. ''I fear I must. I am very sorry, for he has been at the manor for seven years and has been a help to me on many occasions. Two years ago in London, I was involved in a rather foolish liaison. Lawrence carried messages for me and kept my confidence when he might easily have betrayed me to Mama for his advantage. Since then, I have felt obliged to him, and would hate to see him sent up on charges on my account." She put her hand on Kate's arm. "Can you not see why I feel such a terrible responsibility? If I did not close the safe properly, I placed temptation in Lawrence's way. *I* may have caused his downfall."

"If it is true that the footman took the jewels," Kate said gently, "the moral fault is his, not yours. Have you taken your suspicions to your father or to your brother Bradford?"

At the mention of Bradford, Eleanor pulled herself upright. "I am sorry to say that my brother and I have not been on the best of terms of late. And as for speaking to my father—" She paused. "I will, of course, if I must. But I hoped that you might be able to help."

"I?" Kate was surprised. "How could I help?"

Eleanor's shoulders lifted helplessly. "I am not at all sure," she said. "I was hoping that perhaps you might discover whether Lawrence took the jewels, and if he did, how he disposed of them. If redeeming them is not too costly, I may be able to persuade Mr. Fairley to assist. I've come to you because I know that it was through your investigations that the murderer of your aunt was brought to justice, and I thought—"

"I very much fear, Ellie," Kate broke in, "that you overestimate my abilities. In any event, I do not see how I might have the opportunity to do the kind of investigation required in this case. I think you must speak with your father or your brother about this matter, and let them handle it."

Eleanor looked crestfallen. "I suppose you're right. But I did so hope—You're sure, Kate?"

"I have a great interest in mysteries," Kate said firmly, thinking of Beryl Bardwell. "But I am no detective. I fear you must pursue this without my assistance, Ellie." She smiled and deliberately changed the subject. "I trust that your disagreement with your brother is not serious."

Eleanor fanned herself. "Probably not." Her mercurial face brightened and her voice became lighter. "Do you know that he has a romantic interest in you?"

"I doubt that it is a serious interest," Kate said, matching the lightness of her friend's tone. She had long since come to terms with the fact that she was not a beauty. Her face and figure were presentable and her mop of mahogany hair attractive when she bothered to comb and dress it properly (which she did not always do). But she spurned the social arts of flattery and flirtation and said what she thought without worrying much about how it might be received. Hers was not a style that readily attracted lovers, who seemed to wish for more compliance than she was willing to offer. And to tell the truth, she was glad, for she had not met many men, either American or British, whose romantic attentions she would welcome. If spinsterhood was the price for her independence, she was more than ready to pay it.

"It may be more serious than you think," Eleanor said with a mysterious smile. "And have you heard from our mutual friend, Sir Charles Sheridan? Did you know that he has returned from Paris and is staying at Marsden Manor?"

"I had not heard," Kate replied casually, not betraying her interest. Before leaving for Paris, Sir Charles had called twice. They had walked among the ruins on the other side of the lake, where he had found a rare species of bat that interested him greatly. She found him quite attractive and enjoyed his company—had indeed almost thought that he might be a man whose attentions she could welcome. But something told her that it was the bats that brought him to Bishop's Keep, rather than an interest in her. Now, thinking of Sir Charles and remembering his investigative skills, Kate said, "You might speak to Sir Charles about your mother's jewels, Ellie."

Eleanor brightened. "What a splendid idea! Mr. Fairley and I will be going back to the manor on Monday to spend the week. Mama is planning a garden party to introduce him to the neighbourhood."

"Yes, I know," Kate said. "I've been invited."

"I can't be sure, of course," Eleanor went on in a teasing tone, "but I suspect that both Sir Charles and Bradford are interested in you. Tell me, Kate. Which do you prefer?"

Kate returned Eleanor's teasing with a deliberately arch smile. "Oh, come, now, Ellie. Sir Charles is interested only in my bats. And your brother has spent most of the past few months in London immersed in his automobile investments. Faced with such masculine preoccupations, what is a woman to do? I think I shall not prefer at all, but remain exactly as I am, unmarried and independent, answering neither to a baron-to-be nor to a knight who loves bats.''

Eleanor shook her head in despair. ''Oh, Kate, you *are* so wicked. Whatever shall I do with you?''

''Yes,'' Kate said decisively, ''I am very wicked and very unmarried. And I intend to stay that way.''

9

In all good fairy tales, the princess is transformed by a fairy godmother, or a hidden identity is brought to light, or a magical animal brings wealth and happiness. It was thus for the shy young woman of Bolton Gardens, who was transformed by the magical animals she loved and brought to life, and for the children who will forever after treasure her work.

—SARAH TISDELL
The Magic of Imagination

It was raining the next afternoon at the hour that Kate had agreed to walk with Bea. A little while before their appointed time, she went in search, expecting to find her room on the third floor where the visitors' servants were put up—or in the garret, where Bea's ward was no doubt confined. But Kate was surprised when the maid of whom she inquired told her that the room was on the second floor, near the head of the stairs. When she knocked and was bade to enter and did, she was surprised again. Not only was the room on the wrong floor, it was far too handsomely furnished and decorated to be that of a servant. It was hung with rose damask draperies and contained a four-poster bed, carved mahogany furniture, and a blazing fire in the fireplace. And there was no madwoman mumbling insanities in a corner. Instead, stretched out on the hearthrug, in drowsy repose, lay the white rabbit Kate had apprehended yesterday.

"Hello," Bea said, looking up from the sketch pad in her lap, on which she was working in pencil. On the table in front of her sat a small creature, quiet and complacent enough, but with a prickly coat as rough-bristled as a scrub brush and a black snout almost like that of a small pig. "I should have come to find you in a moment or two," she added. "It is much too wet to walk out, don't you think?"

"Yes, it is," Kate said. "I would rather enjoy the rainy afternoon by looking out the window." As she came forward, a brown mouse with large black eyes peeped out from beneath Bea's skirt. "Excuse me," Kate said urgently, and backed up a step. "There's a mouse under your skirt!"

"Oh, dear." But instead of jumping onto the chair and shrieking, as Kate might have expected, Bea pulled her skirt aside and looked down. "Hunca Munca," she scolded, "get back in your house. Can't you see we have a visitor?" When the mouse still sat blinking beadily at her, she scooped it up, rose, and popped it into a small wire cage on the window sill. "You shall have a bit of cheese if you are polite," she said. "But if you persist in making a nuisance of yourself, you shall be put to bed without any tea."

Kate was so astonished that she could only stare. "Do you often talk to mice?" she managed finally.

"It depends upon whether I have anything to say. I more often talk to hedgehogs." Bea went to the table and picked up the prickly creature, which snuggled into her hand.

Kate stepped forward. "What a funny creature," she said, extending a finger. "What is its name?"

"Mrs. Tiggy-Winkle," Bea said.

Kate couldn't help smiling. So *this* was the madwoman in the garret! "She's just like a fat, sleepy little dog."

Bea nodded. "As a model, she's very comical. So long as she can go to sleep on my knee, she's delighted. But if she's propped up on end for half an hour, she begins to yawn pathetically, and then likes to bite."

Mrs. Tiggy-Winkle chose that instant to yawn, showing sharply pointed yellow teeth.

"You're very brave, to make a pet of a creature with such sharp teeth," Kate said. She glanced down at Bea's sketch pad on the table. There were several drawings of the hedgehog. In one, she was wearing a large apron over a striped petticoat and a ruffled mobcap, and her forelegs were soapy to the elbow. "I see you've dressed her up," she added, admiring the skill and humour with which the cunning little animal had been drawn. "How clever. And what a remarkably lifelike figure!"

"Thank you," Bea said. "She's a washerwoman, you see. All my animals have one profession or another." She pulled out another sketch, this one of a frog dressed in a mackintosh and galoshes, with a fishing rod and basket. "The children like my stories better when I write about what the animals do—fishing or ironing clothes—and show them doing it."

"You're a writer!" Kate exclaimed happily, as Beryl Bardwell recognized a kindred spirit. "As well as an artist."

"No," Bea said sadly. "I'm afraid I am neither. I have begged to be allowed to submit a story or two for publication. But unhappily for me my father is actively opposed, and my mother agrees to everything he says. I've only managed to sell a watercolour for a calendar and a few humourous Christmas cards, and I've illustrated some terrible doggerel that a German firm printed on cards at fourpence-ha'penny." She sighed. "When Papa discovered what I was doing, he set up such a horrid fuss that now I only put my pictures in letters. I write for the little Moores, you see. They're the children of my former governess. *They* like my stories."

Kate looked back at the drawings. "But you're so enormously talented. How can you let your parents deny you the opportunity to develop your art?" She didn't add, *and on top of that, you're a grown woman, and ought to be doing as you like*. But she thought it.

Bea gave a melancholy shrug. "How am I to do otherwise? I am entirely dependent on their financial support. I am expected to live with them in Bolton Gardens until I am married." She smoothed Mrs. Tiggy-Winkle's furry ears. "And that becomes less likely each year. They discourage friendships, you see, with men and with women." She twinkled, and the corners of her mouth turned upward. "Not that I mind so dreadfully being a spinster. I have not yet met a man I wanted to marry, and I am perfectly content to live singly. But it *is* difficult, since I am allowed away from Bolton Gardens only in my parents' company."

Now Kate understood why Bea had spoken so triumphantly about her solitary railway journey. "I wonder that they permitted you to come here alone," she said.

"That's because the Hyde-Parkers are cousins and we are frequent visitors here." Bea opened a large wicker hamper with its own little food and water dishes and set Mrs. Tiggy-Winkle inside. "Papa and Mama planned to make the trip, but Mama fell ill with a cold and I begged to be allowed to come alone. Not that I like Melford all that much," she added, pouring a handful of hemp seeds into the hedgehog's dish. "It's grand and imposing, but rather boring, except for the squirrels in the park. Still, it's a chance to be on my own, and I intend to make the best of it. I have brought my sketching materials and Papa's second-best camera, and when the rain stops, I shall go out and see what I can find."

"You are a photographer, then?" Kate asked, thinking of Sir Charles, whose other passion, besides mushrooms and bats, was photography.

"Yes," Bea said. "I enjoy it, but I must confess that I took it up as a means of getting away from Mama when we are on holiday." Her plain face was transformed by a brilliant smile. "She detests driving through the bracken in a pony cart, stopping in the cold wind to photograph a growth of *Peziza* or a gigantic *Cortinarius*." She laughed a little. "Poor Mama. She wearies me so at times, but I do pity her. I could not live confined, as she does."

"I see," Kate said, suddenly struck by the marked contrast between this shy young woman and gay, exuberant Eleanor. But in a way that seemed startlingly clear to Kate's American eyes, these two British young women were very similar. Eleanor married as her parents expected, Bea stayed home. Both did as they were bid, and both were docile enough on the surface; yet both exercised whatever subtle means they could find to resist coercion, to establish their own separateness, their independence. For Eleanor, it was her husband's fortune that gave her a measure of freedom. For Bea, it was her eccentric love of animals, and the art that it inspired.

Kate looked up. An idea was forming in her mind—a most *wicked* idea. "Do you never travel anywhere except to Melford in the company of your parents?"

"Only occasionally with my brother Bertram, and last year to my cousin Caroline, at Harescombe Grange." Her smile was pensive. "After visiting Caroline, I have become dreadfully anxious for more travel. I do love the countryside, and gardens full of flowers, and cottages, and walking by the water."

"Then perhaps," Kate said, "you would like to come to Bishop's Keep for a few days. It is near Dedham, in Essex, about forty miles from here. There are gardens and cottages, and miles and miles of countryside, and a lake and a river— the River Stour—and an estuary, where the Stour flows into the sea. And it is all very beautiful, now that spring is here. The house is large, and you and your friends"—she looked at Peter on the hearth, and Hunca-Munca in her cage—"your *many* friends could be quite comfortable."

Bea's blue eyes were round. "But I am expected to remain here for at least a week! The Hyde-Parkers would not object, certainly. But whatever should I tell Papa and Mama?"

"Do you have to tell them anything, at least right away? If you are wanted, the Hyde-Parkers could telegraph to Dedham and you could receive the message straightaway. And when you returned home, you could as easily take the train from Colchester. Your parents would be none the wiser."

There was a moment's silence. Bea's face was wistful, then thoughtful, and at last determined. "I think," she said, in a small but steady voice, "that it is a splendid idea."

"Wonderful!" Kate exclaimed. "We shall leave on Monday morning, by carriage, and be home in time for tea." She was halfway to the door before she thought of something, and turned. "How funny," she said. "I didn't even think to ask your whole name." She laughed a little. "Or perhaps it is a secret. Perhaps I should simply call you Bea, and not ever know who you really are."

"Oh, it's no secret. I forgot, that's all." Bea laughed. "Mama would be scandalized at my manners." She sat down at the table and took up her sketch pad again. "My name is Beatrix," she said. "Beatrix Potter."

10

County of Essex to wit}
Sir Charles Sheridan, Knight

By Virtue of a Warrant under the Hand and Seal of Harry Hodson, Esquire, Her Majesty's Coroner for the County of Essex, You are hereby summoned to be and appear before him on Monday the twelfth day of May, at twelve o'clock precisely at the Coroner's Court to be held at the Live and Let Live, Lamb's Lane, Dedham, then and there to give evidence on Her Majesty's behalf touching the Death of Sergeant Arthur Oliver, Constable, Gallows Green, Essex. Herein fail not at your peril.

The Live and Let Live, the only pub on Lamb's Lane, was little bigger than a cottage. Its low-ceilinged main room, beams blackened with smoke, was crowded with farmers and villagers, jammed against the walls and the long wooden counter that usually served as a bar. Both windows were open so that the sounds of the lane—the *baa*ing of a passing flock of sheep, the roll of wheels, and the clatter of hooves—were mixed with the indoor drone of voices and punctuated by the occasional loud remark. But the sweet May air could hardly contend with the overpowering scents of sweat and horse and leather jerkin.

At the farther end of the room was a small trestle table, like a desk, and behind it a scarred oak armchair. This seat was reserved for Coroner Harry Hodson. At one end of the table was a stool for the clerk, with paper, pen and ink, and blotting-paper; at the other end was a chair for witnesses. Directly in front of the table, on the plank floor, was a closed pine coffin. Two long benches were arranged at right angles to the coffin for the jurors, who after some commotion at the door and shouts of "Let 'em pass, by Gawd, so they kin earn their two shillings!" were ushered through the crowd to take their seats. At two shillings, the jurors were not overcompensated for their work, for their attendance could be enforced for the entire day if need be. Still, the event gave the day distinction, and those summoned were willing to spend it serving the Queen and her coroner.

It was into this gloomy cave that Charles Sheridan made his way, carrying a leather portfolio. He paused to let his vision adjust from the noonday glare to the inner darkness, and then pushed through the crowd until he found a place to stand not far from the coroner's table. He caught sight of Edward Laken leaning against the opposite wall and waved a greeting, thinking that Edward looked pinched and pale and unhappy. Arthur Oliver had been his good friend.

A moment later, a wisp of a man came through the rear door, perched on the stool like an eager bird, and shouted "Gentlemen, the Coroner!" Anybody who was sitting down stood up until Harry Hodson, who had nearly doubled in girth since Charles had last seen him twenty years before, took his seat with due ceremony in the chair of honour and nodded at the clerk to proceed.

The room became suddenly silent and the wispy man began to recite in a rapid sing-song: "Oyez, oyez, ye good men of this district summoned to appear here this day to inquire for Her Sovereign Majesty the Queen when, how, and by what means Arthur Oliver, Sergeant of the Essex Constabulary, came to his death, answer to your names as you shall be called, every man at the first call, upon the pain and peril that shall fall thereon.''

That done, the coroner read from his list the names of the jurors, each one answering with ''Present, sir,'' meekly or assertively, according to his temperament. Then followed the administering of the oath, in which the jurors promised to render a true verdict without fear or favour, affection or ill-will, to the best of their skill and knowledge, so help them God. The oath taken, the coroner told the jurors that they were to consider three possibilities: homicide, suicide or misadventure, and if they were not satisfied that the evidence warranted any of these, they must return an open verdict. The coffin lid was then raised, and the jurors filed soberly past it and once again resumed their benches. The coffin was closed, and the inquest began.

''Lawrence Black,'' the coroner called. Charles leaned against the wall as Lawrence, splendid in yellow-checked trousers and visibly impressed by his importance in these court proceedings, took the oath, kissed the Testament, and began, in response to the coroner's questions, to relate his discovery of Artie Oliver's body. Everything went as Charles might have expected until the coroner said, ''I understand that you were not alone when you discovered the body, Mr. Black.''

Lawrence's handsome face, which to this point had been animated, went blank. ''Sir?'' he said.

''I understand,'' the coroner repeated patiently, ''that you were accompanied through the hedge by a certain young woman. Is this true?''

A titter ran from one side of the room to the other. Lawrence turned to Edward. ''D' I 'ave t' answer?'' he asked in a loud whisper.

Edward stepped forward and leaned over the table. ''If you don't mind, Harry,'' he said quietly, ''it'd be best for the girl if she were left out of this. I've questioned her, and she can offer nothing new. Her testimony would simply corroborate Mr. Black's.''

''Disregard the question,'' the coroner said, and a disappointed sigh followed the titter around the room. Lawrence Black was excused and stepped down, to be followed by the police surgeon, who reported that death had resulted from a bullet being fired from a revolver into the heart. "It was at close range," he added. He had ascertained this fact from powder burns on the uniform jacket, entered now in evidence, along with the fatal bullet.

Edward was called next. He filled in Lawrence's rather vague description of the location of the body with a more careful account, and offered the speculation that Sergeant Oliver had been killed elsewhere and the body conveyed to the site by a vehicle along the adjacent lane and then through a gap in the hedge. From Edward, the jurors also learned that the victim was thirty-two years old, married, with one young daughter, Betsy, and a wife, Agnes. Oliver had served with distinction in the Suffolk parish of East Bergholt before being promoted to sergeant and posted to Gallows Green. When Edward had completed his testimony, Charles was called.

"I understand, Sir Charles," the coroner said when the oath had been administered and Charles was seated in the witness chair, "that you are a photographer."

"I am," Charles agreed.

"And that on the day in question you received a summons from Constable Laken to photograph the dead body of Constable Oliver at the place where it was found."

"I did," Charles said. "If it please the Court, I have brought enlargements of the photographs with me."

There was a curious stir in the room as he took the prints out of his leather portfolio and offered them to the coroner. For the past twenty or so years in England, photographs had been used in an attempt to identify criminals, with very limited success. Scotland Yard had 115,000 faces in its rogues' gallery, but the collection was in chaos because of the criminals' tendency to give false names. No reliable means of matching a photograph to its real-life subject had yet been developed, and no other uses of the camera were officially contemplated. So it was that Charles's photographs were little more than objects of curiosity to Coroner Harry Hodson and his twelve jurors. Even so, they were passed around and examined and wondered at, as was the triangular piece of red cloth discovered in the hedge, and Mr. McGregor's coat, which Edward brought forward and laid on the table.

At that point, Sir Charles was excused, and Mr. McGregor, wearing a stiff suit of dark-brown corduroy and a red-and-yellow neckerchief knotted under his ear, was summoned and sworn. His testimony was listened to with interest but proved to be of little consequence. That the triangular cloth bit had been ripped from his coat was clear, but it was, after all, his hedge and any fool knew that a man went through his own hedge a dozen times a week. Mr. McGregor's wife's brother's missing pistol was mentioned but not pursued, the police surgeon having determined from the shape of the recovered bullet that it could not have come from a weapon of that type. In answer to the question of whether he had noticed anything suspicious in the neighbourhood, Mr. McGregor offered the same opinion he had offered to Charles and Edward, with a slight but significant variation.

"Allus somethin' suspicious gooin' on," he rasped. "Sheep gooin' missin', poachers, gypsies in th' vale—"

"Gypsies?" the coroner asked sharply. "When was this?"

"Las' week. Two cabbages and a cauly-flow'r was took from me garden, an' Mrs. McGregor's apern an' a sheet off th' line."

"And you think these gypsies might have been responsible?"

"'Twern't rabbits," Mr. McGregor replied smartly, and was rewarded with a laugh. But as to whether gypsies might have murdered the constable, he declined to say, nor could he offer any other helpful information. He was dismissed with thanks. Charles, thinking the inquest at an end, turned to make his way in Edward's direction, when the coroner raised his voice once more.

"Superintendent Hacking," he called, over the murmuring and rustle. There was a silence, and through the crowd came a stocky, distinguished-looking man in the uniform of the constabulary. He went to the witness chair, was sworn, and sat down. The man's grey hair and mustache were luxuriant, his boots were polished, and several decorations glittered on the pocket of his impeccably pressed serge jacket. Altogether, he was an impressive-looking witness.

Charles looked at Edward and raised his eyebrows, curious as to why a superintendent had been called. Edward answered with a shrug. Apparently it was a surprise to him, too—which in itself was odd, considering that the murder, which had been committed in Edward's district, was Edward's case. Superintendent Hacking, who was stationed at district headquarters in nearby Colchester, began with a brief summary of Sergeant Oliver's service and reported that the Standing Joint Committee that controlled the County Force had met upon the matter and determined that the sergeant had met his death while in the execution of his duty. Mrs. Oliver had been granted a pension of fifteen pounds a year, plus two-pounds-ten for the child. The questioning then turned to the incident itself.

"Do you know," Harry Hodson asked, "why Sergeant Oliver might have been in the vicinity of Dedham on the night he was murdered?"

Hacking's face was impassive. "I do," he said.

"Please state it for the jury."

"There was a matter that required the urgent attention of the police in this neighbourhood." Hacking' voice was clipped. "If you press me I will state it, but in the interests of justice, it would possibly be best not to."

Charles frowned. An odd business. Several of the jurors apparently thought so too, for they sat forward on their bench. Edward was even more intent, his face furrowed, lips pressed together.

"You may state the reason," Coroner Hodson said.

Hacking's eyes flicked to Edward. "Sheep have been stolen in the neighbourhood," he said. "In consequence, close attention was being paid. By my special direction, I might add."

Edward sat upright.

Harry Hodson frowned. "No one has offered any evidence suggesting that the murder involved sheep stealing."

"The preceding witness did," the superintendent replied.

The clerk was consulted, Mr. McGregor's testimony was read back, and the superintendent's recollection was confirmed. But when asked to specify whose sheep had been taken, the superintendent only replied that this was the very information Sergeant Oliver had been attempting to procure, so he was no wiser than any of them. However, Chief Constable Pell had taken the case himself, and expected it to be speedily resolved.

Mr. McGregor was recalled from the bench outside the pub, where he was sharing a pint with a friend, and asked for more specifics about sheep-stealing. But he could provide nothing more and was permitted to return to his pint. The jury retired to the back garden and returned a few moments later with the verdict everyone had expected: "Homicide, by person or persons unknown."

People stirred, voices were raised, Sanders the publican opened the tap, and life at the Live and Let Live began to flow again.

11

Never the time and the place
And the loved one all together!
—ROBERT BROWNING
"Never the Time and the Place"

Edward Laken swallowed convulsively. "I don't understand it," he said.

The black coach bearing the coffin had returned to Gallows Green, the curious had gone back to their shops and farms, and Superintendent Hacking had been driven back to Colchester by the uniformed constable who had brought him. The twelve jurors were bellied up to the bar, drinking the convivial pints purchased for them by Harry Hodson and explaining to anyone who would listen the complex logic behind their verdict. Edward and Charles were seated at a scratched deal table in the rear, a pitcher of local beer before them, a dark brew faintly suggestive of licorice and tobacco and with a definitive body. Edward, having had two glasses, was feeling deeply morose.

"I don't understand it," he said again, staring into his glass.

"The sheep-stealing, you mean?" Charles asked.

"Not that, nor the superintendent's giving the case over to Pell, nor—" He leaned back in his chair and bitterly mimicked the super's clipped tone. " 'The urgent attention of police in this neighbourhood.' If Hacking had bloody wanted the urgent attention of the police, he could've had *my* attention. *I'm* the police in this neighbourhood.''

Of all the hurtful things about this case, that had been the worst. To hear his superintendent, in the presence of every male member of the Dedham community, say that Artie had been working *his* patch, trying to solve a crime that *he* had never heard of, and had died in the process. And then to learn that the case was being taken by C.C. Pell! Jesus Mary and the angels. It was bad enough that Artie was dead. It was even worse to think he'd been murdered because he was doing Edward's job, and worse yet to have to wait for somebody else to find the murderer. Christ above!

''You mean,'' Charles said, ''you'd rather have gotten yourself killed than Artie?'' He picked up the pitcher as if to pour himself a second glass, but apparently decided against it and set it down again.

''At least I don't have a wife,'' Edward said, ''and a child. What's more,'' he added forcefully, ''I don't for a minute believe that Artie *was* murdered in this neighbourhood. I think he was killed on his own patch, and dumped here. And whether he was on police business—'' He clamped down on the anger roiling inside him. ''I'm telling you, Charlie. If there's any sheep-stealing going on here, *I* don't know anything about it. And neither does anybody else. You could see that on the faces of those jurors. If an animal goes missing here, everybody for three miles around knows it. Within the half hour, they're out counting their own flocks.'' He said each word emphatically. ''There's been no sheep-stealing hereabouts.''

''You think the superintendent is mistaken?''

Edward made circles with his wet glass on the tabletop. ''How the bloody hell should I know?'' he asked wearily. ''I'm just a country copper.'' He leaned back in his chair and stretched out his legs, examining the muddy toes of his boots. ''Anyway, Hacking's given the case to Pell. I don't have to worry about it anymore, do I? Let Pell knock his head against it.''

''I wonder about that,'' Charles said thoughtfully. ''The body was found in your district. Why would Hacking assign the investigation to somebody else? And especially to a chief constable?''

"And especially to Chief Constable Pell," Edward said. He took another swallow to wash down the bitter taste in his mouth. "Pell's as woolly as a sheep himself." He gave a short, sarcastic laugh. "Got himself disabled in the line of duty. Bloody hero, but damn stupid. Since he wasn't of any use on the beat, they made him a chief constable. Twenty years behind the desk hasn't sharpened him up. The only thing he knows how to do is deny promotions." Pell had been quick enough to deny his. He was still at the level of constable long after Artie had been promoted to sergeant.

Charles lifted his eyebrows. "And that's the man Hacking has preferred to you?"

"That's him, damn it," Edward said wrathfully, and slammed his glass on the table. "Well, let 'em have old Woolly Pell if they want him. But he'll never get to the bottom of this, I promise you. I wouldn't care, either, if it weren't Artie Oliver we're talking about." He shook his head, despairing. "That's the bloody hell of it, Charlie. Artie deserves justice done. And Agnes and that little girl deserve to see the murderer hanged. And I've been removed from the case. Confound and curse it!"

Edward was not a sentimental man, but his heart softened when he thought of Agnes Oliver. Ah, Agnes, Agnes. He'd loved her a dozen years ago, but somehow the time and the opportunity to let her know how he felt had never come together. And then suddenly the banns were being said for her and Artie, and all his hopes had died.

A dozen years, but she was still beautiful. It was the first thing in his mind when he and Charlie took her the dreadful news: how beautiful she was, with that sad, silent dignity that tore at his heart. It couldn't matter now, of course, although he'd lain awake many nights in the intervening years, lonely and longing, wishing for Agnes beside him, and envying Artie with such a woman in his bed. But that had been then, and this was now, and seventeen and ten a year would pay the rent on the cottage but leave nothing for food.

At the bar, the jurors had drunk up Hodson's pint and were

into their own. If they kept on drinking for long, they'd do it on the tick, since most wouldn't have another shilling in their pockets until the end of the week. They were discussing the case loudly, over the rusty wheeze of the concertina someone was playing outside the front door. Sanders the publican—a tall, lanky man in slippers and trousers too short for his legs—was saying to a tenant farmer who had just lost his farm, '' 'Tis no gud gooin' agin th' gentry, Jack. They got th' land an' they got th' money, an' what've you got?'' He spoke with the authority of one who owned his own business, while the dispossessed farmer sadly hung his head and wiped his eyes on a grimy sleeve.

''I wonder,'' Charles said slowly, ''if I could be of some help in this matter.''

Edward gulped the dregs of his beer and poured a third, the last in the pitcher. ''God-awful beer,'' he muttered, slopping it on the table. ''Any more murders 'round here, ol' Harry ought to move th' inquest t' th' Marlborough, where a man c'n get somethin' decent to drink afterward.''

''I had it in mind, Ned,'' Charles remarked, his gaze steadily on Edward, ''to look into Artie's murder myself.''

Edward leaned his head on his hand. His vision was blurry and his tongue felt thick. Sanders probably brewed his beer in the privy. ''Y'did right well th' last time y' took it in mind t' look into a murther, Charlie,'' he said, lapsing into a slurred country idiom. ''Not even th' doctor guessed what 'twas that did for th' Ardleigh sisters.''

Charles was thoughtful. ''I don't suppose you have seen Miss Ardleigh since she received her inheritance.''

'' 'N th' contrary,'' Edward said, rubbing the back of his neck. ''See her quite oft'n.''

Charles looked up, startled. ''The devil you say.''

Edward pursed his lips. If it had been anybody but Charlie, he would not have confided the truth. ''Been teachin' her t' ride a bicycle,'' he said. Miss Ardleigh's request for the lessons had come as a surprise, but he had been glad to help. He understood and honoured the wish for independence that lay behind her desire to ride a bicycle. So it was with pleasure that he had helped her obtain a suitable machine and had de-

voted several delightful Sunday evenings to assisting her wob-
bly efforts. The friendly, casual intimacy of their excursions
had proved a welcome break in the humdrum routine of the
police work that was the centre of his life. He grinned fondly.

"Lovely sight, that, I'll tell ye, Charlie m' friend. Kate Ardleigh on her cycle, weavin' merrily down th' lane from ditch
t' ditch, singin' at th' top o' her lungs. Even rode into Mrs.
Perry's black cow one afternoon. But she's stayed with it,
bless her. Goes flyin' down the High Street, proud as ye
please, basket piled wi' parcels. She's a wonder, she is."

His grin faded slightly and he fell into silence. He was
thinking of Agnes, beautiful Agnes, and how she might look
on a cycle, her hair blowing in the wind, her face alight, flying
beside him down the steep hill toward the River Stour. But
she was a widow now, with a child, and Artie's murder had
broken her heart. What might have been was past and would
not come again, dream as he might.

Edward's reverie was broken by the advent of the publican's
fat wife with a tray of fragrant pies. "All 'ot!" she cried over
the enthusiastic babble that greeted her. "Beef, mutton, an'
eel! All 'ot!"

Thinking that food might serve as an antidote to the beer,
Edward signaled to the woman and received a penny-ha'penny
pie. The woman gave Charles a dimpled smile. " 'Ow about
you, sir? 'Ot eel pie, sir?"

Charles shook his head and watched as Edward wolfed
down his pie. After a moment he remarked, oddly, and apro-
pos of nothing that Edward could think of, "I suppose you've
considered taking a wife, Ned."

Still fuzzy-headed, Edward finished the last bit of pie. "I
have." He thought of the time when he might have asked
Agnes but had not, delaying, believing that she deserved more.
"But life is hard f'r a P.C.'s wife, an' precious little t' show
f'r it. Twenty-two shillings, eleven pence when I began, an'
not much more now. Long duty hours, difficulty, danger. A
wife never knows when her man won't come home." He
shook his head sadly. "An' no station, either, and no respect.
To most, a policeman's low as a crim'nal, his wife none
better."

But Agnes had wedded a policeman, and had lived with the duty hours and the danger, and had not wished for more. Edward sighed, weighed down by an awareness of the time and the opportunity he had missed and feeling that life had somehow grown sadder as he had grown older, alone. He had taken a wrong turn when he might have asked Agnes to marry him and had not, and he was heavy with regret.

For his part, Charles, looking at his old friend, felt sympathy, and beneath that sympathy, sadness. He knew Ned to be a man with a large, warm heart, as well as intelligence, courage, and humour. He deserved an intelligent, courageous wife who would love him and laugh with him, whatever others might think. Charles did not know many such women. In fact, he knew only one, and therein lay his sadness.

Her name was Kate, and Ned was teaching her to ride a bicycle.

12

All art is but imitation of nature.

—SENECA

No great artist ever sees things as they really are.

—OSCAR WILDE

Truth is always strange; Stranger than fiction.

—LORD BYRON

Beatrix was delighted that the Hyde-Parkers took very little notice of her desire to leave with Kate Ardleigh.

The carriage ride from Melford Hall to Bishop's Keep took eight hours all told, including an hour for luncheon at the Polstead Oak Leaf, a dark little inn which offered a greasy kidney pudding and stale Chelsea buns. But there was rhubarb tart and hot elder cordial out of a copper urn, and the fare did not matter in any event. For Beatrix, the journey itself was a notable event, and the company unmeasurably enjoyable.

The carriage, driven by Kate's man Pocket and laden with luggage and Beatrix's animals, fastened up in hampers and cages, wended its way through the countryside. The narrow Essex lanes were bordered by bluebells and banks of blue speedwell, the marshes bloomed with golden kingcups and the large-flowered bitter cress, and the hedges were fragrant with May blossom. As Beatrix and Kate bounced along, their conversation ranged over a universe of subjects and became intimate even before they reached Great Waldingfield.

Beatrix found that Kate, who wore a grey traveling dress and grey felt hat perched on her mane of russet hair, had a way of listening intently, with genuine interest. It was a trait that Beatrix had happened upon very seldom in her life, and despite her shyness, she found it so inviting that she surprised herself by revealing some of her most private thoughts. She told Kate more about her wish to publish a children's book with drawings and a story, about her desire to leave Bolton Gardens, and her fear that she would always have to live with her father and mother.

"Although I love them both," she added, "Papa can be quite fidgety about things, while Mama complains constantly." She sighed, afraid that she was being disrespectful, and began to talk about her wish to have a small stone cottage all her own, with a front garden full of flowers, "which just might be possible," she added. "I was recently given some North Pacific Railway bonds, although they've paid no interest since '93, the company being in the hands of receivers. But there is some hope of realizing a small amount from them."

And Beatrix listened with great eagerness as the carriage rumbled through the early afternoon haze and Kate talked about herself. About her father's death before her birth and her mother's death when she was five. About growing up in New York City in the family of an Irish aunt and uncle (a policeman, of all things! Beatrix had never known anyone whose uncle was a policeman). About working as a governess for two utterly dreadful children, and as a secretary for an elderly German lady, and as an author, until she was asked by her father's oldest sister to come to England, where, upon her aunts' untimely deaths, she inherited the Ardleigh family estate. Really, this American woman was the most amazing creature, so clever, with so much energy and imagination! And so much independence, especially in choosing what she wanted to do!

"You're an author!" Beatrix's sigh was wistful. Being an author was the dream she cherished most. If she could only sell her illustrated stories, she might be able to earn an inde-

pendence something like Kate's. She might remove herself
from the hothouse of Bolton Gardens to a little cottage in the
North, with ducks and geese and pigs and gardens all around.

Kate's mouth compressed. "Perhaps I should not have told
you about my work. No one else in England knows."

"But whyever not?" Beatrix asked wonderingly.

Kate made a self-deprecating face. "Because I write sen-
sational stories. Penny dreadfuls. What you call 'shilling
shockers.' My last story was called *The Conspiracy of the
Golden Scarab*. I wrote it under the name of Beryl Bardwell."
She paused and glanced at Beatrix, as if testing her response.
"It was about a murder, you see."

"How amazing," Beatrix murmured. Her life in Bolton
Gardens had not been so sheltered that she had never read a
shilling shocker. She had, in fact, read any number of sensational tales, for they were in all the popular magazines. (Her
mother, no doubt, would require the smelling bottle if she
thought the purity of her daughter's mind were tainted with
such poisonous stuff.) "I should very much like to read it,"
she added shyly.

"You would?" Kate brightened. "Then you shall. It was
published in America just last month, and I have a copy. But
don't let the servants know, or anyone else. I sometimes use
the people around me as starting points for my characters, and
everyday events seem to have a way of intruding into my
plots."

"They do indeed," Beatrix agreed enthusiastically. "I draw
what I see, and I do it as realistically as possible. That's why
I use living animals and copy mushrooms and flowers from
nature."

Kate smiled. "Where in nature does one find a frog wearing
a mackintosh and galoshes?"

Beatrix returned the smile. "Of course, art is always
stranger than life."

"Indeed," Kate said. "Real life is remarkably lacking in
the sensational. If I were to write what goes on every day at
Bishop's Keep—shopping in the village, seeing to the servants, the gardens, the house—I would have no readers. But
I must settle down to writing very soon, if I am to finish the

story my editor has requested. I am hoping for inspiration."
She frowned a little. "Of course," she said half to herself,
"there *are* the Marsden emeralds."

"I beg your pardon?" Beatrix said.

"Nothing." Kate shook her head, still frowning. "Nothing
I can do anything about, at any rate," she said obscurely.

Beatrix smiled. "Well, then, my dear Kate," she said, "we
shall simply have to have an adventure. Your next story must
be a story of real life. And I shall perhaps find a new idea or
two, and will do better than putting galoshes on a frog."

Kate patted her hand. "So it's resolved," she said gaily.
"We shall have an adventure, and it shall be filled with
enough murder and theft and missing persons to fill the most
sensational of novels."

Bea began to feel anxious. "Perhaps we'd better wait until
we arrive safely at Bishop's Keep," she said. "I should rather
not be adventured *upon*."

The rest of the journey, however, proved to be without adventure or misadventure. They arrived at Bishop's Keep just
before tea. The house itself—a large, grey brick Georgian
trimmed in white—wasn't as grand as Melford Hall, Beatrix
thought, but it was spacious and attractive, and so much lighter
and more airy-looking than Bolton Gardens. A pair of stone
lions stood guard on either side of the steps that led down to
the drive, and the house was surrounded by thick evergreens
and hollies. To one side was a veranda bordered by beds of
brilliant flowers, with roses twining up the pillars. And below
the house, set like a sapphire in the emerald grass of the park,
lay a small lake, on the other side of which loomed an ancient
rock ruin, like a large grotto, shaded by huge copper beeches.
It was, Kate had told her, the ruin of the old Norman keep
that had given Bishop's Keep its name.

Beatrix smiled happily as she left off admiring the vista
and stepped around the carriage to show Pocket which hamper contained Mrs. Tiggy-Winkle. A few days to herself in
this lovely, peaceful spot—no Mama constantly complaining
at her, no Papa telling her what to do, and her new friend
Kate with whom to share confidences. This by itself was all
the adventure she needed!

* * *

As Kate stepped out of the carriage after Bea, she realized how glad she was to be at home. She had enjoyed Melford Hall, especially after she had met Bea. But there were a half-dozen projects underway at Bishop's Keep, not the least of which were the design of a new conservatory and the planting of a garden behind the house, and she was anxious to return to them. And there was her new story to begin; and the business about the Marsden emeralds that she couldn't quite dismiss from her mind; and the other news she had received from Eleanor, that Sir Charles Sheridan had returned to Marsden Manor and might soon be—

"Welcome back, Miss Ardleigh."

Kate spun around. As if she had conjured him up, there was Sir Charles, dismounting from a bay horse. He was a tall, lean man in his mid-thirties with deepset eyes, regular features, a closely trimmed brown beard, and brown hair curling nearly to his collar. As usual, he wore a shapeless brown felt hat and Norfolk breeches and a brown canvas jacket whose pockets were lumpy with the gear and tackle of an amateur scientist. He had gained a knighthood by taking some sort of photograph of the Queen at her Jubilee. But the honour seemed to matter very little to him, to the point where he always seemed surprised when he was addressed as Sir Charles, as Kate did now.

"Sir Charles," she said, trying not to show how pleased she was. "How kind of you to call."

"I was on my way to visit the ruins," he remarked, gathering the reins in his hand, "and saw your carriage. I understand you've been at Melford Hall for the week."

"Yes," Kate said, disappointed. Of course he had not come to call, but merely to continue his study of the bats. Eleanor's remark to the contrary, Sir Charles had no interest in women, and certainly none in her. Science was his mistress. Bea came around the carriage, carrying Mrs. Tiggy-Winkle's wicker hamper, and Kate turned. "Sir Charles, I would like you to meet—"

"Miss Potter!" Sir Charles exclaimed, his voice deepening with pleasure. "How *very* good to see you—and Mrs. Tiggy-Winkle, of course. What brings the two of you to this corner of Essex? I thought you never strayed far from Bolton Gardens. Has your father come with you?''

Kate was struck with surprise, and surprised even more when she looked at Bea, who had flushed nervously. Clearly Sir Charles and Bea were old friends, and judging from Bea's blush, she was very glad to see him.

"Oh, dear," Bea said, so flustered that she nearly dropped the hamper. "Sir Charles! How delightful to see you again! No, Papa has not come with me, I'm afraid. That is . . . I mean—" She stopped.

"He is not ill, I hope."

"No, quite to the contrary." A dimple flashed in Bea's cheek, and her plainness was transformed to something close to prettiness. "I fear I have been very naughty, Sir Charles. I took leave of Melford without informing Papa or Mama. I have not told them that I have come to Bishop's Keep. Should you happen to see them, I beg you not to give me away."

Kate looked from Bea to Sir Charles. "You have been long acquainted?" she asked.

Sir Charles nodded. "We met through Sir Henry Roscoe, Miss Potter's uncle and a chemist of distinction. He showed me her drawings of fungi, including one of a clump of *Peziza Aurantia*. Most remarkable, I must say. Extraordinarily precise. A very faithful reproduction of nature." He turned back to Bea. "And I thank you for the copy of your paper on the propagation of mould spores, Miss Potter. I found it quite intriguing. I hope we will have time during your visit to discuss it."

"Mould . . . spores?" Kate asked.

"Indeed," Bea replied happily, more animated than Kate had seen her. "I have recently been considering lichens, as well, Sir Charles, and I am anxious to have your views on my theory that they are dual organisms, fungi living in close association with algae. Uncle Henry says I should discuss the matter with Mr. Thiselton-Dyer, the Director at Kew."

Sir Charles nodded. "I should certainly like to hear your ideas, Miss Potter. But in the meantime—" His eyebrows drew together and his face became sober. "You will no doubt hear the news from your housekeeper, Miss Ardleigh. But perhaps I should set you right on the matter first, so that you will not be overly distressed when you discover that your maid Amelia and the Marsden footman, Lawrence—''

''Lawrence!'' Kate exclaimed, remembering Eleanor's suspicion. ''And Amelia?'' Could she be involved in some kind of wretched jewel-robbing scheme?

''I trust you won't make it hard for the girl. She and Lawrence meant no great mischief.''

''I think, Sir Charles,'' Kate said grimly, ''that you had better tell me exactly what they *were* up to.''

An apologetic look crossed his face. ''I am afraid,'' he said, ''that they discovered a dead man.''

Bea gasped. ''A dead man!'' Kate exclaimed, forgetting all about the emeralds.

''Yes,'' Sir Charles said soberly, and told them.

''Oh, how appalling!'' Kate cried, clasping her hands. ''Poor Agnes Oliver!''

''You know the widow, then?'' Sir Charles asked.

''I do,'' Kate said. ''I met her at St. Mary's Church. She has helped me carry on Aunt Sabrina's work.'' Kate was Irish and had grown up in an Irish family, but she had given up attending Mass years before. Under the gentle influence of Vicar Talbot, the Episcopal vicar in the nearby village of Dedham, she had continued her aunt's practice of giving generously to the support of needy people in the surrounding villages and hamlets. ''I must call on Agnes tomorrow,'' she said. ''How very dreadful! And whatever will the poor woman do to earn a living?''

''She is to be given a police pension, I understand,'' Sir Charles said. ''Fifteen pounds a year, and two-and-ten for the child.''

''This Sergeant Oliver,'' Bea said tremulously, ''this friend of yours—you said he was *murdered*, Sir Charles?''

''I'm afraid so,'' Sir Charles said. ''The coroner's inquest was held yesterday. The jury returned a verdict of homicide.''

''Does Constable Laken yet have an idea why the sergeant was killed?'' Kate asked. The death of the constable and the loss of the jewels seemed to her unusually coincidental. Perhaps they were connected. If so, the constable would soon discover it. She pulled herself up short. No, he wouldn't, for he couldn't know that Lady Marsden's emeralds were missing. No one but she and Eleanor—and the thief—knew that. She would send a message to Eleanor immediately and let her know what had happened. Lady Marsden must be told about the theft, and the constable informed. The business was very possibly connected to the murder

"Laken has been taken off the case and the investigation handed over to some bureaucrat in Colchester," Sir Charles said. "Some ridiculous political thing, no doubt. Ned's terribly upset by it, of course, for he was Oliver's friend. But his hands are tied."

"I don't suppose," Kate remarked, thinking that Lady Marsden might find it easier to talk to Sir Charles about the missing emeralds than to the constable, "that *your* hands are tied."

A smile flickered briefly across Sir Charles's face. "You are right," he said. "I intend to find out who killed Arthur Oliver." He went back to his horse and stepped into the saddle, and Kate thought that his eyes seemed to linger on her. "I am sorry to have been the bearer of bad news, Miss Ardleigh, so shortly upon your arrival." He shifted his glance to Bea with a smile. "I won't forget those lichens, Miss Potter. We must talk soon."

As she said good-bye to Sir Charles, Kate was thinking about Agnes Oliver and her daughter Betsy, and whether they needed help. And Beryl Bardwell—the irrepressible Beryl, whose imagination was fired by even the slightest of mysteries—was deeply intrigued. Why had Sergeant Oliver been killed? What did his murder have to do with the theft of the emeralds? Was Lawrence involved in either, or both? And what of Amelia?

As Kate turned to go up the stairs to Bishop's Keep, her mouth firmed. She had work to do. And she knew exactly where to start.

13

And so he made off with the rubies and left his sweet love behind, never to be the wiser, never to know why her miscreant lover had flown.

—HARRIET PAXTON
The Perjured Heart

"Amelia," Kate said firmly, "I am not overly concerned with the impropriety of your leaving the party to walk in the lane with Lawrence. What I am concerned about is the fact of the sergeant's death, and any connexion Lawrence might have had with it."

Amelia's tear-filled eyes widened. "Lawrence! Oh, miss, there's no connexion, none! He didn't even *know* th' pore man! He was told later, by Constable Laken an' Sir Charles."

Kate eyed her maid narrowly. She knew Amelia for a truthful girl and a good one at heart. Kate was sure that she was telling the truth. What she could not be sure of, however, was how much of the truth Amelia might *not* know. Lawrence, with whom Kate was little acquainted, might be very devious and canny. Perhaps he had murdered the constable when he was discovered with the emeralds, then disposed of the body and arranged to stumble on it himself, in the company of an innocent witness. He would thereby avoid all suspicion of guilt.

Kate softened her tone. It would do no good to frighten the

girl, or alienate her. "How long have you known Lawrence, Amelia?"

"A few months, miss," Amelia said nervously. "Since the magic lantern show."

"And you have become well acquainted with him?"

She ducked her head. "Not to say *well*-acquainted, miss. We 'uv got t' be friends."

"How long has he been with the Marsdens?" No, wait. She knew the answer to that. Eleanor said he had been in their employ for seven years.

Amelia was shaking her head. "I can't say, miss. All I know is that he's th' footman, an' well-liked. But he's valetin' fer Sir Charles right now."

Kate looked up sharply. "For Sir Charles?"

"Yes, miss." Amelia shifted. "Sir Charles didn't bring a valet. Lady Marsden give him Lawrence."

"I see." Kate thought for a moment. "Do you and Lawrence have future plans, Amelia?"

Amelia went rosy. "Oh, no, miss," she said, flustered. "I'm sure I—I mean, he hasn't . . ."

"If you were to marry, would he stay in service?"

Amelia looked shocked. "Of course, miss! How else would we live? Service is how we earn our living."

"Thank you, Amelia," Kate said. If Lawrence had made off with the emeralds and planned to use them to finance a new start in life, he had not told Amelia, of that Kate was certain. But Beryl Bardwell's imaginative mind did not for one second take that to be a guarantee of the man's innocence. He wouldn't be the first man to fly with his booty and leave both his service and his sweetheart behind.

Still, Kate had discovered something interesting from her questioning of the maid: Lawrence, it seemed, was temporarily serving as Sir Charles's valet. Eleanor had said that she planned to inform Sir Charles about the theft of the emeralds. Kate wondered whether he might have some immediate impression of Lawrence as a possible thief—or murderer. For Beryl Bardwell was persuaded that there was a link between the two.

So as Kate directed the maid's unpacking, she had something else to think about: the conversation she planned to have with Sir Charles regarding Lawrence, the emeralds, and the dead police sergeant. She sat down at her desk to write him a note and ask him to call tomorrow—in the afternoon. For in the morning she must offer her condolences to Agnes Oliver.

At the thought of Agnes, Kate felt a deep sympathy. How hard it must be for her to be left in the world without the one she loved and depended upon for her livelihood. But at least she had her pension, Kate reminded herself as she sealed the note to Sir Charles and rang for Mudd to arrange for it to be sent. When a woman lost her husband she was very likely to lose everything else, as well.

14

Throughout the late 1800s, the average British citizen had little respect for the effectiveness of the police. Lack of training and opportunity, bureaucratic corruption, low pay, and even lower social status made it difficult to recruit good policemen. This was compounded by a reluctance to adopt modern scientific methods for criminal investigation and identification, and a lack of interest in new technologies of communication and transport. Most people felt that the police, taken all in all, were a sorry lot.
—GERRARD BINDLE
The Police in Nineteenth Century England

Dudley Pell turned in his chair and contemplated the detailed map of the County of Essex that hung on the plaster wall of the borough office in the Colchester Town Hall. On the map, each of the county's boroughs was outlined in red: the half-dozen smaller ones, like Braintree and Bishop's Stortford, and the larger ones, Chelmsford and Colchester. Within each borough, the police districts were outlined in green, with clusters of coloured pins to represent each location of the constabulary. He had risen from humble beginnings as a simple constable in the District of Great Baddow—a black pin, as it were—to the position of chief constable of the Colchester Borough—the *only* green pin. And he now had the enviable and useful authority of deploying and overseeing two red pins (inspectors), five blue pins (sergeants), and forty black pins (constables). Forty-seven pins in all, the entire borough force. His contemplation of the map was coloured with a certain justifiable pride.

The success that had come Chief Constable Pell's way in the last two decades had not been without cost. His leg, but more than that, his time and energy, leaving him with none to spare: he spent it all in work, one way or another. Much of this expenditure was invisible to those beneath him, who imagined that what he did in this office—signing his name to papers, drinking tea, speaking with his subordinates—was all that he did. They had no imagination. They couldn't conceive of his *real* work: all that went on in this office and outside it, beyond the formal perimeters of the job, as it were.

For of course the four hundred pounds a year plus fifty in allowance that the borough paid Dudley Pell did not come close to providing the kind of life—the house, the servants, the carriage—desired by his wife. Upon their marriage, she had brought him a meager but potentially profitable family interest in marine transport, which interest he had expanded over the years so that it now made up the difference between his salary and his wife's expenditures, with a nice bit left over for his own pleasures. This enterprise required that he spend the latter part of each afternoon at the quay at Wivenhoe, below Colchester, an altogether profitable activity, taking the long view of it. And even if his several undertakings did not require his full attention, he would have found something to keep him away from home. No matter what luxuries he bought her, Mrs. Pell grew more pettish every year, no joy after a long day at the office, on the quay or in the field. So the chief constable was in the habit of spending even longer days doing the various things he did, and very little time lounging in slippers and shirtsleeves at home, where Mrs. Pell could set upon him.

Chief Constable Pell withdrew his attention from his private affairs and looked again at the map, pulling at his black whiskers. At the moment, he was faced with a problem in the deployment of manpower. Sergeant Arthur Oliver, of the district of Gallows Green, had unfortunately gotten himself killed. Most unfortunately, for his was a record of exemplary service to the force. But there it was, he was dead, and Chief Constable Pell must assign his replacement. For the time being, P.C. Bradley from Manningtree could take on the district of the deceased in addition to his own, for Gallows Green and Manningtree were contiguous. Bradley was young and inexperienced, to be sure, but not unsuitable for the chief constable's purposes, for he was ambitious and had a young family to support. Superintendent Hacking had been set on Edward Laken, whose Dedham district also adjoined Gallows Green. But Laken would not do at all, and Pell was glad to have succeeded in bringing the super around to his way of thinking. It was Bradley, then. Pell would keep his eye on the boy and see how he got on.

Pell turned to his desk and picked up his pen to execute the appropriate order. He had just dipped it into his inkwell when there came a knock at the door. Upon his bidding, it opened, and P.C. Nutter put his head through.

"A gentl'man t' see ye, sir," he said respectfully.

"On what business?" Pell asked, not looking up. He signed the order with a flourish, blotted it, and held it out. "Take this and see that it's taken care of."

"Yessir." P.C. Nutter took the order. " 'E says 'tis th' business o' Sergeant Oliver's death, sir."

Chief Constable Pell pushed his lips in and out, considering. "Oh, very well, then," he said at last. "Show him in."

The man who came through the door had the easy, unconscious grace of a gentleman, but he did not wear a gentleman's clothes. His shapeless brown jacket was missing several buttons, his boots were muddy, and his brown felt hat a ruin. The chief constable, who required those about him to be neatly turned out, was not impressed.

"Well?" he demanded, leaning back in his chair. "What's this about Oliver?"

The man sat down and took off his wreck of a hat. "My

name is Charles Sheridan. I am an old friend of Artie Oliver. I took the photographs of the body.''

"Photographs?"

"Of the body," Sheridan repeated distinctly. "Entered in evidence at the inquest."

"Ah, yes, *those* photographs." Pell had little use for the camera as part of a policeman's kit. A sharp eye, that's what was wanted. He regarded the man. "Well?" he asked.

Sheridan's lips tightened. "I have come on the widow's behalf to ask about your plans for the investigation of her husband's death."

"Ah, yes." Chief Constable Pell gave a heavy sigh. "Poor woman. I understand she has a child."

"Yes."

"But the Standing Joint Committee has recommended a generous pension."

Sheridan leaned forward and put his elbows on the chief constable's desk. "The investigation," he said pointedly, "is my concern at the moment."

The superintendent gave the man's elbows a distasteful look. "My dear, ah, Sheridan," he said. "While the widow is due every sympathy, surely she cannot expect me to jeopardize the investigation by revealing its details."

"Details are not necessary," Sheridan said. His eyes were hard as brown-bottle glass. He fixed them on the chief constable. "A general outline will do."

Pell frowned. "I am afraid," he said carefully, "that I must refuse your request. I—"

"To whom have you assigned the investigation?"

"Why, I—" Pell's frown became a scowl. "I quite fail to see why it is any concern of—"

"To whom?"

The chief constable felt cornered. "P.C. Bradley, from Manningtree, will be doing the legwork," he said stiffly. "I, of course, will be informed of each development. Now, I must insist that you—"

"I met Bradley at the funeral. He's a boy. Why was Laken taken off the case?"

The chief constable puffed out his cheeks, feeling his face

redden. "I am not in the habit of discussing police affairs with civilians. Now, if you will be so good as to—"

There was another knock on the door, and the chief constable felt a great relief. P.C. Nutter came in. "Sorry fer th' int'ruption," he said. "Superintendent Hacking has sent fer ye, sir."

The chief constable did not rise. "Inform the superintendent that I shall be there shortly," he said. "And show this gentleman out, Constable Nutter. Our business is concluded."

Sheridan got up and jammed on his hat. "You're making a mistake. Laken is your best man."

Pell did not answer. For several minutes after Sheridan had gone, he sat musing. Then he hoisted himself up and faced the map. He took down one blue pin and moved a black pin a precise quarter of an inch to the left. He surveyed the map for a moment, his lips pursed. In his careful planning, had he overlooked something he should have considered? He thought not. At last he turned and walked, stiffly, to the door.

15

"Ha! I have a theory. These flashes come upon me at times."
—SHERLOCK HOLMES
Sir Arthur Conan Doyle, *The Sign of Four*

Charles Sheridan, his hat pulled down over his ears, rapidly took the stairs to the basement of Town Hall, where he pushed his way through the door of the Colchester Department of Police. A stout sergeant wearing a too-tight uniform jacket looked up from a stack of papers on his desk and gave him a weary nod of recognition.

"Morning, Sir Charles," he said, moving his elbows. As he did so, several sheets cascaded to the floor and he bent to pick them up. In the process, his pen flipped out of the inkwell, raining droplets of ink on the desk. With an even wearier look, the sergeant resumed his seat. "How c'n I be o' service, sir?" He picked up the pen wrong end first and looked dismally at the ink on his fat fingers.

"Why don't they buy you a fountain pen, Battle?" Charles asked. He took out a handkerchief and offered it. "Is Inspector Wainwright in?"

"With respect, sir," Battle said, "th' budget's a bit tight with regard t' fountain pens." He wiped off his fingers and made as if to return it. Then, noticing with some confusion the inky stains on the snowy cotton, he pulled it back and stuffed it in his pocket. "I'll see if th' inspector's available," he said, red-faced. As he stood, he dislodged a ledger that fell from the corner of the desk, knocking over a can and spilling dirty sand and the chewed stubs of cigars onto the floor. A moment later, when he returned with the news that the inspector was in, he had a broom in his hand and a resigned look on his round face.

The inspector's basement office was a square, dingy room with one window let into the wall near the ceiling and gridded over to hinder access from the street. His desk was a table piled with papers, boxes of evidence, and a crumpled paper parcel that from the look of it had recently contained eel pie and baked potato. Inspector Wainwright stood in the corner, taking down two crockery cups from a shelf over a gas burner on which a chipped enamel kettle was beginning to steam.

"Tea?" he asked morosely.

"Yes, thank you." Charles sat down on one of the two chairs. "It's good to see you in such high spirits."

Wainwright gave his caller a sideways glance as if to determine whether he was joking. But he apparently found nothing to smile at, for his long grey face remained gloomy. "No biscuits," he remarked, and poured boiling water onto a spoonful of tea leaves in a cracked pot.

"I can do without biscuits," Charles said. "Tell me about Pell."

Inspector Wainwright's face, if possible, grew even more gloomy. He put the lid on the pot.

"Well, then," Charles asked, "what about Hacking?"

Wainwright's thin mustache drooped. He put his hands in his pockets and stood stoop-shouldered, pondering the teapot. After several moments, he took his hands out of his pockets and poured the tea, then carried the cups to the table, where he pushed papers aside to clear a space. He still had said nothing other than "Tea?" and "No biscuits."

Charles sat back in his chair and regarded the inspector. They shared a fairly recent acquaintance, having jointly apprehended the killer of an unfortunate foreign gentleman whose remains had been discovered in an archaeological dig. During the investigation, their relationship had grown from mutual suspicion to grudging respect. But even on the crime's resolution, Wainwright had not seemed cheered by their success. In the several months Charles had known the inspector, he had yet to see the man smile.

Charles accepted his cup and looked around for the sugar. "I take it," he said mildly, "that you do not have a high opinion of either of your superiors."

With a long sigh, the inspector broke his silence. "Th' Colchester Telephone Exchange has signed on twenty-seven subscribers." He took a packet from his pocket, mournfully counted out four cubes of brown sugar into his tea, and handed the packet to Charles. "The Colchester Police haven't yet subscribed. 'Twill be next month, th' superintendent tells me. But he's very mean as to ha'pence, and that's what he's been tellin' me for th' past year. Next month." He stirred his tea with a bent spoon.

"I see," Charles said. When he had first met Inspector Wainwright, the man was hoping for a typewriter to assist with mountainous paperwork. But judging from the stacks on both his and Sergeant Battle's desks, his hopes had been disappointed. "It appears that neither Hacking nor Pell has a great interest in making the force more efficient."

The inspector gave his bleak assent.

Charles shook his head. "Well, I suppose I can understand. Little money, less imagination. But why in God's name did Hacking put Pell in charge of the Oliver murder? And why did Pell take Laken off the case and replace him with a green recruit?"

"Sheer baboonery," Wainwright said with an infinite sadness. "Pell's too wrapped up in his shippin' business t' take any notice of what's afoot, an' Hacking's too bone-lazy t' care. Doubt we'll see any improvement in th' force until they're gone, which won't be in my lifetime." He sighed heavily. "But at least they don't have sticky fingers, as they do at th' Yard." Wainwright never failed to bring up the moral corruption of the Metropolitan Police Force, whose scandals were regularly exposed in the newspapers. It was in his nature to be heavily burdened with the melancholy knowledge that all men—even, on occasion, the police—had their dark side.

Charles leaned forward. "What have you heard about the Oliver case?"

Wainwright sipped his tea. "Sheep-stealers," he said.

Charles frowned. "But if there were sheep-stealers about, I don't understand why Constable Laken wouldn't have known. The two districts are contiguous, and Laken is a careful policeman."

"Careful as may be," Wainwright replied. "But there are gypsies abroad, and where there are gypsies, there are sheep-stealers. At least that's the theory."

"Whose theory?"

"Hacking's. And Pell's."

"But I don't see the evidence for it," Charles persisted. "Laken tells me that no one has reported the theft of an animal. And if Oliver had received such reports, he would have informed Laken."

Wainwright shrugged. "Well, it's Hacking's theory, and he's not the sort to require a lot of evidence. Pell told him, I guess. Pell is the one who set Oliver to work on it, anyway."

"So it's Pell's theory?"

"Pell or Hacking, what does it matter?" Wainwright was philosophical. "Theories are easy. They come like flashes. It's the evidence that's harder."

"Is something being done to discover evidence?"

"You'll have to ask P.C. Bradley. That's his business."

"I will." Charles finished his tea and stood. "You'll send word if you hear anything?"

The inspector nodded. His eyes were large and sad, like those of a bloodhound. "I could send it faster with a telephone."

"No, you couldn't," Charles said. "There's no telephone yet at Marsden Manor. Not likely to be for quite a while yet, either."

Wainwright looked into his cup, found it empty, and pushed it away with a sigh. "By th' bye, what d'you hear of Miss Ardleigh?"

"I have a note from her," Charles said, "asking me to call this afternoon. She seems to be adapting admirably to her responsibilities at Bishop's Keep."

"Is that right?" Wainwright replied doubtfully. "Sergeant Battle rather wondered when he heard."

"Heard what?"

Wainwright's shrug was eloquent. "That she was seen in a lane just at dark, riding a bicycle." He paused, and raised his glance. "In the company of Constable Laken. Battle thought there might be something between them."

"Ah," was all Charles said, and made his face as blank as the word. But within himself, he felt the stirrings of something that could only be envy.

Ned Laken was a very lucky man.

16

I want to prove that all sections of Society poach. Magistrates, policemen, keepers, farmers if they get the chance. It's in our nature as Englishmen. It is in our Nature to Cop what We Can.

—JAMES HAWKER
A Victorian Poacher

Kate knew Agnes Oliver well enough to have formed a high regard for her, and, added to that, a strong sense of obligation. Gallows Green was one of the nearby hamlets where Aunt Sabrina's benevolent presence had often been felt. The villagers were for the most part agricultural labourers, and while they did not think of themselves as poor, poor they were, the weekly wage seldom amounting to more than ten shillings. Aunt Sabrina had provided blankets in the winter and garden vegetables in the summer, and clothing and shoes for the children throughout the year. Kate was eager to continue her aunt's philanthropic work.

"It seems little enough to offer," Kate had told the vicar, "when I consider how much I've been given." Life had been difficult growing up in her uncle's household, for Sergeant O'Malley's wages as a New York policeman never quite stretched far enough to meet the needs of a wife, six children, and a niece. Kate had always expected to work hard for her own living. Finding herself an heiress had been a shock. She was anxious to make use of her legacy in a way that would bring credit to the memory of her aunt, and Agnes Oliver, who knew almost every family in the district, had helped her to do so by identifying those in the greatest need.

So it was that on the morning after their arrival at Bishop's Keep, Kate and Beatrix took a gingham-covered basket into the gig and set off toward Gallows Green, two miles to the northeast by lane, less by the footpath. The hamlet nestled into the shoulder of a long, gentle slope above the River Stour, the expanse divided by pollarded hedges and stone fences into neat fields. The morning was warm, and the horse chestnut trees on the green in the center of the village were masses of white blossom. The twenty or so cottages, the inn, and a small general grocery shop with a postal office in the rear were ranged in a rectangle around the green. There was no church or school, for these were in Dedham, close by.

At the far end of the rectangle sat the Olivers' whitewashed cottage with its thatched roof and diamond-paned windows with green shutters, the dooryard bright with foxgloves, irises, and daisies. Agnes Oliver answered Kate's knock wearing a plain black cotton dress under a grey apron. Her brown hair framed a face that was lined with grief, but she managed a small smile. "It was good of you to come, Miss Ardleigh."

"I only heard of your loss upon my return yesterday," Kate said, taking Agnes's hand in hers. "My dear Agnes, I am so very sorry. I hope you'll let me do everything I can."

"Thank you," Agnes said simply. She stepped back. "Will you come into the kitchen? I'd ask you into the parlour, but—"

Kate understood. Sergeant Oliver's body would have lain for a time in the parlour, for friends to visit. It would not be a happy place for Agnes for some while.

Kate introduced Bea and they followed Agnes into the small kitchen. An antique eight-day clock with a single hour hand ticked pleasantly in the corner. A braided rug of red and blue rags warmed the stone floor. Six bright oranges were heaped in a blue bowl on the table, and the room was tangy with their fragrance. The kettle was boiling, and while Agnes put tea leaves into a green teapot and added boiling water, Kate set her basket on the table.

"Mrs. Pratt sent biscuits and sweets for Betsy and a pudding and some mutton for your supper," she said.

"That's very kind," Agnes said. She put the teapot on the table, and took three white china cups and saucers from the corner crockery cupboard. She looked up as the door opened and a small girl shot into the room, sandy brows pulled together in a furious scowl. She was wearing a grey sacking shirt and boys' patched trousers held up by a pair of red braces. Her hair was braided into two tight, carroty braids. At her heels was a small brown collie with alert eyes.

"Betsy," Agnes said gently, "please. Act a lady. We have visitors."

Betsy's scowl deepened. "I'm not a lady," she said indisputably, "so I can't act one. Ladies never get their hands dirty. I'm a girl." And she held out grubby, berry-stained hands to prove it.

"Those," her mother said distastefully, "are not the hands of a girl. They belong to a ragamuffin boy. Go and wash." As Betsy went, sighing, to the basin, Agnes added, "You remember Miss Ardleigh from Bishop's Keep. This is her friend Miss Potter. They've brought some sweets."

Betsy acknowledged the introductions with a nod. "Uncle Ned brought oranges," she said, making clear where her preferences lay. She washed her hands and dried them on the linen towel that hung under the basin, then sat down on a stool, the collie settling at her feet.

"She's gone again," she remarked somberly. "I've looked and looked. She's not to be found."

"I'm sure she'll turn up," Agnes said, beginning to pour the tea. "She always does, you know."

Betsy looked at Kate, her mouth pulled down, her eyes—a startling lavender blue—intent. "Where would *you* lay your eggs if you were a duck and you were tired of having them found and carried off?"

"I think I should want a quiet place," Kate replied thoughtfully. "And if I expected to raise a family, I should certainly want to be clear of cats."

Beatrix leaned forward. "A duck?" she asked curiously. "What's her name?"

"Jemima," the girl said. "Jemima Puddle-Duck." She looked at Beatrix, her glance giving nothing away. "You like ducks, then."

"Most decidedly," Beatrix said. She rose. "If you like, I shall help you search."

The girl accepted the offer with a neutral shrug. "Well, come along, then," she said, sliding off the stool. The collie got up. "You stay here, Kep," she commanded. "Jemima won't take tupp'nny from you." To Bea, she said, "Kep's trained as a tracker, you know. He can track people. He always tracked my father, in fun, of course." She nudged the collie with her toe, her voice scornful. "But he thinks Jemima is foolish, so he won't track her." The dog who refused to track ducks lay back down again with a resigned sigh and watched as the girl and Beatrix went out of the room.

"She's taking it hard," Agnes said, with a sad look. "She's always been her father's girl, and not much girl at that. Always fancied herself more boy. With his encouragement, too."

"There's something to be said for that," Kate said. "In the long run, Betsy's spirit of adventure may stand her in good stead."

"Perhaps," Agnes said. "But in the short of things, it's bound to bring her trouble. She needs to learn decent manners if she's to get work in the world."

Kate took her cup from Agnes. "Mrs. Pratt tells me that you are to receive a police pension."

Agnes sat down. "I fear it is in doubt."

"In doubt?" Kate exclaimed. "But why?"

Agnes bit her lip. "Because," she said in a low voice, "of what P.C. Bradley found in the shed."

"Who is P.C. Bradley?"

"The constable from Manningtree who's looking into Artie's murder—instead of Ned Laken, who ought to do. He was here very early this morning. Out in the shed, he found two hares and a net."

"Two hares and a—" Kate set the cup down hard, and tea slopped into the china saucer. "A *poacher's* net?"

"Yes. But it wasn't Artie's!" Agnes said passionately. "He

never, *never* brought game for me to cook. It's no secret that almost everybody in the village takes a hare from the Marsden park now and again, or pheasant. But never Artie. He was proud of being a police sergeant. He was an honest man.''

This was a serious business, Kate knew. The possession of a net was generally taken, *de facto*, to mean that its possessor was engaged in poaching, which carried serious penalties. If the Police Committee decided that the net and the animals had belonged to Sergeant Oliver, they might well deny Agnes her pension.

"Perhaps someone put the net and the hares in the shed," Kate said. "Perhaps—" She was interrupted by a knock at the front door. As Agnes went to open it, she sat back, glad that she had not finished her sentence. It was not right to involve Agnes in speculation about her husband's killer. The poor woman had enough to worry about as it was.

When Agnes came back, Edward Laken was with her, bearing a paper-wrapped parcel.

"Miss Ardleigh," he said, his grey eyes smiling. "Kate."

"Hello, Ned," Kate said. In the past months since her aunts' deaths, she had come to count Edward Laken as a friend. He was a dependable man, a man of kindness and common sense. He was patient too, even with a novice cyclist who habitually rode her machine into the ditch.

Edward held out the parcel to Agnes. "I've brought Artie's things," he said, sober-faced. "The police surgeon has done with them."

"Thank you," Agnes said. Her face was pale but her voice was steady. "Miss Ardleigh, I've gathered together Artie's clothing. I wonder if you would take it to the vicar. He promised to see that it was distributed to those in need."

"Of course," Kate said, and watched as Agnes undid the parcel and took out a bloodstained uniform jacket.

"This can be cleaned and mended," Agnes said matter-of-factly, and laid it aside. "Artie would not want it to go to waste, when others are going cold." She went through the rest of the parcel until she found a cheap silver-plated watch on a long chain. She fingered it lovingly for a long moment, then searched through the parcel again. "Where is his sovereign?" she asked.

"I don't remember that he had a sovereign about him, Agnes." Edward looked uncomfortable. "There were only a few shillings in his pockets."

"On his watch chain, it was," Agnes said, holding it out. "Just here. It was his father's lucky coin, you see, with a nick in the edge. Betsy should have it."

"I'll ask after it in Colchester," Edward said, but he sounded doubtful.

"Perhaps it's in a pocket," Kate said. She picked up the jacket and pushed her fingers into a pocket. "Nothing in here but chaff," she said, pulling it out, "and some grains of wheat. If you'll give me the other things, I'll see that the vicar gets them."

When Agnes had gone up the narrow stairs, Kate turned to Edward. "You've heard about the hares and the net?" she asked in a low voice.

Edward's mouth was taut. "It's a nasty business, Kate. The committee could deny Agnes her pension."

Kate was silent for a moment. She could think of two possible explanations for the presence of the equipment and the dead hares hanging in the shed. The things could have been placed there to distract attention from the real crime—the theft of the emeralds, say. But even Beryl Bardwell had to admit that this was unlikely. The other explanation was much more probable.

"Is it possible," she asked, "that the sergeant discovered a poaching ring? Could that have been a motive for his murder?"

"It could," Edward said. "Times have been hard these last years. Poached game is free meat. And good money, too. It's sold by the hundredweight to shops in London."

"Who would know?"

Edward shrugged. "The local farmers, usually. They don't often tell, however. They hate the gentry for their ruinous game preservation practices. They see poachers as Robin Hoods."

There was yet a third possible explanation. "Sergeant Oliver himself couldn't have been involved?"

Edward's reply was firm. "Not Artie. A man of greater scruple never lived."

"Well, then," Kate said conclusively. "We shall have to discover who hung the hares and the poaching net in the shed." Whether it had been done to conceal another crime, or was connected to the crime itself, the objective was obviously the same. Find the one who did it, and the killer was found.

Edward looked at her. "You must stay clear of this business, Kate. A police officer has been murdered."

Agnes's step on the stair kept Kate from replying, but she had no intention of staying clear. Agnes Oliver was her friend.

"Here is the clothing," Agnes said. "I've kept several shirts to make over for Betsy. But the rest of these things should go to the vicar." She turned to the kettle. "Let me make you a cup of tea, Ned." She was pouring it when Betsy danced into the kitchen, cradling a white duck in her arms.

"We found her!" Betsy exalted. "Miss Potter discovered her under the cabbages at the back of the garden!"

"And we found this as well," Beatrix said, holding up a large white egg.

"You'll let Jemima keep the egg, won't you, Mother?" Betsy asked anxiously. "She *does* so want to start a family."

Agnes took the egg and put it into a basket on the window sill. "I'm afraid not, Betsy. Ducks are very poor sitters. Jemima would never stay on the nest for the twenty-eight days it takes to hatch the eggs, and they would all be wasted. If you want ducklings, we'll save the eggs and set them under a hen."

Betsy's eyes grew stormy but she said nothing. Beatrix was introduced to Edward Laken, Agnes fetched another cup, and while Betsy took Jemima outside, the grown-ups had their tea. When they finished, Kate added the bloodied jacket to the clothing Agnes had brought downstairs, and she and Beatrix prepared to leave.

"You'll call on me if you need anything, won't you, Agnes?" Kate asked, taking the other woman's hand.

"I shall," Agnes said. "Thank you."

Edward gave Kate a warning look. "And you'll remember what I said?"

Kate did not reply. Edward looked as if he were about to say something, then thought better of it. Good-byes were exchanged, Kate put the clothing into the gig, and Beatrix climbed in beside her.

"What did Constable Laken mean by that last remark?" she asked as the pony moved smartly down the lane.

"He meant that I shouldn't meddle in the investigation into Sergeant Oliver's murder," Kate said.

Beatrix turned to look at her. "And are you?"

"Not yet," Kate said. "But I am very concerned about Agnes." She told Bea about P.C. Bradley's find in the Olivers' shed and the possibility that Agnes might lose her widow's pension.

"Without the pension, how could she live?" Beatrix asked, in the horrified voice of one for whom money was abundant, even if she herself had little.

"On charity," Kate said thinly, flicking the pony's rump with the reins. She could support Agnes and Betsy, if it came to that. But Agnes was a proud woman: She and her daughter would have to be very hungry and cold before she accepted money from a friend.

That was the last that was said of the matter until Kate returned to the gig from the vicarage, where she had left Sergeant Oliver's clothing. Bea was holding the bloody coat.

"You forgot this," she said.

"I thought to keep it for the time being," Kate replied. She climbed into the gig and picked up the reins. "Will you mind if we make one other stop before we start home?"

"Not at all," Beatrix said. "Where are we going?"

"To call at the McGregors' cottage," Kate said.

"Isn't that where the constable's body was found?"

"Yes," Kate said. She lifted the reins and the pony moved down the lane. But when she brought him to a stop a mile or so later, beside the hedgerow, there was no cottage to be seen.

"I thought we were going to call on the McGregors," Bea said.

"This is their back garden," Kate replied, getting out of

the gig. ''I wanted to see for myself the spot where the constable was found, and I thought it inadvisable to announce our presence.'' She looked around, trying to visualize what must have happened here several nights ago. The sun was warm on her face and the late morning was bright around her. But inside she felt a dark chill as she conjured up in her imagination the killer's furtiveness, the fear of being seen, the stomach-turning horror, perhaps, at the savagery of what he had done. The inert weight of the dead man, the snapping of twigs as the body was dragged through the hedge to be abandoned in the copse on the other side. And then the hurried escape, the hasty command to the horses, the flight into the darkness, unseen—to where?

The bright sun slipped behind a cloud and Kate shivered against the bleak reality of her imaginings.

Where had the killer gone? Where was he now? Was he smugly gloating, knowing that he had so far successfully eluded all the efforts to identify him?

Who was he?

17

The gamekeepers, whose numbers had risen to well over 15,000 by 1895, outnumbered the police in many rural counties. As the elite of the estate employees, they often behaved arrogantly and with little regard for the rights of the tenants. Feared and distrusted by the farmers, gamekeepers were a law unto themselves.

—CYRIL PADGETT
The Victorian Gamekeeper

The copse still showed evidence that something had lain there, and the marks of the dead body's removal were still evident in the grass. But when Kate and Bea examined the ground in the area, they found nothing of real interest.

"I think," Kate said, "that we should find Mr. McGregor." They walked down the lavender-bordered path toward the cottage. As they came to the corner, Kate held up her hand. They could hear voices.

"All I want to know, McGregor," a high, thin voice was saying, "is whether you know where he is."

"I haven't seen 'im, and ain't like to," a different voice said, as raspy as a rusty file. "Leave it, Tod, an' be gone wi' ye. I'm off t' th' Manor."

The thin voice became peeved. "There's no call t' take that tone with me, McGregor."

"I'll take any tone I please wi' intruders on my place. Now be gone!"

Kate stepped around the cottage, trailed by Bea. "Mr. McGregor?" she asked.

Two men stood looking at her, their faces reflecting their surprise at the sudden appearance of the two women. One man was tall and thread-paper thin, with a sharply pointed chin, coppery whiskers along his jaw, and a brush of reddish hair under a green felt hat. The other was stooped and surly with a grey beard. In one hand he held a long-barreled gun and in the other the reins of a grey horse. He was the one who spoke next, in a crabby tone.

"I'm McGregor."

"Good morning, sir," Kate said. "I am Miss Ardleigh, of Bishop's Keep."

McGregor grunted. "I know who ye are. I seen ye ridin' yer bicycle." He gave a sharp chuckle.

Kate didn't like the tone of his voice, but she behaved as if she had not noticed it. "And you, sir, are—?" She turned to the other man.

"Tod, ma'am." The copper-haired man swept off his hat with a foxy smile. "Russell Tod, at your service, ma'am."

"To be sure, Mr. Tod." Kate recognized the bailiff who had organized the workers who picked apples during last autumn's harvest. The yield had been heavy, and the villages and hamlets roundabout could not provide enough labourers. Mr. Tod had been hired to bring in navvies and gypsies and other itinerant workers to speed the picking.

Tod replaced his hat and turned to McGregor. "If you see him, tell him he's wanted tomorrow night."

McGregor growled something inaudible. Tod nodded to Kate and departed without a word.

Kate turned back to the surly man. "You are Lord Marsden's assistant gamekeeper, I understand."

McGregor nodded and laid his gun across the saddle. "Been so fer a dozen years," he said, putting his foot into the stirrup.

"Then," Kate said, "I suppose you are aware of whatever poaching might occur in the vicinity?"

McGregor's eyes grew flinty. "People got no respect fer propity." He swung onto the horse. "There's allus poachers. That's me job, t' keep th' poachin' down. Keeps me busy."

Kate looked up at him. "What do you know of poaching in regard to Sergeant Oliver's death?"

McGregor's eyes shifted to Bea and back again to Kate. His mouth twitched in something like a smirk. "Oh, so *that's* wot ye want t' know," he said. "Come t' think o' it, I *did* hear summat about a net an' a hare er two hangin' in th' sergeant's shed." He pulled his brows down fiercely. "There's plenty o' crooked coppers these days. Wudn't surprise me if he was one of 'em. Now, 'f ye'll 'xcuse me, I'm expected at th' manor." He turned his horse's head and rode off down the lane.

Bea looked at Kate and wrinkled her nose. "A thoroughly unlikable and arrogant man," she said. "His eyes are shifty."

"He reminds me of a ferret," Kate said. They began to walk back through the garden to their gig and pony waiting in the lane.

"But ferrets are quite fetching creatures," Bea objected, "and not at all arrogant. My brother, Bertram, had one once. Its name was Filbert, and its gaze was most direct."

Kate frowned. "Well, I hardly think we could call Mr. McGregor a fetching creature," she said. "I think the man knows something." She quickened her step. "But we must hurry. It's past time for lunch, and I've asked Sir Charles to call this afternoon."

The ride from Colchester toward Dedham was a pleasant one, through narrow lanes under the blossoming hawthorn, loud with the midday cries of linnets. But Charles scarcely noticed the beauty of the countryside, for the business about sheep-stealing was still in his head. Had Artie been investigating theft when he was killed? Or was it more than that: Had he been killed *because* he was investigating theft? If so, someone in the farm district of Gallows Green ought to know something. But short of questioning each farmer, one by one, how could the matter be uncovered? And if the business were so surreptitious that Artie had not told Ned about it, would the farmers be any more free with their tongues?

Charles frowned, remembering that in fact someone *had* talked already of sheep-stealing: McGregor, in whose garden Artie's body had been discovered. At the thought, his mouth hardened. Was there a connexion, after all, between McGregor and the murder? Perhaps not. Perhaps it was entirely coincidental that the murderer had chosen his garden in which to abandon the victim's dead body.

But there was also the possibility that McGregor himself knew something more than he admitted—that he had been one of the killers, or knew the killers. He might have agreed to placing Artie's body in his garden until it could be moved elsewhere. The question certainly warranted more investigation. He would search out McGregor after he had spoken with Miss Ardleigh at Bishop's Keep. And after he had talked with P.C. Bradley, the constable at Manningtree.

Charles pulled out his watch. It was early yet to call on Miss Ardleigh, but Bishop's Keep was quite nearby. He would go there next, and then to Manningtree. But as he turned a sharp bend, he had to pull up sharply to avoid a smartly-stepping pony and gig.

"Sir Charles!" Miss Ardleigh said, pulling the pony to a stop. "Good afternoon."

"Good afternoon," Charles replied. He tipped his hat. Miss Ardleigh looked quite pretty, with russet tendrils curled loose around her face, cheeks flushed, eyes bright. He thought of Ned and looked away. "I was just on my way to Bishop's Keep."

"As are we," Miss Potter said in her sweet, cheerful voice. "We have just come from calling on Mr. McGregor."

Charles frowned. Miss Ardleigh was a charming and intelligent woman, but her cleverness could get her into difficulties which charm could not resolve. "If you don't mind my asking," he said stiffly, "what took you to see McGregor?"

Miss Ardleigh's reply was cool. "We went because we are concerned about Agnes. This morning very early, the constable from Manningtree found a pair of hares and a net in the Olivers' shed."

"Hares and a net!" Charles exclaimed.

"Yes. Agnes may lose her pension if the authorities believe

that her husband was involved in poaching. Mr. McGregor is a gamekeeper. He seemed the logical person to ask.''

Charles stared at her. The woman might as well be a detective, such a nose she had for information. ''Well?'' he asked, ''what did you learn?''

''Disappointingly little,'' Miss Ardleigh admitted, ''although Mr. McGregor gave me reason to suspect that he knows more than he's willing to tell.''

''His eyes were shifty,'' Miss Potter added in explanation.

Miss Ardleigh checked the pony. ''Have you made any progress in your investigation, Sir Charles?''

''Not as much as you have,'' Charles replied honestly. ''I've only just come from talking with the chief constable in Colchester.''

''Oh, yes,'' Miss Ardleigh said. ''I suppose he is the one who took Edward off the case. What did you learn?''

Charles spoke with more heat than he intended. ''That Pell is incompetent and too busy about his own affairs to be much bothered with his official duties. He has assigned a young and inexperienced policeman to the case—P.C. Bradley.''

''Yes.'' Miss Ardleigh nodded. ''The one who found the hares and the net.''

''But Mrs. Oliver says that her husband would never have been involved with poaching,'' Miss Potter said.

Miss Ardleigh looked at Charles. ''You knew Sergeant Oliver. Do you agree?''

''I do indeed,'' Charles replied. Honesty was one of the traits Artie had shared with Edward Laken. Many police officers might take a little something in tribute. But never Ned, nor Artie.

Miss Ardleigh tilted her head. ''That means that either he stumbled onto poachers and took the hares and the net as proof of their wrongdoing, or that someone has—''

''Constructed the evidence in such a way as to deliberately implicate him.'' Charles finished the sentence for her.

''Exactly so,'' Miss Ardleigh said. She raised her eyebrows. ''But there is something else that may complicate this situation, Sir Charles, and that is why I asked you to call at

Bishop's Keep. It has to do with some emeralds that are missing from Lady Marsden's safe."

"Emeralds!" Charles exclaimed.

Miss Ardleigh nodded. "When Eleanor returned a ring she had borrowed from her mother, she saw that the other jewels were missing from the set, although she knew them to have been there shortly before." She gave him a narrow look. "She suspects that Lawrence might have taken them. She has not mentioned this to you?"

"Eleanor is not expected at the manor until tomorrow," Charles replied. "I could not swear that Lawrence is not a thief. But if he took the emeralds, I do not believe he would stay to risk discovery." He regarded Miss Ardleigh. "You are supposing that the theft of the emeralds is somehow connected to the murder of Sergeant Oliver?"

"I thought it possible when I learned that it was Lawrence who discovered the body." Miss Ardleigh pursed her lips. "I am not in a position to investigate the theft of the emeralds, Sir Charles. You are. Perhaps you could look for a connexion to the sergeant's murder. And perhaps I could pursue the poaching business and discover whether our murderer—"

"Miss Ardleigh," Charles broke in hastily, "I must congratulate you on the impeccable logic with which you have analysed the situation. But this is not *your* murderer. You must stay out of it. You might find yourself in serious danger. Or you might—"

Miss Ardleigh's hands tightened on the reins. "Muck things up?"

It was not a word Charles would have expected a lady to use, but it certainly fit the circumstance. "I fear so," he replied.

"Oh, really, Sir Charles," Miss Potter said earnestly, "Miss Ardleigh's efforts scarcely warrant—"

Miss Ardleigh's tone became sharp. "The man has made up his mind, Bea. It's pointless to attempt to reason with him." She raised the reins and chirruped to the pony. "Let's go home."

Charles scarcely had time to tip his hat before they had driven away. For a moment he sat, looking after them in sheer surprise. Then, as he turned to ride off in the opposite direction, he caught himself chuckling.

18

Policemen are but men, their pay but scanty, their situations precarious, and it would be too much to expect that all are so pure as to decline to make a little money when favourable opportunities present themselves.

—*St. James Magazine,* 1865

The twin villages of Manningtree and Mistley lay at the mouth of the River Stour, where it ceased to be a well-defined river and lost itself among the reeds of Seafield Bay, sheeting like hammered silver across Jacques and Copperas and Holbrook Bays, and thence into Harwich Harbour before spilling into the stormy grey waters of the English Channel. At Manningtree and Mistley, the upper reaches of the Stour estuary were deep enough to accommodate ocean-going vessels, and as Charles rode down the hill and through the twisting streets into the town, he could see the forest of masts along the quay. The air had a salt taste, and gulls wheeled over a recently arrived fishing boat, raising a hungry clamour.

The police station and gaol were in the rear of a plastered building at the foot of Wharf Street, which housed an apothecary's shop in the front and dentist's and doctor's offices above. Charles reached it by taking the cobbled alley to the rear and stooping under a low lintel. A narrow hallway gave directly onto a square room with one window and a barred cell at the back, quite chilly, where the atmosphere was acrid with coal smoke. A uniformed man was down on both knees, putting a light to a coal grate. He scrambled to his feet when Charles came in.

"Sir Charles Sheridan," Charles said in a crisp, old-school voice. He did not offer his hand. "You are P.C. Bradley, I assume."

"I am," said the constable. He was a smart-appearing young man with pale grey eyes and blond hair combed slickly back. He had a certain arrogance, as if he were accustomed to having attention paid to him. He was, however, at some little disadvantage, for he was bootless. "Help you with something?" he asked, somewhat carelessly.

"I wish to speak with you."

The constable's eyes measured the distance to his boots, which stood on the other side of the grate, drying. Apparently deciding that he could not surreptitiously retrieve them, he muttered "Excuse me," reached for them, and took the required measures to put them on. Appropriately attired, he went behind his desk and asked, with a curl of his lip, "In regard to what business?"

"The death of Sergeant Oliver."

The constable's jaw tensed. "I have no information on the matter," he said stiffly.

Charles sighed. He did not want to be coercive, but he had no choice. He pulled himself up in a barrister-like stance. "I wish you to tell me," he said, "on whose authority you recently invaded the home of Sergeant Arthur Oliver, and removed two hares and a net from a shed."

P.C. Bradley's eyes blinked rapidly. "I am not at liberty to give information about a current investigation to—"

Charles held up his hand. "You are aware, are you not," he said coldly, "that the rights of property are jealously guarded by the law of England?"

"Well, I—"

"And that any unwarranted interference with the rights of property—even by the police—is a tort for which an action can be brought?"

The young man's eyes went from one side to the other. "But I understood that—"

"Just how was it," Charles asked, "that you determined it necessary to search the sergeant's property?"

The P.C.'s mouth twitched. He wore a cornered look. "I was given intelligence that I would find evidence of wrong-doing on the part of—"

"You were given *intelligence*," Charles said with a heavy emphasis. "Pray, Constable Bradley, *who* gave you this intelligence?"

"I . . ." The constable swallowed. "I cannot say, sir."

"You will not say?"

"I cannot." The P.C.'s voice had become shrill. He made an effort to bring it down a notch. "It was in a letter, sir."

"A *letter*," Charles said. The colour he gave to the word implied doubt as to the constable's veracity. "I don't suppose you are still in possession of this, ah, vital evidence?"

P.C. Bradley hesitated, obviously of two minds about the matter. He took three indecisive steps to a nearby table, opened a drawer, and took out an envelope. As Charles held out his hand he made a move to draw it back, but Charles persisted.

"Oh, very well," P.C. Bradley said irritably. "I don't suppose it can do any harm for you to see it."

The envelope was directed, in a sloping hand, to Police Constable Bradley, Wharf Street, Manningtree. The *B* was shaped with a flourish and the *t*'s were crossed with decorative twists. The envelope had not been posted.

"How was this delivered?"

"Don't know." The P.C. was sullen. "Found it in the door yesterday."

Charles opened the envelope and found inside a folded sheet of plain white paper, upon which was written in the same hand that had directed the envelope the terse intelligence that if the P.C. betook himself speedily to the shed behind the home of the recently deceased Sergeant Oliver, he would discover certain evidence unmistakably indicating the aforesaid sergeant's unlawful attempt to augment his earnings by engaging in the lucrative side-line of poaching, in which effort the writer had no doubt that the victim had met his untimely end. The letter was signed, "A Dutiful Citizen."

"You have no clue to this dutiful citizen's identity?" Charles asked.

"None, sir," the P.C. said. He held out his hand for the envelope. "Now if you will be so kind as to—"

"One moment." Charles reached into an inside pocket in his bulky jacket and took out a small box. In it were bits of charcoal and folded sheets of a lightweight, nearly transparent paper that he frequently used to make rubbings of certain interesting fossils. He took the letter to the window and proceeded to trace the script with a pen, taking care to reproduce it as exactly as possible.

The constable was alarmed. "With respect, sir, you can't be allowed to—"

"I'll square it with Pell," Charles said over his shoulder. "Don't worry, old chap, I shan't get you into difficulties with the chief constable."

"But that letter is evidence in a murder investigation. You can't—"

"Of course it's evidence," Charles said soothingly. "That's why I *must*." He finished his work and handed the letter back to the constable. "And here you are. None the worse for a bit of copying."

The constable's lips thinned. "Who *are* you, sir, to take it upon yourself to behave in this high-handed manner?"

"Who am I?" Charles asked. He looked down at the note in his hand. "A man who is interested in justice," he said, and turned and left the room.

19

Mr. B, Mr. B! riddle-me-ree!
  Flour of England, fruit of Spain,
Met together in a shower of rain;
  Put in a bag tied round with a string,
If you'll tell me this riddle, I'll give you a ring!
                              —BEATRIX POTTER
                          The Tale of Squirrel Nutkin

That afternoon, Kate and Bea explored the ruins of Bishop's Keep and walked into the nearby woods, looking for interesting fungi for Bea to draw. While Bea sat down to sketch a large mass of rust-coloured toadstools against a mossy rock, Kate picked meadow buttercups and yellow heartsease, feeling herself almost contented.

But several nagging thoughts continued to intrude into her mind. One had to do with Sir Charles, whose patronizing objection to her investigative efforts still rankled. Another had to do with Agnes, whose future security depended upon her husband's posthumous reputation. Surely there was something she could do to ensure that Agnes kept her pension, even though Sir Charles had so pointedly told her to stay out of the affair. And the third had to do with the emeralds.

So when they returned to Bishop's Keep that afternoon, and while Bea was giving Peter Rabbit an airing in the shrubbery, Kate summoned her butler to the library. Mudd, she had found, could be counted upon to supply almost any information she might need about the local environs. While he was young for his position and clearly a climber, she knew him to be reliable in difficult circumstances and she respected his intelligence and good judgment. She had come to this assessment when he had assisted her in apprehending her aunts' killer a few months before.

"Mudd," she said, "I am greatly concerned about the welfare of Mrs. Oliver. I assume that you know her situation, and what is being said about her husband's off-duty pursuits."

Mudd inclined his head to show that he did. "A very sad business."

Kate eyed him. "What credit do you give the rumours about the sergeant's involvement in poaching?"

"None, mum," Mudd said firmly. "It's only the riffraff talking." Mudd was from London, and rather inclined to scorn the villagers, feeling himself their superior in station, manners, and intelligence.

Kate went to the mantle and stood staring down at the fire. "I have spoken with Lord Marsden's assistant gamekeeper, Mr. McGregor. What do you know of the man?"

Mudd pulled a long face. "He's a shrewd one, that Matthew McGregor. He has his hand into many a pot, I hear. People say they wouldn't put a spot of murder past him."

"But I understand," Kate said, "that the sergeant's body was discovered in Mr. McGregor's garden. One would scarcely think that a murderer would abandon a body on his own doorstep, would one?"

" 'Twas said at the inquest," Mudd remarked judiciously, "that the sergeant was shot elsewhere and left in the garden. But that was the constable's interpretation. If anybody saw what happened, they haven't put themselves forward yet."

"Suppose that theory isn't correct," Kate said, thinking out loud. "Suppose the sergeant *was* shot in the garden and left there with the intention of bringing a cart through the lane to take him somewhere else, probably at night, when no one was about. Only the business was somehow interrupted, and Lawrence and Amelia discovered the body before it could be disposed of."

"Could've been," Mudd agreed. "There's Mrs. Mc-

Gregor's brother, too. He's an unsavoury sort."

"Mrs. McGregor's brother?" Sir Charles had mentioned a brother in his telling of the story, but Kate did not recall the details.

"Tommy Brock," Mudd said, "called Mr. B by some. It was his gun that was first thought to be the murder weapon, but wasn't. He was gone for a time from the area, but he's back again. Or so Pocket's father says," he added. "He's the brewer's drayman, you see, and goes from pub to pub."

Kate had ceased to wonder at the marvelous efficiency of the information network that linked the villages and hamlets in the district so that news traveled as fast as by telephone in the city. Now she thought briefly of the copper-haired Mr. Tod, who had come to McGregor's inquiring after someone. Perhaps he had been looking for McGregor's brother-in-law.

"I would be obliged if you could inquire at the pub," she said, "into the matter of Mr. Brock's reappearance. I should like to know if the man seems to have any connexion to the crime."

Mudd was perfect for such an errand, because he had the interesting capacity of being able to mimic the speech and manners of those with whom he spoke. In any event, Kate herself could hardly visit The Live and Let Live without creating a local sensation. Even her completely innocent bicycle rides with Edward Laken had caused a great many raised eyebrows. And while Beryl Bardwell's female characters sometimes disguised themselves as males to gain information, Kate did not intend to do anything quite so *outré* when Mudd was available, willing, and excellently dependable.

Mudd gave her a canny glance. "I should have to go to the pub specially," he remarked. "I don't have another half-day until next month."

"Then go this evening," Kate commanded, "and tell me what you learn." She went to the desk drawer, took out a purse, and found two florins. "And use these to purchase a round," she added, giving Mudd the coins. "Perhaps a pint or two will loosen a few tongues."

Mudd straightened his shoulders. "Very good, mum," he said.

"And one more thing," Kate said. "What do you know about Lawrence, the Marsden's footman?"

Mudd's mouth reflected his displeasure. "A light sort, mum. He has played fast and free with Amelia's affections." Mudd might look down on the villagers, but he was unfailingly kind to the household staff.

"Aside from your opinion," Kate said, stressing the word, "what do you know of him?"

Mudd became rather more cautious. "Only what I see of him at the pub. He's likable enough. He's been in service hereabout for seven or eight years."

"I would not want you to mention this question to anyone else," Kate said, "but I wonder whether . . ." She paused and chose her words carefully. "Has there been any rumour of Lawrence's coming into a sum of money?"

"If he has, he's keeping it close," Mudd said sagaciously. "He's been drinkin' on th' tick. On credit, mum," he added. "He did not appear to be in funds."

"Thank you," Kate said. "And is there, do you think, any possible connexion between Lawrence and Mr. Brock?"

Mudd's brows came together. "I saw them drinking together once. A year or so ago, it was."

Kate nodded. "Thank you, Mudd," she said. "That will be all."

Mudd retired, leaving Kate standing alone beside the fire, speculating about the mysterious Mr. Brock. How did he figure in this increasingly complicated situation? Was it possible that he was somehow connected to Lawrence? Were the two of them related in any way to the emeralds? And were the emeralds connected to the sergeant's murder?

Kate walked to her desk, wondering how Beryl Bardwell might resolve this puzzle. If this were a novel, however, the plot would likely need more thickening before it was done. Wanting to feed her readers' taste for sensation, Beryl might add another murder, or perhaps a kidnapping, and a few exotic characters—a pirate or two, perhaps. But in the end, no matter how many complications she introduced, the solution would be as neatly wrapped and pleasing as a pudding. It was a pity that the mysteries of real life were not resolved so easily as Beryl Bardwell's penny dreadfuls.

20

O put not your trust in princes, nor in any child
of man: for there is no help in them.
—*Prayer Book*, 1662

In all of her nine years, Betsy Oliver had prayed on only
one occasion. Mister Browne, her pet owl, had flown off in
a huff after she had taken a live baby rabbit from him and
substituted a dead lizard. Betsy had petitioned God for his safe
return, and God (who in her imagination bore a remarkable
similarity to Father Christmas, the chief difference being that
He wore a white robe instead of a red fleece suit and was
somewhat less rotund) saw fit to respond by recalling Mister
Browne to his perch in the shed before another night was out.

This minor success notwithstanding, Betsy was not given to
prayer. It was not that she did not trust God to reply (for
evidence of the efficacy of prayer, she had only to look to the
safe return of Mr. Browne), but rather that she questioned the
ethics of the transaction itself. For instance, telling God that
you would be a good girl all day in return for marmalade
biscuit for tea, when all Mother could put on the table was
plain biscuit—wasn't that selfish and unjust? It seemed rather
shabby to ask God to slip it into Mother's head that she ought
to be supplying marmalade biscuit when she couldn't, with the
consequence that Mother felt sad when she had to serve up
plain, or spent more on marmalade than she ought. Or force
God to expend divine effort on a marmalade miracle, which

was admittedly more mundane than loaves and fishes but no doubt required every bit as much divine ingenuity.

Having reached this conclusion and despite the vicar's benevolent example and the exhortations of Miss Bottle, her Sunday School teacher, Betsy resisted putting God into such a sticky wicket. So when all the other Sunday scholars dutifully bowed their heads and repeated the Lord's Prayer after Miss Bottle, Betsy always sat with head up, eyes forward, and mouth resolutely shut. The murder of her father, however, tested her resolve. For several days after she learned the awful truth, it was all she could do not to fall on her knees and beg God for his return, intuitively feeling that while He could find an errant owl in the dark, it was asking too much to request Him to return an escaped soul to the body. Still, she was impressed and even somewhat comforted by the solemnity of her father's funeral at St. Mary's in Dedham, and by the gravity of the neighbours as they put the pine box with him in it into a muddy hole in the churchyard, and especially by the vicar's somber but fervent prayers for her father's soul.

Well. Her father had been loving, and far kinder than her friend Baxter's father, who fell to flogging his unfortunate wife and children when he got home from the pub on a Saturday night. Betsy had no doubt that a fair and incorruptible God would assign him a premier place in heaven, where he could enjoy his pipe and the view in comfort.

But Betsy was less certain about her mother's welfare, and it was that which led her to rethink her position on the matter of prayer. Her mother's seventeen pounds ten a year was not to be dealt out by God, but by the Standing Joint Committee of the County Police Constabulary. A skeptical realist whose experience as the daughter of a policeman had early introduced her to the darker side of human nature, Betsy did not trust the committee's good will. Not only that, but last Sunday's "O put not your trust in princes" still echoed in her mind. So she decided to call God's attention to the matter of the pension while there was still time for Him to have a hand in things without having to flex a great deal of divine muscle, and went to church to lay her petition before Him.

But it was not to St. Mary's in Dedham that she was going,

her collie dog, Kep, trailing after. The God who lived in such a lofty church might be too grand or too busy to be bothered by the difficulties of small people. So that morning, she followed instead a winding lane that led away from Gallows Green in the direction of the River Stour, to a very old, very plain church built of red brick and flint rubble. She and Kep and Mr. Browne had explored the building and its adjacent cemetery quite often, although this was the first time she had come on official business. She left Kep at the door and went in. Inside, it was chilly and dim, the only light coming through the narrow windows of the nave and the rose window above the altar. She went down the north aisle to the tiny Lady Chapel, where she slipped behind the rood screen, knelt at the undecorated altar, and said what was on her mind.

"God, I wish You would keep Your eye on the people who are supposed to be giving Mother her pension, because it looks as if they are trying to cheat her out of it, which would be a very bad thing. Amen."

Having thus succinctly put her case, she remained still for a minute, waiting to see if God planned to give her some sign that He had heard—a dove, perhaps, or even a pigeon. When nothing happened, she stood. She had done what she could. The rest was up to the Almighty.

21

Fifteen men on the dead man's chest
Yo-ho-ho and a bottle of rum.
—ROBERT LOUIS STEVENSON
Treasure Island

Kate pulled up the pony and she and Bea sat gazing at the little church, quiet in the morning sun. "It's very old," she said. "Aunt Sabrina donated a large sum to help shore up the tower, but it still needs work."

"Churches always want shoring up, don't they?" Bea observed realistically. "Our vicar is continually asking for money to keep the tower from falling down." She climbed out and took a heavy bellows camera and tripod from the gig. "Is there a particularly good view?"

"Over there," Kate said, pointing to a little knoll from which could be gained a picturesque vista of church, meadow, and estuary. "But let's look inside first. There are one or two inscriptions I want to show you, and the north aisle offers some very nice stone detailing."

Inside, they spent several minutes examining the carved inscriptions around the stone baptismal font and a commemorative plaque set into the wall. Kate was leading Bea up the north aisle for a better look at the stonework when they were both startled by a sudden apparition: a small girl in stiff pigtails, pumpkin-coloured shirt, brown corduroy trousers, and muddy boots.

"Oh!" Bea exclaimed, stepping back. "Betsy!"

"Why, hello," Kate said. "What are you doing here?"

"Praying," was the crisp answer. "What else do people do in churches?"

"Oh, lots of things," Kate said. She wanted to ask what Betsy was praying for, but she thought she knew, and the little girl's face did not invite casual inquiries.

"Did you come to pray?" Betsy asked, with more interest now, as if she might enlist the two of them in her petition to the Divine, whatever it was.

Kate smiled. "We came to see what we could see. And we're very glad to see *you*."

"Yes," said Bea. "How is your mother? We will be stopping there to visit later this morning."

Betsy's *I-suppose-she's-all-right-but-not-quite* shrug was perfectly comprehendible. "I can show you around," she offered, with a proprietary air. "There's a sundial and some very old gravestones. One's a pirate."

"We'll see the pirate," Kate said. "But first, let's look at the stonework."

A few minutes later, having admired the interior of the church, they went outside and were met by Kep, who escorted them to the back of the cemetery. The pirate's headstone bore an engraved name, a ship, and a cryptic bit of doggerel.

> He longed for Distant Places,
> He sought the whole World round.
> Pieces of Eight he was after,
> Eternal Peace he's found.

"I suppose," Bea said thoughtfully, "he really *must* have been a pirate."

Betsy turned to look out across the estuary, calm and gleaming in the late morning sun. "There's lots of pirates around here."

"There used to be, you mean," Bea said, bending over to examine a clump of silvery fungi. Kep looked at it with her, sniffing to see if it might be something he should remember and come back for later.

"No," Betsy said. She clearly did not appreciate contradictions. "Now."

"I really don't think there are pirates anymore," Kate remonstrated gently. She thought of Beryl Bardwell. "Except in novels, of course."

Betsy gave her a stony look. "You really don't *know*."

"How do *you* know?" Kate returned. "Have you seen them?"

"Of course." Betsy folded her arms across her chest. "Two nights before my father was killed." She pointed across the field in the direction of a stone barn, a half-mile away. "Over there. At Highfields barn."

"At night?" Kate frowned. She didn't ask *What were you doing out here at night?* for she wasn't Betsy's mother. But the question did cross her mind.

"Mister Browne was hunting," Betsy said. "It was mizzling, so I came with him. He sometimes catches baby rabbits on mizzly nights, and I take them away from him."

Kate frowned, trying to imagine who Mr. Browne might be and why he was so interested in baby rabbits that he'd go out on a rainy night to look for them.

Bea laughed at Kate's mystified look. "Mister Browne," she told Kate, "is Betsy's owl. I met him when we went looking for Jemima Puddle-Duck."

"Oh," Kate said. "I see." She looked at Betsy. "What were the pirates doing?"

Betsy turned to gaze out across the meadow at Highfields Farm. Kate followed her glance. The barn was only one of several buildings clustered together. Some distance away was a farmhouse with smoke coming from the chimney.

"They were drinking rum," Betsy said. She frowned. "But they weren't pirates exactly. They were more like smugglers. There were five of them. They whispered the whole while, drank rum out of a bottle, and they had horses and a wagon. But it wasn't loaded with dead men's chests. It was loaded with sacks. They drove it down to the river and carried the sacks onto a boat."

"But smugglers smuggle things *into* a country," Bea objected. "Not *out*."

"Maybe they plan to smuggle them into Spain," Betsy said.

"Why Spain?" Kate asked.

"Because," Betsy said, "one of the men was a Spaniard. They called him Juan. He drank the most rum."

Kate looked at the little girl. "Did you recognize any of the others?"

"They had their hats pulled down because of the wet. But one was very thin and had a pointy chin and red whiskers. The other one had the same name as yours." Betsy looked at Bea.

"Beatrix?" Bea asked, surprised.

"Of course not." Betsy's tone added *you ninny*. "B-E-E. 'How doth the little busy bee.' Mister Bee."

Bea looked at Kate, her eyes wide. "Red chin whiskers? It must be Mr. Tod, the bailiff!"

"And Mister B. might be Tommy Brock," Kate said. This morning, at breakfast, Mudd had reported to Kate and Bea what he learned at the pub the night before: that Tommy Brock (Mr. B. to his friends) seemed to have access to a large supply of shillings, which was quite remarkable since he had not worked since the last harvest, when he was employed by Mr. Tod. If Betsy were correct in her identification, the source of those shillings might be the pirates or smugglers or whatever they were, of whom Tod was one.

She frowned. It certainly looked as if Tommy Brock and Mr. Tod might be involved in something illegal—theft or smuggling, or both. But did that mean that they were connected with the death of Sergeant Oliver? And were the two of them involved with the theft of the emeralds as well? Or was that an altogether separate matter, unconnected to this one? And what of Lawrence? What was his role in all of this?

As Kate and Bea drove on to Gallows Green that morning, they had a long list of unanswered questions to discuss. But their discussion brought them no nearer to a solution.

22

A chapter of accidents.
—EARL OF CHESTERFIELD
Letter to his son, 16 Feb. 1753

Eleanor Marsden Fairley was in a dilemma. She had arrived
at Marsden Manor the evening before in the company of
her husband (the rather dull company of her husband, it had
to be admitted). She had come with the full intention of laying
her discovery of the theft of her mother's emeralds before Sir
Charles Sheridan, whom she knew to be a man of great logical
ability and an acute observer of human nature.

But this proved to be impossible, for when Eleanor had come
downstairs to dinner that night, she learned that Sir Charles had
gone to Dedham to spend the evening at the vicarage. Frustrated
and feeling that she could no longer carry the knowledge by
herself (the *guilty* knowledge, for she had by this time con-
vinced herself that if she had not accidentally left the safe unlocked, Lawrence would not have yielded to temptation), she
took the opportunity to approach her brother, Bradford, after
Papa and Mama and Ernest had gone upstairs to bed.

Bradford, ten years Eleanor's senior, was an extremely
handsome man with large blue eyes, blond hair and side-
whiskers, and a charming smile. But the smile and charm were
singularly absent just now. He was standing in front of the
fireplace in the library, staring at the flames, with his hands in
his pockets and a dark, brooding look on his face.

"I need to speak with you, Bradford," Eleanor said, "on a matter of great importance."

She spoke diffidently. Since the events of the week before, she and Bradford had not been on the best of terms. She had been dreadfully sorry that Ernest had refused Bradford's request for a loan, because it had seemed quite reasonable to her. But the money was Ernest's, of course, and Bradford should not be angry with her merely because she had been forced to convey her husband's refusal.

But then Bradford had seemed distant and angry a great deal of late. She did not expect him to share his feelings with her, however. The two of them had never been close. They were too distant in age for that, and Bradford had been sent away to school while Eleanor and her younger sister, Patsy, received their desultory and piecemeal education from various governesses. And of course Bradford was a son, the only son, and had always known that he would carry on the Marsden baronetcy and the Marsden traditions. He hadn't seemed to welcome that responsibility, and for over a decade had resisted his mother's efforts to find a suitable wife for him. But he must come to his senses soon, Eleanor knew, and seek a bride.

And if her suspicions were accurate, his choice had fallen upon Kate Ardleigh. Eleanor was sure she was right, for she had seen him look at Kate with speculative interest when they were together. From her brother's point of view, it would seem a good match: Kate was a lovely woman—a bit old, perhaps, at twenty-seven, but still quite pretty, with all that russet hair— and wealthy enough, now that she had inherited Bishop's Keep. Her estate bordered the Marsden lands along the north and would extend them considerably. And from Eleanor's point of view, the match was a romantic one, for Kate was her friend, and an American, and quite the most lively and adventurous woman Eleanor had ever known.

But it could not be Kate that Bradford was thinking of just now, for there was a fierce look in his eyes and his brows had come together. Love did not make a man look so stern.

"What is it, Ellie?" he growled.

"I . . . I have discovered something dreadful," she said. "I should have told Mama or Papa straightaway, but I didn't, and now I wish I had. But I shall tell you, and perhaps we can decide what to do.''

Bradford scowled at her. ''Whatever are you carrying on about?''

Eleanor pulled in her breath. ''It's Mama's emeralds. They're missing.''

Bradford stared at her, his scowl deepening. ''How do you know that?'' he demanded brusquely. ''Have you been snooping in her safe?''

''No, no, of course not,'' Eleanor said too quickly. She had not been snooping, exactly, although she admitted to having browsed through Mama's diamond and pearl cases, admiring the stones that would one day be shared between her and Patsy. ''She had loaned the emeralds to me, and I returned all but the tea ring. When I opened the safe to return the ring as well, I discovered that the box was gone.''

Bradford gave her a sidelong glance. ''You did not speak of this to Mama?''

''No, I . . .'' She caught her lower lip between her teeth. She had concealed the truth too long. It was best to confess all, without reservation. ''I very much fear, Bradford, that I am at fault.''

To her surprise, Bradford threw back his head and laughed—not a very nice laugh, at that. ''You!'' he exclaimed. ''Yes, indeed you *are* at fault, you little goose, grievously at fault. If you had not—''

But Bradford did not finish his sentence. He was interrupted by the butler, Howard, a tall, haughty man of impeccable speech and dress. He bore an envelope on a silver tray.

''A telegram for you, sir,'' he said, bowing.

''Thank you, Howard,'' Bradford said, and the butler withdrew. Eleanor watched her brother open the envelope and saw his face change, grow even darker than before. Swiftly, angrily, he wadded up the paper, threw it on the fire, and flung himself into an arm chair.

''What is it, Bradford?'' Eleanor asked anxiously.

But her brother did not answer her, and after a few moments Eleanor quietly stole from the room, leaving him as she had found him, staring into the fire.

23

Lord Fawn was always thinking, not exactly
how he might make both ends meet, but how
to reconcile the strictest personal economy with
the proper bearing of an English nobleman.
Such a man almost naturally looks to marriage
as an assistance in the dreary fight, and he soon
learns to think that heiresses have been invented
exactly to suit his case.

—ANTHONY TROLLOPE
The Eustace Diamonds

Bradford Marsden felt as if he were poised on the edge of
a very high, very steep cliff, with breakers frothing angrily
across sharp rocks below, while behind him roared a pack of
savage hounds. He could be smashed on the rocks or torn limb
from limb. The telegram that had arrived the night before had
informed him that Concerto, publicly posted at twenty-five-to-
one and privately assessed at two-to-one, had loped last and
latest across the finish line. He had exhausted his final fragile
hope. Nothing whatever could save him now—unless he could
prevail upon his friend Charles.

Bradford got up from the carved oak desk where he had
been staring at his accounts ledger and walked to the French
doors opening out onto Marsden Manor's lovely south park,
with its vista of meadow and field and rich woodland. To the

right, in the elaborate latticed garden house, he could see his mother and sister directing the servants in the laying of the tables for the garden party that afternoon. A short distance away, complacently observing the activity that was being conducted in honour of his and his wife's visit, stood Eleanor's stout husband, Ernest Fairley.

At the sight of Mr. Fairley, Bradford's lip curled. One would imagine that the scion of Fairley's Finest Fancy Candies—the well-heeled scion, still quite clearly besotted with love—would be willing to lend a spot of financial assistance to the brother of his dearly beloved, especially if the dearly beloved pleaded prettily. But no. Mr. Ernest Fairley, it seemed, was implacable, even when his wife laid an urgent case before him. He could also quote Shakespeare, and after he had given his *no* to Eleanor last week to convey to Bradford, he had taken the opportunity of a pause in the dinner table conversation to whisper in his wife's brother's ear a piece of avuncular advice from *King Lear*: "Keep thy foot out of brothels, thy hand out of plackets, thy pen from lenders' books, and defy the foul fiend." Mr. Fairley's counsel had been delivered in great sincerity, Bradford believed, but that didn't keep him from wanting to whip the fish off his plate and across the very sincere face of his parsimonious brother-in-law.

The difficulty that Bradford faced, the one he had tried to solve by applying to his brother-in-law, had to do with his mother's emeralds—the emeralds that Eleanor had discovered missing. They were not stolen, of course. They had been placed by Bradford himself on deposit with the Messrs. Attenborough in Chancery Lane in return for the sum of five thousand pounds, which he had used to answer a margin call on stock he owned in the Paramount Horseless Carriage Company. To no avail, however. Paramount had gone irretrievably defunct, taking with it all of Bradford's liquid assets.

Of course, when Bradford purchased the stock, Paramount had seemed to promise a very good return. It had been capitalized the year before, when Mr. Harry Landers, a British entrepreneur, had acquired certain valuable French automotive patents. The company was underwritten by the Bank of England and Wales and the Assurance Trust Corporation, as well as a number of shareholders belonging to the peerage. Bradford's acquaintances at the *Financial News* had been quite bullish about Paramount's potential, for the horseless carriage, they assured him, heralded a very profitable industry which would inaugurate innumerable other industries. A great new era of prosperity was about to dawn upon the land.

There were, however, several spanners in the works. The motor car was vigorously opposed by factions both in the press and in the Parliament: the pro-steam lobby, for instance; and those who believed that the motor car spelt doom to horses; and those fearful of speeding automobiles running down women and children. In response to these fears, Parliament had passed the Red Flag Act, decreeing a speed limit of four miles an hour in open country and two miles an hour in populated areas and requiring a man to walk twenty yards in front of any vehicle with a red flag. Few people cared to drive a vehicle that had to be preceded by someone on foot.

And Harry Landers himself was a spanner of a different sort, a blustering, brassy egoist who could not be trusted. Unfortunately, Bradford had discovered this only after his shares in the Paramount Horseless Carriage Company had become worthless, leaving him with nothing except his stock certificates and the pawn ticket from Attenborough & Attenborough.

And now his mother had become urgent about the damned emeralds, imploring him to restore them by the next day but one, when she was expected to wear them to have her portrait taken. And when he asked her if she thought his father might advance him five thousand pounds to redeem the jewels, her horrified reaction affirmed his own glum perception: that Baron Marsden, president of the Essex Horse Breeders Association, would die before he saw a single Marsden shilling devoted to motor cars.

This was why Bradford had wagered more than he ought on Concerto. And it was in this context that he had begun to think about marriage. The idea was not new to him: He had been brought up to know that he must assure the continuation of the lineage. But for nearly a decade, he had managed to elude the eligible young women thrust upon him by the machinations of anxious mothers, not to mention those of his own mother on his behalf. He had kept his heart free until now, when it seemed that he must bestow it upon an heiress whose land and fortune would allow him to pursue his investments in the motor car industry. Fortunately, one such lived in the neighbourhood.

Of course, it was not her fortune or her estate that rendered Kathryn Ardleigh attractive. It was her person: her intelligence, wit, and courage—and the rich abundance of mahogany hair that made her almost beautiful. Still, the fact that she was an heiress added to her natural attractions and made her nearly irresistible, in spite of the fact that she was an American, and Irish—neither of which were likely to sit well with his parents. But he was confident of bringing them around. Marriage to Miss Ardleigh would not pull him out of his immediate predicament nor obviate the need for continued strict economy with regard to his own funds. But they could live quite nicely on her fortune until he came into the Marsden estate and could do what he liked.

Yes, Miss Ardleigh was the perfect choice. He could only thank Providence for having seen fit to place her so conveniently at hand.

Now, if he could just resolve the problem of those damned emeralds!

24

Englishmen are strange creatures. I doubt if they ever really fall in love; they marry of course; but generally from a prudent motive.

—MAUD DE PUY
to her mother, 1883

Charles opened the door of Bradford Marsden's study. His friend was standing by the French doors looking out, hands thrust into his pockets.

"May I intrude?" he asked.

Bradford turned from the window. "Ah, Charlie," he said heartily. "Sit down and solve a problem for me, will you?"

Charles sat down by the fire and put both feet on the fender. "I came to ask you to solve one for me." He pulled out his pipe. "But let's hear yours first. What is it?"

"What else?" Bradford went to the sideboard and poured two glasses of brandy. "Money."

Charles wasn't surprised. Lord Marsden had settled an allowance on his eldest son but it almost never went far enough to support Bradford's expensive tastes. From time to time, his friend had applied to him for the funds he needed to get him out of a tight place, and Charles had always been glad to oblige. Without exception, the money had been repaid.

"How can I help?" Charles asked. He took the brandy snifter from Bradford and placed it on the inlaid table at his elbow.

Bradford sat down in a leather chair and put his booted feet up on a gros-point ottoman. "Lend me five thousand pounds. Interest at the current rate, of course."

Charles raised both eyebrows. It was the largest loan his friend had asked of him. As a younger son, Charles had long ago accepted the fact that his elder brother Robert would inherit the bulk of the Sheridan estate and money—as he had, upon the death of Charles's father several years before. But Charles was not without fortune, for his father had settled a house and an allowance on him, and he had received a sizable legacy from his maternal grandmother. His public status as a second son functioned to keep him single, while his private fortune set him at liberty to enjoy his bachelor existence as an amateur scientist, amateur photographer, and amateur criminologist. Still, he had to live on his income. And five thousand pounds was quite a lot of money.

Bradford's face was grave. "I wouldn't ask you if you weren't the final resort," he said. "And this is the last request you'll have of me." He swung his feet to the floor and sat forward in the armchair, his eyes lightening. "I've decided to marry, Charlie. The woman on whom I have settled my choice is well-established. We should be able to do quite well on her income until I come into the baronetcy."

Charles raised his glass. "I thought I'd never live to see the day! Good for you, Marsden! Who is the lucky lady?"

Bradford stood up. "She is Miss Ardleigh, of Bishop's Keep."

Charles stared, his thoughts turning around a hollow center that had suddenly opened inside him. Bradford and Miss Ardleigh were to be married! But what about *Ned* and Miss Ardleigh? Had the woman been engaged in some sort of flirtatious game, playing the offer of one suitor against another?

But even as Charles asked himself that question, he answered it. He did not know Kate Ardleigh well, and now was not likely to do so. But he knew, at least, that she was not capable of a duplicitous dealing in hearts. He had not seen Ned Laken since yesterday morning. There had been plenty of time for her to honourably refuse one man and accept the other. She was perfectly within her rights to do so—and wise, too, at least as the world would see it. Ned was a very good man, but Bradford was, or would be, a very rich one.

"I . . . see," he said. The hollowness within him seemed to echo in his voice, and he cleared his throat. "When will the wedding occur?"

"As soon as is convenient. I may have taken my time to settle my choice, but now that I know my mind, I do not intend to linger. I plan to make the proposal in the next day or two."

"I see," Charles said again. So she had not yet committed herself.

"But you may expect the bargain to be struck most expeditiously," Bradford added. "I have called on the lady once or twice and found her gracious and willing. I know of no other suitors. And of course the match is logical and quite prudent, since our properties adjoin."

As if from a distance, Charles heard himself ask, "Do you love her?"

"Love her?" Bradford sounded surprised, as well he might. It was not a question that one gentleman would ask another. "I don't know. Haven't given it any thought. I suppose I will, once we are married. People do, don't they? Now, about the loan . . ."

"Consider it done," Charles said. He covered his feelings by searching in his pockets for tobacco. "I'll obtain a bank draft for the funds immediately."

Bradford's sigh of relief was almost audible. "Many thanks, old man. You can't think how you have eased my mind." He stood and went to the window, looking out on the preparations for the garden party that was to take place on the manor grounds that afternoon. "And Mama's, although she doesn't know it yet. I'll need the money tomorrow, if possible, so I can retrieve her bloody emeralds from Attenborough's greedy clutches."

"Emeralds?" Charles asked. He paused in mid-gesture, his tobacco pouch in his hand. "*You* took Lady Marsden's emeralds?"

"Of course," Bradford said. "Did you think Mama would carry out such an errand herself?" He turned, frowning. "What do you know of the emeralds, Charlie?"

"Well, I—"

Bradford's face darkened. "You have no need to answer. It was my sister, wasn't it? *She* told you they were gone." His chuckle was sour. "No sense at all, women. She came to me last night, claiming they had been stolen."

Charles finished filling his pipe before he spoke. "It was not Eleanor who spoke to me about the matter," he said. "It was Miss Ardleigh. Eleanor confided to her a fear that Lawrence might have made off with them."

"Miss Ardleigh!" Bradford pulled at his mustache, scowling. "Confound that Eleanor," he muttered. "Can't keep her mouth shut. Probably carried the tale to that husband of hers, too. Suppose I'll have to set her right."

"That would relieve her of the concern that Lawrence took the jewels," Charles said.

Bradford swallowed the last of his brandy and set the glass on the sideboard, turning to face Charles. "Well, then. You have solved my problem, and handily, at that. Now let me have a shot at yours. What is it?"

Charles lit his pipe and pulled on it, giving himself a moment to flush Kate Ardleigh out of his mind and call up the matter that had brought him to Bradford's study.

"What do you know of poaching?" he asked.

"Poaching?" Bradford poured himself another brandy. "In general, you mean, or hereabouts?" He held up the decanter. "Another brandy?"

Charles shook his head. "Hereabouts," he said. "And tell me about your assistant gamekeeper, McGregor. Have you had him long?"

"McGregor has been in service for a decade or so," Bradford said. "My grandfather set sport above all else. When he died, a dozen liveried gamekeepers headed his funeral procession." Bradford chuckled dryly. "They are nearly gone, though. McGregor and Peters—the chief keeper—are remnants. Papa's passion for horses supersedes every other. He has no time for anything that does not involve a horse. But he does insist on a minimum of preservation—maintaining the game coverts and the deer in the park, and holding down the poaching where possible.'' He glanced at Charles. "What's this about, if I may ask?''

''It has to do with Sergeant Oliver's death.'' If the emeralds were not a possible motive, as Miss Ardleigh had suggested, the only thing left that resembled a clue was the connexion to poaching.

''Ah, yes. Sad business, that. Are the police making any progress?''

''Precious little. The constable from Manningtree received an anonymous tip, and when he went to investigate, he found a pair of hares and a net in Oliver's shed. Artie wasn't the sort to be involved in anything dishonest, but it looks very bad. The police committee could well deny his widow's pension. If so, it would go hard with her.''

''In Grandfather's day, possession of the net alone would have sent the man to Australia for seven years, policeman or no,'' Bradford remarked. He frowned as he took a cigar from a gold case on the table beside him. ''Is there a suggestion that McGregor is involved in the murder?''

Charles drew on his pipe. ''No evidence, only suspicion.'' He did not want to say whose suspicion it was.

''The man's a shifty devil,'' Bradford said, sniffing the cigar appreciatively. ''I don't recall the details, but there was trouble some years back when he beat one of the tenants for cutting down a game shelter. When Papa learned of it, he stopped the practice of planting shelters in the middle of the fields.'' He applied a match to the cigar and pulled on it. ''One has to think of the tenants' livelihood. It's to the detriment of the crops when the land becomes nesting and feeding grounds for game.'' His smile was rueful. ''My grandfather would have had me caned for such heresy, of course.''

''McGregor has a brother-in-law, Tommy Brock. What can you tell me about him?''

''Only that he is a neighbourhood nuisance. He was accused of stealing several sacks of thrashed grain some while back. But there wasn't enough evidence to have him up, so the matter was let drop.''

Charles hoisted himself to his feet. ''You will keep your

ear to the ground and let me know of anything you hear about either McGregor or Brock?''

''I will,'' Bradford said. He stood too and held out his hand. ''My dear Charles, many thanks for the loan. You have saved me from a rather nasty circumstance.''

''You are quite welcome.'' If Lady Marsden's emeralds were at stake, Charles did not doubt that the circumstance was indeed nasty. He had known for some time about Bradford's financial interest in Harry Landers's various motor car schemes. It wouldn't surprise him if the recent failure of the Paramount Horseless Carriage stock figured prominently in his friend's need for money—and if that need figured equally prominently in Bradford's decision to marry. Not that Miss Ardleigh herself were not attraction enough, he reminded himself with a great sadness.

''Well, things may be a bit rocky just now, but all will be well once Miss Ardleigh and I are wed.'' Bradford clapped Charles on the shoulder. ''Will you be the chief groomsman, Charlie? I can think of no friend I would better like to stand beside me on that great occasion.''

Charles met his friend's eyes with as much candour as he could summon. ''I would be honoured,'' he said.

''I knew I could count on you, old man,'' Bradford said. ''Knowing the esteem in which you are held by Miss Ardleigh, I am sure that she will agree to your place in our wedding party.''

''Thank you for the compliment,'' Charles said, and escaped.

25

A Dog may be trained by the trailing or dragging of a dead Cat, or Fox, (and in case of necessity a Red-Herring) three or four miles . . . and then laying him on the Scent.
— N. COX
A Gentleman's Recreation, 1686

Having been recently at Long Melford, with its constant luncheons, teas, and dinners, Kate was not anxious for another party so soon. But she *was* anxious to convey to Sir Charles the information she had learned from Betsy that morning, and to hear from him what he had learned about the stolen emeralds. When she and Bea returned from visiting with Agnes, after their encounter with Betsy at the church, she immediately submitted herself to Amelia for the tedious ritual of dressing for the garden party at Marsden Manor. When she emerged, impatient with the maid's fussing but pleased with the result, she was wearing a grey silk dress with a lace cape over full sleeves, caught at the breast by a red silk rose. She wore elbow-length grey gloves and a wide-brimmed, tulle-trimmed hat. Bea was simply dressed, in a light shade of blue that exactly matched her eyes.

"Do you think we will see Sir Charles?" Bea asked, as she and Kate were handed into the carriage by Pocket. To Kate's pragmatic mind, it had seemed silly to order the carriage for a three-mile drive. But to have driven themselves would have offended their hostess.

"I certainly hope so," Kate replied, settling her skirts with a rustle. "We have a little matter of murder to discuss with him—whether he wants to hear it or not."

She glanced at Bea, whose face wore an anticipatory look. Remembering how Sir Charles had patronized her at their last meeting (*muck things up*, indeed!) Kate resolutely turned her eyes forward. If Bea liked the man, that was her business. Her own eagerness to see him had entirely to do with finding Sergeant Oliver's killer and helping Agnes out of her trouble. However fervently Sir Charles might wish her to stay out of it, he would simply have to listen.

The garden of Marsden Manor was laid out in the elegant French style, with velvety expanses of lawn bordered by formally trimmed hedges and brilliant flower beds. An ornate temple stood on one side, suggestive of aristocratic pastoral fantasies, and on the other was a latticed white pavilion sheltering elaborately decorated tables laden with ices, sandwiches, cakes, and drink. In a nearby rose-covered pergola, a small group of musicians played Mozart and Bach. Linen-draped tables centered with crystal bowls of flowers were scattered conveniently about so that guests could sit and sip champagne and seltzer or lemonade while they recovered from the exertion of strolling about the gardens and the shrubbery.

Upon their arrival, Kate and Bea were immediately swept up by a bubbling, diamond-decked Eleanor. "I have been waiting especially to see you, my dears!" she cried, embracing Kate and warmly pressing Bea's gloved hand. To Bea, she said, "I hope you are finding more to interest you at Bishop's Keep than at Melford." To Kate, she said in an enigmatic whisper, "Never mind about the emeralds, Kate. All has been explained, and I am absolutely mortified at my ignorance."

"Ignorance?" Kate asked with great interest. "Of what? How was it all explained?"

"It was explained by my brother," Eleanor said. Without waiting to hear the other questions that came to Kate's lips, she led them toward Lord and Lady Marsden. They were stationed on the marble stairs that led from the upper gardens to the lower, surrounded by masses and pyramids of flowers in an exquisite profusion of perfect bloom, arranged in great vases that might have been stolen from the Arabian Nights. The baron was a bluff, balding man whose ample girth and apple cheeks testified to his love of fine food and wine. Lady Marsden was as brittle as porcelain but rock-hard, her aristocratic nose slightly beaked, her chin jutting, her grey eyes glinting.

"Miss Ardleigh, Mama," Eleanor said, "and Miss Potter."

Lady Marsden smiled graciously and gave her hand to Bea. But to Kate, she only inclined her head, withholding her glance. Kate detected a distinct coolness in the gesture and was puzzled. She had been invited to tea and to dinner at the manor several times before Eleanor was married, and had exchanged easy pleasantries with Lady Henrietta on those occasions. Those conversations had been threaded through with Lady Henrietta's unthinking assumption of superiority, which Kate had noticed but had not bothered to resent, since it was so obviously bred into the woman. Today's response was haughtier and more chilly, and Kate wondered what she had done to earn Lady Henrietta's disapproval.

Under another circumstance, Kate might have asked Eleanor what was behind her mother's cool greeting. But there was no time for that now, for Eleanor whisked Kate and Bea away from the baron and baroness and trotted them around from one glittering cluster of guests to another, all extravagantly dressed and jeweled and gay. The Marsdens had invited many of their Society friends, and Kate found herself in the company of such notables as Sir Hwfa Williams, the founding genius of the new Sandown Race Course and a special friend of the baron's; to Louisa, the lively, amusing Duchess of Manchester; and to the charming, witty Lady Brooke, the Countess of Warwick and (Eleanor whispered to Kate) the current mistress of His Royal Highness the Prince of Wales. To Kate's surprise, the countess (whose handsome husband, Lord Brooke, was animatedly discussing politics with Lord Marsden) was not only elegantly beautiful, but seemed to possess a brain beneath her elaborate confection of a hat. Kate was intrigued to learn that she was an elected trustee of the Warwick Board that governed the local workhouse and that she proposed to take the prince on a tour of its awful wards.

Eleanor raised her eyebrows when she heard that news. "I was not aware that the prince had an interest in such matters," she said delicately.

The countess sighed and fluttered her ivory fan. "I fear you may be right. But that shall not excuse His Majesty. I have vowed to do all in my power to make him see how wretched the poor really *are*."

Kate stared at her, thinking how incongruous it was that those words should be spoken by a titled lady with a half-dozen rings on her fingers, a rope of enormous pearls around her alabaster neck, and diamonds dripping from her pretty ears. But Lady Brooke herself seemed oblivious to any contradiction. She went on to chatter with enormous enthusiasm about her schemes for educating poor children, providing jobs, and improving housing.

"There is a great deal of work to be done," she said, her voice ringing with passionate conviction. "People's minds must be changed, their hearts touched. People, that is, who have the power to make changes in the government."

"That may prove difficult," Kate said quietly. "Society—in this country and in America as well—has a habit of caring chiefly for its own."

The countess regarded her thoughtfully. "A perceptive remark, Miss Ardleigh. You are exactly right. But that is why we need to make *examples* of those who care. And we need persons to carry the message!"

"I regret to interrupt your exhortations, Daisy," said Lord Brooke, coming up to place a hand under her elbow. "But you must leave off talking about your causes and come. You are wanted by Lady Henrietta."

The countess tossed her head. "We must speak of these things again, Miss Ardleigh," she said with a bright smile, and went off with her husband.

There might be some incongruity between the countess's person and her message, Kate reflected as she watched her go, but her concern was decidedly genuine. Speaking with Lady Brooke was the high point of the party, however. It wasn't long before Kate was quite weary of the entire affair and longed to sit down.

"There's an empty table beside that holly bush," Bea pointed out.

"We shall take it," Kate decided, thinking of her chief reason for coming to the party, "and see whether we can spy out Sir Charles."

But just as Kate and Bea reached the table, they were waylaid by Bradford Marsden, resplendent in black frock coat, grey trousers, pink satin waistcoat, silk hat, and silver-topped walking stick. His blond hair was combed smoothly back, his blond mustache and side-whiskers carefully groomed. His handsome face bore the impress of aristocracy, a man with a look of vitality, confidence, and the authority bestowed by fortune and family tradition.

"Ah, Miss Ardleigh." He bowed over Kate's hand with a flourish of feeling that was at odds with his mother's cool greeting. "It has been far too long since I have seen you. Far too long," he repeated, engaging her eyes as well as her hand.

"Miss Potter," Kate said, "may I present the Honourable Mr. Marsden?" She withdrew her hand and gave in to a mischievous urge. "I must warn you, though," she added. "Mr. Marsden has a passion for motor cars. If he has his way, we shall all be on wheels by the turn of the century."

Bea raised her eyebrows. "I have seen only one motor car," she said. "It smelt of paraffin and made a great deal of noise."

"To be sure," Bradford Marsden said smoothly. "But those are minor engineering defects and will be conquered shortly. In a year or two, it will be possible to ride in a motor car in ease and comfort." He turned to Kate and extended his arm with a courtly gesture. "I would be delighted, Miss Ardleigh, if you and Miss Potter would walk with me through the gardens. My mother has engaged the best gardeners money can obtain to impress her guests. It would be a pity to waste their efforts."

"Oh, please," Bea begged, "I would prefer to sit and be quiet." She turned. "Here is Sir Charles. Perhaps he will sit with me while the two of you walk."

"Miss Potter." Sir Charles, not nearly so elegantly attired

as Bradford Marsden, bowed in greeting. His eyes met Kate's and quickly moved away. "Miss Ardleigh. How good to see you."

Bradford Marsden took Kate's hand and placed it on his arm with a proprietary air, so swiftly and confidently that she could scarcely retrieve it without calling attention to herself. "Miss Ardleigh and I were about to tour the gardens," he said.

Sir Charles's glance flicked to Kate, her hand on Bradford Marsden's arm, and then to Bea. "Well, then, Miss Potter, perhaps you will sit with me and tell me about your observations on lichens. You have not yet outlined your theory to me," he added, "and I am most curious."

"Lichens," Mr. Marsden said and shook his head. He smiled at Kate. "It's best that we leave them to it, Miss Ardleigh."

Kate cleared her throat. "Perhaps before the afternoon is out we could talk briefly, Sir Charles," she said with greater stiffness than she had intended. "I have some information to share with you." She turned away, wishing in spite of herself that she could stay and contribute an interesting remark or two about lichens.

When Kate and Mr. Marsden walked away, Beatrix took a frosty lemonade from a tray offered by a liveried footman and settled herself to enjoy a productive exchange of scientific ideas with Sir Charles. This was not their first such conversation, for her uncle Henry Roscoe had seen to it that they were conveniently seated together whenever they happened to dine at his house, which of late had been once or twice a month. The most endearing thing about Sir Charles, she thought as she sipped her lemonade, was his unquestioning acceptance of her expertise in such odd corners of scientific inquiry as animal behaviour and lichens. It was an acceptance she coveted, for making some recognized contribution to science was another of Beatrix's cherished desires—along with her hope of publishing her drawings and stories and using the earnings to escape from Bolton Gardens.

But after some little conversation, she noticed that Sir

Charles's attention was not entirely fixed upon their discussion. He was answering her eager questions in an absent-minded way, while his eyes followed Kate and Mr. Marsden as they wandered through the gardens and finally disappeared into the temple on the other side of the lawn. She carried on for a few moments, but the cause was clearly lost.

"Sir Charles," she said at last, when he had failed to answer a question the second time she asked it, "are you troubled by something?"

He turned toward her. "Troubled? No, not at all, Miss Potter. Why do you ask?"

Beatrix had never considered herself brave, and she was fully aware of the strictures placed by social etiquette upon their discourse. But there were things that had to be said, prohibited or not.

"I ask," she replied gently, "because you have been waiting for some minutes for Miss Ardleigh and Mr. Marsden to emerge from the temple."

Sir Charles laughed a little. "Come now, Miss Potter, I hardly think—"

"You *are* quite transparent, you know," Beatrix said, gaining courage.

The redness that suffused his jaw showed her that she was correct. "Oh, I *must* say—" he began.

She leaned forward. "Why haven't you told her?"

He paused. "Because there isn't anything to tell," he said. Then he stopped, considering. When he spoke again, his tone was straightforward and direct. "That is a lie," he said. "I have not spoken because there are other claims on the lady's affections. They take precedence to mine."

Beatrix had been about to drink from her glass. Now she set it down, surprised by his use of the plural. "Claims? Miss Ardleigh has suitors other than Mr. Marsden and yourself?"

The sudden flicker of pain in Sir Charles's eyes raised him in Beatrix's esteem more than a thousand scientific discourses might have done. He could deny his feelings to himself or hide them from others, but he obviously felt them deeply.

When he spoke, his voice was gruff. "She has not mentioned . . . Edward Laken?"

"Only in passing," Beatrix said. She frowned. "But we are not so intimate that we have shared *all* our secrets." She looked up. "Please forgive me for probing," she said quickly. "I am sure it is quite forward of me, but I only wish your happiness, and hers. And forgive me when I say that I truly fail to see why *you* should take it upon yourself to decide which claim should be preferred. I have always understood that decision, Sir Charles, to be the prerogative of the lady."

He turned his glass in his hands. He did not look at her, but Beatrix could sense his deep unhappiness. "The other gentlemen are close friends of mine."

"I see." Bea picked up a pansy that had fallen from the crystal bowl. The delicate purple and yellow petals had always looked to her like children's faces, and she pressed it to her lips. "Yet I still feel that you must press your own claim." She glanced obliquely at him. "To be fair to the lady, that is to say. What if she should prefer you to the others?"

Sir Charles sat still for a moment, as if he were weighing what she had said. A shadow crossed his face. Then his mouth lifted in an attempt at a smile and he placed his hand over hers in a gesture of intimacy that both surprised and gratified Bea.

"Thank you, Miss Potter, with all my heart. I value your advice most highly, although I fear that it cannot alter my intention. I trust you will safeguard my secret?"

Hesitant, aware that she was transgressing the bounds of propriety, she tried once more. "I cannot persuade you to declare yourself?"

His hand tightened over hers. "You must promise not to speak of this to Miss Ardleigh."

She pulled in her breath. "Really, I—"

"You must promise, Miss Potter." His voice was light, as if he were joking, but sharply intent. "This secret must remain between us. Otherwise, not another confidence you will worm out of me."

She sighed. "Oh, very well," she said crossly. "But I—"

"Thank you," he said, and a smile lighted the depths of his brown eyes. He released her hand with a satisfied nod. "Now, what were we saying about lichens?"

* * *

In the temple, Bradford Marsden used his silver-topped walking stick to direct Kate's attention first to the splendid stained-glass windows ("the work of William Morris, from a Burne-Jones design"), then to the richly detailed wainscoting, then to an antique marble cherub imported from Florence. But while she appreciated his commentary on the temple's art, her thoughts were with the couple they had left. She desperately wanted to talk to Sir Charles, and she was afraid he might leave before she returned. As quickly as she could, she made an excuse to go back.

"Of course," he said. He turned toward the door. "But grant me one favour first, please."

"And what is that?"

His eyes were on hers. "That you will allow me to call upon you in the next few days, Miss Ardleigh."

Kate was not easily taken aback, but Mr. Marsden's question caught her unprepared. The man seemed to be asking permission to court her. But that was impossible! As a prospective member of the peerage, he was obligated to make a choice that would please Society. And while she enjoyed his friendship, he was not at all the kind of man she would consider marrying. On neither side was it a match.

"To call?" she repeated slowly. "But Mr. Marsden, I—"

"My dear Miss Ardleigh." His smile was confident, self-assured, and almost (but not quite) surprised. "I trust you do not object?"

She hesitated, even more sure (and even more astonished at the thought) that he meant to court her. "Really, Mr. Marsden, I don't think—"

A shadow darkened the door and a cultivated voice said, "Miss Ardleigh, Mr. Marsden! How nice to see you worshiping the gods of the garden."

The speaker was Vicar Barfield Talbot, a stooped, leathery old man with a mane of silvery hair, a silver mustache, and an ebullient energy that belied his seventy-plus years. He was carrying a champagne glass in one hand and a white lily in the other. He had obviously been enjoying both the refreshment table and the garden.

"Ah, vicar," Bradford Marsden said dryly. "Good afternoon." He turned aside, but the vicar, a friend of Kate's, had more to say. It was several moments before she could manage to interrupt the old man's flow of words and pull herself and Mr. Marsden away.

As they left the temple, Mr. Marsden put his hand under her elbow. "Since you have no objection, I shall call," he said. Before Kate could reply, he added, "The sooner the better, I think. I have business in London tomorrow. Shall we say, the day after that?"

Kate nodded. She could hardly tell him here that she did not wish to be the subject of his attentions. She would have to tell him when he called. Or perhaps she was imagining the whole thing. Perhaps his call was a purely social visit. Perhaps he meant to bring Eleanor, although he had not mentioned doing so.

Mr. Marsden cleared his throat. "There is another matter I wish to clarify with you," he said, somewhat stiffly. "It has to do with something my sister told you. About my mother's emeralds."

"She mentioned to me that she had discovered them missing and feared them stolen," Kate acknowledged. "This afternoon, she told me that she had been mistaken, but she did not explain."

"Yes," he said. "Ah, yes." He twirled his walking stick, not quite meeting her eyes. "Well, y' see, the clasp on the necklace was broken, and Mama asked me to have it repaired for her while I was in London on business. I took it to a jeweler, and that's where it is. I will retrieve it tomorrow when I go up to London."

The clasp might well have been broken. But why had that necessitated the removal of the other pieces in the set? Still, if Eleanor were satisfied, she must be, as well. And the matter clearly was not connected with the murder of Sergeant Oliver.

"I see," Kate said quietly. "I am most gratified to hear that it was merely a misunderstanding."

Mr. Marsden's voice was hearty and his eyes, when he turned them on her, guileless. "Nothing at all of consequence, I assure you," he said. "Poor Eleanor has suffered the pangs of self-reproach quite unnecessarily. And now shall we join the others?''

A moment later, Bradford Marsden seated her at the table beside the holly bush. ''I shall look forward to our conversation,'' he said meaningfully. He smiled at Bea and nodded to Sir Charles, then walked jauntily away, turning his stick between the fingers of one hand.

Kate was acutely aware that Bea and Sir Charles were watching her. ''I am pleased to see that you are still here,'' she said to Sir Charles. She coughed slightly, to cover her embarrassment at Bradford Marsden's last remark. ''Mr. Marsden and I were waylaid by the vicar, and were gone rather longer than I had expected.''

Sir Charles signaled a footman and obtained a glass of lemonade for her. ''I assume that the information you have for me has to do with Sergeant Oliver's murder,'' he said. There was a certain wryness in his tone, as if he were remembering that he had directed her to stay out of the affair.

Kate glanced at Bea. ''You have not told him of our discovery?''

Bea shook her head. ''We had something else to talk of. Anyway, I thought you would wish to tell him.''

Kate leaned forward. ''We have learned of a curious nocturnal activity at a place called Highfields Farm,'' she said, ''about a half-mile from Gallows Green, just above the river. Our informant is Betsy Oliver, who witnessed it.''

Sir Charles frowned. ''Ah, yes, Betsy. An adventuresome child. One might expect her to rove about at night.'' His frown deepened. ''What kind of activity? When?''

''Two nights before the sergeant's murder,'' Kate replied. ''Five men drove a wagon from Highfields barn down to the river, where they removed a number of sacks from the wagon to a boat. According to Betsy, one of the men was called by the name of Juan. Another was called Mr. B.—the familiar name, I am told, of Mr. McGregor's brother-in-law, Tommy Brock. Betsy also described a third, who sounds very much like Mr. Tod, a local bailiff who organizes the crews that travel from farm to farm at harvest and planting time.''

"We thought they might be pirates," Bea put in excitedly, "Or smugglers!"

"But smugglers usually move goods into the country," Sir Charles said, "to avoid the tariff."

"Yes," Kate replied. "The question is, what were they doing? And what is the connexion between their activity and the death of Sergeant Oliver?"

"Precisely," Sir Charles said. "And you suspect that the poaching—"

"Might be merely a device to divert attention from the real crime to something else. A red herring, as it were." Kate sipped her lemonade. "How did Constable Bradley come to discover the poaching equipment and the animals in the Olivers' shed?"

"It was a tip, an unsigned letter." Sir Charles looked at Kate, his eyes intensely bright. "A red herring," he said thoughtfully. "Indeed, Miss Ardleigh, you could be right."

"If I am," Kate reflected, "then it is of vital importance to discover the writer of the unsigned letter. Were you able to examine it?"

"I was," Sir Charles said. "I was also able to make a copy."

"A copy!" Bea clapped her hands. "How fortunate!"

"It would seem, then, that we are pursuing the wrong quarry with this poaching business," Sir Charles said. "A quite different scheme is afoot. But I should tell you that the murder has nothing to do with stolen emeralds, which have turned out not to be stolen at all."

"So I am informed," Kate said. She looked at him. "It seems that Mr. Marsden has taken the necklace for repair. Is that your understanding?"

Sir Charles coughed. "Something of the sort," he said.

It was obvious to Kate that Sir Charles had a different idea about the emeralds, but she did not pursue it. "Well," she said, "if poachers are not our quarry, who is?"

"I have not the slightest idea," Sir Charles said. "Perhaps you would agree to examine the copy of the letter Constable Bradley received and give me your opinion on the matter."

Kate looked at him, her head to one side. Was it possible

that he was actually taking her seriously? Then perhaps he would be willing to listen to her other ideas.

"I would indeed," she said. "And there is an additional matter to consider. I wonder if you examined the sergeant's jacket—the one he was wearing when he was murdered."

"Yes," he replied, "in a rather cursory way. I recall that there was a small amount of grass seed intermingled with the dried blood on the front of the jacket, around the entry wound. There was no grass at the site where the body was found. It would appear that the sergeant fell face down onto a grassy area and lay in that position for some little while before he was moved."

"Did you look in the pockets?" Kate asked.

"I did not." He looked at her. "I suppose, from the tone of your voice, that you have done. But how did you come into possession of Artie's coat?"

"Agnes gave it to me, together with her husband's other clothing, to deliver to the vicar. I kept the coat, however, thinking that there might be more to learn from it. Perhaps if you were to examine the contents of the pockets under a microscope—Do you happen to have a microscope with you on this visit?" He had mentioned at one point that he usually traveled with a microscope.

"I do." Sir Charles pushed back his chair and stood. "I shall dispatch Lawrence with the copy of the letter this evening, and he can fetch the coat to me."

"Thank you," Kate said, standing also, and feeling a deep satisfaction. She had come today feeling that she might have to force Sir Charles to listen to her ideas. She was leaving with the sense that he had not only heard them with respect, but welcomed and valued them highly.

Bea got up. To Sir Charles, she said, oddly, "It has been a revealing afternoon."

"Indeed." Sir Charles held her glance for a moment. "You will remember your promise?"

"Yes," Bea said. But from the look on her face, Kate guessed that she was not pleased by the pledge which Sir Charles had extracted from her, whatever it was.

26

In the last half of the nineteenth century, a wave of investigative curiosity broke over the world, a need to examine, to weigh, to measure, to *know*, definitively. This new vision slowly began to affect methods of detection and the new science of criminology. When Sherlock Holmes employed a magnifying glass to scrutinize a flake of latakia tobacco discovered on the Smyrna rug in the Boscombe Valley Affair, and spoke of having written a little monograph on 140 varieties of tobacco ash, he was not just speaking as a fictional detective. He was a proponent of the scientific method in the investigation of crime.

> —MARTIN DiLISI
> "Science and the Detective"

Lawrence must have hoped that his trip to Bishop's Keep would serve more than one purpose, for when the valet returned that evening, he was deeply perturbed. Charles, who was clearing off the small table in his bedroom where his microscope sat, smiled a little.

"You have seen the fair Amelia, I suppose?"

Lawrence held out a brown-paper parcel. "Hit don't bear talkin' about, sir," he said with dignity.

Charles took the parcel, regretting that his question had been so lightly and unfeelingly phrased. "Were you prevented from seeing her?"

Frustration was written across Lawrence's face, mixed with disappointment. "Hit's the 'ousekeeper," he growled. "Missus Pratt. She don't want Hamelia seein' me."

"On account of what happened the last time you were together?"

Lawrence's lip curled slightly. "On haccount o' Missus Pratt's a narrow-minded ol' misery wot cares more f'r happearance than f'r wot's true."

"I know Mrs. Pratt a little," Charles said. "My impression is that of a woman intent on doing her duty. Perhaps if I spoke with her, or better—" He paused, considering. "Or better, with Miss Ardleigh. Under the appropriate circumstances, there might not be any objection to your seeing the girl. With supervision, of course."

Lawrence shook his head sadly. "No disrespect, sir," he said, "but 'ow wud ye like t' do yer courtin' wi' some sharp-eyed ol' woman lookin' on, allus tellin' ye t' mind where ye put yer 'ands?"

Charles sighed. He was not likely to be doing any courting at all—at least, not in the immediate future. Miss Ardleigh seemed to have a surfeit of suitors. But Lawrence's point was well-taken. "I'll see what I can do," he said.

Lawrence thanked him and was leaving the room when Charles thought of something and called him back. "Do you happen to know Tommy Brock?" he asked. "The brother-in-law of McGregor, the assistant gamekeeper?"

Lawrence's face grew dark. "Ol' Tommy? Sure I know 'im. 'Ee's a bugger, is Tommy. Ye don't want t' run afoul of 'im on a dark night."

"Is that right?" Charles asked with interest. "What can you tell me about the man?"

What Lawrence could tell, it turned out, both was and was not material to the matter at hand. He and Tommy Brock had been acquainted before Lawrence came to work at Marsden

Manor, when he was a man-servant in the home of a certain Mr. Dalton, a wealthy ship owner in Manningtree. Tommy Brock was an agent in Dalton's shipping business. He was given to gambling at cards and had covered his losses from Dalton's receipts. When the money was discovered missing, however, there was not sufficient evidence to take him before the magistrate, so he was discharged with a stern warning. He had remained in the area, doing whatever work he could find and applying frequently to his sister for assistance.

"Do you know where he lives?" Charles asked.

Lawrence shrugged. "Mayhap McGregor knows. Or Mrs. McGregor. Or ye might ask after 'im at th' Live an' Let Live on a Sattidy night. 'Ee's usually there."

When Lawrence had gone, Charles laid the parcel on the bed and opened it. Inside, neatly folded, was the jacket Artie had been wearing when he was shot, the bloodstain on the front left breast still matted with seeds and what looked like bits of grass stem. But when Charles scraped off a sample and looked at it under the microscope, he saw that what he had taken to be grass stems were the broken pieces of thick, golden stems of wheat. The seeds were most certainly threshed grains of wheat.

He went back to the jacket to investigate further. There were pockets, one on each side and one on the right breast. When he carefully turned each one out onto a sheet of paper, he found a great deal more grain: so much, in fact, that he could only conclude that it had not got into the pockets when Artie was shot and fell to the ground. It looked as if Artie had deliberately scooped a handful of grain into each pocket. Why would he do such a thing? What was there about the grain that made it worth keeping?

Charles spent the next few minutes with his microscope, giving a cursory examination to the grain from each pocket. What he saw both puzzled and intrigued him. The material in each sample—mostly wheat seeds, a few other seeds, and some chaff—appeared to differ substantially from the material in the other two samples. Artie had somehow managed to acquire samples from three different sources. How had he done this? Why? Did this material hold any clue to the reason for his death, or to the identity of his murderer?

These questions intrigued Charles to such an extent that he spent the next several hours, until well after midnight, performing what he was accustomed to call a "population analysis," a technique he had developed in his work in paleontology. In studying different rock strata, he had learned that the populations of different organisms varied from strata to strata. The strata could be compared by identifying and counting the organisms. Using the same technique, he carefully sorted the grain, seeds, and other materials—mostly bits of grass and stem. When he had finished and recorded his results, he had a profile of each sample: so many grains of wheat; so many round, brown seeds; so many pointed yellow-green seeds; so many tiny burrs; and so on.

And when Charles compared the material in each sample to the other two, he discovered something equally intriguing. The grains of wheat from Artie's breast pocket were fuller and more round than the grains of wheat from his right pocket, while the grains from the left pocket were much darker in colour and heavier. In one sample, there were yellow-green seeds and no burrs; in another, many burrs and no yellow-green seeds. The conclusion was clear. Artie Oliver had carefully filled each of his three pockets with three very different samples of grain: so different, in fact, that the contents of each pocket might have come from a different field, perhaps even a different farm.

For a moment, Charles stood staring down at what he had found. What on earth was Artie doing with all this grain in his pockets? Where had he got it?

But the grain yielded no answer, and the longer Charles stared, the less distinctly he saw. And when he finally lay across the bed and fell asleep, he dreamed of Artie Oliver, tramping from field to field, filling his pockets as he went.

27

"The rats get upon my nerves, Cousin Ribby,"
said Tabitha.

—BEATRIX POTTER
The Roly-Poly Pudding

"I should like," Kate said to Bea at breakfast the next morning, "to make an excursion. It is time we talked to Mrs.
McGregor."

"What can she tell us?" Bea asked from the sideboard,
where she was serving herself a generous portion of Mrs.
Pratt's scrambled eggs and herring from a silver dish.

"She is the sister of Tommy Brock. The mysterious Mr.
B." Kate said, spreading marmalade on toast. "She ought to
know where he is to be found."

Bea added some stewed apples to her plate and sat down at
the table. "But what would we do once we have discovered
his whereabouts?" She paused, and after a moment, added,
uneasily, "Do you intend that we should actually confront the
man?"

Kate added another spoonful of marmalade to her toast. Bea
had lived her entire life with a father who oversaw her every
move and a mother who continually fretted about her health
and welfare. Seen in that context, her decision to visit Bishop's
Keep, alone and without their permission, had been a brave
and daring act. Kate did not want to push her to the point
where she might regret her adventure. Beryl Bardwell might

be all for bearding the elusive Mr. Brock in his den (wherever it was), but Kate had to take her friend's nervousness into account.

"Well, then," Kate replied, "perhaps we could enlist the aid of Sir Charles."

"A capital idea," Bea said more comfortably. "We can discover where to find this Tommy Brock, and Sir Charles can take the matter from there." She looked at Kate. "It isn't that I'm not brave, of course." She laughed a little. "Or is it? *You* were brave enough to confront a killer." Kate had told her about her encounter with her aunt's murderer. "Perhaps I am simply too timorous."

"No, no," Kate said. "Looking back, I shudder at what I did. It strikes me as incredibly foolhardy now, although at the time it seemed quite necessary." She busied herself with the teapot. "But I have another idea. What would you say to a nocturnal expedition in addition to our morning excursion? Please say no straightaway if you wish," she added hurriedly.

"A nocturnal excursion?" Bea smiled. "Now, that's something to which I *am* accustomed. My brother Bertram's ferret—quite a fascinating creature, really—had been trained by his previous owner to hunt rats. At night, after Papa and Mama had gone to bed, Bertram and I often took Filbert into the alley behind Bolton Gardens so that we might observe his behaviour. Bertram is quite as taken with animals as am I." Her eyes shone with mischief. "Poor Mama. She would have perished with fear had she known that I went ratting with Filbert and Bertram." Her face darkened and she shook her head, sadly musing. "Poor Mama indeed. I doubt if she has ever been abroad at night after nine, except to go with Papa to the opera."

Kate felt heartened. Bea was not quite the timid person she might appear. "In that case, the excursion I propose might be of interest to you. Its purpose is to observe rats—of a sort."

"Of a sort?" Bea raised both eyebrows. "I take it that you are speaking of metaphoric rats. We are likely to encounter criminals?"

"If things happen as I anticipate, we might observe a certain amount of criminal activity," Kate conceded, feeling it best to be honest. "I should not expect the criminals to observe *us*, however. We will be quite safe."

Bea finished the last of her eggs and herring, appearing to give the matter careful consideration. When she finally spoke, it was with resolute anticipation.

"I have learned by experience," she said, "that it is prudent to wear dark clothing when one goes ratting at night."

Their morning excursion began a half-hour later. Kate and Bea drove the gig down sun-dappled Lambs' Lane and around the corner to the McGregors' cottage, stopping in front and looping the pony's reins around the slender trunk of an ash tree. A pair of large grey geese accompanied them to the door, the gander stretching out his neck and hissing with a show of authority, the goose announcing their presence with loud cries.

With such a noisy escort, they were hardly required to knock. The door was opened by a short, plump woman in a black dress, white apron, and flat white cap. She acknowledged their introductions and invited them into the parlour, a small, tidy room with a vase of daffodils on the mantel and an unlit fire neatly laid in the grate. Not a speck of dust could be seen on the small tables arranged on either side of the old-fashioned green plush sofa; the square window panes were crystal clear; and the flagstone floor was swept clean and covered with a scrap of blue wool carpet. Across the back of the sofa was an odd carriage-rug of a beautifully striped grey fur that Kate could not identify.

"Oh, that?" Mrs. McGregor replied when Kate asked. "That's tabby-cat skins, a dozen of 'em." They had been cured and prepared by her husband, who practiced the trade in the course of his profession as gamekeeper. In fact, all the cats to which these skins belonged, most of them wild, had been caught in the traps Mr. McGregor set for vermin. Mrs. McGregor had matched the skins and sewn them together.

"I've made many a rug of badger skins, an' ladies' muffs of fox skins, an' waistcoats of moleskin f'r gent'lmen," she said proudly. "Moleskin work is tedious work, though, f'r each little skin is no bigger'n th' palm o' yer hand, an' has t' be done separate. When ye've collected sev'ral score, there's th' sewin' together, an' the cuttin' an' the linin'.'' She stroked the cat-skin rug. ''I'd ruther do cats than moles, were it left t' me.''

Seeing that Bea was troubled at the thought of so many innocent foxes and moles sacrificed to warm a lady's hands or a gentleman's midriff, Kate hurriedly broached their reason for calling. But she did so obliquely, for if Mrs. McGregor knew their true motive for inquiring after her brother, she would never tell them what they wanted to know.

''I find myself in need of another pair of hands at Bishop's Keep,'' Kate said, giving the reason Bea had helped her invent during their drive to the cottage. ''The work will be steady and the remuneration substantial. I am informed that your brother, Mr. Brock, might be the right person for the position. I wonder if you could tell me where I might find him.''

Mrs. McGregor's face lighted up with such unabashed delight that Kate felt ashamed of the lie. ''Sartin'ly I kin tell ye,'' she said. ''If 'twer an idle reason I wudn't, 'cause Tom Brock is a man wot seeks his privacy an' niver wants people t' know where he lives. But steady work, now, that's diff'rent, it is. Tommy 'ud want me t' jump at it.''

''Well, then,'' Kate said, ''where may I call to speak with him?''

''Behind th' Pig 'n' Whistle, in Manningtree,'' Mrs. McGregor said. She paused, thinking. ''I misdoubt ye'll find him in t'day, though. Best wait till t'morrow, I'd say.'' She smiled guilelessly, showing a broken front tooth. ''He's got a job t'night, as I heard him tell Mr. McGregor. Yes, best wait till t'morrow.'' She stood up, obviously eager to please the lady who might be her brother's employer. ''Now, how 'ud ye ladies like a cup o' tea?''

When Kate and Bea returned to Bishop's Keep, Kate dispatched Pocket with word to Sir Charles that Tommy Brock might be found behind the Pig and Whistle in Manningtree.

28

To do the bulk of the labourers bare justice it must be stated that there is a certain bluff honesty and frankness among them, which entitles them to considerable respect. At the same time, the labourer is not always so innocent and free from guile. There are very queer black sheep in the flock, and these force themselves, sometimes most unpleasantly, upon the notice of the tenant farmer and the landlord.

—RICHARD JEFFERIES
Hodge and His Masters, 1880

Charles woke groggily the morning after his midnight session with the microscope. He washed and shaved in the basin of hot water a morose Lawrence brought him, renewed his promise to speak to Miss Ardleigh about Lawrence's suit, and took himself down to breakfast, which was spread on a sideboard in the morning room. He had removed the top from a silver tureen of hot deviled kidneys and was helping himself when Bradford came into the room, whistling.

"I'm off to London on the ten o'clock train," he announced cheerfully. He clapped Charles on the shoulder. "Thanks to you, Mama's emeralds will be back in her anxious hands this evening."

Charles added scrambled eggs and a rasher of bacon to

his plate, took a roll from a covered basket, and sat down at the damask-covered table while the butler poured coffee into his cup. After a moment he remarked, not looking up, "I take it from your remark to Miss Ardleigh yesterday that she has consented to your calling."

Bradford pulled out a chair and lounged on it, accepting the coffee the butler handed him. "Of course," he said lazily. "Why should she refuse?"

Indeed, Charles thought, staring into his plate of kidneys. Why should she refuse? The Marsden estate bordered Bishop's Keep, the Marsden fortune was substantial, the Marsden name socially prominent, the Marsden heir handsome and debonair . . . Bleakly, he abandoned his fruitless enumeration of the advantages to Miss Ardleigh of a marriage to the Marsden baronetcy and turned his attention to breakfast, while Bradford regaled him with a story he had read in the newspaper of a possible German plot to invade the south of England. A bit farfetched, Charles thought, only half-listening. The Germans might have designs on portions of the Empire, but only if they could lay their hands on them without a great deal of effort. And it was foolish to imagine an invasion of the south when a landing on the East Coast offered a clear way into the industrial Midlands.

When he had finished eating, he pushed back his plate and brought up the matter which had kept him up so late the night before. "I would like to have your permission to speak with your estate manager, Marsden. I am in need of some information."

"With Carter?" Bradford leaned forward and began to pull grapes off an elaborate pyramid of fresh fruit and flowers in the center of the breakfast table. "Of course, although the old man's a bit foggy."

"He's been with you for some time?"

"Since Grandfather's day. Much of the arable land that is not let has been turned back to meadow to feed Papa's horses. But we still plant some grain, even though the American wheat imports hold prices down. And of course there are the swine and the dairy, though those operations too are small, in comparison to the old days." He waved his hand like a man clearing away a swarm of vexing problems. "What kind of information are you seeking?"

Charles held out his cup to the butler for more coffee. "It has to do with the murder of Sergeant Oliver."

Bradford pulled out an elaborately engraved gold watch and consulted it. "I do hope you are not planning to accuse Carter. The man's too decrepit to have killed anyone—recently, at any rate. And too old to go to jail for it, if he did." He put the watch back in his pocket.

"No accusation," Charles said. "I want to pick his brain about harvest practices hereabouts."

Bradford drained his coffee cup and stood up. "Well, dear chap, I don't profess to know how the harvest might be connected to that wretched murder. But if you think Carter can help, by all means have a go at him. As for me, I am off to London to redeem Mama's emeralds." He went to the door and turned. "Eternally grateful, Charlie. You've saved me once again."

Charles was left with his thoughts about murder, the harvest, and Miss Ardleigh.

Carter had once been a thickset man with a face the colour of brickdust and whiskers and hair of the same tint. Now, his girth had softened and sagged into belly, his ruddy complexion was lined and faded like a dried pippin too long on the tree, and the fringe of rusty whisker beneath his jaw was streaked with white. He wore a round black felt hat, made in the old broad-brimmed style, an ancient green smock-frock, thick green trousers, and black boots, well-oiled. Charles found him standing at the corner of a field, shading his eyes to look out over a gang of men at work with a noisy, hissing steam plough that turned the dark, rich soil in even rows. The plough was drawn back and forth on a cable strung between two traction engines posted on either side of the field and followed by a crowd of raucous black rooks, searching the turned-up clods for worms and grubs. The old man leaned on a carved oak stick, looking from the ploughmen to the northern sky, and back again.

"A good day for ploughing," Charles remarked, when he

had introduced himself and mentioned his errand. The sun was bright, the breeze gentle, and the air sweet.

The old man turned flint-blue eyes on him. "No, 'tant."

Taken aback by this gruff reply, Charles asked "Why not? The sky is clear."

"No, 'tant," Carter said again, and gestured toward the north. "See that grey cloud wind'ard? Th' glass be fallin', too. By afternoon, it'll be dank an' foggy, an' termorrer there'll be rain. Got t' plough this field an' the next afore then. Don't do t' have th' steam plough mired in, er th' men."

Charles thought to himself that he preferred the sights and sounds of the horse-drawn ploughs of his childhood, when teams of horses, each with a boy at the head and a ploughman behind at the shafts, moved up and down the field, striping the pale stubble with widths of darker furrows—and with none of the menacing hiss and clanking of the steam plough. But the machinery had its advantages.

"I suppose the machines have reduced the labour requirements," he said out loud.

Carter gave a sharp, sardonic cackle. "So say some," he replied. "But th' steam plough don't work itself. See those two engines? Want a man apiece t' manage 'em, an' another to go wi' th' watercart t' feed the boilers, an' others wi' th' wagon f'r coal. Th' drill wants men, too—experienced ones—an' horses t' draw it, an' th' horses want men. An' the threshin' machine wants a reg'lar troop to feed it." He shook his head mournfully. "In better days, th' men an' horses 'ud work past midnight, 'til they were too fagged-out t' walk home. But they cared about gettin' th' oats in or rickin' th' hay, an' they cared about doin' it right, an' all f'r ten bob a week." He took out a large pocket-handkerchief and blew his nose. "Now they want four shillin's extra an' a cottage free o' rent."

Charles pursed his mouth thoughtfully. "Do you hire the men yourself?"

"No, worse luck." The old man pulled out a chipped pipe and applied a match to it. "That's why they have t' be watched—so ye know th' work's done as ye'd want it. Have t' rely on bailies like Russell Tod t' supply th' labour. Every harvest, he combs th' country, hirin' as many as he kin get from th' villages an' fillin' in where he kin't wi' navvies an' gypsies an' such. He supplies the machines, too. Hires 'em wherever he kin find 'em sittin' idle.''

Charles considered for a moment, thinking about his errand and the problem he was trying to solve. Carter's morose description of the coordinated system used to bring in the harvest had shed a new light on it. ''The harvesters, then, are not necessarily local people?'' he asked.

''Happen not.'' Carter pulled on his pipe, his face grim. ''Nobody wants t' do field work anymore. 'Tis too hard. Folks 'ud rather fly off t' London t' hire out as grooms an' footmen. They make more money cleanin' rich folks' boots than farmin'.'' He spat. ''Among them that are left are a few black sheep, lazy idlers, er worse.'' A chaffinch uttered a bold challenge from a nearby hedge and from a nearby copse came the deep hollow bass of the wood pigeon. Carter paused to listen for a moment, then turned back to Charles. ''Was it plantin' ye wanted t' ask me about?''

''Actually, it's the harvest I'm interested in,'' Charles said. He took several envelopes out of a pocket in his coat. ''Would you mind taking a look at these and telling me what you see?''

His gnarled, stubby fingers surprisingly nimble, Carter opened the envelopes one by one and inspected the contents of each. ''Looks like ord'nary red wheat,'' he said judiciously. ''A mixed lot, I'd say. Not too good, not too bad. Last year's harvest. Comes from diff'rent fields, o' course.'' He peered at Charles. ''That whut ye want t' know?''

''That's it exactly,'' Charles said. ''You say it comes from different fields. Where, precisely? Can you tell?''

'' 'Course I kin,'' Carter said with a contemptuous look. He fingered the contents of one of the envelopes. ''Take this lot, now. Comes from th' far side o' Manningtree, along o' the estuary.''

''How can you tell?''

'' 'Cause a bit of spurrey's mixed wi' th' wheat.'' To illustrate, Carter licked the tip of his old blunt finger, pushed it into the envelope, and pulled it out with a brown seed stuck to it. ''Spurry grows where th' soil's light an' sandy, near th' coast. Sandwort, some call it. An' this lot—'' He looked into another envelope. ''Th' western edge o' th' district, as far west as Melford, I'd reckon. See how shriveled an' brown is th' seed? There was almost no rain t' th' west last summer. Th' buyers at market remarked that th' wheat from there was poor an' overdry.''

Charles nodded. ''So these samples,'' he said thoughtfully, ''came from various parts of Essex.'' It was a good fifty miles from the estuary to Melford.

''And into Suffolk as well,'' Carter replied, as he opened a third envelope and peered into it. ''Th' thistle here—mean thistle, it is. It's mostly been cleaned out, but you'll still find it t' the north o' East Bergholt, where th' land's unthrifty.''

''I see,'' Charles said. His dream came back to him. But would Artie have tramped from field to field? Wasn't there another explanation? ''Where might I be likely to find all these different lots of grain together in one place?''

Carter shrugged. ''Market comes t' mind. Farmers bring samples of their harvest t' market, f'r buyers t' look over.''

''Where else besides market?''

''Well, there's th' shippin' depot warehouse. When th' farmer's sold his harvest, he hauls th' sacks t' th' depot, where 'tis stored a-fore bein' shipped. Whut's stored has been brought in from all corners o' th' district.''

''Are there any depots in this vicinity?''

Carter shook his head. ''You'll find 'em in towns wi' warehouses, on th' railway. Colchester, Ipswich, Chelmsford, an' other such like.''

Charles had not yet heard what he needed to hear. ''And where else besides market and shipping depots?''

''Nowhere else.'' Carter pulled out his pipe and grinned, showing cracked, yellowed teeth. '' 'Cept where there's rats in th' granary.''

''Rats?'' Charles asked.

The old man spat again, derisively. ''Thieves, sir, thieves,'' he said.

That was what Charles had needed to hear.

29

How now! a rat? Dead, for a ducat, dead!
—WILLIAM SHAKESPEARE
Hamlet, III, iv

Kate spent the afternoon in the person of Beryl Bardwell, shut up in the library at her Remington typewriter, working on her new story, which now bore the intriguing title of *The Corpse in the Garden, Or, The Gamekeeper's Fatal Secret*. The story was well underway; that is to say, it had a beginning: Two lovers, out for an afternoon ramble, stumble upon the body of a gamekeeper at the foot of the constable's garden. Beryl could not bring herself to do further damage to Agnes or Betsy by making a fiction of the sergeant's death. But the story itself was so interesting that it begged to be told, and Beryl could not but oblige it.

Kate and Bea began their nocturnal adventure about eight in the evening. Wearing dark dresses with narrow skirts and with dark shawls thrown over their heads, they took the gig once more and drove away. Kate had instructed Mrs. Pratt not to prepare dinner, since the vicar had invited them for a visit and an informal late supper. She was sorry to deceive her kindhearted housekeeper, but Mrs. Pratt would be deeply perturbed if she knew the real purpose of their excursion. It was kinder to lie than to tell the truth. To stave off hunger, she and Bea had eaten a large tea and pocketed several small sandwiches and biscuits.

It was nearly dark when they set out in the direction of Gallows Green. By the time they reached the hamlet, a ground fog had risen from the low-lying areas and thickened to treetop height. But the sky above was clear, and the full moon, just rising, eerily silvered the landscape so that it took on a mysterious quality. That was the way Beryl Bardwell would have expressed it, Kate thought. "The night had an enigmatic quality," she might have written, "as if little were known and much were to be guessed."

Bea did not speak. Where her hair showed under her shawl it was beaded with mist, but her face was shadowed so that Kate could not read it. Kate also said little, preoccupied as she was with the plan she was trying out in her mind. But finally she gave up trying to think through what they would do when they got where they were going. There were too many circumstances that could not be predicted. All they could do was feel their way along, watch what they had come to see, and observe what occurred.

Suddenly the face of Sir Charles Sheridan rose before her, the sherry-brown eyes, the thick brows, the flash of a smile, half-cynical. What would he say to their expedition? Yesterday, he had shown himself sympathetic to her efforts to save Agnes's pension. But his sympathy would likely not extend to tonight's sortie. Ladies of breeding did not drive down lonely country lanes in the dark, unaccompanied. He would certainly order them home. It was a good thing that he would not know what they had got themselves up to.

At Gallows Green, Agnes Oliver ushered them into her kitchen with pleased surprise but some little embarrassment, for she and Betsy had eaten their suppers a while ago, and Betsy was already in her bed in the loft.

"Had I known you were coming," she said, "we could have stayed our supper. May I fix you something to eat, or a cup of tea?"

"Please, no," Kate said, perfectly aware that there wasn't any extra food in the Oliver cupboard. "We had quite a substantial tea."

"We thought Betsy might like to have these for her breakfast," Bea said, taking out a packet of shredded beef and a small jar of gooseberry jelly Kate had spirited from the pantry. She set a tin of tea beside them. "And this is for you."

Kate pulled off her dark gloves, put them in her pocket, and got straight to the point of their visit. "We have come," she said, "because we would like to borrow your dog for the evening."

Agnes stared at them, astonished. "Kep? But whatever for?"

Bea gave her a dimpling smile. She looked, in fact, as if she had gotten over any trepidation she might have felt and was quite enjoying this odd adventure. "Miss Ardleigh and I are going ratting," she said.

"Ratting?" Agnes's surprise turned to puzzlement. "I am not sure I understand you."

"I think it would be better," Kate replied carefully, "if we spared you the details, Agnes. Simply let me say that we hope to clear your husband's name, if we can, so that your pension need no longer be at risk."

Agnes pressed her lips together and her eyes filled suddenly with tears. "Oh, Miss Ardleigh, do you think you can do that?" she whispered. "Living would be hard without the money. But even harder would be the agony of knowing Artie judged as a criminal, when he was a decent, law-abiding man!"

"I am not sure what we can achieve," Kate replied honestly. It would not be fair to raise Agnes's hopes, when the outcome of their night-time investigation was so uncertain. "All I can speak to is our intention."

"Thank you," Agnes said. She took out a scrap of white cotton handkerchief and blew her nose. "Yes, by all means take the dog, and the rope Betsy uses to leash him. Whatever rats you are after, I pray he will help you catch them. And keep you safe," she added, with a half-smile. "Kep is small, but ferocious."

"Thank you," Kate said, touched by her earnestness. "There's one other thing, if you don't mind. I remember that you kept several of your husband's shirts to make over for Betsy. I wonder if we might borrow one."

"Artie's shirts?" Agnes's face was a study in emotions.

"But then you must think that the dog . . . that is, you must have some knowledge of where Artie . . ." She bit her lip and looked from Kate to Bea. "Are you sure that what you are doing is entirely prudent?"

Bea put her hand on Agnes's arm. "Perhaps it is not," she said gently. "But prudence may not discover what must be discovered."

Agnes managed a small smile. "Then you are very brave," she said. "And I will give you something more to your purpose. I still have his nightshirt. I have not been able to bring myself to wash it since—" Her mouth trembled.

"Thank you," Kate whispered, and folded her in her arms.

When Kate and Bea embarked once more into the dark and misty night, they had with them Arthur Oliver's nightshirt. And beside the gig, looking alert and pleased to be taken on a late-night expedition, trotted Kep, the collie dog who was trained to track.

Bea was silent for a space of time, whether it was because she was occupied by her thoughts or because the darkness somehow seemed to silence speech, Kate did not know. Finally, as they drove down the lane past the church, its bulk shadowy in the moon-silvered fog, she spoke.

"It seems, Kate, that you intend to use the dog to track the sergeant. And we are on the way to Highfields Barn. Does that mean that you believe him to have been killed near there?"

"I think it is possible," Kate said, "that Sergeant Oliver may have been in the barn before he was killed, or perhaps *when* he was killed. His pockets were full of grain and chaff—the sort of thing one associates with barns. Betsy claimed that Kep could track her father—remember?"

Bea's voice was dubious. "But even if the dog has that ability, it has rained since the murder. It doesn't seem likely that the scent will remain."

"I am sure you are right," Kate said. "If we were to try to track him out-of-doors, we should fail. But the barn is enclosed. If there is anything inside pertaining to Sergeant Oliver, Kep may be able to show us what it is. I know it sounds far-fetched," she added. "But we have nothing to lose and everything to gain. If we can prove that the sergeant was not killed because he was a poacher, Agnes's pension will be secure.''

''To be sure,'' Bea said. ''But what of the pirates, or smugglers, or whatever they are?'' She glanced at Kate, her mouth apprehensive. ''Betsy saw them at the barn. Perhaps they will be abroad tonight?''

''It's entirely possible,'' Kate conceded. ''In fact, when we came upon Tod and Mr. McGregor, Tod was mentioning that—''

''—that the man he was looking for, who must have been Tommy Brock, was wanted for an urgent job *tonight*!'' Bea clutched at Kate's arm. ''But, Kate, what if they come to the barn while *we* are there?''

''Not *we*,'' Kate corrected her. ''While *I* am there. Kep and I will go to the barn and quickly look around. You will remain with the horse and gig. When I return, we will find a safe place from which to observe anyone who comes to the barn tonight.''

Bea sat up straight. ''Don't be ridiculous,'' she said smartly. ''I have faced my fears this entire evening. And I have gone too far in this journey to quit it at the point of our arrival. I will *not* let you go into that place alone.''

''But really, Bea,'' Kate objected, ''I think it would be far better if you—''

''I am coming,'' Bea said with a decided firmness. ''If there is danger, we will face it together. We will be a true Sherlock Holmes and Dr. Watson.''

In spite of herself, Kate had to chuckle. She knew there was very little similarity between herself and Bea Potter—two women groping about in the foggy dark, pursuing they knew not what—and the cool, supremely logical characters of Conan Doyle. But Beryl Bardwell, who had been making mental notes all evening for Chapter Two of *The Corpse in the Garden*, could not help but be flattered by the comparison.

''Very well, then, come,'' Kate said, ''and welcome. But I am sure we will face no more real danger than do Holmes and Watson in their fictional adventures. It was barely nine by

Agnes's clock when we left her kitchen, and must be no more than nine-thirty now. I doubt that any self-respecting pirate will be out and about before midnight. We ought to be able to see what there is to see in the barn, leave it, and safely conceal ourselves in an observation post before the business begins. *If* there is business at the barn tonight," she added carelessly, "which may very well not be the case."

Bea stifled a giggle, and Kate glanced at her. "My dear Bea," she said, "what can possibly be funny?"

Bea's shoulders were shaking under her shawl. "I was thinking of Mama," she managed finally, "and what she would say if she saw me riding down a dark country lane in search of rats. Quite *nasty* rats, at that!"

Kate was saved from answering by the emergence out of the silvery fog of a cart track leading away from the lane in the direction of Highfields Barn. Kate followed it for a hundred yards, and then pulled the pony into a clearing well off to the side. Bea shielded the flickering lantern with her shawl, glancing apprehensively into the thick shadows around them, while Kate tied the rope Agnes had given them around Kep's neck and bundled Sergeant Oliver's nightshirt under her arm. They followed the cart track in the direction of the barn, Kep pulling ahead, head up, ears pricked attentively. When they came close to the barn, Kate held up her hand and stood listening for a moment.

Save for the eerie hoot of a nearby owl and the distant tolling of a fog bell on the estuary, she could hear nothing. There was not a light anywhere. The farmhouse was some distance away across the ploughed field. It was a silent silhouette against the darker woods. Kate shivered in the otherworldly, fog-softened silence, under the half-light of the moon.

"It seems safe enough," she whispered. "But let's move quickly and be ready to leave at any moment. If someone does come, it wouldn't do to be trapped inside."

The barn was a huge half-timbered building, two stories high, with a loft above. With Kep's leash in her hand and Bea directly behind, carrying the shielded lantern, Kate moved cautiously along the wall to a small side door. She pushed it open. They stepped quickly through and stood within, listening intently.

After the damp chill of the foggy night, the barn felt dry and almost warm, and the air had a soft, furry quality. As Bea held up the lantern, Kate saw that there was a heavy double door at one end, made of wood, with a bar across it, fastened with a rusty hasp. The dirt floor was littered with straw, and two spotted cows stood in stalls in a far corner, their liquid eyes turned curiously to the light. Somewhere a rooster clucked nervously, and there was a stirring in the straw in the loft.

"Rats," Bea whispered. "They're not nearly as nice as mice. It's hard to make a pleasant drawing of a rat."

But Kate was not concerned with rats at the moment. She had dropped to one knee and was holding Sergeant Oliver's shirt out to the collie dog. "Can you sniff him out, boy?" she asked, with not the least idea in her head what to expect. The whole affair might be a wild-goose chase. "Can you find him?"

But if Kate had not the proper confidence, Kep did. Sensing a great game, the dog thrust an eager nose into the shirt and snuffled with enthusiasm. He stood still for a moment, his head cocked as if he were considering the matter, then dropped his nose to the barn floor and began to move in a zigzag fashion, randomly at first, then with greater design, and finally with purpose, his tail a silken flag.

Standing beside Kate, Bea raised the lantern. "It looks as if he has discovered something!"

Kate watched the dog with mounting excitement. This expedition had been a very long chance. Had she been a wagering woman, she would not have placed high odds on the outcome. But it looked as if Kep had succeeded in finding a scent. Was it that of his master? He was near the far wall, beside a stack of filled sacks, pawing at the floor and whining eagerly.

Kate ran to him in a rush, followed by Bea with the lantern. It took considerable effort to move him away from the spot in the earthen floor that so excited him—a clear space that had been swept free of the hay that littered the floor elsewhere. In the center was a large, irregularly-shaped dark stain, where something had been spilled onto the earth. As Kate raised her eyes, she saw that the partially-cleared track extended from this point across the floor to the side door, like a path. Something heavy had been dragged from this point to the door. A body!

Bea bent over, holding the lantern low for a better view of the dark spot. "Kate," she whispered, touching it with a fearful finger, "can this be a *blood* stain?"

Kate stood up. "I believe it is," she replied. "I believe we have found the spot where Sergeant Oliver was shot."

Beside Kate, Kep stiffened and growled low in his throat. From the other side of the door Kate could hear the murmur of low voices. She and Bea froze, staring at one another in petrified fright.

While they were occupied, the pirates had crept up on them and blocked the door. They were trapped in the barn. And there was no way out!

30

I smell a Rat, sir, there's juggling in this business.

—*The Voyage of Vaughn*, 1790

"Grain thieves, you say?" Edward Laken asked, turning away from the small coal stove where he was making a supper of cabbage, potatoes, and plump pieces of sausage. It was late evening when Charles had located him in his whitewashed two-room cottage behind the Dedham gaol.

"That was Carter's idea," Charles said. "It sounds reasonable to me." He watched with no little admiration Edward's deft stirring of the pot. He himself had always had to endure the tender mercies of one cook or another. Once when he had dared to reconnoiter the kitchen in search of tea and a sandwich, the cook had been so horrified at his effrontery that she had served notice on the spot.

"And to me," Edward said, and fetched the bread from the cupboard. "There've been rats in the granaries many times before this."

Charles indicated the envelopes spread out on the table. "My guess is that Artie came upon a large cache of wheat somewhere—sacks of grain stolen from several different farms. To authenticate his discovery, he filled his pockets with samples of the grain, intending perhaps to lay watch and apprehend the thieves. But he was surprised and murdered."

"It makes sense." Edward spooned out a plate of cabbage and potatoes and added a chunk of satisfyingly greasy sausage.

He set it in front of Charles. "A crew takes the threshing machines about from farm to farm, on hire. The wheat is cut and threshed and sacked and tallied in the field, then stored in the farm's granary until it is sold or used. And of course there's no guard on it."

Charles poured mugs of the ale he had brought. "So anyone can help himself to a dozen sacks or so," he said, pushing the ladder-back chair to the table and sitting down. "It isn't difficult to juggle the tally, either, so the farmer never misses it."

"A dozen sacks from a dozen farms amounts to a fair harvest, especially when you've not the expense of ploughing and planting." There being a deficit of chairs, Edward sat on an overturned box. "But a cache of stolen grain might be hidden in any granary hereabouts," he added, slathering butter on a crusty slab of bread. "I wonder where Artie happened on it?"

"I've got an idea about that," Charles said. "After supper, we can walk there. It's no more than a mile." He began to eat. "By the way, I've located Tommy Brock."

"You don't say!" Edward exclaimed. "The elusive Mr. B. comes to light at last. How did you manage that?"

Charles glanced up from his cabbage and potatoes. "Actually, it was Miss Ardleigh who managed it—how, I have yet to discover. She sent word this morning that Brock has a cottage behind the Pig and Whistle in Manningtree. I haven't actually talked to him yet, however. I rode over this afternoon, but he was out working, according to the landlady. She expected him back on the morrow."

At the mention of Miss Ardleigh, Charles saw, Edward's face had become thoughtful. Charles applied himself to his supper, trying to decide what to say. If Ned did not already know about Bradford Marsden's suit, it would be kind to give him advance notice so that he might prepare himself for the likely outcome. Miss Ardleigh, however, was more independent than any woman Charles had ever known. She was perfectly capable of refusing a baron-to-be and accepting a village constable, if that was where her affections lay.

Charles frowned. But if Ned had won her heart, why the devil had she given Marsden permission to call? One would have thought that she would have the wit to reject Marsden's proposal before he made it. The whole thing was such a muddle that he finally decided to say nothing. He and Ned finished their supper in silence, smoked the cigars Charles had brought while they did the washing-up, and set off into the silvery dark, their path half-lit by a moon high above the ground fog and by Ned's bull's-eye lantern, which cast a golden halo around their feet.

31

Anything like the sound of a rat
Makes my heart go pit-a-pat!
— ROBERT BROWNING
"The Pied Piper of Hamelin"

"Oh, Mother, Mother, there has been an old
man in the dairy—a dreadful 'normous big rat,
Mother, and he's stolen a pat of butter and the
rolling pin."

— BEATRIX POTTER
The Roly-Poly Pudding

Contrary to her mother's belief, Betsy Oliver was not in bed when the Misses Ardleigh and Potter called to borrow Kep. She was, in fact, sitting at the top of the narrow stairs in her pink-flannel nightdress, her elbows on her knees and her fists jammed under her chin, listening to what was said in the kitchen. When Miss Potter remarked that she and Miss Ardleigh intended to go ratting, Betsy scowled horribly for a moment or two, then stood up and squared her shoulders.

If they could take Kep ratting (although she couldn't fathom why they fancied Kep—the dog was a *tracker*, not a ratter, and a lazy layabout where work was concerned), she could take Mr. Browne on the same errand. And when the hunting was all done and over, they could compare their catches (although not where Mother could hear), and she could gloat. And gloat she would, to be sure, for the owl was a superb hunter who much preferred rats to mice and larger rats to smaller, and could be counted on to best that lazy Kep any night of the week. Her father had once read her a poem called "The Pied Piper." When he had come to the lines where the sound of the rat made his heart go pit-a-pat, she had laughed out loud. She and Father had agreed that it was exactly how Mr. Browne must feel when he made to dig his talons into a cowering rat.

The spirit of the game dispelled any sleepiness, and she ran lightly to her tiny corner room under the low thatched roof, skinned out of her nightdress, and pulled on a pair of breeches and a dark-blue shirt. She tucked her hair up under a black woolen cap and climbed out the window. Her descent down the drainpipe was executed with the careless panache of long practice. When she reached the ground she darted toward the shed, keeping to the shadows, and slipped through the door. As she did so, she heard the voices of Miss Ardleigh and Miss Potter, who were leaving by the front way.

"Who?" Mr. Browne inquired querulously from his perch by the window. Jemima Puddle-duck, nesting for the evening in a box of straw, pulled her head out from under her wing and uttered a drowsy quack.

"And where have *you* been?" Betsy demanded, hands on hips. Jemima had gone missing that afternoon. Betsy had searched everywhere for her, to no avail.

Jemima put her head under her wing again. Of course she wouldn't tell where she had been, for she was still trying to find a place to lay her eggs undisturbed and raise a family. Probably she had found one, and she intended to keep it secret.

"Pay no attention to Jemima," Betsy told Mr. Browne. "She's obsessed with ducklings." She slipped her hand into the leather gauntlet sleeve her father had contrived for her. "*We're* going ratting."

Mr. Browne's golden eyes glittered and he clicked his sharp beak in anticipation of dinner. She found an old gunnybag, then released the owl from his perch. With the bird on her arm, she stole through a hole in the garden hedge, went around the brick wall at the back corner, and set out through the fog.

Fifteen minutes later, under a misty moon that turned the drifting fog phosphorescent and set the trees to glimmering as if they had been dipped in mercury, Betsy and Mr. Browne crossed the pasture and fetched up at the stone wall above the barn at Highfields Farm, where she knew the hunting to be better than anywhere else in the neighbourhood. When the owl returned with his prey, she planned to drop his kill into the gunnybag. Allowing Mr. Browne an interim snack or two would only delay him and dull his appetite. If their catch of the night were to exceed that of Kep and his two borrowers, the owl's desire for dinner would need to remain sharp.

The night was chilly, but for the next little while, Betsy kept warm by busying herself with the owl. In fact, the two of them were enjoying quite the most remarkable success—a success at least partly attributable to the fog that was draped like a diaphanous shawl over the trees and fields, softening even the ominous sound of the owl's wing beat.

Indeed, it might have been the fog that explained what happened next. For to Betsy's great surprise, while she was sitting on the wall, waiting for Mr. Browne to return from his third sortie (his first two quite dead victims were safely in the bag), she glimpsed the shadowy forms of a dog and two shawled women—one of them carrying a lantern that cast huge, wavering shadows against the barn wall. They crept furtively along the side of the barn, opened the door, went inside, and shut it behind them. The moon moved behind a cloud.

Betsy stifled a surprised exclamation. She should have thought that Miss Ardleigh, who had evidenced quite a little interest in the barn, would think to go hunting there, and coming along the lane, would be considerably delayed. Her surprise also held not a little envy. Why hadn't *she* thought to take Mr. Browne into the barn, where he might hunt in the warmer, drier place? A seat in the hay would have been far more comfortable than her perch on the fence, where the cold of the stones penetrated through her breeches and the silvery dark was distinctly chilly. And there were far more rats in the barn than in the hedgerows. She drew down her brows and gritted her teeth. Her opponents had displayed a devious ingenuity with which she had not credited them.

Mr. Browne came back crestfallen and empty-clawed from his third flight. But Betsy praised and stroked him anyway, and released him with a special word of encouragement. As if to show her his gratitude, he returned with a brown mole of substantial size, with enormous whiskers and a very long tail. Betsy congratulated him on his skill and cunning, popped the mole into the bag with the rats, and released the owl once again, confident that she and Mr. Browne would outshine the ratters in the barn. *They* were unlikely to find a mole.

And it was in that mood, with the celebration of victory in her heart, that the second surprise of the evening overtook Betsy. It was a scratchy burlap sack that smelled horribly of fish, dropped over her head. She bit and spit and cried and wriggled, but despite her efforts to escape she was flung to the ground, held down by an invisible knee and several hands, and rolled up in the sack as neatly as if she were the raisin-and-currant-and-sugar-and-butter filling in the roly-poly puddings her mother made with a rolling pin: her ankles trussed, her arms pinned to her sides, her nose and mouth filled with the stink of rotten fish, and her heart pounding in terror.

The rats had put Betsy in the bag.

32

No female Rat shall me deceive
Nor catch me by a crafty wile
                    —*Roxbury Ballads*, 1866

"So it's Highfields Farm you have in mind," Edward said
over his shoulder, as they strode purposefully along the
ridge above the River Stour.

"What's your opinion?" Charles asked. He was trying to
walk close enough behind Edward to utilize the lantern light,
but far enough back to avoid treading on his heels. "If you
were caching stolen wheat, would the barn at Highfields be a
reasonable place to hide it?"

"It would," Edward replied decidedly. "The barn is only
a field's length up from the river. And it's below the locks,
giving easy access to the estuary and the quay at Manningtree.
If a barge or a flat-boat were pulled in below the barn, grain
could be hauled there by wagon and readily ferried to a larger
boat, or even to a ship moored at Manningtree."

Charles negotiated a rickety stile after Edward. "Who owns
the farm?"

"Sir Thomas Morrell, of Ipswich. He let it last year to a
man named Napthen, who comes from over Harwich way. It's
said that Napthen isn't much of a farmer, and the evidence
points that way. The fields are idle, save for the odd cow."
He skirted a fresh pile of dung in the path. "How'd you get
onto Highfields, Charlie?"

Charles grinned into the dark. "Miss Ardleigh again, I fear."

Edward turned back a surprised face. "Indeed?"

"Quite," Charles said dryly. "She heard word of it from little Betsy." It was interesting to speculate how much of the information regarding this matter had come from the distaff side.

Edward stopped in the middle of the path. "I don't suppose I should ask how the child came by such facts," he muttered.

Charles chuckled. "It appears that the young lady was out prowling with her owl one night when she saw a group of men—including, it seems, the elusive Tommy Brock—driving a wagon. They were hauling sacks from Highfields Barn to a boat on the river. Exactly the scenario you surmised."

Edward's mouth was set, his voice sour. "Her father let her roam too freely, like a boy. Agnes will have to curb that one."

"I hope not," Charles heard himself replying rather to his own surprise. "A young woman growing up in these times needs a sense of adventure."

The thought of Miss Ardleigh came unbidden to his mind. If Betsy grew up with anything like Kate Ardleigh's sense of adventure, she would be fortunate. On the other hand, she might also find herself in serious trouble now and then—especially if she took after Kate's apparent interest in criminal mischief. He grinned wryly. That was an interest that would likely be curbed, however, when Kate became Lady Marsden.

Edward wheeled about with an impatient sound and started off again. "Adventure be damned. A girl who goes prowling about at night may not live to grow up. These people, whoever they are, have already killed once—and a police officer, at that. Who's to say they wouldn't murder a child?"

Or a woman, Charles thought, remembering that Miss Ardleigh had persisted in ignoring his earlier admonitions of caution. But that was something he could not worry about just now.

"I see no boat," he remarked, looking down the hill where the broad, green meadow gently shelved into the river. "No sign of a barge."

"Are you expecting activity tonight?"

"I don't know," Charles said. "But the barn is just up the way there. It might be well to shutter the lantern."

A little distance down the path, Highfields Barn emerged, a solid shape out of the shrouding, silvered fog. The silence was broken only by the heavy beat of an owl's wings and its sharp predatory cry, uttered once and then again.

"There's a side door," Edward whispered, his voice eager, a man ready for action. "And no sign of life. The farmhouse seems dark, too. Shall we risk a look inside?"

"By all means," Charles said. "My guess is that if our quarry were on the premises, there'd be a wagon. Anyway, if they're in there, we've cornered them."

"Like rats," Edward said feelingly.

Charles moved forward, carefully, looking all around. But caution did not seem warranted. No boat, no wagon, and the countryside was cloaked in a profound stillness, as thick and palpable as the fog. At the door, they paused once more.

"I'll go first," Charles said. "You follow." Edward seemed about to say something, then nodded. Cautiously, Charles pushed the door inward with his foot and flattened himself against the wall. Hearing nothing, and seeing that the interior of the barn was dark as pitch, he stepped quickly over the threshold, Edward on his heels.

Inside, there was the thick, dusky odour of animals and stored hay and paraffin, as if a lantern had been recently extinguished. All was quiet, cloaked with a heavy, foreboding stillness, and the air itself seemed to have weight. From a nearby corner came the sound of a large rat rustling in the hay. Charles took an uneasy step forward, groping along the wall. He was overtaken by the intuition that he and Edward were not alone in the barn, and the hair rose on the back of his neck.

Then he heard it, a throaty, menacing growl. He stopped, and Edward bumped into him.

"Someone's here," Charles said.

"Could merely be a dog shut in to guard the animals," Edward said quietly. "Or kill rats. I heard one rustling just a moment ago—a big one."

"Someone's here," Charles insisted, low. "I feel it."

His insistence was corroborated with a sharp, light sneeze. A *female* sneeze. Charles scowled. "The lantern, Ned," he said.

Edward unshuttered the lantern and held it up. "Show yourself," he commanded. "In the name of the Crown."

At the very edge of the lantern's pale circle, Charles caught sight of a hesitant form. He took two steps forward.

"Miss Ardleigh?" he demanded, incredulous.

For answer, there was another sneeze.

"Miss Ardleigh!" he exclaimed.

Kate Ardleigh stepped into the circle of the lantern's glow. "Good evening, gentlemen," she said with consummate courtesy, as if this were her drawing room and he and Edward her guests. The brown shawl that covered her head fell back to reveal her russet hair, tendrils escaping untidily around her face, framing it. Behind her Miss Potter stifled another sneeze, and a collie dog—Agnes Oliver's dog Kep—wagged its tail furiously at the sight of Edward. "We did not expect guests," Miss Ardleigh added dryly. "I fear you were not properly announced."

Edward chuckled. Charles, however, was too out of sorts to be amused by the woman's deuced playfulness or swayed by her physical attraction.

"Don't you two have the sense to know that you are in danger?" he asked roughly. "What in God's name brought you out in the middle of the night?"

"We have come ratting," Miss Potter said. "Anyway, it is not the middle of the night. It is scarcely ten."

Charles ignored her. "What the devil gave you the idea to come here?" he demanded of Miss Ardleigh. "This is no place for a woman."

But as he heard the harshness in his words, he knew also the passion and ambivalence that prompted it. If the woman lacked the sense to fear for herself, he feared *for* her. He feared because he cared. And he cared, paradoxically, because she had the courage and fortitude to undertake adventures like this one, when other ladies of far less heart were flirting through a waltz or being escorted to dinner by a handsome partner. What irony! He could not have her here, in danger, and yet he would not have her anywhere else. And the worst of it was that she was not his to command or protect. He could not in good conscience concern himself about her, more than in a friendly way.

But Miss Ardleigh could know nothing of the conflict that swirled within him. She pulled herself up, her grey eyes cool and steady, and spoke with a dignified reserve.

"We came here in search of the spot where Sergeant Oliver was killed. And we have found it."

"You *what*?" Edward was incredulous.

"We found the very spot where the sergeant was murdered," Miss Potter put in excitedly. She pointed. "Over there. By the wall. There's a bloodstain."

"Yes," Miss Ardleigh said. "Beside those sacks." There was a deep sadness in her voice. "After they shot him, they dragged him to the door. You can see the track of the body."

For the space of three heartbeats, Charles stared where Miss Potter pointed. And in that brief instant, he saw it all, just as it had to have happened. Artie bending over to fill his pockets with samples from the grain sacks. The grain thieves coming upon him in the dark. Artie turning, the thieves shooting point-blank. And then instead of loading sacks into their wagon, they loaded the dead Artie and drove off with him.

"But *why* was he shot?" Miss Potter asked. "What could have been the motive?"

Miss Ardleigh looked at Charles. "It was the grain, wasn't it?"

"Yes," Charles replied. His irritation was gone, and his anger. How could he be angry at her for having the courage to search for the truth? "It looks as though a ring of thieves was stealing grain from granaries throughout the district and storing it here. Artie discovered the crime, and was murdered."

"I see," Miss Ardleigh murmured. "And Tommy Brock was one of the thieves?"

"So it appears," Charles said.

"And the farmer who owns this barn," she added. "I hardly think that grain could have been stored here without his connivance."

Charles nodded. "Agreed."

She was thoughtful. "And all this can be proved? I ask, of course, because of the need to refute the false charge of poaching and protect Agnes's pension."

"It *will* be proved," Edward said with determination, "when we apprehend the criminals. And that should be shortly."

"Excellent." Miss Ardleigh pulled her shawl closer. "There is one more thing," she said. "When the bailiff Tod spoke to McGregor, he intimated that Tommy Brock was wanted for tonight. Miss Potter and I intended to set up an observation post, but since you are here—"

"Since we are here," Charles said, "we might as well stay and see what is to be seen, and allow you ladies to return home."

"Exactly." Smiling, Miss Ardleigh turned to her companion. "Well, then, Bea, I think we should leave the matter in the capable hands of Sir Charles and Mr. Laken. Do you agree?"

The relief was plain on Miss Potter's face. "I do indeed," she said vehemently, gathering her skirt in her hand. "We have had quite enough adventure for one evening!"

33

"Tell me, what sort of match is it?"

"An unspeakable match, my dear, utterly abominable. It has turned his mother's hair silver and made his father into a pallid wretch."

"But could no one remonstrate with him? Could no one dissuade him from his intention?"

"Sadly, no one. The affair is an absolute tragedy, and it bids fair to sink the whole family."
—BERYL BARDWELL
Amber's Amulet

True to his word, Bradford Marsden placed his mother's emeralds in her hands the next morning, immediately upon his return on the early train from London.

"Thank you, dearest Mama," he said, "for the loan."

Lady Marsden, still in her bed with a lace shawl around her shoulders, tried to hide her relief. She had not wished to let Bradford have the emeralds, but he was her only son and dearest joy. Her mother's heart had been touched, and she had offered to help—but impulsively, without fully understanding what was needed. That she had been sorry afterward was not something she wanted him to know. So she only said, in the acerbic tone she used to mask her sentimental feeling for him, "I hope, Bradford, that you have learned your lesson."

With a toss of his head, Bradford gave her his usual insouciant grin. "I have, dearest Mama." He sat down on the edge of her bed and reached for her hand. "At any rate, there will be no more need of loans. You will be glad to know that I have come to a decision about my marriage. The lady in question has an ample fortune, which should be quite an adequate supplement to my own."

Lady Marsden's hand flew to her heart. Like every other mother, she had longed for the day that her only son should wed, should make a match that would not only bring him happiness but bestow honour and fortune upon the Marsden house and perpetuate the family name and title. To that end, she had scrutinized all the great families for suitable candidates and studied each acceptable young woman who was presented during the season. But even though she had identified three or four promising candidates each year—as many as five or six in a good year—none had suited Bradford. Their hair was the wrong colour, or their teeth were crooked, or they could not dance, or they laughed too often or not often enough. Last year, when he attained his thirtieth birthday and was still a bachelor, she had almost despaired of his marrying. But of course that was impossible. He bore the responsibility for carrying on the Marsden name. He *had* to marry, and she was delighted—indeed, jubilant—that he had chosen to do so now, when Eleanor was safely wed and she could devote a mother's loving attention to the nuptials.

"Bradford, my dear!" she exclaimed, seizing his hand and bringing it to her cheek. "How very wonderful! Oh, *do* tell me! Is it Miss Poulett?" Lady Hermione Poulett, the charming daughter of Lord and Lady Poulett, had been her favourite candidate this season. Lady Hermione and her gracious sister Lady Ulrica had been going about with Lady Damer, wife of Sir George Damer, who had been so long at the Foreign Office. Lady Hermione was remarkably pretty, with violet eyes and pale gold hair, and her ball dresses were an absolute wonder. Lady Marsden had fastened her maternal hopes upon Lady Hermione the minute she saw her.

Bradford's glance was teasing. "No, Mama, it is not Miss Poulett. Guess as you like, you are not likely to discover the lady's identity. It will be a complete surprise to you."

"Then it must be Miss Dyke," Lady Marsden said decidedly. While Lady Poulett might have been a better choice, she could feel no real disappointment, for Miss Madeleine Dyke was one of the Queen's Maids-of-Honour, quite intellectual, it was said, and certainly the possessor of a pleasant face and figure and fortune—her own, in addition to the thousand-pound dowry bestowed by the Queen on her Maids of Honour. Miss Dyke's dresses were not the equal of those of Lady Hermione, but they were quite nice, and she danced delightfully.

Bradford leaned forward and laid his finger gently on her lips. "No, Mama," he said. "Please, conjecture no more. The object of my affection, the lady who has won my heart, has no connexion with the Court, and none with Society. You are not likely to think of her when thinking of a match, although I am sure you will believe, with me, that it is most suitable."

Lady Marsden stared. "No connexion with Society!"

"That is correct, Mama." Bradford sat back and stroked his blond mustache with a pleased expression on his face. "She is in fact your own near neighbour. Now can you guess her name?"

"My own—!" Lady Marsden felt herself go pale as a searing pain lanced her heart.

"Indeed, Mama." Bradford's smile was triumphant. "She is Miss Kathryn Ardleigh, of Bishop's Keep."

"Miss Ardleigh!" Lady Marsden cried. "Miss Ardleigh!" Her voice rose into a shriek. "No, Bradford, no! Not Miss Ardleigh!"

At that moment, the door opened and Eleanor came running in. "What's happened?" she cried. "I heard a cry. Is there a fire?"

"No, no fire, sister," Bradford said. "I have just told Mama of my intention to marry Miss Ardleigh and—"

"Oh, no, no," Lady Marsden moaned, pressing her hands

to her heart, where she had been wounded mortally. "Not Miss Ardleigh! Never!"

Bradford stood, frowning. "Really, Mama, there is no need for hysterics. Miss Ardleigh is a—"

"Miss Ardleigh is Irish!" Lady Marsden cried, opening her eyes wide in an agony of loathing.

Eleanor frowned. "No, Mama," she said, "she is an *American*, and American women have married into the best British society. Your own dear friend Lady Churchill, for instance—"

"We are not speaking of Lady Churchill!" Lady Marsden cried, clutching at the counterpane as if it were all that shielded her and hers from the direct onslaught of a thousand mad Irish. "We are speaking of the common Kate Ardleigh, who was brought to Bishop's Keep to be her aunt's *secretary*!"

Eleanor's face darkened. "Mama, you are being utterly unreasonable! Miss Ardleigh is an uncommonly fine—"

"Eleanor," Lady Marsden said cuttingly, "you are to stay out of this. I have observed Miss Ardleigh worming her way into your friendship by the devices of flattery and ingratiation. Your perception of this affair is not to be trusted."

Bradford's tone was stiff. "Am I to understand, Mama, that you oppose—"

"Oppose!" Lady Marsden pulled in a gasping breath, clenched her ringed fingers, and steadied herself. Over the years, her only son, her dearest boy, had given her much cause for grief. But nothing he had done in the past held as much potential for future disaster as this. It was incumbent on her to deploy whatever force was needed, to use whatever ammunition was required to deter him from this folly. She weighted her voice with all her maternal authority.

"I do more than oppose this match, Bradford. I utterly forbid it. You certainly know that she allowed her cook to ride in the Ardleigh carriage."

"Mama," Eleanor said patiently, "I have *told* you. That was a special occasion. Miss Ardleigh does not as a matter of course allow the servants to—"

Lady Marsden swept on. "And have you not heard that she goes about in *bloomers*, and rides her bicycle in the public lanes?"

Bradford's mouth quirked. "I have also heard that the Countess of Warwick, the Prince's Daisy, wears bloomers and finds them extraordinarily comfortable. And that *she* has ridden her bicycle on Rotten Row."

Lady Marsden perceived that she had made a strategic mistake. She had not put the matter in its strictest terms. She straightened her shoulders and chose a better angle of attack. "I say again, Bradford, I forbid this match. As would your father, should you dare to mention it to him. I advise you, if you value his high estimation of your judgment and hope for his continued generosity, that you banish Miss Ardleigh from your mind. She is utterly unacceptable."

"But Mama," Bradford said, "you are not accurately assessing the advantages of—"

"There are *no* advantages in this match, Bradford." Lady Marsden's voice was steel now, her words ice, and she brought up her big gun from the rear. "Surely you have heard the wretched tales that are told about her."

"Tales?" Bradford asked.

"What tales?" Eleanor echoed.

Lady Marsden lobbed her last and best shot. "That the despicable woman is to wed the village constable."

Eleanor gave a little shriek. Bradford seemed stunned.

"You are sure of this?" he asked.

"Utterly," Lady Marsden lied. "I have it on the best authority. They are to be married within the month. There. Does this not reveal the sort of low, uncultured person she is? Whatever foolish hopes you may have squandered on—"

But her salvo had hit home. Bradford turned on his heel and left the room.

34

Mordre wol out.
—CHAUNTACLEER
Geoffrey Chaucer
"The Nun's Priest's Tale"

It was the morning after their discovery of the grain sacks in the barn, and Charles and Edward were on their way to Highfields Farm, in the fly Charles had brought from Marsden Manor. After the departure of Miss Ardleigh and Miss Potter, their vigil had been unproductive, and they had abandoned it at three in the morning.

The lane was open to green fields on the one side and hedged on the other with hawthorn, its white blossoms mixed with the pink of wild roses. A tall elm stood beside the gate of Highfields Farm, its branches laden with rooks' nests, a dovecot fixed in the fork. Beyond the elm, on the far side of the farmhouse, was a muddy sty containing two portly Berkshire pigs.

The farmhouse itself was small and built of brick, the tiles of its roof furred with lichen and moss. A thin smudge of blue smoke rose from the chimney and into the misty morning. In the orchard, a hen cackled, cheerfully announcing a fresh egg.

"Napthen, you say?" Charles pulled back on the reins and slowed the horse. Bradford's groom had fitted him out with a smart high-stepping filly this morning, eager to show her mettle.

"That's the name," Edward replied. "Said to have been a ship's carpenter at Harwich before he rented this place."

"Why would a man leave a dependable trade for the uncertain rewards of farming?"

"He's one of these new four-acre farmers," Edward said. "I heard he means to make the farm into a market garden." He was thoughtful. "The scheme might work, at that. The farm is close enough to Colchester and Manningtree, and vegetables bring a good price all season. He could crop fodder for gentlemen's stables on the rest of the acreage and do well enough. It's a wish I've had for myself for some time now," he added. "A market garden, a few pigs and chickens, and a small dairy—" He paused. "But a man can't manage all that alone. I should need a wife."

"You should indeed," Charles agreed in an even tone, trying to picture Miss Ardleigh in an apron, making cheeses or curing bacon. But Bradford planned to press his suit this afternoon, and any sensible lady would surely prefer to live on a manor than a farm. For Ned's sake, he was sorry. For his own, he was sorrier.

"The thought of taking a wife has come to me more and more since Artie's death." Edward's voice was wistful. "I doubt, however, that she would want to—"

But Edward's reflections were interrupted by the sound of hammering. They had arrived at the house. Charles stopped the fly and got out and tied the horse, and he and Edward followed the path around the back. A man in a leather jerkin was pounding nails into the windlass frame that stood over the well, rebuilding it, from the look of the rotten pieces of wood scattered on the ground. Several black hens and a red rooster with iridescent green tail feathers pecked greedily at the wood, digging out grubs.

Edward raised his voice. "Mr. Napthen?"

The man in the jerkin turned, his hammer poised. He was slender and loose-limbed, the sleeves of his grey shirt, too short by inches, exposing skinny wrists covered with a coarse mat of dark hair that extended onto the backs of his hands. The corner of his mouth twitched nervously under a brush of dark mustache, and his eyes were deepset under a thicket of black brows that grew together in the middle.

"I'm Napthen." His voice was a boy's tremolo, although he was a man of nearly middle age.

Edward introduced himself and Charles. "We have come to inquire about the grain in the barn."

"Grain?" Napthen asked. His dark eyes flicked from Edward, who was uniformed, to Charles, who wore his khaki jacket and Norfolk tweeds. He went back to Edward. "There's no grain i' th' barn, Const'ble," he said roughly. "I didn't sow last year—only sold th' hay, standin'."

"I know you didn't sow, Mr. Napthen," Edward said, patient. "The fact remains, however, that your barn is stocked with over a hundred sacks of wheat. At least one load has already been hauled from there to the river, where it was carried onto a—"

"If yer sayin' I'm a thief," Napthen broke in violently, "yer wrong." He slammed the hammer onto the ground in an unconvincing show of anger. The chickens fled, clucking and fluttering, all but the rooster, who stood his ground, flapping his wings. "If there's grain i' that barn, it's none o' mine," Napthen shouted over the noise. 'Twas put there wi'out my knowin'."

"Theft isn't the only issue here," Charles put in, watching the man's face. "A constable was murdered in your barn."

Napthen's eyes opened wide. "Murdered?"

"You are aware of Sergeant Oliver's demise, I presume," Charles said. Of course he was aware. Everyone for miles around knew of the murder.

"I am." Napthen swallowed fearfully, his Adam's apple a bony knob in his neck. "But I ha'n't . . . I mean, I di'n't . . ." His mouth jerked. "'Pon my honour, if murder was done here, I'm ignorant!" The rooster crowed, and several hens came out of hiding for another go at the bugs in the rotten wood.

"Your honour!" Edward leaned forward, his voice flinty. "A *constable* was murdered here, and you have the gall to talk about honour!"

"I don't know nawt! I swear't!" Napthen was swallowed up by his fear. His teeth chattered. "I *swear*!"

"Murder was done," Charles said softly, "in your barn. We have the evidence to prove it in a court of law."

"Gawd oh Gawd oh Gawd." Napthen's voice cracked into a soprano whimper. "I told em, I *told* 'em . . ."

"*What* did you tell them, Mr. Napthen?" Edward asked.

The man leaned against the half-built windlass as if all the strength had gone out of his thin legs. "I *told* 'em 'twas risky. I *warned* 'em ter be careful. I was afeered . . ." The words died into a long shudder. A drop of spittle hung on his mustache.

"Told *who*?" Edward asked sharply. When Napthen did not answer, his voice became grim. "Do you want to be tried at the summer assizes for Constable Oliver's murder? Come on, man. *Talk*!"

"The grain, yes." Napthen wiped his mouth with the back of his furry hand. His eyes were dark with panic, his voice tinny. "They wanted th' barn t' store th' wheat till it cud be moved, an' they offered a fair price. But I had nawt t' do wi' *murder*!"

"Did you know the men to be thieves?" Edward asked.

Napthen looked down at his feet. "Not 'xactly. They said th' barn was wanted f'r extra storage."

"Did you know they were moving the grain at night?"

"We—ll . . ."

Charles could hear in that lengthy syllable a whole paragraph of admission. Of course the man had known. He had known he was letting the barn to thieves, and that the grain was being smuggled to a ship in the estuary. Perhaps he had helped steal the grain. Perhaps he had even rented the farm for the purpose of obtaining the barn to store the stolen wheat until it could be smuggled out by boat. But the extent of Napthen's guilty involvement could be determined later. Other matters took precedence.

"To whom did you let the barn?" Charles asked.

Napthen licked his mustache. "Name's Tod," he whispered. "Russell Tod." The rooster crowed again, jubilant over a newfound cache of grubs. He picked up the fattest one and laid it at the feet of one of the hens, who pecked at it greedily.

"Who else was involved?" Charles asked.

"Tod paid th' money. But there were a man wi' 'im. Brock, 'ee were called. I niver saw any o' th' others."

Napthen was sullen now, conscious of his betrayal and profoundly aware of the consequence. Charles understood. Even if the man could convince a jury of his peers that he was innocent of Artie's murder, he could not continue to work this farm, nor live in this county. For the villagers and farmers roundabout, betrayal was a heinous crime. Having cast his lot with thieves, Napthen was honour-bound to keep his mouth shut. That he had not doomed him, and he knew it.

The rooster crowed once again.

35

Novel-writers are a devious lot. Just when the question seems resolved and the answers all known (or nearly all), a new difficulty is often introduced, startling the reader out of his complacency and throwing order into chaos once again.

—LENORE PENMORE
Secrets of the Narrative Arts, 1892

Kate was at her rolltop desk in the library shortly after ten that morning, ostensibly to write the second chapter in Beryl Bardwell's *The Corpse in the Garden*. But even though she was pleased with the plot, featuring as it did grain thieves and midnight excursions into the fog-shrouded countryside, she was not making much headway in the writing, for her attention was distracted by the prospect of Bradford Marsden's call that afternoon. She had already mentally composed three or four pretty speeches of rejection and rejected them all. She was at work on yet another when Mudd came into the room with the dignity he affected when he was carrying out an official duty. He bore an envelope on a silver tray.

"A message, mum," he said, "just arrived from Marsden Manor." He bowed and took a backward step, waiting to see if there was an answer.

The envelope was sealed with red sealing wax embossed

with the Marsden crest. Inside was a five-line note scrawled in a hasty hand. "My dear Miss Ardleigh," it said. "I very much regret that I will not be able to call this afternoon. I have been summoned to London upon extended business and am unsure when I shall return. Please accept my sincerest apology for any inconvenience I may have caused you." The note was signed, "Yr humble servant, Bradford Marsden."

Kate's eyebrows went up and her mouth quirked. It wasn't hard to guess what had occasioned the writing of the note. If the situation had been as she had suspected, Bradford had most likely spoken of his call to his mother or father and found them in whole-hearted opposition to it, as they should be. He was destined for a Society match, and Bishop's Keep was not enough of a bait to attract Lord and Lady Marsden.

She stood and went to the fireplace to drop Bradford's note into the flames. "There is no reply," she said to Mudd.

"Very good, mum," the butler replied and withdrew.

Kate stood for a moment staring at the flames licking the note, savouring the relief of knowing that she would not after all have to make excuses to Bradford Marsden. Briefly, she wondered whether losing so advantageous a match ought to make her unhappy. Most women would regret the loss, of course, particularly unmarried women of her age. But she was not most women, and the thought of living singly the rest of her life held no terror for her. She had meant what she said to Eleanor at Melford Hall. She valued her freedom to come and go as she pleased, to defer to no one's opinion, to respect no one's authority but her own. Singleness was a gift she would not readily relinquish unless . . .

Unless . . .

Kate leaned her head against the mantle as Bradford Marsden's note disintegrated into flimsy black ash and fell through the grate. *Unless she truly loved the man.* She thought of Sir Charles Sheridan and admitted to herself—reluctantly, because it seemed almost traitorous to her independence—that she could love *him.* Sir Charles was a man of great intelligence and intensity, devoid of guile, one who kept himself to himself, who did not give himself easily or frivolously. It was that very privateness, that depth and substance, that drew her to him, for in it she felt a call to her own depths.

But that privateness was a wall, as well, and the person behind it was remote and complex. He had many dimensions, many strengths. The woman whom he loved (if he ever allowed himself to love or be loved, which Kate somehow doubted) would have to be as strong as he to hold her own against him, and as multi-faceted as he to hold his interest. Would there not be a constant conflict between two such persons? Would not their relationship be a battle of wills from the very beginning, eventually abrading away the affection that drew them together?

Kate pulled her shawl around her shoulders. The questions were academic, as least as far as she was concerned, for Sir Charles had obviously concluded that she was a meddlesome woman who pushed her way into matters that did not concern her. She would not be the one to whom he gave his heart—and against whom he tested his mettle. It was time to stop thinking of such things and return to her typewriter.

But when she sat down to her desk, she found herself considering, not the fictional murder of the surly gamekeeper in Beryl Bardwell's thriller, but the real one she had been occupied with for the past days: the slaying of Sergeant Arthur Oliver in Highfields Barn. It was a sad death, and she could only feel a great relief that the truth of it had been discovered and the nonsense about poaching finally laid to rest. The case could not be solved until the killers had been apprehended and brought to justice, of course, but Edward and Sir Charles would see to that. Far more important was the fact that Agnes's pension was now secure, and she and Betsy could be assured of a comfortable life.

Beryl Bardwell turned to the typewriter and rolled in a fresh sheet of paper. Across the top of the page, in capital letters, she typed the words GRAIN THIEVES IN THE BARN. It was time to begin a new chapter.

While Kate and Beryl Bardwell were wrestling with marriage proposals and murders, Beatrix was in the kitchen, toasting her toes before the fire. It was a rare privilege for her, and one she greatly treasured. At home at Bolton Gardens she was never allowed in the kitchen for fear of antagonizing Cook, who ruled below-stairs with an iron fist and whose kitchen was sacrosanct. Mrs. Pratt had, to be sure, a quite similar demeanour, but she also had a strong affection for Kate. This affection was extended to Beatrice in the form of an invitation to visit the kitchen whenever she liked.

To Beatrice, the kitchen at Bishop's Keep was exactly what a kitchen should be. Every morning since her arrival, Beatrice had taken her sketch pad and pencils and gone to sit beside the fire to watch Mrs. Pratt and Harriet, the sweet little scullery, go about their homely work—washing up the breakfast dishes, preparing the luncheon soup, rolling out dough for a sweet tart, and readying the evening joint for an afternoon in the oven. While they worked, she sketched the cave-like fireplace hung with iron pots and copper-bottomed kettles; the red and green braided rugs on the stone floor; and the cupboards filled with neat rows of jam pots, mustard jars, and—topping the whole delightful display—a rose-sprigged china biscuit barrel.

While she sketched, Beatrix soaked up as much of the cozy warmth as she could and thought wistfully of the kitchen she coveted in her very own small cottage somewhere in the North, perhaps near Sawrey, where she had gone several times with her father—not a cottage to share with a husband or child, but a cottage of her own, where she could keep her animals and study fungi and write little books and have tea whenever she pleased.

But to break away from her parents and obtain the cottage, Beatrix knew that she must have an independent source of income. She had hoped that perhaps her botanical work, particularly her paper on the spore germination of the *Agaricinea*, might open the door to recognition in the world and to freedom. Besides, it was a subject in which she was passionately interested, and which she had studied so deeply that she knew more about it than any botanist in England. But her work looked to be going nowhere, even with the help of Uncle Henry Roscoe and Sir Charles. There was too much opposition from the scientists—and not even valid opposition, at that. It was not the merit of her research that they seemed to find wanting, but the merit of her person, her sex. Even Uncle Henry said so, and angrily too, for he was offended at their cavalier attitude toward her paper.

At any rate, she was forced to conclude that botany was not to be the career that would set her free. But the stories— She bent her head over her sketch with renewed energy. If only her stories could earn money, as did Kate's. She was still amazed when she thought of Kate's writing enterprise. It was no secret that women actually earned money by writing, but *she* had never known one who did, and the thought of it gave her courage and a renewed determination. For some time, she had been thinking of a story about a cat called Tabitha Twitch-ett. Mrs. Pratt's stove polished to a jetty brilliance that must have required pounds of blacklead, would perfectly illustrate one of the scenes in Tabitha's story.

Mrs. Pratt herself was humming over her paste-board and rolling pin at the table, Harriet was peeling a pot of potatoes in the stone sink, and the kettle was whistling merrily on the back of the stove. There was a sharp rapping at the back door. Beatrix looked up.

"'Tis Old Willie Hogglestock, the peddler," Mrs. Pratt said, not pausing in her attentions to the tart. "Tell him I'll be out in a shake, Harriet."

Beatrix followed Mrs. Pratt and Harriet out into the flagged dooryard, under a leaden sky that threatened rain. Old Willie Hogglestock was a man of nearly sixty, with a white beard and a lank figure covered neck to knees in a white apron. His cart was laden with quite an amazing stock of fruit and fish: lovely rich grapes and pears and peaches and oranges, and fish in mother-of-pearl colours and queer shapes—John Dorys, and Yarmouth bloaters, and cod, and haddock, and live eels—and tomatoes. Beatrix enjoyed tomatoes, both the scarlet and the yellow, and they often had them at Bolton Gardens. But Mrs. Pratt scorned them: "tommytoes," she called them, "proper rubbish," and wouldn't have any. There was a lovely basket of field mushrooms too, but she turned those down quite as sharply.

Mrs. Pratt completed her purchase of cod and grapes and

gave Old Willie a smile with her shillings. "You'll sit fer a cup, will you?" she asked.

"I'll 'ave th' cup, thank'ee," the old man said, "but not th' sit." He looked up at the sky. "Got t' be on t' th' Manor afore th' rain begins i' earnest." He went with them into the kitchen, where he leaned his lank self against the wall and accepted a cup of tea. "Ye've heard th' news, I reckon," he said.

"What news?" Mrs. Pratt asked, picking up her rolling pin. "We've had no news from the village yet this mornin', only a messenger from the manor."

Beatrix went back to her sketching with a secret smile. The messenger from the manor had made a stop in the kitchen, and now all the servants knew that Mr. Marsden would not be calling today. Beatrix, to whom Kate had confided her thoughts about the call, was pleased at this outcome. Whether Mr. Marsden had lost his enthusiasm for the match, or his parents had voiced an opposing opinion as to its suitability, or Sir Charles had somehow acted to stop him, she did not know. But however it had come about, one of Kate's suitors had departed the field, leaving only Constable Laken standing between Sir Charles and Kate. And while the affections of the constable were certainly to be respected, Beatrix knew that Kate's heart leaned toward Sir Charles, as his toward hers. The only problem she now faced was getting the two of them to recognize the truth.

Old Willie had been staring mournfully into his teacup. " 'Tis sad news," he said, "from Gallows Green. Pore Agnes Oliver is beside 'erself worryin'." He sighed. "As well she might do."

"Agnes Oliver!" Beatrix exclaimed, looking up. "Why?"

"Why? Because lit'le Betsy's gone missin'," Old Willie said. "That's why."

"Betsy!" Beatrix and Mrs. Pratt exclaimed in unison. Harriet dropped a potato on the floor and it rolled under the stone sink.

"Aye," Old Willie said sadly. "A second trag'dy, fallin' on th' same 'ooman in such short time. Wot's th' pore thing t' do, I'm sure I doan know."

If the old man knew other details, Beatrix did not wait to hear them. She spilled her sketching materials on the hearth and flew to the door. Where was Betsy? And poor, poor Agnes, what was she feeling?

She and Kate must go to Gallows Green, straightaway!

The Dedham gaol was only a mile or so from Highfields Farm, but Edward was officially off the case, and Charles knew it wouldn't do to haul James Napthen there. The next nearest gaol was in Manningtree, and since P.C. Bradley was heading the investigation, that was the logical place to incarcerate the man. Edward tied Napthen's hands, and they loaded him into the fly. They made the five-mile trip to Manningtree without event, save for a drenching. The rain was beginning to come down rather hard, and Charles wished earnestly for his mackintosh.

"James *who?*" Bradley asked, looking from one to the other as the three of them dripped puddles onto the floor. In front of him on the desk were the greasy remnants of an early luncheon—a parcel of fried fish, a slice of heavily buttered bread, and a baked potato—which had no doubt been sent down from the pub on the High Street. He cast about for something on which to wipe his hands and failing to find it, wiped them on his trousers and then looked guilty, as if he wished he had not. He stood up and hastily buttoned his uniform coat.

"James Napthen," Edward repeated patiently, "of Highfields Farm. Oliver's murder took place in his barn." He coughed. Charles could see that the stove was not drawing properly. The air was smoky, and every now and then a blue cloud puffed out around the door.

"It was a grain-stealing ring, you see," Charles said, feeling some sympathy for Bradley. The P.C. had buttoned his coat crookedly, and it gave him the look of a boy who had been caught out by the upper form. "Sergeant Oliver got onto it and was surprised while taking samples. They shot him in the barn, loaded him into a wagon, and dumped him in McGregor's garden."

Bradley pushed his blond hair back with his fingers, leaving a trace of oily grease across his forehead. His toilet completed, he became more confident. "Oliver was poaching," he said. "I collected the evidence myself. Two hares and a net. There's the note, too, of course."

"No," Edward said crisply. "The grain thieves wanted you to *believe* Artie was poaching, to keep you from nosing around and stumbling on the truth. They planted the hares and net and wrote you the note."

Bradley blinked his pale grey eyes several times, very fast. "But I don't understand how you know that—"

"You will," Charles assured him, "when you see the evidence."

"But—"

"Believe it," Edward snapped, in a tone Charles had never heard him use. "Question him." He jerked his head at Napthen. "He'll tell you."

Bradley blinked again. A momentary confusion flashed into his eyes, followed by a tightening of the mouth that registered an almost imperceptible anxiety. Charles frowned. Was something going on here that he and Edward had overlooked?

Bradley recovered himself and looked at Napthen, standing with hands tied behind him, head hanging, the picture of dejection. "Who else was involved besides this man?"

"Russell Tod and Tommy Brock," Edward said. "Tod's a bailiff who assembles the harvest crews and sends them round to all the farms. Brock's one of his hired men. Napthen gave us the names, but they were already under suspicion. Another witness saw them moving grain from the barn to a barge on the river and will give corroborating testimony."

Bradley cleared his throat. "A corroborating witness?" His young voice was thin. "Who?"

Edward jerked his head toward Napthen with a cautioning gesture. "Later," he said. "Out of his hearing."

Bradley nodded reluctantly. Charles wondered what his reaction would be if he knew that the corroborating witness was a child, a girl, at that. But it wasn't necessary to reveal Betsy Oliver's name at the moment, or her role in this. And perhaps not at all, if Tod and Brock were apprehended and made to confess.

Bradley seemed to recollect himself. He straightened his shoulders and reached for a large metal key hanging on the wall behind him. "Come on, you," he said to Napthen, with unnecessary roughness. "I'm locking you up."

The act of propelling Napthen into the cell and locking the heavy oaken door—without either untying the prisoner's hands or removing his rain-soaked coat—seemed to return to Bradley some of his self-importance. When he came back to his desk, he hung up the key with a flourish, sat down, and shoved the parcel of fried fish to one side.

"I'll need a written statement of everything you know," he said to Edward, taking a printed form out of a drawer. "Make it complete. It'll go to Colchester with Napthen."

"To Colchester?" Edward asked, surprised. "You're taking him there?"

Bradley busied himself with papers. "Yes, well, I'm not in charge, you know. It's Chief Constable Pell's case—he asked for it. I'm sure he'll want to question the suspect."

Charles regarded the young constable thoughtfully. So Pell himself had asked to take the case—it hadn't been a whim of Hacking's, or some sort of punishment for Ned. But why had he wanted it? What was it to him?

Edward sat down and took up the pen Bradley handed him. "You can have your statement," he said sourly. "But before you go trotting Napthen off to see Pell, don't you think you'd better collar Tod and Brock? We brought the prisoner here in a fly. On the way we passed a dozen people, and a dozen more saw us in the High Street. Not to put too fine a point on it, but word of his arrest won't take an hour to reach the other two, and any others who might be involved."

Bradley chewed his lip nervously. "Yes, yes, I see the difficulty. Er, are you available to help? It's a matter for more than just one officer, I should think. And this case isn't the only problem on my hands. It's been a busy morning."

"It has?" Charles asked, looking around. The constable's office didn't appear busy, and the lunch testified to at least a quarter hour of leisure. "What's happened?"

Bradley shifted. "I don't suppose there's anything I can do about it, at least not at the moment, although I'll have to institute a search if she doesn't turn up. It's a missing child over at Gallows Green." He glanced at Edward. "You were a friend of Sergeant Oliver's, weren't you? Did you know his daughter Betsy?"

Edward's face went white. He stood up abruptly and his chair fell over with a clatter. "Are you telling me that Betsy Oliver—"

"Afraid so," Bradley said ruefully. "Gone missing. Happened last night, apparently. Sounds a bit improbable, I admit, but it seems she was in the habit of slipping out the window and down the drainpipe after dark. Her mother's in a bit of a panic, and sent over to ask for help."

"Gone missing!" Edward roared, "and you sit here stuffing yourself with fried fish!" He ran to the door and yanked it open. "Come on, Charlie!"

"But the report!" Bradley exclaimed. He snatched up the paper Edward had been writing on and waved it frantically, like a white flag. "I can't take this man to Colchester without your written statement! I don't know any of the details!"

"Damn the bloody details," Edward snapped, his eyes flashing. "Come *on*, Charlie! Agnes'll be beside herself. I must be with her."

And there, in Edward's anguished face, was written the truth that Charles had not grasped until now. It was not Miss Ardleigh that Edward cared for, it was Agnes Oliver. But Charles was not conscious of any relief, for his belly had twisted with cold fear for the child's safety. Betsy Oliver was a witness to the theft that had motivated her father's slaying, and now she had disappeared. Had the thieves who killed the father taken the daughter, as well?

Charles held up his hand. "Wait," he said. "We have a man here who may know something. Napthen."

Edward whirled. "Of course!" he cried, snatching the key off the wall and running to Napthen's cell.

But whether Napthen knew something and would not reveal it, or whether he knew nothing at all and could only deny, they could not tell. After ten minutes of fruitless questioning, Napthen was flung into his cell once more and Edward and Charles hastened to Gallows Green.

36

"It is a frightful turn of events, I very much fear. She has been missing for nearly a full day."

"A full day! Has all expectation of her safe return been given up?"

"Not yet, not yet. But it would be wrong to entertain false hopes. All seems very dark."
— BERYL BARDWELL
Missing Pearl, Or, The Lost Heiress

From the summer-like sunshine of the days before, the weather had turned cold and drizzly. Wisps of mist haunted the lanes like vagrant ghosts, and diamonds of rain-drops dripped from every twig and thorn. It began to rain in earnest halfway to Gallows Green, and Kate was glad she had asked Pocket to drive her and Bea in the closed carriage. They carried with them a full basket supplied by Mrs. Pratt, who had insisted on sending the food she had prepared for their luncheon. Kate had brought it, although she knew Agnes would have little appetite. Some of the searchers might need food, though—for of course there would be searchers.

And there were. When Kate and Bea alighted from the carriage, a crowd of men was just setting off from the Oliver cottage, booted and mackintoshed against the wind-driven rain. Kate and Bea went into the kitchen where Agnes was huddled beside the fire in the company of her neighbour, Mrs. Wilkins, a stout woman with a face like a cauliflower and a nose as red as a radish. Her rolled-up sleeves revealed arms that rivaled those of her husband, the hamlet's smith, but her touch was gentle. She clucked softly to Agnes, petting her as if she were a child.

"She went looking for the duck, I am sure," Agnes was saying wearily when they came in. "If the duck can be found, Betsy will be found too." She began softly to cry, and Mrs. Wilkins pulled her to her ample bosom.

"There, there, dearie," she said, "doan take on so. Like as not she'll be found quickly. Or else she'll come dancin' 'ome on 'er own, an' you'll 'ave th' pleasure o' stroppin' 'er fer givin' ye such a fright." With that practical observation, the fruit of nearly two decades of motherhood, she tucked the rug over Agnes's knees, greeted the visitors, and went to pour the kettle into the tea pot.

Kate took Agnes's cold hands in her own. "Tell me about the duck," she said.

"The foolish thing was gone yesterday afternoon." Agnes wiped her eyes. "Betsy looked everywhere. The child was still looking when I called supper, and it was all I could do to get her to bed, just before you came. I found her nightdress on the floor this morning, and her shirt and breeches missing."

"I'm sure she's all right," Bea comforted. "She's a very level-headed child, and she knows the fields and river."

Agnes's face was thin-lipped. "That is why I fear so," she said in a ragged whisper. "I am quite sure she isn't lost. No child ever knew her way more surely than Betsy."

The door burst open and the rain and wind gusted in. "Agnes!" Edward cried, and was across the room in two steps. Sir Charles lingered at the doorway, looking on.

"Oh, Ned," Agnes sobbed, letting herself be gathered up and held in Edward's strong embrace. "First Artie, and now Betsy. How can I endure it?" She buried her face in his shoulder, while he pressed his lips against her hair.

"We will endure it together, dear heart," he said, so low

that Kate was the only other who heard. "And when she is found we will be glad together." There was a long silence in the room while he stroked her hair and she clung to him, both oblivious to all else.

At last Mrs. Wilkins coughed. "Well, now," she remarked sagely. "Here is the tea, and I shall be off." She poured five cups, found her shawl, and left, with a nod at Kate and Bea and a long look at the constable, still on his knees now beside Agnes's chair, her hands in his.

There was a catch in Kate's throat when she looked up, feeling Sir Charles's eyes on her. She blushed, remembering her thoughts of that morning, and looked away again quickly.

"What's to be done?" she asked.

"The entire hamlet has mustered for the search." Sir Charles's brown coat was wet, and water dripped off his hat and onto his shoulders. "There's no doubt she'll be found." He paused and stepped closer. "Edward has arrested the man who let Highfields Farm," he said in a lower voice, "a man named Napthen. We fetched him to the gaol at Manningtree this morning. He says he knew nothing about Artie's murder, but he admitted to letting the barn. He named Tod and Brock in connexion with the grain stored there."

Kate glanced toward Agnes. She was gazing at the fire, her hand still in Edward's, and did not appear to be listening. Agnes had enough to bear without knowing this—at least, not yet. "They'll be arrested quickly?" she whispered.

"Before the day is out, I hope."

Kate was glad that the sergeant had been exonerated from the charge of poaching, and glad that progress was being made toward the apprehension of his murderers. But the gladness could not lighten her heart just now. Sir Charles's declaration that Betsy would be found sounded confident enough, but she felt a coldness settle in her as she remembered that it was Betsy who had seen the grain thieves, had heard their voices and their names, and could identify them. If Tod and Brock had somehow learned what she knew, and discovered that they were implicated in the constable's murder—

Kate felt her throat tighten. "If only we had known about

them before . . . '' Her voice trailed away, but Sir Charles took her meaning and nodded.

"Yes,'' he said softly. "If only we had known, we could have apprehended them before yesterday evening. But we did not.'' He touched her arm. The slightest touch, but deeply intimate, it seemed to her. "There was nothing we could have done, Miss Ardleigh, knowing only what we knew.''

Biting her lip, Kate turned away. But *she* had known. She had known that Betsy was a witness to nocturnal activities in the barn, and had suspected that something illegal was involved, and that it was somehow connected with the sergeant's death. She could have come immediately to Agnes and warned her to keep her daughter safe. Or she could have told Edward to watch out for the little girl, or Sir Charles. Or she could have taken on the task herself, and kept an eye on Betsy. She could have done many things, *should* have done them, but she had done nothing—except to think how she might turn the events of last night into material for Beryl Bardwell's foolish novel.

Heartsick, Kate turned to the grey window, silvered with cold rain. Betsy was somewhere out there in that chilly damp—not a fictional girl, a character in one of her sensational stories, but a flesh-and-blood child, whose alert, curious attention to the world around her had lured her into very real danger. Thinking of the possibilities, Kate's heart twisted within her.

Was Betsy alive, or was she dead?

37

We have left undone those things which we ought to have done; And we have done those things which we ought not to have done; And there is no health in us.

—Prayer Book, 1662

Edward at last released the weeping Agnes and stood. His heart was heavy and dull as lead within him, but he could not simply sit beside the fire and let others carry on searching. He put his hand on Agnes's shoulder.

"She'll be found," he said, with all the conviction he could summon.

"I pray, Ned, oh, I pray." Agnes closed her eyes and rested her forehead on her hand. "If only I had penned the duck."

Edward stood for a moment looking down at her, at the way the soft brown hair curled away from her face, at the lines of worry that etched her forehead. Sweet Agnes, who could in her innocence believe that Betsy had strayed after the duck, while he feared in his policeman's heart, darkened by the knowledge of too many ill deeds, too much rank disorder, that the truth was much harsher. Why hadn't he seen to the child's safety? Charlie had told him what Betsy knew, and he had sensed immediately how dangerous such knowledge could be. But he had done nothing to protect her, not the least thing, when it was his *business* to do it, as well as his heart's desire! In his haste to apprehend Artie's killers, in his hurry to show

Pell that he could succeed where Bradley would inevitably fail, he had caused Betsy harm and Agnes torment, and the thought of his negligence ripped like a mad dog at his insides.

Grim-faced, Edward stepped across the kitchen to the door, where Charles stood waiting, his shoulders sodden with wet. "Come on," he said, low.

"To Tod's?"

"If Bradley isn't going after the blighter," Edward said between his teeth, "we will." He led the way diagonally across the soggy turf of the village green, skirting muddy puddles. A pair of sheep tethered on the new grass shied as he and Charles splashed toward the smithy, which sat back from the dirty lane under a wooden sign-board painted with a pair of iron tongs and an anvil. Wilkins, the grey-haired, leather-aproned smith, was standing just outside his shed, the sleeves of his sacking shirt rolled to the elbows, feet wide apart, muscular arms akimbo. He was a massive man, well over six feet, heavy and bull-necked. Behind him, an apprentice was pumping an enormous bellows. The forge was roaring and the fire blazing, a bright sight on a dark and chilly day.

"Any sign o' th' child?" Wilkins called in a voice like a rusty file.

"Not yet." Edward came up to the smith. "We're looking for Russell Tod. He rents from you, does he not?"

" 'Ee does that," Wilkins said with a nod of his grizzled head. "The lit'le cottage at th' foot o' th' garden. But if ye'r wantin' t' see Tod, ye'll be disappointed. He's not t' 'ome. Went out early this mornin' and an't been back."

"Was Tommy Brock with him?" Charles asked. Behind the smith, the apprentice, a pocked, narrow-shouldered lad of twelve or so, left off the bellows, prodded the fire, and stood listening.

The smith scratched his grey mustache, trimmed short against the possibility of sparks. "Brock?" He squinted, considering. "Don't b'lieve I know 'im. Tod went alone, anyways. I saw 'im ride away. Near nine this mornin', 'twas."

"What about last night?" Edward asked. "Was he at home?"

Wilkins's snort was petulant. "A man 'ires a cottage, not a

keeper. Wot business o' mine is it whether he's t' 'ome or away?''

Edward could feel his patience fraying. "A child is missing," he said. His voice hardened as he thought of Agnes's daughter in the hands of her husband's killer. "We have reason to suspect that Tod's involved. Was he at home last night?"

Wilkins's look was somber. "Wudn't know," he said. "'Ee cud o' bin 'ome, 'ee cud o' bin gone, f'r all o' me.'' His gold tooth glinted. "But th' girl, that's another matter, 'tis. She was 'ere yesterd'y arternoon, lookin' out 'er duck, an' 'er dog was 'ere this mornin', lookin' out '*er*.''

"The dog?"

"Th' girl's collie dog. Th' boy took 'im 'ome an' tied 'im up proper, behind th' shed.'' He sighed. "I'd be searchin' fer th' girl too, pore thing, 'f I din't 'ave a job t' be done by nightfall.''

The apprentice, wearing a black-wool cap, ragged breeches, and a shirt with no sleeves, came forward out of the gloom of the smithy. "Ye'r askin' 'bout Mr. Tod?''

Edward looked down on him. He was too frail to be a smith's apprentice, with those broomstraw arms and delicate hands. But hamlet boys counted themselves lucky not to be in the fields. Likely this one preferred the deafening roar of the forge and the ring of the hammer to the back-breaking labour of ploughing and harvesting. And likely those wrists would thicken in the next year or two.

"I am." He added, in a more kindly tone, "Do you know something that might help us find the girl?"

"Not th' girl, no,'' the apprentice said, and wiped his nose on his sleeve. "But I know that Mr. Tod was gone las' night, f'r a while, leastways." He jerked his thumb upward. "I sleeps in th' loft above th' forge on chill nights. I was there last night. I saw summat—a lantern, an' Tod, an' sev'ral men.''

"Did they have a wagon?" Charles asked eagerly.

The apprentice shrugged. "All I know is, 'ee went away, an' 'ee come agin a while arter, an' then I went asleep.''

"Thank you,'' Edward said, thinking how easy it was for deeds to be done at night, when the countryside was dark and decent folk were snoring in their beds. He turned back to the smith. "We'll be taking a look around the cottage."

"Ye'r the constable," the smith said.

A low hedge of elder separated the cottage from the neat garden with its rows of lettuces and cabbages and carefully-mounded potatoes. The roar of the forge could not be heard here, and there was no other sound except for the gossipy chatter of rooks in a nearby large elm and the irritated hoot of an owl awakened from its daytime slumbers.

Edward paused to peer first into one low casement window, then another. There were only two rooms, but they were neat and relatively clean, and the flagged floor was covered with a nearly-new coconut mat. A hearth opened to both of the rooms, of such size that several sides of bacon might be smoked in the chimney at once. An oak table stood in one room, a narrow bed in the other, a chair and in each a small wooden dresser. Beside the bed stood a washstand with a basin; on the wall over it a shaving glass, on the floor beneath it a boot rack and boot jack. The bedclothes were flung aside as if Tod had risen hastily and flown.

"Nothing here, looks like," Edward said. What had he expected to find? A clue to Betsy's whereabouts? A trail of white duck feathers? Desperation seized him, and he sagged against the wall. "Where *can* she be?"

"Anywhere," Charles said flatly. He gestured toward a small lean-to shed behind the cottage, so overgrown with creeper that the windows, if there were any, were completely covered. "There, perhaps."

They went toward the shed, against one side of which was piled a heap of sodden coal. An empty coal scuttle stood nearby, and a stack of faggots had tumbled onto the ground and were wet through. The shed door was built of panels of sturdy oak with a hasp and padlock. Edward tried it, but it was locked fast. He picked up a rusty spade and was about to break it open when he heard a loud shout. He turned. It was the apprentice, rounding the corner at a run, waving his wool cap like a black flag.

"They found 'er shirt," the boy cried. "In the river, where the willows grow aslant! They say she's drownded!"

Edward gave one loud, heart-stricken groan, and his blood froze in his veins.

Charles put out his hand. "Ned," he said gruffly, and with deep sympathy.

"It's my fault, Charlie." Edward was filled with a whirling misery that sucked all the breath, all the strength out of him. "I might have prevented this. If only I had gone to Agnes last night, after you told me what Betsy saw—if only I had cautioned her that there was danger." He closed his eyes and leaned his forehead against the shed, giving himself up to the anguish. "My fault, my fault." The words of the Prayer Book were like a litany in his mind. *I have left undone those things which I ought to have done. And I have done those things which I ought not to have done; And there is no health in me.* He began to weep, great wrenching sobs, for the child who was lost, and the dead father, and the living mother, and himself. *No health in me, no health in any of us, no health in the world.*

Charles gripped his shoulder. "It is the fault of those who did it," he said fiercely. "If Tod had anything to do with this, he will pay, Ned. We will find him and *make* him pay!"

That was cold comfort, Edward knew, when he could pull himself above the black whirlpool that spun in his gut. But it was all he had to offer Agnes.

38

I am a brother to dragons, and a companion to owls.

—Job 30:29

Kate and Bea were weary and somber when they climbed into the carriage and started back to Bishop's Keep late that evening. The Oliver cottage had filled with women after the awful news arrived from the river. They brought food and the softly murmured comfort of those who keep daily company with birth and death, joy and bereavement. Edward had returned for a little while, drawn and stoop-shouldered and with nothing at all to say, but he and Sir Charles had left when summoned by a message from Constable Bradley at Manningtree. As they went, Vicar Talbot, a close friend of Kate's, arrived to sit by the fire and read aloud from Psalms and the Book of Job and the Prayer Book: ancient, measured words that seemed to bring dignity to death and enfold them all within a sense of larger purpose.

But it was an illusory seeming, Kate thought bitterly, a magician's trick to ease a mother's pain, to explain the inexplicable. Whatever words the vicar might summon, no purpose could be served by a child's death—especially if, as she suspected, that child had been killed by those who feared that she might name them as her father's murderers.

But Agnes did not know what Kate knew, or guessed. Agnes grieved a daughter who was accidentally drowned while searching for her duck. The vicar's presence appeared to bring the mother some small comfort, and her sobbing lessened as the old man read on, until at last she fell asleep in her chair, worn out by grief upon grief.

There was nothing more to be done. Agnes was surrounded by women who cared, who had lived through their own terrible losses, as she would. The river was being dragged by men who had dragged it before, on other sad occasions. And because the site of the drowning had occurred in the short stretch between the lock at Flatford and the lowest lock near the mouth of the estuary, they held out hope of finding the body.

"They allus turn up," Mrs. Wilkins told Kate, as she and Bea went out to the carriage. "Th' Sawyer lad fell int' th' millpond three year a-gone. 'Ee 'twas two days under th' water, but 'ee turned up." She became confidential. "They float, y'know, even if they be tangled in weed. The belly arter a while bloats, and they won't be kep' down."

Kate said a hasty good-bye, fearing that the grisly details of drowning would be too much for Bea on the heels of such a dreadful, wearying day. But Bea was only sad, and thoughtful.

"It's queer, you know," she remarked, as Pocket climbed up to his seat and chirruped to the horses, "about the owl."

Kate arranged her skirts and settled into the seat. "The owl?"

"Betsy's owl," Bea said. "Mr. Browne. He lives in the shed. There's a ring that clips around his leg, fixed to a chain on his perch. I went to release him, not wanting him to go hungry if Agnes did not think to feed him. But he was gone."

"I shouldn't think that's unusual," Kate said. "Perhaps Betsy let him loose yesterday."

"Perhaps," Bea said thoughtfully. "But Betsy's gauntlet was missing as well."

"Her gauntlet?"

"A leather glove made by her father. She wore it on her arm so that the owl could perch there, like a medieval falcon, when she took him hunting. She was quite proud of it."

Kate frowned. "And it's gone?"

Bea nodded. "I wonder," she said. She fell uncomfortably silent. "Perhaps it was—" She looked at Kate, doubtful. There was a worried crease between her eyes. "You don't suppose—"

"I can't suppose anything," Kate said crossly, "until you finish one of your sentences and I know what we're talking about."

Bea looked out the window into the grey twilight of the late afternoon. "We told Agnes last night that we intended to go ratting. 'Miss Ardleigh and I are going ratting,' I said. That's the reason we gave for wanting to take the dog."

"Well, yes, I suppose that's what we *said*," Kate replied, "but it was only a manner of speaking. I really fail to see . . ." She paused, thought. "Do you think Betsy might have overheard the conversation?"

"If she did," Bea said, "she could have decided to go herself, and take her owl."

"But it was dark," Kate objected, "and drizzly."

"Dark and drizzly didn't deter us, did it? And I doubt that it would have deterred Betsy, either. She is . . . was a daring child, more boy than girl, don't you think?" Bea sighed. "And fortunate to be encouraged in her daring by her father, when so many girls are sentenced to the mother's tender mercies. Afternoons in the parlour are hideously boring. One quite envies Betsy, actually."

Kate heard in Bea's words her unframed wish for greater freedom. Then she frowned. "I wonder," she said, "if Betsy would indeed have followed us."

"I think it quite possible," Bea said. "Should we not go—"

Kate did not require Bea to finish that sentence. She leaned forward and signaled Pocket with a tap. When he ducked down and slid open the window, she said, "We'll go home by way of the old stone church, Pocket, and up the lane toward Highfields barn."

So that was how Kate and Bea happened to come once more to the barn, this time in full daylight, and to find Betsy's leather gauntlet discarded beside a stone wall. And one child's boot, and a gunnybag with two dead rats and a long-tailed mole, and signs in the muddy earth of a fierce scuffle.

It was small comfort to know what had happened, but there could no longer be any doubt. Betsy had not gone into the river by accident.

39

All tragedies are finished by a death.
                                    —LORD BYRON

When they arrived at Bishop's Keep, Kate immediately sat down and wrote a note to Sir Charles and another to Edward. She posted Pocket in one direction and Ben, the newly-hired gardener, in the other. Both returned three quarters of an hour later with the news that neither man was at home, and that the notes had been left. This word came just as Kate and Bea were sitting down to a late supper served by Mudd and a subdued Amelia. Both of them were acquainted with Agnes Oliver.

"Pocket didn't say when Sir Charles might return?" Kate asked.

"No, mum," Mudd replied, serving Bea's soup. He placed the tureen on the table so that they could serve themselves if they wished, and stepped back. "But Ben learned that the constable is still away with Sir Charles. They have gone to Colchester, to the police headquarters."

"I see," Kate murmured, and at the thought of Sir Charles turned slightly pink. He had touched her arm when he spoke to her in Agnes's kitchen. And he had spoken with a deeply intimate tone, as if in his mind this anguish had somehow drawn the two of them closer.

She looked up to find Bea's eyes on her, and felt herself blushing even pinker. "I suppose that they have gone to instigate a search for Tod and Brock," she said briskly. "Thank you, Mudd. We will ring when you are wanted.''

"Well, we've done all we could," Bea said, when the servants had left the room. "If Constable Laken and Sir Charles
are searching for Tod and Brock, I wish them good fortune!"
Her voice became low and fierce. "If I were a man, I'd like
to be the first to lay hands on them! I'd have them dead!''

As the evening wore on, however, Charles began to suspect
that fortune was not to smile on Edward and him that night.
While they were still at Agnes's, after the news of Betsy's
drowning had arrived, a message had come from P.C. Bradley.
Edward was to meet him in Inspector Wainwright's office at
Colchester, to receive certain intelligences regarding the
whereabouts of Tod and Brock.

They arrived at nearly five to find the inspector there but
the P.C. delayed. While they waited, they dispatched Sergeant
Battle to the pub for several two-penny pigeon pies, a half-
dozen boiled eggs, cake, and bottles of East India ale. Edward
could scarcely eat for impatience, but Charles fell to his meal
with a good appetite, not sure when he would have another.

It was nearly six when P.C. Bradley arrived, breathless and
damp. He explained that Chief Constable Pell, when notified
by wire that Napthen was in custody and had named Tod as
the leader of the grain-theft ring, had wired back that a police
informer believed Tod to be in Wivenhoe, a port village at the
mouth of the Colne, a few miles to the east and south of
Colchester. Bradley and Edward were directed to go to The
Flag, a pub on the wharf there, and apprehend Tod when he
appeared, expeditiously.

"Expeditiously?" Edward growled. "Does Pell take us for
asses?"

"Perhaps Sergeant Battle can be spared for duty," P.C.
Bradley said. He cast a hungry look at the half-pie that re-
mained on Edward's plate, the crust crumbling, juices oozing.
"You've been eating, I see," he added unnecessarily.

"Battle?" Wainwright snorted, contemptuous. He stood up.
"Battle is not your man. I'll go myself.''

"Right, then," Bradley said, as Charles too got up. "We're
off." But he remained staring at the food.

"For God's sake, man," Edward said, already at the door.
"Wrap the damned pie and eat it on the way. Let's be gone,
or we'll miss the bloody devil!"

It was still drizzling and very dark as they made their way to
Wivenhoe, Charles and Edward in a fly, P.C. Bradley and
Inspector Wainwright in a gig. The road was mire and the
wind chill, and Charles sincerely hoped that their journey
might not be in vain.

The Flag, whose sign-board bore the storm-beaten sem-
blance of the Union Jack, was located on the wharf at Wivenhoe, not twenty paces from the moorings of the dozen or so
wooden-hulled ships that were crowded into the narrow harbour. The pub consisted of three cramped rooms, one behind
the other. The ceilings were barely higher than Charles's head
and the roaring fireplaces rivaled the blazes of perdition. The
rooms were crowded with all the crews of all the ships in the
harbour (or so it seemed), every man suffering from a quench-
less thirst.

After the chill freshness of the damp night, the place was
stifling and rank with the odour of men, cigars, and stout. The
din of voices in the first two rooms was loud. From the third
room (which appeared to be a separate establishment, with a
doorway connecting it to the pub) came the noisy thumping
of boots on a board floor, to the accompaniment of a seaman's
ditty, brayed out by a concertina and fiddle. A half-dozen
Jacks turned and churned around the floor, clutched by and
clutching robust women, young and old. As Charles peered
over the heads of seated imbibers, the dancers lined up for
heel and toe, heel and toe, and in a minute were back to the
churning and turning again. The concertina gave one last
wheeze, the fiddle one final wail, and the shout of *rum! boys,
rum!* was heard.

The landlord was a man of sly face and a girth unusual
even for a publican, with a ring of coarse black hair encir-
cling a bald head. He resembled nothing so much as a stout,
happy friar, Charles thought. When P.C. Bradley identified
himself and desired information, the landlord wiped his

hands on his white apron and professed himself eager to be of service.

"*Any* service, sirs," he added, with a crafty grin, his look taking in all four of them. "I'd ruther be on th' gud side o' th' law than th' bad." He gestured with his head to a painted and feather-decked lady, pretty, but not as pretty as she once had been, smoking a brown cigarette and being courted by two drunken sailors. "Jenny's fond o' a kiss an' fonder o' a crown," he confided. "Her sisters live 'round th' corner an up th' stair. Jes' tell 'em George sent ye, an' they'll treat ye right."

P.C. Bradley, heaven help him, blushed to the tips of his ears, and Charles wondered whether he should alter his estimation of the young man who had seemed so worldly and self-assured.

"That isn't the kind of information we're looking for," the P.C. said rather stiffly.

"Ooh, ah, ye're 'ere fer *that* business, are ye?" The publican delivered himself of a heavy sigh, together with his hope of a tip for special services rendered. "Why they'd send four o' ye fer such a mite of a job, an' late too? 'Ee warn't a fighter, as it turned out, an' Smokey over there already give 'im th' boot. 'Ee jes' wanted a row, was all. 'Ee didn't mind 'oo it wur with, er wot it wur fer. But Smokey moved 'im on."

Edward pushed forward, clearly impatient. "We weren't sent here to keep the peace," he said. "We're looking for a man named Russell Tod."

"Tod, eh? Russell Tod?" The publican screwed up his face, considering. After a moment's reflection, he shook his head. "Tod, Tod. Niver 'eard of 'im."

"But we were told he would be here," Bradley said angrily. "We've come all the way from—"

"Decker!" The publican beckoned with a beefy hand to a wizened, wily-looking man enveloped in a brass-buttoned greatcoat several sizes too large for him. "Decker! These gennulmen o' th' law want ter know 'bout somebody named Tod." To Bradley he said, "If Tod's t' be known, Ol' Decker'll know 'im. 'Ee knows ever'body, 'ee do."

The wizened man dragged himself to the bar. "Wery dry," he whispered in a voice like the Sahara.

Edward snapped his fingers. "Give the man a pint," he ordered.

The pint was delivered, and Old Decker refreshed himself, but when he was questioned as to the whereabouts of Tod, it fell out that he, like the publican, had niver 'eard of 'im, and he shuffled off to cradle his pint by the fire, where he could bask in the warmth of Jenny's perfumed laughter.

"But I don't understand," Bradley said desperately. "We had certain intelligence that Tod would be here."

"Ooh, intelligence, is it?" the publican remarked. "Well, then, sirs, p'r'aps it's only a matter o' time a-fore yer man shows 'is face. Whyn't yer 'ave a pint an' wait?" He peered at them. "Wot's 'ee wanted f'r, that brings out four o' ye?"

"Theft," Bradley said.

"Murder," Edward growled. "The killing of a constable and the drowning of a child."

The publican's eyes opened. "Ooh, aye," he muttered. "Well, then, best ye look sharp. 'Ee sounds a very untoward gen'leman, 'ee do."

They took their pints to a table in the corner from whence they could oversee the comings and goings of pugnacious sailors and pliant Jennies, but the untoward Mr. Tod failed to materialize, nor did any of the men whom they questioned acknowledge ever having heard of him. Two hours later, despairing of doing what they had come for, Edward pushed back his chair and stood up.

"You and Wainwright can stay if you like," he told Bradley, "but Charles and I are going back to Gallows Green. We'll do as well watching Tod's house as sitting here. Maybe better."

The P.C. scrutinized his third pint. "Well," he said thickly, "p'r'aps that's best. Inspector Wainwright an' I can stay here an' see what we see."

Wainwright, as cheerful as Charles had ever seen him, agreed. "We might walk down the wharf," he remarked, "and inquire of another pub."

"You do that," Charles said, "and if you come upon Tod, apprehend the man." He grinned dryly. "Expeditiously."

"Of course," Bradley said with great seriousness. "And you do the same."

"Ah," Wainwright said, "expeditiously." And raised his glass in signal for another.

But even though Charles and Edward drove hard back to Gallows Green, it was close to midnight when they arrived. If Tod had been at the cottage at all that evening, he was not there now. The place was dark, and only the querulous hooting of an owl broke the silence, and on a wall across the green, the shrill cacophony of courting cats.

Without speaking, they set up a concealed watch where they could observe the door of the cottage and waited there in the damp night chill until a pale dawn silvered the morning mist. But they waited in vain, for their quarry failed to return home that night. And of all the reasons that Charles imagined as he waited, the only one he did not consider was that Russell Tod, he of the sharp chin and coppery whiskers, was dead.

40

She's as headstrong as an allegory on the banks
of the Nile.

—RICHARD BRINSLEY SHERIDAN
The Rivals

"Wi' respects, mum—"

"With respect, Amelia," Kate broke in crossly, "I
shall wear what I please. Now tell Pocket we shall want the
gig. Immediately." As the maid left the room, Kate shook her
head. Of course, Amelia hadn't actually *said* anything about
the costume she had chosen, and she likely wouldn't have
dared. But her agonized look had spoken volumes.

Bea gave her a slight smile. "If you don't mind my saying
so, your dress does invite comment."

Kate looked down at herself. She was wearing a version of
the garment that Mrs. Bloomer of Seneca Falls, New York,
had devised almost fifty years before as part of her program
of rational dress, designed to free women from the confines
of their costumes. The trousers were fashioned like knicker-
bockers, buckling neatly at the calf. The jacket was snug but
comfortable, with reasonable sleeves. Both were cut of sturdy
green tweed.

"The Society cyclists are wearing this in Hyde Park," she
said, a bit defensively. She had seen a drawing of the costume
in *The Queen*, with a caption that reported that titled debu-
tantes had taken to riding between the Achilles statue and the

powder magazine in Hyde Park every morning in bloomers. On a bicycle, a full skirt was an invitation to a tumble.

Bea raised both eyebrows. "There's a great difference between Hyde Park and an Essex village," she remarked in a practical tone. "People in London are used to emancipated women, but in the countryside, ladies who wear such costumes are thought to be—well, headstrong, at best."

"And at worst, beyond the pale." Kate couldn't help smiling. "I'm sure you're right," she added. "I am always surprised by how easily the villagers work themselves into a lather about things. But still—"

She sobered, remembering why she had decided to wear her tweed bloomers. "I do want to join the search for Betsy, and a full skirt is inappropriate for probing a muddy river bank. I would be weighed down by pounds of muck." She looked down at the black stockings that showed above the high tops of her boots. "If people want to be offended by two inches of leg, for pity's sake, let them. There are more important things to worry about in this world."

Betsy's awful fate, for one. The capture of the man or men responsible for her death, for another. She thought of Sir Charles and Edward and wondered whether they had been successful in their search for Tod and Brock.

Bea sneezed. "I would join you at the river if I dared, Kate. But it's mizzly this morning, and I have been overtaken by a cold. I think I should not walk about in the wet." She pulled on her gloves. "I'll stay with Agnes, while you do whatever you must."

"Agnes needs you." Kate pinned her tweed cap to the curls she had massed on the top of her head. "Losing Betsy is such a horrible thing, almost incomprehensible." She took up her aunt's heavy walking stick, which she had decided might be useful in her search.

"How dreadful it must have been for her last night," Bea said sadly. "What will she do with her life now? How can she live, having lost both husband and child?"

Kate didn't say so, but if there was any good thing about this miserable business, it was that Agnes did not yet suspect that both of her loved ones had been taken from her, and by the same evil hands. She must know, of course, sooner or later. Kate found her gloves in a pocket and pulled them on. But let her first become accustomed to the magnitude of her loss, before she was burdened with an even greater pain.

They went outside and climbed into the gig Pocket had brought around. Kate picked up the reins and they headed toward Gallows Green, where she left Bea with a pale, silent Agnes. With a heavy heart, she drove on to the River Stour below Highfields barn. There, a subdued group of men and boys were working from barges, dragging the river bottom with heavy iron hooks. The banks had been searched yesterday, but as Mrs. Wilkins had so graphically remarked, the river clung to its dead and often yielded them up tardily. The banks would be searched daily until Betsy's body was found, and Kate wanted to do what she could.

So while the sad grey sky wept overhead and her heart wept within her, Kate climbed out of the gig and tied the horse to a tree. She walked to the riverbank, ignoring the stares of the village lads, who were clearly astonished by her costume.

"Nothing yet?" she asked of a muscular, round-cheeked man who seemed to be in charge. She recognized him as the owner of the tiny grocery on the corner of the green.

The grocer leaned on his pole, which had a hook on one end. "No, mum," he said, "if wot ye mean is have we found lit'le Betsy." His mouth was sad. "We did find 'er boot, though. Pulled it up on our first drag this mornin'."

"I see," Kate said gravely. Betsy's shirt, her boot. If anyone had doubted the child's fate, it could be doubted no longer. "Has anyone walked the south bank this morning?" The river, which marked the boundary between the counties of Essex and Suffolk, was quite wide at this point; it was not very likely, Kate thought, that Betsy's body would be found on the Suffolk side, along the north bank.

The grocer shook his head. "I was about t' send my lad t' do't."

"Let him stay and work," Kate said. "I shall search."

"Beggin' yer pardon, mum," the grocer said, alarmed. "It's hardly a woman's affair. Ye might find her an'—"

And what? Kate thought. Cry aloud at the sight of a dead

body? Shriek? Faint? But she smiled as courteously as she could.

"Thank you for your concern," she said, and started down the footpath that followed eastward along the winding course of the river toward Manningtree. The distance to the mouth of the Stour, where the river broadened into the estuary, was only two miles. The footpath was clearly trodden into the grass. She walked along it with attention, prodding the clumps of reed and willow on the riverbank with Aunt Sabrina's walking stick. But her probes yielded nothing more than sodden hanks of black weed and the occasional startled cry of a river bird frightened from her reedy nest. The river was stubborn. Or if it had given up Betsy's body, it was not along the south bank.

When Kate came to the river's mouth, within sight of the quay at Manningtree, she stood and looked out for a long moment over the quiet water, thinking of the secrets it held—the secrets of pirates and grain smugglers and of one brave girl, as headstrong and daring and truly emancipated as any bloomer-clad young lady who dared to cycle in Hyde Park, and whose last adventure had taken her far beyond the pale.

Back in Gallows Green, Kate drank the obligatory cup of tea and endured the suspicious scrutiny of the two women who had come ostensibly to offer Agnes their condolences but more likely to learn some new piece of information. Mrs. Wilkins, who had been so cordial the day before, averted her eyes from the sight of Kate's ankles. The other was a pinched, shriveled woman named Mrs. Bentley, her hair netted with black chenille at the back of her head and her thin shoulders draped with a black knitted shawl. She glared at Kate, and as she passed the biscuit tray, muttered something that sounded like "shameless, shameless." But Vicar Talbot, who had stopped in with a pot of soup prepared by his housekeeper, gave Kate a smile and a sympathetic glance. And Agnes, true to her generous nature, remarked that she had always admired the practicality of rational dress—yes, even bloomers—and hoped one day to have the opportunity to try it for herself.

"Practicality and comfort come first, I believe." Her smile was wan. "Betsy enjoyed the freedom of boys' clothing, and

I shall always be glad that she took her comfort while she could.''

Mrs. Bentley's dark face went darker. ''Yes, an' look wot 'appened t' 'er,'' she said in a voice as grating as a rook's. '' 'Eadstrong, she was, 'eadstrong as a young 'orse. Needed a rein.''

''Marjory, Marjory,'' Mrs. Wilkins chided. ''She were just a child, an' she's gone from us. Now's not th' time fer hard words.''

Mrs. Bentley lifted her chin. ''Well, but I have t' say't, don't I, Flora? An' Agnes 'as to 'ear it. It's a sad time, indeed it is, an' I'd be th' last t' cast stones. But let it be a lesson.'' The glance she threw at Agnes, if not a stone, was stone-like and accusatory. ''It weren't just th' breeches, neither. The child used t' whistle goin' past my window, loud, like any boy. I said t' Mr. Bentley, I said, 'Crowin' 'ens an' whistlin' girls. Ye know wot their ends be,' I said.'' Her nod was confirming and her eyes glittered. '' 'Eadstrong. Too 'eadstrong by 'alf.''

The vicar cleared his throat. ''And the greatest of these,'' he remarked into his teacup, ''is charity.''

Mrs. Wilkins stood. ''Marjory Bentley,'' she said with dignity, ''I am truly ashamed o' ye, lettin' yer hard mouth run ahead o' yer Christian heart. Now, come along an' leave this pore woman t' 'er grief.''

When they had gone, the vicar turned to Agnes. ''You must not take Mrs. Bentley to heart, my dear. Be glad that Betsy was as she was—a carefree and happy child.''

''And headstrong,'' Agnes admitted ruefully. ''Perhaps I should have reined her in, or asked Artie to be harder with her.'' She looked down at her hands. ''Perhaps she would be here now if I—''

''Please,'' Kate said, reaching for Agnes's clasped hands. ''You can't blame yourself.''

Agnes sighed. ''Yes, I know. But it is most difficult.''

Bea sneezed twice and blew her nose. ''I fear I really am perishing with this cold, Kate.''

''Then it's time we started for home,'' Kate said. She squeezed Agnes's hand. ''You'll be all right?''

Agnes nodded. "You will come back when . . . when there is news?"

"Of course," Kate replied. Good-byes were said, Bea was tucked into the gig with an extra robe over her lap and an umbrella, and Kate took up the reins. They started off, the pony's hoofs splashing thick brown mud.

"I think," said Kate as they rounded the corner of the green, "that we should go home by way of Crayford Lane. It is less traveled and perhaps less muddy, and certainly shorter."

It was on Crayford Lane, not far from the Dedham Gas Works, that they found the body.

41

Nobody could call Mr. Tod "nice." The rabbits could not bear him; they could smell him half a mile off. He was of a wandering habit and he had foxey whiskers; they never knew where he would be next.

—BEATRIX POTTER
The Tale of Mr. Tod

The corpse sprawled beside the cart track was that of a man, as Kate could see from her seat in the gig. He was clad in dark trousers, a dark blue jacket, and muddy boots with a hole in one leather sole, and he lay sprawled on his back some little distance from the road, his limbs twisted and bent as if he had been hurled from a vehicle in some violent roadway accident.

"Oh, dear!" Bea exclaimed, wide-eyed. "Is he dead?"

"I had better see," Kate said. She jumped down and touched the body gingerly, finding the skin cold. When she raised the wrist to search for a pulse, the arm was stiff.

The man was indeed dead. And justly so, Kate could not help but feel as she rose and stood staring down at the sharp-pointed chin, the coppery hair. A hot, angry revulsion rose like a volcano inside her.

"Kate?" Bea called anxiously. "Kate, is it someone you know?"

"It's someone we both know," Kate said, "at least by

sight.'' She pulled her gaze away from the body with a deep shudder. ''It's Mr. Tod.''

Bea gasped. ''The man who—''

''Yes,'' Kate said bleakly. ''The man who may have murdered Betsy.'' She clenched her fists, hard, nauseated by anger. ''But now that he's dead, he's beyond the punishment of the law.''

Bea's voice was firm. ''Now that he's dead, he is within the hands of the Law. And he *shall* be punished.''

''Tod?'' Vicar Talbot asked, incredulous. He stepped back down from the gig into which he was climbing, in front of Agnes's house. ''You think Russell Tod killed the little girl?''

''That's right,'' Edward said grimly. ''And her father, too. Have you seen him?''

''Not in the past few days,'' the vicar said. He frowned. ''I have to admit, although it's not Christian of me to say it, to not liking the fellow. He seems to have a wandering habit, here a year, there a year. Of late, he's been courting the Widow Dayle. The banns are to be said in two weeks. I have had my reservations about the marriage and have spoken to Mrs. Dayle. But to no avail. She is determined to wed again.''

''I fear the widow must remain a widow,'' Edward said remorselessly, ''unless she wishes to be widowed yet again. When Tod is apprehended, he will be jailed. If the case against him can be proved, and I believe it can, the man will be hung for his crimes.''

''Oh, I *say*,'' the vicar protested. He was known to resist capital punishment. He looked distressed. ''Still,'' he muttered, ''to kill a child and an officer of the law. Such things cannot be tolerated in a society that is governed by law.''

''I will go to see Mary Dayle,'' Edward said, ''and ask her if she knows where Tod might be.'' He paused, thinking how women had to bear the burden, over and over, of such awful losses. Mary Dayle's first husband, Will Drummond, had fallen on a hay fork and been carried home on a barn door, dead. She had nursed her second husband, George Dayle, through a cancer, to lose him two years ago on Christmas Eve. ''Will you come with me?'' he added, thinking that it might be easier to face the woman with the vicar at his elbow.

The vicar sighed and stepped back into his gig. "Of course," he said. "I—"

"Constable! Constable!" The boy was thin and freckle-faced and out of breath. "Come quick! There's somebody dead down by th' Dedham Gas Works!"

Edward started. "Dead!" he exclaimed, thinking of Betsy. "A little girl?"

"No, not a girl," the boy said. "A man. Miss Ardleigh found 'im. She gave me a shillin' to come fer ye."

"Miss Ardleigh!" Edward and the vicar exclaimed in unison.

"Yes," the boy said. "Hurry!"

"Who is the dead man?" Edward asked. "Do you know him?"

The boy shook his sandy head. "Not me," he said. "But the Miss knows 'im. Said to tell you he's the one you've been lookin' fer."

"Tod!" Edward roared, thunderstruck. "Not Tod!"

"That's 'im," the boy replied, now hopping on both feet. "That's 'oo she said. Mr. Tod, with red whiskers and a pointy chin. Come on!" He raced off.

Edward followed swiftly after, leaving the vicar sighing to himself and thinking of what he would say to the Widow Dayle.

Charles received the message as he was shrugging into his coat in the back hallway of Marsden Manor, on his way to collect the horse that the Marsden stablemaster had saddled for him. He was about to leave for Manningtree to learn from P.C. Bradley whether Tod had been apprehended at Wivenhoe the night before. It had been damned frustrating for him and Ned to wait all night in the shrubbery outside Tod's cottage, shivering in the damp air, listening to the wispy hoot of an owl, and not catch even a glimpse of the wretched fellow. They would have done as well to have sat in the warmth and raucous conviviality of The Flag. At least there they would have been dry, and not thirsty.

Lawrence approached. "From th' constable, sir," he said, handing over the folded piece of paper. He cleared his throat and glanced over his shoulder as if to ensure that he was not overheard. "If ye don't mind me askin', Sir Charles," he said in a low voice, "I was wond'rin' wot word ye'd 'ad wi' the lady."

"What lady?" Charles asked, inattentive. He unfolded the paper.

"Wi' Miss Ardleigh," Lawrence said. "About th'—" He coloured deeply. "Ye know."

"Oh, quite," Charles said, remembering. "About Amelia."

Lawrence nodded eagerly. "Hindeed, Sir Charles. Hamelia."

"I must confess, Lawrence, that the pressure of events drove the matter right out of my mind. I have not yet spoken to Miss Ardleigh of it. But I shall. Rely on it."

Lawrence's face fell. "I wouldn't press it, sir," he said glumly, "but th' ol' misery—Mrs. Pratt, that is—says she's not t' come out wi' me, ever agin." He shook his head. "Times've come round 'ard when a man's kept from courtin' th' 'ooman of 'is 'eart."

"I'm sorry, Lawrence," Charles said with genuine feeling. "I will see what I can do. Thank you for recalling the matter to my attention."

The heavy sigh that issued from Lawrence's lips seemed to convey both a lack of confidence in Charles's ability to intervene between his loved one and the self-appointed guardian of her chasteness, and the simultaneous belief that this ability was his only hope. "Thank 'ee, sir," he said, and walked away with a dragging step, the picture of the despondent lover.

But Lawrence, however dejected, was not so easily conquered. Charles could not know that once out of sight, Lawrence straightened his shoulders, his eyes became flinty, and his determination hardened. Mrs. Pratt or no Mrs. Pratt, it was time to take matters into his own two hands.

Left to himself, Charles opened the envelope and read the brief message from Ned. It said simply, "I have just received word that Russell Tod is dead. Crayford Lane, near the turning to the Gas Works. Come at once."

Charles stared down at the hastily penciled scribble and felt a sharp, almost physical relief. Tod's capture was inevitable, his trial a certainty, his execution by hanging—a savage, ugly act, even when well deserved—the most probable outcome. However death had come to Russell Tod, it had relieved the Crown of the burden of prosecution and saved Agnes from the agony of a trial.

But his relief was mixed with a ragged frustration and a profound regret. Alive, Tod had held the key not only to the father's death but also to the daughter's disappearance. Now that the man was dead, would they ever know for a certainty how Betsy had died—in the struggle by the stone wall or in the cold river? He thought of the little girl and was almost overwhelmed with sadness, not only for her but for her grieving mother. If this question were not answered, its long shadow would darken Agnes's heart for the rest of her life.

42

Death always comes too early or too late.
                                        —English Proverb

Edward Laken frequently encountered death in the course of his duties, and he had learned to hold himself apart from it—from its violence, its pathos, its pain. But this time, he reveled in the grim satisfaction that churned in the pit of his stomach as he stood beside Tod's contorted body, arms and legs flung wide as if he had been thrown from a horse. The man was a thief. He was implicated in Artie's murder— was most likely the murderer himself. And in Edward's mind, he was the man responsible for what had happened to Betsy. The only thing the least bit wrong about his death was that justice had not administered it. Now that it had come, though, Edward was glad of it, and glad that Agnes would be spared the brutal business of a trial.

Still rejoicing, he bent over the twisted body. Russell Tod's head—mouth open, eyes staring—was flung back and to one side, pointed chin tilted upward, face colourless in the grey light, coppery hair and side-whiskers rain-slicked. The man had died, it appeared, from a blow to the left side of the head: the skull had a queer, caved-in look, the depression badly bruised and discoloured. There was blood, although not much of it, at the nostrils and at one corner of the mouth. Perhaps he had been thrown from his horse and struck his head on a rock, or had ridden under an overhanging tree limb. But there were no trees in the vicinity, nor any rock substantial enough to have inflicted that damage. More likely, he had been kicked in the head by his horse.

Edward turned as Charles came up, camera in one hand, tripod over one shoulder.

"Ah, Charles," Edward said, relieved to see him. Standing alone beside Tod's body, so close to the man who had wrecked Agnes's life, was a dangerous business. There was a maelstrom of feeling inside him, an ungovernable flood of it, capable at any moment of sweeping him away. "So we've come to the end of it," he said, with a half-guilty, ill-concealed satisfaction.

"Perhaps," Charles replied somberly. He set down his gear. "But perhaps not. How did he die, do you think?"

"Kicked by his horse, it would seem." With an effort, Edward shut out the feeling. "No sign of the horse, though. No report of it, either." He didn't say so, but it did seem a bit odd. In this area, where the country people knew animals and respected them, a saddled, riderless horse would be caught and penned and immediate word sent to the owner.

Charles said nothing, only bent to the body.

Edward looked down at his friend and shook his head. He knew himself to be a good policeman. He kept the Dedham peace by being the kind of man the villagers could respect. He cautioned the rowdies at the pub and hauled them off for a night in gaol when a cautionary word did not suffice. He kept a watch on the nomad gypsies that ranged his rural district and on the scores of casual labourers that thronged the village at harvest time. But while Edward was ambitious, there was almost no opportunity for the kind of real detective work that Charles relished, even if he had been trained to it. The great bulk of the crimes that happened on his patch were crimes of passion or opportunity, not crimes of stealth, and the criminals were easy to identify.

Under other circumstances, Edward might have been on his knees beside Charles, peering at the body. Now, more than a little guilty for having been glad of Russell Tod's death and anxious to go to Agnes and tell her that her pain was ended, he shifted from one foot to the other and scowled. Russell Tod was dead, and only Mary Dayle would mourn him. His death had ended the anguish, the sorrow, the unimaginable heartache of Betsy's loss, of Artie's death. There was no point in dragging it out by this inch-by-inch, hair-by-hair investigation in which Charles was so deeply engrossed. Nothing more was to be learned than what they could see with their eyes, unaided.

Finally, Charles stood up. "I doubt it was a horse, Ned."

"A stone, then," Edward said quickly. "He fell."

"No. The area of discolouration and depression is far too small. The object that caused this death was little more than an inch in diameter. The man was killed when he was hit by something the size of a poker."

Edward closed his eyes and wished he could close his ears, wished, irrationally, that he had not summoned Charles to the scene. But that was wild foolishness. He was a policeman, and his job was to see that justice was done, fall upon whom it might. He opened his eyes and said, "You think he was murdered, then?"

"Most probably," Charles said. "What did you find when you searched the area?"

Edward looked at him. "I haven't."

Charles's nod was sympathetic. "He's dead. That's something." He paused. "Death always comes too early or too late. Pity he can't tell us about Betsy."

"Yes," Edward said. He looked down at the body. "Murdered to keep him from telling what he knew, d'you think?"

"Someone higher up, perhaps, in the ring of thieves." Charles was thoughtful. "I wondered at Tod, a simple bailiff, being able to arrange for a boat to receive the grain."

"Napthen, then. He worked on the docks in Harwich. He'd know how to arrange it."

Charles shook his head. "Not Napthen. He spent the night in the Manningtree gaol."

"Then Brock." Edward looked at the sprawled body, trying to imagine how it might have happened. A falling-out of thieves, angry words, an impulsive blow. The body loaded into a cart and flung out, so that the murder could be mistaken— by a policeman anxious to bring an end to the business—for an accidental death.

"Perhaps," Charles agreed. "Yes, perhaps Brock." He bent

to examine the ground around the dead man, found something that interested him, and studied it carefully. "Who discovered the body?" he asked.

Edward chuckled dryly. "Who do you think?" He didn't wait for an answer. "Miss Ardleigh, of course."

"Ah, yes." Charles turned, eyebrows raised. "I might have known. The woman is ubiquitous."

"Indeed," said a wry voice.

Edward turned, startled. "Good afternoon again, Kate. I thought you and Miss Potter had gone home."

"We had." Miss Ardleigh stepped off her bicycle, leaned it against Edward's cart, and crossed the ditch toward them. She was wearing the same remarkable tweed costume she had been wearing when Edward arrived on the scene, summoned by the neighbouring farm boy whom she had dispatched with the news of her gruesome discovery. Edward had to confess to being nearly as stunned by the sight of her ankles as he had been by the sight of the dead man. Even now, his glance was drawn inexorably to her lower limbs, and he had to wrench it away, feeling his face colour.

"Miss Potter has a dreadful cold," she went on. "I took her back to Bishop's Keep, saw her to bed, and organized her tea." She looked down at the body, frowning. "But I could not get this . . . this business out of my mind. I came to see what you had learned."

"I wonder," Charles said, "if I may examine your boots."

Miss Ardleigh looked at him for a moment before speaking. "I hope you don't think *I* killed the man."

"I doubt it," Charles said evenly. "Did you?"

"No," she said. Her mouth tightened and she glanced at the body with something like the fierce satisfaction that Edward himself felt. "But I must say that I'm glad I wasn't given the opportunity."

Edward thought he had given up being surprised by Miss Ardleigh. But he could not help being surprised now. She bent down, unlaced her stout black boot and pulled it off, balancing on one foot in an altogether unladylike posture. He averted his eyes from her slender black-stockinged foot, a part of the female anatomy that he had seen only once or twice before in his life and found, to his dismay, inordinately provocative. She handed the boot to Charles, who dispassionately inspected its broad, flat heel and handed it back.

"Did Miss Potter approach the body?" he asked.

"No," Miss Ardleigh said. She bent over to lace up her boot again. "She remained in the gig."

"Did you see any woman in the vicinity?"

"No," Miss Ardleigh replied. She straightened, her grey eyes puzzled. "Why do you ask?"

Edward frowned. A woman? What reason could Charles have to think that a woman had anything to do with Tod's death?

Charles did not directly answer the question. "I should like to cast your boot heels in plaster," he said to Miss Ardleigh. "I have some back at the manor, for the field work I plan to do in fossils." He turned to Edward. "Your heels too, Ned."

Edward nodded. "But I should like to know," he said slowly, "why you have taken such a sudden interest in shoes."

"Because of this," Charles said, pointing to a deep, round indentation, a half-inch in diameter, in the soft earth. "And this." He pointed to another. "And this."

Chagrined, Edward bent to look. He was here on police business. He should have seen the indentations himself. But he had been so swept up by his feelings that he had not paid even a routine attention to the site, and scarcely more to the body. He had not even gone through the pockets.

Miss Ardleigh bent over. "Heel prints!" She straightened, her eyes widening in an expression of surprise. "A woman's prints! You don't suspect . . ." She stared at him and her voice trailed off. "Do you?" She was clearly frightened.

Edward stiffened. A woman's prints! Was it possible that—?

No, no, of course not. Whatever else the shoe prints meant, they could not mean *that*. He drew in his breath and controlled his feelings with an effort. Agnes was too calm, too composed, too level-headed to have done something like this. And besides, she did not know the details of her husband's murder, nor suspect that Betsy's drowning was anything but an accident. Without that knowledge, she had no reason to kill Tod. He frowned, thinking back to the conversation in Agnes's kitchen, when Tod's name had been mentioned within her hearing.

But she hadn't been listening—had she?

Charles shoved his hands into his pockets. "There's not enough evidence to suspect anyone, man or woman, at this point." He did not look at Edward. "But I think it a good idea to preserve these prints after I have taken photographs of the body. And also to cast the heels of the three of us, for purposes of comparison, and of anyone else who may have been near the body."

Miss Ardleigh was pale. She stood still for a moment, then said, with the air of a woman who had just made up her mind to something, "I'll ride to the manor for your plaster, if you like."

Edward was too deeply engrossed with the questions running through his head to question her intention. But Charles's quick smile lightened his sober face, and his voice was teasing.

"You'd let Lady Marsden see you cycling, in that get-up?"

Miss Ardleigh tossed her head. "I am sure that Lady Marsden already believes me unredeemable," she retorted. "A bicycle and a bit of ankle won't make her think any the worse of me. And since I intend to wear this comfortable 'get-up' regularly, everyone had better become accustomed to it."

Charles chuckled out loud. "Right, then. The plaster will be found in my science kit, on the table in my bedroom. Lawrence can get it for you."

"I'm off," Miss Ardleigh said briskly, and left them.

Charles unpacked his camera, set up the tripod, and took a half-dozen photographs of the body and several more of the puzzling round prints. Finally he finished, repacked his gear, and straightened up. He looked at Edward and spoke for the first time since Miss Ardleigh had gone. His words went straight to the heart of Edward's worry.

"I don't see how Agnes might have killed him, Ned."

Edward felt a relief wash through him, so great that his knees actually felt weak. "No, no, of course not. She knew nothing about Tod's connexion to—She had no motive." He cleared his throat loudly, too loudly. "I'll search the body now, if you've done."

Charles stepped back. "It's yours, Constable."

Edward knelt beside the body and ran his hands into the pockets of the jacket, the dark trousers. He found nothing except a few shillings, a small silver pocketknife, much worn, and a grimy handkerchief. But when he pulled out the handkerchief, tied into the corner was a gold coin with a nick in the edge.

"Artie's gold sovereign," he exclaimed, holding it up. "That corks it!"

"I suppose it does," Charles said. "Now all we have to do is find the person who corked *him*."

Edward pocketed the sovereign, the knife, and the handkerchief. "If you're done with your picture-taking, you can help me load the body into the cart. I'll take it to the police surgeon at Colchester, and make my report while I'm there. I'll telegraph Bradley, too."

"Right," Charles said. "I'll wait here for Miss Ardleigh, and cast the heel prints. God knows we can't go peering at every female boot in the county, but the casts may come in handy."

It wasn't until he was halfway to Colchester, the body wrapped in a canvas and angled awkwardly in the back of the cart, that Edward realized what Charles had really said, and felt as if he had just driven into a cloud of icy, roaring blackness.

Charles had not said that Agnes had not killed Tod. He had said that he didn't see *how* she might have killed him.

Between the two there was a world of difference, a spectral world haunted by Agnes's motives. Artie and Betsy. Both beloved, both dead, both at the hand of Tod.

Now Tod was dead, too. Agnes, if she had known what he had done, could very well have killed him. And Charles, persistent and perceptive as he was, and dedicated to the art of detection, would undoubtedly discover the truth of the matter—even if it destroyed her.

And at that moment, Edward hated his friend.

43

"How did you come here?" asked Pigling Bland.

"Stolen," replied Pig-Wig, with her mouth full.
                              —BEATRIX POTTER
                              The Tale of Pigling Bland

Arthur Oliver and Russell Tod were indeed dead, and nothing more was to be done for them in this world.

But Betsy was not.

Yes, Betsy Oliver was alive, although not at all happy with her lot in life. She lay trussed like a plump harvest pig, with a rag tied in her mouth in place of a baked apple, on a heap of dry, scratchy hay in a lean-to shed a short distance from the smithy. Her shirt was gone and her boots, and a filthy, scratchy blanket smelling of horse had been thrown over her.

Still, until the last few hours, Betsy had not been unbearably uncomfortable. Although she was securely bound and her feet and hands had long since gone numb, she was warm and dry, and she had not been lonely. The man with the pointed chin and scraggly red hair had twice come into the shed to remove her gag and feed her porridge and brown bread and give her milk to drink. And yesterday afternoon, through a crack in the board by her head, she had watched Uncle Ned and Sir Charles arrive. They were just about to break open the door and rescue her, when the smith's boy (a loud, loutish creature, frightfully inconsiderate of small birds and lizards) had galloped around the corner, waving his black cap and shouting that she had drowned.

What utter nonsense, she had thought angrily. How could anyone imagine that she might drown when her father had always boasted that she could swim as well as any pike? But no one seemed to raise that question. Voices from the smithy drifted into her prison: she heard that her boot had been found, as well as her shirt, and that the river was being dragged for her body. This intelligence was far more painful than the ropes that bound her, because she knew how sad and grief-stricken and lonely her mother must be. She longed to run home and fling her arms around her mother and tell her that the sharp-chinned man had only made it appear that she had drowned and she was perfectly alive. And not only alive, but less lonely, likely, than her mother, for she had Jemima Puddle-duck for company, and Mr. Browne, who sat on a limb outside the shed, hooting a raspy encouragement.

It was perhaps not surprising that Mr. Browne should have followed Betsy and her captors and stationed himself as a watchful guard outside her prison. Or that Kep, such a good tracking dog, should sniff her out and stay close by until the stupid smith's boy had laid hands on him and taken him away. But how did it happen that Jemima Puddle-duck had located her so speedily?

Betsy could give herself little credit for this fortuitous turn of events. The fact was that there was a small opening in one of the boards at the back of the shed, and Jemima—determined duck that she was—had discovered it. This event had apparently occurred several days before, for four large eggs lay like polished ivory in a nest in the dry straw. This morning, Jemima had slipped through the hole and settled herself amiably upon her four eggs, evidencing no surprise at finding Betsy in the audience. She sat there for an hour, yawning occasionally, now preening a wing, now her breast feathers. When she had finished her motherly duty, she got up and examined her fifth egg, nibbling it fondly with her orange bill. She then carefully covered all the eggs, quacked a maternal farewell to them and to Betsy, and went out briskly in search of her breakfast.

With Jemima's cheerful company, the heartening calls of
Mr. Browne, and the sharp-chinned man's porridge and bread,
Betsy had been less worried about herself than she was about
her mother. But the sharp-chinned man had not come back
since his dispute with the other man last night, and she was
beginning to fear that he might not come back at all, especially
considering the circumstances under which he had left.

Betsy had been asleep in the velvety darkness, dreaming
that she was at home with her mother and father, having a late
tea at the kitchen table. At first she had thought that the
voices—the whispers and hisses and muttered curses—were
somehow part of her dream. She even heard her father's name,
and he heard it too. In the dream, he got up from the table
and reached for his policeman's hat and said he would be back
when he had done an urgent errand. But then she woke and
pulled herself into a little ball under her scratchy blanket, realizing that her father was in the dream but the voices were
real. The men who spoke were in the cottage on the other side
of the shed. She looked through the crack and saw them,
standing in front of the window, the light behind them.

At first Betsy was frightened by the harshness of the voices,
that of the sharp-chinned man and the other. But her fear wore
off a little as they kept on arguing, the voices rising and falling, only a word here or there distinguishable. This had gone
on for a long time, while Betsy dozed and woke and dozed
again. Then she woke to see them come out of the cottage,
carrying a lantern. In the circle of light, their figures were quite
clear: the sharp-chinned man and the other, a stoutish man
with black whiskers and a hobble. They went around the corner of the cottage, and a moment later she heard the muffled
hoofs of a horse. The sharp-chinned man had not come back.

That had happened last night. It was now mid-afternoon,
judging from the clamour of the school children across the
way and the loud rumbling of her empty stomach, and Betsy
was feeling horribly hungry and thirsty. Jemima's ivory eggs
lay beside her, lightly covered with straw, tempting. If worse
came to worst, she might somehow contrive to break an egg
and eat it, although the idea of raw egg was not particularly

appealing, and the notion of eating one of Jemima's babies even less so.

But still, one did what one had to do. And with that last resort in mind, she lay back to watch an industrious brown spider who came out of a crack in the wall and began to drape a silver web between a protruding nail and the broken handle of a rusty garden rake, preparatory to trapping and trussing up unfortunate bluebottles.

44

There will never be any love lost between Tommy Brock and Mr. Tod.

—BEATRIX POTTER
The Tale of Mr. Tod

Bea's cold was not dangerous, but her nose was as red as a berry and she was plagued with great sneezes, so she confined herself to her bedroom. On the morning after their discovery of Tod's body, Kate joined her there, and Amelia brought in their breakfasts: tea, crumpets and fresh strawberries, and the Colchester newspaper. On the front page was an article about their grim find. It concluded with Chief Constable Pell's speculation that Russell Tod had been the mastermind of the grain thieves who had plagued the Dedham area.

"Now that he is dead, the ring is likely without a leader," the Chief Constable was quoted as having said. "The police are to be congratulated upon resolving this matter." Kate read the statement once more out loud, wondering exactly what it was that the police had resolved, and how.

"I suppose it was Brock who killed him," Bea said thickly, and sneezed. "They must have argued over money. Perhaps Tod refused to pay what he had promised." She accepted a cup of hot tea from Kate, laced heavily with lemon and honey. "It is the sort of criminal act one might expect to read in one of your novels, Kate."

"Yes," Kate replied, testy. "But Beryl Bardwell would not

leave a clue like that woman's heelprint if Brock were the killer.'' She buttered a crumpet and put it on her plate.

Bea sighed and took her handkerchief out of the pocket of her dressing gown. ''*Agnes* is the only woman we know with a reason to kill that man.''

''I'm afraid you're right,'' Kate said regretfully. ''But suppose there was another woman about whom we know nothing—perhaps a woman scorned or abandoned. I am certain that such a man as Tod is perfectly capable of that sort of thing. Perhaps it's worth looking into, if only to distract attention from Agnes.''

Bea stared at her. ''You don't *really* believe that Agnes . . .'' Her voice trailed off and her watery blue eyes grew large. ''You *do*!''

''No,'' Kate said, ''of course I don't.'' She poured herself a cup of tea and added cream to it before she spoke. ''But I fear that others may believe it. Especially when they discover that she has no alibi.''

''No alibi?''

''She cannot prove where she was the night Tod was killed,'' Kate said. ''On my way to Marsden Manor to fetch Sir Charles's plaster, I stopped to ask.'' The visit to Agnes had been, in fact, the reason for Kate's volunteering to go to Marsden Manor. She wanted to reach Agnes before anyone else.

Bea's voice was worried. ''And what did she say?''

''That she was restless and went for a walk along the river very late in the evening—hoping, I suppose, that she might find some trace of Betsy.''

''I suppose the next question has to do with boots.'' Bea blew her nose.

Kate tried hard not to reveal the concern she felt. ''She has a pair of black ones with small round heels, which she wears to church. I did not pursue the matter because I did not wish to alarm her. I can only hope that the heels do not match Sir Charles' plaster casts.''

Bea sat back in bed with an irritated look on her face. ''One could wish that Sir Charles were not so diligent in his detecting.'' She picked up her cup and sipped her tea. ''Not that I believe for a moment that Agnes did it, of course.''

Kate nodded and finished her crumpet. ''It's really most unfortunate that Sir Charles was summoned. Edward was so relieved to find Tod dead that he was not inclined to examine the scene very carefully. When he first arrived, he was sure that Tod had been killed in an accident with a horse. Without Sir Charles, those heelprints would have been trodden underfoot when the body was removed.''

Bea pulled a bowl of strawberries toward her. ''Well, then,'' she said with resolve, ''you must not linger, Kate. If the evidence Sir Charles has discovered seems to point to Agnes, then the evidence is surely wrong. Brock is the murderer, I'm sure of it. It's up to you to find the clues that point to his guilt. You'd best get on with it.''

Kate stood. ''You won't mind if I leave you all alone?''

''I'm hardly alone,'' Bea replied with a little laugh. She pointed to the hedgehog curled into a ball in the middle of a pillow, her shiny prickles smoothed flat. ''If Mrs. Tiggy-Winkle proves unsociable, there's always Hunca Munca. And I have my sketchbook. I was thinking of beginning another story.''

''Well, you've had plenty of adventures to draw upon,'' Kate said as she turned to leave the room. ''You shouldn't run out of ideas.''

Bea gave a sad little sigh. ''My dear Kate,'' she said, shaking her head, ''when I wished for adventure, someone should have thrust a handkerchief in my mouth.''

''Well, but I can't help it, can I?'' P.C. Bradley demanded irritably. ''It's not *my* idea to question the woman. I was ordered. All I'm asking is your company during the interrogation, and that was ordered too.''

Edward could feel the anger welling up within him like molten lava. ''For God's sake, man, it's insane! No one in his right mind could accuse that poor, bereaved woman of—''

''No one has,'' P.C. Bradley broke in wearily. He shook his head. ''I'm just supposed to ask a few questions, that's all. It's part of the investigation.''

Edward spoke very quietly, damming his fury. "What questions?"

Bradley looked uneasy. "What she knew about the victim. How much she knew about her husband's affairs." He hesitated, and added slowly, "Where she was on the night Tod was killed."

Edward felt as if he were drowning in a sea of fire. "You can't be serious! What makes you think she knew *anything* about—"

"For God's sake, man, I don't know." Bradley's mouth went firm. "Take your complaints to Colchester. I'm just doing what I'm told to do." He reached for his hat. "Are you coming, or am I to tell Chief Constable Pell that you have disobeyed a direct order?"

Garbed in a split tweed skirt, (not quite so comfortable but less controversial than bloomers), Kate rode her bicycle to Manningtree. The Pig 'n' Whistle was situated in a wide, open street, facing the quay. It was a Tudor building with generously pargeted stucco panels, window boxes filled with spring flowers, and gleaming diamond-paned windows. The Dutch door hung open and a black-and-white cat sunned itself on the stone step, which had been worn deep by the tread of many feet.

The publican's wife was stoutish, with sallow skin and a sour mouth. "Tommy Brock?" She frowned and indicated a direction with her head. "In the cottage behind, if he's t' home." Her dark eyes glinted suspiciously. "Wot 're ye wantin' him for?"

Kate fell back on the lie she had invented for Mrs. McGregor several days before. "His sister has given me to understand that he might be available to do some work. She is the one who directed me here."

The woman's face brightened. "Oo, aye!" she exclaimed. "By all means, then, go an' see if ye kin knock him up, an' if not, leave yer name an' where he kin reach ye, an' I'll see that he does."

Surmising that the landlady's enthusiasm might have something to do with payment of the rent, Kate gave her name and

directions to Bishop's Keep, and went out into the graveled
alley and around the back. Tommy Brock's dwelling was a
board shack tilted to one side under the weight of a large
creeper vine, which covered the roof and the adjacent brick
wall. The vine was full of blue tits, who fled with shrill peeps
at Kate's approach. She tapped at the open door, then called,
and then, with a cautious glance over her shoulder, pushed it
wide and went in.

The two-room shack was dark and chilly and smelled of
damp. Other than the bed, the table, and a few items of clothing hung from pegs in the wall of the second room, Kate saw
nothing unusual, and certainly nothing to connect Brock with
Tod's death. She had just come out the door and was closing
it behind her when she found herself face to face with the
ugliest man she had ever seen. He was short and hefty-looking,
with a face like a bulldog, a bristly black beard, and a fresh
cut over his left eye. He was carrying a bottle of ale in one
hand and a stout oak staff in the other.

'' 'Oo be ye?'' the man growled, and brandished the staff.
''Wot be ye doin' in me 'ouse?''

Kate recoiled from the man's alehouse breath. ''My name
is Kathryn Ardleigh,'' she said with as much dignity as she
could muster. ''I was looking for Mr. Brock.''

''This be Brock,'' the man said, indicating the front of his
filthy navvy's coat with a jerk of his thumb. He bared yellow
fangs in a ferocious grin. ''Wot d'ye want wi' th' bastard?''

''I understand from your sister,'' Kate said faintly, ''that
you might be available for work. I am seeking to fill a position
on my—''

But Kate did not get to finish her sentence. Unexpectedly,
Tommy Brock threw back his ugly head and exploded into a
shout of rough laughter. ''Work!'' He slapped his hand on his
thigh. ''Work, th' leddy sez! Work!''

Kate pulled herself together. ''I see nothing amusing about
an offer of employment.''

''Amusin'!'' Brock cried. ''Nothin' amusin' 'bout employment, the leddy sez!'' He lifted the bottle of ale to his mouth
and pulled a generous swig. ''Tom Brock woan't be workin'
agin.'' He belched heavily. ''Not til 'ee's drunk up 'is money

from 'is las' job. An' that'll take sum time, I'll wager, sum time. Tom Brock, 'ee's a rich man. Very, very rich, 'ee is.''

"I see," Kate said with a show of respect. "And what kind of work have you been doing that has earned you so much money, Mr. Brock?"

A guarded look came into Brock's eyes. "Bit o' this, bit o' that," he said. He downed another swig of ale and slung the empty bottle against the wall of the shack, where it shattered. "Be orf wi' ye, leddy. Ye'll get no work from Tom Brock this day. He's gorn t' sleep, like th' gud 'eathen 'ee be." And he lurched toward the shack and pushed open the door. A moment later, there was a thud, followed by a loud crash, as if he had flung himself across the bed and it had collapsed under him.

As Kate got on her bicycle and pedaled down the cobbled street, it occurred to her that P.C. Bradley might be interested in the news that Tommy Brock had recently earned enough to keep him in ale for some time. As to what kind of work the man had been doing, Kate was sure she knew. He was a confederate of Tod's, and Betsy had identified him as one of the grain thieves. He could be a murderer, as well. That gash over his eye—so raw it hadn't begun to scab yet. Had he got it when he struggled with Russell Tod? Had that heavy oaken staff in his hand left the round prints that Sir Charles had found beside Tod's body, and mistaken for the prints of a woman's boot? She pulled in a sharp breath. Had that staff, which Brock had brandished in her face, been the murder weapon? It was possible, Kate thought excitedly, and more than possible. It was very likely!

But when Kate arrived at the police station, out of breath and eager to share her information with the constable, she was informed by a hand-printed notice pinned to the door that he had gone to Gallows Green and would not return until later in the day. She frowned at the paper, nervously chewing on her lower lip. What errand had taken him to the hamlet? It couldn't have anything to do with Agnes, could it? She stood for a moment indecisively, then climbed back on her bicycle and rode off in the direction of Gallows Green.

45

"This my child was dead, and is alive again; was lost, and is found."

—Matthew 15:24

"I have told you," Agnes said gently, "but I will tell you again. All I know of the man is his name. I had not even heard of his death until you told me."

P.C. Bradley shook his head. "Surely, now, Mrs. Oliver, that cannot be. Word travels fast in a hamlet like Gallows Green, and Mr. Tod was found yesterday afternoon. You must have heard." He shifted uncomfortably. "Or perhaps you already knew," he blurted.

Edward strained forward, barely managing to hold his rage in check. The interrogation had gone from bad to worse, as Bradley managed to insinuate (without actually saying so, of course) that Artie had had dealings with Tod and that Agnes had known of them. And now he was suggesting that Agnes knew of Tod's death before anyone else! Edward, a man of usually calm demeanour, completely forgot that he was a police officer. He was about to stuff Bradley's insulting words back down the man's throat with his fist when Agnes spoke.

"And *you* must have heard, constable," she said with simple dignity, "that I have lost my daughter as well as my husband. I have been in this house, waiting for news of the recovery of her body. I have no interest in other events, of whatever magnitude, not even the death of the Queen. And how could I have known of this man's death before I was told? That is nonsense.''

Bradley had the grace to look ashamed. ''I did not mean to suggest, ma'am—''

''Perhaps you did not,'' Agnes said, wearily passing her hand over her eyes. ''We are all on edge these days. I wish, Constable, that I could be of more help in your investigation. But if you have come to me hoping for intelligence about this man who has died, you shall certainly be disappointed, for I know nothing.''

Bradley pulled himself together. ''Yes, ma'am,'' he said. ''Begging your pardon, ma'am—'' He blushed furiously, fumbled with the hat he held in his hand, and tried again. ''Begging your pardon, ma'am,'' he burst out, ''may I see your boots?''

It was too much for Edward. With a roar, he lowered his head like a bull and charged full force at P.C. Bradley.

Kate made a circuit of the village green, looking for Constable Bradley's cart or horse. She was bicycling past the smithy when she caught a flash of something white slipping under the currant bushes along the path to Mrs. Wilkins's garden. Betsy's duck!

Without thinking, Kate braked quickly, jumped off her bicycle, and pursued the duck. Jemima had been missing since the afternoon of Betsy's disappearance. She should be caught and returned home where she could be penned up, away from the village dogs. So Kate gave pursuit through the currant bushes, alongside the raspberry patch, and down the walk between Mrs. Wilkins's lettuce and cabbages and freshly mounded potatoes.

But Jemima was clearly determined on conducting her own personal business and upon remaining free to do so. She waddled nimbly through the garden and around a small stuccoed cottage, past a row of cold frames, and around the corner of a small lean-to shed. Kate, however, was equally determined. She stayed close enough to see the duck disappear through a hole at ground level at the back of the lean-to. Quick as thought, Kate knelt down, thrust her arm through the hole, and felt around, hoping to catch hold of a wing or a webbed foot and pull the bird out. But it was not upon a duck's wing that her grasping fingers fastened. It was a warm, bare ankle!

With a little cry, Kate pulled back. She sat for an instant, her heart beating fast, then bent over and put her face to the opening. What she saw in the dim twilight of the shed made her cry out with joy. For what she saw when she looked in was the grimy, tear-streaked face of a little girl, lying on her side, looking out.

46

The terrorist and the policeman both come from the same basket.

—JOSEPH CONRAD
The Secret Agent

P.C. Bradley proved to be more injured in pride than in person by Edward's attack. He had gone back to Manningtree to write his report and, without a doubt, to accuse his fellow officer of violent assault. Edward still sat in Agnes's kitchen, nursing a jammed thumb and a cup of hot tea.

"I have made it the worse," he said miserably.

"Only for yourself," Agnes said. She went to the fire and stirred it. "What will they do to you?"

Edward managed a half-smile. "Force me to endure Pell's berating," he said. It would be worse than that, of course. Edward could be charged not only with assaulting a policeman, but with obstructing justice. It meant the end of his police career.

She sat down at the table across from him. "Someone actually did murder the man, then?"

"Yes," Edward said. "Someone wearing narrow, sharp-pointed heels."

"It's no wonder that the constable wanted to see my boots," Agnes said. "This dead man, this Mr. Tod—" She studied her laced fingers. "Is it thought that he killed Artie?"

"Yes," Edward said, devouring her with his eyes. Her face was lined and pale, her eyes sunk deep in their sockets, as if she were starved for sleep. But her skin had the translucence of fine porcelain and her brown hair was like silk. He ached to touch it.

She did not look up. "And it is thought he may have had something to do with Betsy's . . . death?"

Wordlessly, Edward nodded.

The words were drawn out thinly, like wire. "Does the constable *really* believe that *I* could have killed him?"

Edward never knew what he might have answered. Indeed, he was spared from answering at all, for at that moment, the latch rattled loudly and the door burst open. Betsy, shirtless and shoeless and with bits of straw stuck in her hair, flung herself with a cry across the room and into her mother's arms.

Edward stood, dumbfounded, and knocked his chair over with a crash. Then he shouted "Betsy!" and clasped both mother and daughter to his breast in an incredulous embrace, while a beaming Kate Ardleigh, holding an improbable white duck under one arm, looked on.

The next few minutes were a chaos of incredulous tears and wondering laughter. But after a little, calm was restored, and Betsy was wrapped in her mother's shawl and seated at her mother's knee. Kep sat on one side of her, released at last from the tie rope behind the shed, which the churl of a smith's boy had fastened around his neck—and which had kept him from tracking Betsy to Tod's shed. A cup of hot milk in one hand and a large piece of bread and butter in the other, she began to tell her story, helped in the task with questions from her mother, Kate, and Edward.

"But he *did* feed you," Agnes said worriedly. "You *did* have something to eat."

"For a while," Betsy said with her mouth full. "Until he went away night before last. After that I didn't have anything at all." She cast a guilty glance in the direction of the duck, to whom Miss Ardleigh was serving a bowl of milk and bits of bread, and lowered her voice. "I was thinking of eating one of Jemima's eggs."

Edward leaned forward, his eyes narrowing. "You didn't happen to see Mr. Tod go away, then?"

"Well, yes, actually I did." Betsy swallowed what she had in her mouth. "I was hoping he would think to bring me a biscuit before he left, but he was too busy arguing."

"Arguing?" Kate asked.

"With whom?" Edward demanded eagerly.

"I don't know," Betsy said. She yawned and tugged at her braid. "With a man. They were rather angry."

"Do you remember anything about the man?" Edward asked, trying not to show how intent he was upon her answer.

Betsy yawned again. "He had black whiskers and—"

"Black whiskers!" Kate exclaimed. She turned to Edward. "It *is* Tom Brock! If you hurry, you can find him still asleep in his shack behind the Pig 'n' Whistle."

Agnes turned to Edward, eyes large in a white face. "You believe, then, that Betsy saw the man who killed Mr. Tod?"

Betsy sat quite still. "Mr. Tod is dead?"

"Yes," Kate said simply. Agnes knelt down beside Betsy and pulled her daughter into her arms. She looked at Edward over the child's head, and Edward could read the pleading in her eyes. *Enough of death*, she was saying. *She's had too much already.*

But Edward could not allow himself to be moved. "We need to know what you saw, Betsy," he said as gently as he could.

Betsy rested her forehead against her mother's shoulder. "He wasn't a nice man," she said in a muffled voice, "but he brought me food, and I don't think he really intended to hurt me. Whatever he did to make the other man angry, he didn't deserve to get killed." She sighed and straightened up. "No one does."

Edward stood and looked down at Betsy. "Do you think you would know the other man if you saw him again?"

"Yes," Betsy said drowsily. She rubbed her eyes with her hands. "He had a queer stiff walk." Her yawn was huge and her head began to droop.

"A stiff walk?" Edward put out his hand and shook Betsy's shoulder, gently, to wake her up. "How did he walk, Betsy?"

Betsy sagged against her mother's breast, her eyes almost closed. "His leg," she said in a blurry voice. What she said next stunned Edward into speechlessness. He stared at her, disbelieving.

"You're sure?" he asked. "You're quite sure?"

Her only answer was a sleepy nod.

Kate looked at him. "What does it mean?" she asked. When he told her, her eyes widened.

Agnes gave an incredulous gasp. "You don't suppose she was dreaming, do you?" she asked. "Or that she saw something and invented the rest? She's given to making up stories, you know."

"No," Edward said softly. "Betsy did not invent the man. He's quite real. Quite real indeed."

47

The extraordinary drama of murder is always played against the backdrop of ordinary life.
—LORD DUTTON
The Queen's Barrister

The Live and Let Live, which had been crowded at the inquest into Sergeant Oliver's death, was jammed to the rafters now, several days after the murder of Russell Tod. Three chairs had been set up at the far end of the room, in front of the trestle table that would serve as a desk for Coroner Harry Hodson. With deference to the women and the girl-child who were expected to be seated in those chairs, the coroner had ordered Russell Tod's coffin placed out-of-doors, where the jury could view it before they took their seats on the long benches arranged at right angles to the table.

Sanders the publican, in his usual too-short trousers and heelless slippers, his bald pate gleaming, was briskly clearing away the last of the glasses and bottles from the bar. His fat wife was collecting the remains of the beef and mutton pies that had graced the tables and promising, *sotto voce*, that more would appear as soon as the inquest ended, sooner, if the suppliant would walk to the kitchen.

Outside, above the babble of voices and the clatter of horses and harness, came the rusty voice of Old Willie Hogglestock. Old Willie had discarded his apron for the occasion and donned a green corduroy waistcoat as long as a groom's, buttoned to the throat with brass buttons. Much to the dismay of the publican's wife, Old Willie had pulled up his cart directly over the way and was plying not only his regular trade of fish, fruit, and vegetables, but offering as well ha'penny slices of pineapples, ham sandwiches for a penny-ha'penny, and baked potatoes from a brass potato can that was hung over an iron fire-pot, the whole contraption ingeniously suspended from the back of the cart. Beside him, cleverly stationed to bask in the reflected glory of the brass potato can, was a young boy with a basket of walnuts, lifting his brown-stained fingers and crying in a musical voice, "Fine warnuts! Sixteen a penny, fine war-r-nuts." And beside him, cross-legged on a blanket surrounded by pairs of old shoes, sat a swarthy man, a gypsy with a red neckerchief and blue-checked shirt calling, "Boots fer tuppence, fourpence a pair. Buy boots!"

It was into this jangle of sights and sounds that Kate came with Agnes, little Betsy wide-eyed between them, Edward close behind. Bea had wanted to attend, but her cold had prohibited her, as well as the prospect of possible newspaper publicity.

"It would not do to have my father read my name in a newspaper in connexion with a murder," she had told Kate. "For all he and Mama know, I am safely at Long Melford, sketching squirrels." Edward had discussed the matter with the coroner and both agreed that Bea's presence would not be required so long as Kate would testify to the discovery of Tod's body.

As Kate pushed her way among the crowd of people outside the Live and Let Live, she made mental note of the sights and sounds that turned the ordinarily quiet Lamb's Lane into a bustling fairground, intending to tell Bea about it in detail. She was not surprised at the commotion, for the village of Dedham and the hamlet of Gallows Green had been humming with speculation about the manner of Tod's death and his possible connexion with Sergeant Oliver's murder and Betsy's kidnapping. The expectation that all would be revealed had lent to the inquest the electric excitement of a magic lantern show. The villagers, to a person it seemed, had turned out for it.

Inside, the spectators opened a corridor for Kate and Agnes to pass through. The publican, acting as both host and bailiff, showed them to the chairs in front of the table. They were barely seated when a wispy clerk perched on his stool and silenced the din with his shouted "Gentlemen, the Coroner!"

Magisterial in girth and manner, Harry Hodson appeared, seated himself in the oak chair, and signaled the clerk to read the proclamation. Upon its conclusion, the coroner began to call aloud the names of the jurors who were to be empaneled. It would be sufficient, Kate knew, for a verdict to be returned by twelve men. Owing to the importance and opacity of this case, an extra four had been summoned. One of the four did not appear, and the coroner, without regard to any excuse he might offer, levied a forty-shilling fine. Of the remaining fifteen, a white-bearded elderly man named Walter Dutton did not appear willing to participate.

"Sir," he said, in answer to the name that had to be twice shouted at him, "my presence here is purposeless. I am deaf, sir. Stone deaf."

Harry Hodson did not hesitate. "Then you are excused," he whispered, in a voice so low that Kate hardly heard it. The deaf man rose from the bench and made for the door.

The coroner pounded his gavel on the table. "Mr. Dutton!" he roared, "take your seat or stand in contempt!" Chagrined, Mr. Dutton sat down once more and the coroner administered the jurymen's oath. Meanwhile, Kate sat nervously, her gloved fingers clutching the folds of her sedate dark-lavender dress.

"Do you go first?" Betsy whispered.

"Perhaps," Kate said, looking down at the pale, freckled face. Since she had discovered the body, it was likely that she would be the first to testify.

"Are you afraid?"

"A little. Are you?"

Agnes had not wished Betsy to appear in open court, especially in view of the fact that she alone was able to identify Tod's killer. In fact, for the days since Betsy's safe return, Agnes had not let her daughter out of her sight, and Edward himself had forsaken his other duties to stand guard over the house. But Coroner Hodson had required the little girl's presence, and Edward reluctantly endorsed his decision. Confronted by the coroner's authority and Edward's concurrence, Agnes could not refuse.

"Ye-e-s," Betsy said, apprehensive. She glanced over her shoulder as if she were looking for someone.

Kate took her cold hand. Tom Brock sat sullenly in a chair not fifteen feet away, on one side of P.C. Bradley. His hands and feet were manacled and he wore such an ugly look that Kate shuddered when she looked at him. On Bradley's other side sat the thin, anxious-looking man she knew must be James Napthen.

"You don't need to be afraid," she said reassuringly to Betsy. "Your mother and I are here with you, and Uncle Ned is just over there." Standing by the wall with Sir Charles, Edward lifted his hand to them. Betsy smiled shakily and waved back.

The inquest did indeed begin with Kate's testimony and she was called to sit in the witness chair at the coroner's right hand. The clerk, bearing a leather-bound Testament, got down off his stool and came around the table to administer the oath in a sing-songy voice.

"The evidence which you shall give to this inquest on behalf of our Sovereign Lady the Queen touching the death of Russell Tod shall be the truth, the whole truth, and nothing but the truth. So help you God."

Kate assented, and the coroner began his examination. His questions about the circumstances of her discovering the body were not new to her; they were the ones she herself would have asked had she been the coroner. She answered them simply, clearly, and with dispatch. Nevertheless, she was glad to be done and excused.

"There, you see?" she whispered to Betsy when she returned to her chair. "It was not so bad, after all."

"Not for you," Betsy said tremulously. She looked around once again. "You didn't have to say who it was that killed him."

48

The game ended, kings, queens, bishops, knights,
and pawns are all pell-melled with great confusion into the box.
—WILLIAM WATT
Epistles on the Sins of Gaming, 1711

Standing beside Charles against the wall, Edward scanned
the crowd, watchful, on his guard. Tom Brock had already
been arrested and was sitting with P.C. Bradley, whose handsome face was strained. After today's inquest, Brock would
be duly charged and brought to arraignment for his crimes.
James Napthen sat on the other side of Brock, similarly manacled. Betsy, pale and apprehensive, was seated between her
mother and Miss Ardleigh, in front of the coroner's table. The
police surgeon was just stepping off the stand, having followed
Miss Ardleigh in the order of testimony. Inspector Wainwright, more nervous and melancholy than usual, was standing
at the end of the bar wearing a weary look, for he had been
quite busy in the last few days. Chief Constable Pell was with
him, smiling and grand, his blue uniform brushed to a fare-
thee-well, his brass buttons shining proudly. Even Inspector
Wainwright's sergeant, Battle, was among the throng, as were
several other carefully-chosen men, all watching the proceedings with an air of nervous anticipation. But of them all, only
Edward, Charles, and Wainwright knew why they had been
summoned.

Harry Hodson looked up at Edward and gave an almost imperceptible sign. Edward stepped forward, thinking that he was gladder now of his relationship with the man than he had ever been before. He and Harry had not been boyhood chums, as had he and Artie, nor manhood friends, as he and Charles had grown to be; they were instead acquaintances whose professional relationship was based upon respect and admiration, each for the other's abilities. He had more than once seen Harry handle a difficult courtroom situation where justice and a man's life were suspended between a lie and a half-truth, and had watched him tease out the knot of fact that eventually unraveled the whole story. After Edward and Charles had worked out their theory of the present crime and the two of them had laid it before Harry, it was only a moment or two before the coroner said, in his gruff, blunt way, "Right, then. Let's get on with it, boys. Demmit, what the deuce are we waiting for?"

So now, when Harry summoned him to the witness chair, Edward stepped forward smartly, saluted, and gave his name and rank. Then, in simple language chosen to make the complex matter easier for the jury to understand, he told the story of Tod and Brock and the grain thefts, confirmed by the confession taken by P.C. Bradley from the prisoner James Napthen; of Artie's discovery of the grain stored in Napthen's barn at Highfields Farm and of his murder there; of the argument at Tod's cottage between Tod and an as-yet-unidentified man, with whom he was last seen before his death.

"It would appear," Edward said in careful summation, "that it was this unidentified man who murdered Russell Tod, or who has at the least withheld from the police material information regarding the cause of his death."

There was a stir along the bar, a subtle shifting of space and bodies as men rearranged themselves. A feeling of expectation began to rise in the crowd, as it does when the spectators of a chess match sense that checkmate is near, or the audience of a play feels the denouement draw near. Edward kept his eyes fixed upon Harry Hodson, who straightened the papers on the table before him and spoke with a judicious frown.

"But even if this man were to be identified, Constable Laken, it would appear that any accusation of him would be entirely circumstantial. Is that not the case?"

"Not entirely, sir," Edward said. "There was a witness to the argument, one who can identify the man whom we are seeking."

The room quieted, and Edward was suddenly conscious of how stifling it had become. In the front row, Betsy's face was white as paper, her mouth pinched and frightened; beside her, Agnes clutched the child's hand as if both of them were drowning. Someone at the bar fell suddenly into a fit of coughing and moved a pace or two toward the door to get some air. But several others closed against him, pressing for a better view of the coroner's table, and he was pushed back, still coughing.

"A witness," the coroner said musingly. He consulted his papers. "Would that be the child Elizabeth Oliver?"

"It would, sir," Edward said.

"Thank you, Constable," Harry replied. "You are dismissed. Call Mistress Elizabeth Oliver," he said to the clerk.

The clerk stood beside his stool and raised his tinny voice over the stir of the crowd and the rasping cough of the afflicted man, who had made yet another frustrated effort to push his way through the crowd to the door. "Call Mistress Elizabeth Oliver!"

Edward stood down. An earnest Betsy was sworn and took his place, her white ruffled pinafore neatly starched over a blue gingham dress, worn black boots carefully buttoned and polished with Edward's own boot black.

The coroner smiled in a kindly way over the half-rounds of his gold-rimmed spectacles. "P'rhaps it'd be best, Mistress Oliver, if you were to tell me what you saw, from the beginning. If I am unclear as to what you have said, I may interrupt you with a question, but I will endeavour to do that as little as possible." He leaned back and tented his pudgy fingers under a fold of chin. "You may begin."

Betsy began, in a thin, piping voice, to tell the story of her night-time ratting expedition to Highfields barn, accompanied by Mr. Browne. ("My owl, sir," she explained, in answer to the coroner's question.) While the crowd listened, riveted by her narration, she related what had happened to her: how she had been suddenly sacked and trussed and tossed into a wagon and later into a mound of hay in the shed; how she had heard the smith's boy proclaim her drowned an instant before the constable and Sir Charles Sheridan were about to liberate her; how she had been visited by Jemima Puddle-duck, whose maternal longings had led her to build a nest in the very same shed; how the sharp-chinned man with copper whiskers had got into an argument with the man with black whiskers and—

"Ah, but Mistress Oliver," the coroner objected, "if you were, as you say, bound and gagged and locked into the shed, how was it that you were able to see this black-whiskered man with whom the deceased argued?"

"I saw them out the crack," Betsy said.

"A large crack or a small?"

"A duck-size crack, sir," Betsy said, holding up her hands to demonstrate. A titter ran through the crowd. "The hole Jemima came and went through, you see."

"Ah, yes," the coroner said, and hid a smile. "Since you were able to witness this argument through this duck-size crack, p'rhaps you can tell us more about the gentleman with whom the deceased argued. He had black whiskers, you say?"

"Yes, sir," Betsy said. "And a limp. You see, sir—"

"Ah, a limp," said Harry Hodson, with the air of a man who was finally getting somewhere. "What else can you tell me of this black-whiskered man who limped?"

The crowd at the bar began to stir. Betsy glanced in the direction of the commotion and bit her lip.

The coroner leaned forward. "Don't be afraid, my child. Simply tell me what you saw."

"Yes, sir. Well, sir, he limped because he'd got a wooden leg."

"A wooden leg!" the coroner exclaimed, over the sudden noise of the crowd. He banged his gavel hard. "Silence!" he roared. "There will be order in this court!"

The crowd quieted somewhat, except for the group at the bar, where there seemed to be some kind of stir.

"Mistress Oliver," the coroner said, "please stand on your

chair and look out over the courtroom. Tell me if you see that man.''

The wispy clerk came around the table and gave Betsy his hand. Obediently, she climbed up on her chair, looked out over the crowd, and then suddenly pointed. ''There he is,'' she exclaimed, ''over by the bar! The man in the blue uniform.''

''That's ridiculous!'' the man shouted furiously. ''She's lying! She's only a child—she's not to be believed!''

Confusion rumbled like thunder in the courtroom. ''Let the record show,'' the coroner bellowed to the clerk over the din, ''that the witness has identified Dudley Pell, chief constable of the Essex Constabulary.''

49

Quod erat demonstrandum.
Which was to be proved.

—EUCLID

For Charles, to whom none of this was a surprise, the proceedings had taken on the quality of a stage drama. For the audience, tense with anticipation, the scene was fraught with the excitement of unexpected revelation. For the players, who had not been given a playbook but only the vaguest suggestion of what might unfold, there was uncertainty and great uneasiness. And for the directors and producers of the drama—Charles, Edward, Inspector Wainwright, and Harry Hodson—there was a great anxiety about what would be revealed, and whether the revelation would be of such strength that it would sweep events to their desired conclusion.

From his vantage point against the wall, Charles saw Wainwright, whose face wore a look of exquisite torture, instruct one of his constables to move through the melee and block the exit. Sergeant Battle, his jaw slack in utter astonishment and consternation, took two reluctant steps toward Chief Constable Pell and stopped, hands hanging in trembling helplessness. At Wainwright's whispered urging, he managed two more steps but seemed quite unable to raise his arms. The publican's fat wife, about to put a tray of washed glasses on the shelf behind the bar, gave a shriek of dismay and dropped the tray with a resounding crash.

The chief constable failed to notice the smaller dramas around him. He was too caught up in his own outraged innocence. "It's a falsehood!" he cried, gesturing with his fist. "The child is lying!"

Betsy stared at him. "I may be only a little girl," she said with enormous dignity, "but I know what I saw."

Beside Charles, Edward gave a muted cheer. "That's my girl!" he exulted under his breath. With the assistance of the clerk, Betsy climbed down from the chair and returned to her seat. As she sat down, her mother gathered her into her arms and pulled her close. For all her composure, Betsy buried her face against her mother and burst into tears.

Harry Hodson pointed his gavel at the chief constable and fixed him with a stony look.

"While your emotions are understandable in view of the serious accusation against you, I will tolerate no further outbursts. In due course, you shall be permitted, although not required, to testify before this inquest. Until that time, you will remain silent. Inspector Wainwright, confine the accused."

Wainwright nodded with a great sadness to Sergeant Battle. Battle, whose intention seemed to have been stiffened by the coroner's words, grasped Pell's arms. Another uniformed constable materialized out of the crowd to assist him.

"Get your hands off me!" Pell shouted, struggling against their hold. "I refuse to testify. It's absurd to require an officer of the law to demean himself by answering such a spurious accusation!"

The courtroom erupted into another noisy babble. The coroner pounded his gavel. "Order! There will be order, or I will clear this court of spectators." The room gradually became quiet as the two constables pinned the chief constable's arms behind him. Hodson scowled at Pell.

"This inquest is not a trial, so you will not be required to give evidence which might incriminate you. But you *will* be required to remain silent. Sergeant, do your duty!"

The sergeant and the constable maneuvered Pell, still resisting, to the seat between Napthen and Brock, which had been vacated by P.C. Bradley. The coroner shifted his bulk in his chair and faced the wide-eyed members of the jury, who coughed and fidgeted and moved their feet under his stern glance, shifting their astonished gaze from the prisoner to the coroner and back again.

Harry Hodson spoke with a ponderous solemnity, as if he were a headmaster speaking to a lower-form classroom. "Gentlemen, you have just heard a female child of tender years lay a most serious charge against a respected member of the community. In view of the standing and reputation of the accused, you may feel this accusation to be incredible and wish to discount it immediately."

He paused and pushed his lips in and out several times, as if he were considering what he had just said. Then he leaned forward and his tone became more stern. "However, it is my duty to remind you that you must hear it, and hear it without bias or prejudice."

"But she's a child!" Pell shouted. He would have jumped up, but Sergeant Battle, who was standing behind him, placed his hands on the chief constable's shoulders and brought him down again. Under the coroner's imperative glance, Pell subsided. Hodson continued his remarks to the jury.

"It is the tradition of the law, gentlemen, that guilt is established by the witness of a responsible individual or by the confession of the accused. However, not all crimes are committed in the presence of a witness, and not all accused persons are inclined to incriminate themselves. The crime must then be proven, if proven at all, by other evidence. This evidence—this *proof*—must be of such a persuasive nature that it leads a reasonable man to but one conclusion. To this end, gentlemen, I call the next witness." The coroner turned to the clerk. "Summon Sir Charles Sheridan."

Charles pushed himself away from the wall, picked up his portfolio and leather satchel, and was sworn. He seated himself in the witness chair.

The coroner adjusted his gold-rimmed glasses on his short nose and peered over them at Charles. "Sir Charles Sheridan, it is my understanding that you are an accomplished practitioner of the art of photography, and that you in fact received your knighthood for this skill."

"That is correct, sir."

"I further understand that you employ photography to record detailed scientific observations of antiquities and fossils, and that you have used these photographs to support your findings in learned papers presented to and favorably received by the Royal Academy."

"Yes, this is also true."

"And were you summoned to the place where the body of Russell Tod was discovered, shortly after the event, to assist Constable Laken in the investigation and to document the scene with your camera?"

"I was."

Harry Hodson settled back in his chair. "Tell us, then," he said, "what you observed and what you concluded from your observations."

"I took a number of photographs of Tod's body and of the scene of the crime." Charles reached into his portfolio and took them out. "These are the enlargements showing the body and the scene."

The coroner examined each print in turn, then handed it to the clerk, who dispatched it to the jurors. They handled the photographs with as much gingerly distaste as if they had been the dead man himself, then returned them to the clerk, who placed them once again before the coroner.

"And what, if anything," said the coroner when the last photograph was returned, "did you find remarkable about the body?"

"As the police surgeon indicated in his testimony," Charles said, "there was a depression in the area of the left temple. The skin was heavily bruised but not broken." Charles picked up a photograph and pointed to the wound, much enlarged. "The depression appears to have been created by a blow from a blunt object no larger than one inch in diameter."

"Such an injury would be consistent with a blow from the butt of a handle of some type of implement?"

"Quite so," Charles replied. "As there was no such implement at the scene, I concluded that it had been removed. The fatal blow would seem, therefore, to have been inflicted intentionally—or, at the least, the fatality intentionally concealed."

Harry Hodson's "I see" was judicious. "And did you find anything remarkable about the scene of the crime?"

"There was a small quantity of blood at the victim's mouth and nose and on the ground beneath his head. Since I surmised, and the police surgeon has confirmed, that the injury was almost instantly fatal, I concluded that the victim was struck and died at the scene." Charles glanced at Pell, who had arranged his face into a supremely contemptuous disregard, giving no hint that he was attending to the testimony.

"I see," Hodson said again. "Was there anything else?"

"Yes," Charles said. "Around the body there were a number of shoeprints impressed in the soft earth which was fortunately of a consistency that captured them in fine detail." He took up another photograph and pointed. "Among these shoe prints, there were a series of deep, round indentations which I took to be the heel prints of a woman's boot. You can see them here." He pointed again. "And here." He passed the photograph to the coroner, who examined it. "Upon reflection, however, I decided that this view was incorrect."

The coroner regarded him thoughtfully. "And what led you to this judgment, sir?"

"I made casts of all the impressions using calcium sulfate—plaster of Paris." Charles glanced at the jury to assess their understanding. Seeing a few puzzled looks and wanting to be sure they understood, he added, "Plaster of Paris is a powdery compound, which upon the addition of water becomes quite hard. It can be used to capture a negative impression of any surface onto which the fluid compound has been poured."

"And you have brought these casts with you?"

"Yes." Charles took the casts out of his satchel and set them on the table. This part of his testimony was complicated and he had been concerned about making it as straightforward as possible, knowing that juries often rejected scientific evidence simply because they did not understand it.

"There are five pairs of casts, three of which belong to the persons who visited the scene after the body's discovery: myself, Constable Laken, and Miss Ardleigh." Charles set them to one side. "I am confident of this identification because I made casts of the shoes themselves for the purposes of comparison," he added. "I can produce these if you wish."

"Enter the three identified pairs in evidence," the coroner said to the clerk, who numbered each in order with India ink. "You may provide the matching casts to the clerk after this hearing," he told Charles. "Please continue with your explanation."

Charles picked up another pair of casts. "These two prints belong to the victim and are matched by the casts of the shoes he was wearing." He set them down and picked up another pair, one in the shape of a shoe sole, the other oddly shaped, something like the heel of a boot or the leg of a stool protruding from a circular base of white plaster. "That leaves us with these two, which remain unidentified."

"Enter the victim's shoe prints, the unidentified shoe print, and the unidentified object," the coroner directed the clerk, who numbered them as he had the others. "Go on, sir."

"Once the casts were made, I studied, paired, and typed all the impressions, seeking a left and a right example of each. As I did so, however, I realized that the unidentified right shoeprint had, as it were, no mate. Each time it appeared, it was associated with this impression, which I originally took to be the heel print of a woman's boot or shoe."

"And your conclusions from this examination, sir?"

Charles paused. The courtroom had gone perfectly still, and the entire crowd seemed to have left off breathing. Pell's arms were folded across his chest, his gaze unwaveringly fixed upon some point over the coroner's right shoulder, disdain written on his features.

"I believe," Charles said, "that these impressions were in fact made by a man with a shoe on the right foot and a wooden stump in place of the left."

The taut stillness erupted into a loud buzzing chatter. Above it came a piercing "The copper's got a wooden leg!" from the publican's fat wife, followed by the publican's frantic shushing. The coroner picked up his gavel and used it violently, at last achieving a measure of quiet. He glared around the room as if ready to execute every spectator, then turned to Charles.

"That is all well and good, Sir Charles. But how can you

be sure that the man with the wooden leg did not visit the scene before or after the victim's demise?''

Charles glanced at the jury. He had their attention. He did not want to lose it. ''You know that leaves fall to the ground every year.'' One or two of them nodded wisely. ''And you also know that this year's leaves fall on top of last year's leaves.'' The man who had claimed to be deaf was leaning forward, intent, also nodding.

The coroner frowned. ''And what have leaves to do with footprints?''

''Only this, sir,'' Charles said. ''The footprints of persons visiting the site after the discovery of the body were intermingled. Where these particular tracks are found together with those of the victim and the man with the wooden leg, they are laid upon them—just as we would expect, having been made at a later point in time. This year's leaves, as it were, on top of last year's leaves.'' He picked up a photograph and pointed to the clear impression of several prints, including the curious round one, which had been partially obscured by Miss Ardleigh's and Edward Laken's prints. ''The footprints of the victim and the one-legged man, however, where they occur together, are intermingled. They were laid down at the same time—last year's leaves, as it were.''

The deaf man sat back and several jurors nodded with looks of understanding.

Hodson studied the photograph for a long moment, rubbing the bridge of his nose with his thumb so firmly that Charles wondered why it was not completely flattened. ''So,'' the coroner said finally, ''you believe that the victim and the one-legged man were at the scene together.''

''Yes,'' Charles said. He looked at Pell, who was examining his fingernails.

Hodson peered at Charles over his glasses. ''Are you able to shed any light on the identity of this man?''

''I believe so.'' Charles picked up the cast that he had once thought to be a woman's boot heel. ''This cast is a detailed and faithful reproduction of the lower four centimeters of a wooden leg. You will note that it appears to be fashioned with a protective cup of some sort on the tip, probably made of rubber. And if you look closely here''—he took out a pen and pointed at the cast—''you will see that this cup itself has split and separated.''

The coroner leaned forward and took the cast from Charles. ''It appears,'' he said thoughtfully, ''that a part of the rubber tip has been lost.''

''Exactly,'' Charles said. ''The man who accompanied the victim seems to have worn a wooden leg with a damaged rubber tip.''

Charles looked once more at Pell, who was no longer absorbed in his fingernails. His face had gone grey, his mouth was thinly pinched, and he was staring at Charles with a look of wild-eyed panic. The room was so quiet that Old Willie Hogglestock's cry of ''Fresh fish today,'' in duet with the gypsy's ''Boots fer tuppence,'' could be easily heard.

The coroner leaned back in his chair and for a very long time studied the cast in his hand. Finally he laid it down and spoke.

''Chief Constable Pell, I will not require you to give sworn testimony which may be used against you in a later trial. However, as the Crown's coroner and representative of Her Majesty the Queen, I require you to surrender certain evidence that may be matched against the cast taken at the scene. Do you elect of your own free will to testify before this inquest, or do you choose to yield up your leg?''

Dudley Pell, chief constable of the Essex Constabulary, gave a low moan and covered his face with his hands.

50

I have made many books about well-behaved
people. Now, for a change, I am going to make
a story about two disagreeable people, called
Tommy Brock and Mr. Tod.

—BEATRIX POTTER
The Tale of Mr. Tod

Bea stood beside the carriage that was taking them to the
railway station at Colchester, directing Pocket in the
placement of her bags and Hunca Munca's and Peter's cages.
Mrs. Tiggy-Winkle's basket she held in her hand.

"I am so dreadfully sorry to leave you and Bishop's Keep,"
she told Kate, "just as I was beginning to feel at home here.
I am concerned for the state of Mama's health, but I confess
that I can hardly bear the thought of returning to Bolton Gardens." Her face became mournful. "It feels as if I am returning to prison."

"I am sorry, too," Kate said, with genuine feeling. She
knew that Bea's presence was required at home, but that did
not make her regret the loss any the less, for they had grown
very close. Pocket finished stowing the baggage, came round
the carriage, and handed the ladies in. "I felt I had found the
sister I truly wanted."

"Well, you have done *that*, at least," Bea said. She settled
herself in the seat and put Mrs. Tiggy-Winkle's wicker basket
on the floor at her feet. "We must correspond often, Kate, and

you shall come to visit when you come up to London. I shall want your advice on getting my little books out into the world. And I feel a deep curiosity about how matters will turn out between you and Sir Charles.''

Kate raised her shoulders and let them fall. ''How matters will turn out? My dear Bea, I must confess to being curious as well.'' She had thought from the way he looked at her that afternoon at Agnes's that perhaps he had an interest in her. But it had been several days now, and not a word. And all that time, she had felt vaguely restless and discontented, despite the outcome of the inquest and the assurance that Agnes's pension would be paid. ''I understand that he has gone off to Chelmsford.''

''He may have gone to Chelmsford,'' Bea said with composure, as the carriage rattled off down the lane. ''But he has hardly departed for good. In any event, he has merely gone for the arraignment of the chief constable, has he not?''

Kate nodded. ''I believe it was scheduled for today. He is to give the same evidence, I understand, that he gave at the inquest.''

The source of her information was Amelia, who heard it from Lawrence. At the thought of Amelia and Lawrence, she smiled a little. She had spoken to Mrs. Pratt about the situation that morning. There was no reason why the two should not be permitted to see one another openly, so that they could stop creeping about. Mrs. Pratt was a dear soul, but rather too severe when it came to the maidservants.

Bea shook her head, obviously still thinking about the inquest. ''What a business.'' She made a *tch*-ing noise. ''Who in the world would have thought it possible that an officer of the law could be so villainous as to engage in theft and murder!''

''Apparently the theft was of long-standing, too,'' Kate said. ''Sir Charles told me after the inquest that Pell had been involved in grain-stealing for several years, and not only in this area, but to the south and west as well. As far as Chief Constable Pell was concerned, of course, the beauty of it was that he was so remote from the crimes themselves, and yet received quite substantial sums of money for providing both a means of shipping the grain and protection from the law."

"I find that wonderfully fascinating," Bea said. "Since he employed bailiffs like Russell Tod to manage the actual thefts, he was involved only in arranging for the shipment and sale of the stolen grain—and that through his wife's shipping business. Such an ingenious entrepreneur! To use his occupation as a police officer for the protection of criminals and to enhance his wife's shipping business—and to reap the profits from both ventures!"

"Indeed," Kate said ruefully. "And apparently most of those bailiffs never knew his identity. It was Russell Tod's bad luck that he was curious enough to go to Wivenhoe, the headquarters of the shipping firm, and nose out the real name of his employer. That is apparently why he was killed."

"Brock has confessed that he and Tod killed Sergeant Oliver?"

"Yes, and to kidnapping Betsy—although he is not quite clear as to what he and Tod planned to do with her. They seemed to think that if the law closed in on them, she might become necessary to their escape. In the meantime, they made it appear that she had been drowned in order to curtail the search and possible discovery."

"I am not sure I understand," Bea said, "to what extent other policemen may have been involved in the thefts."

"That is the saddest part," Kate replied. "When Edward realized that it was Pell whom Betsy had seen arguing with Russell Tod the night of Tod's death, and when Sir Charles determined that Tod had been accompanied to his death by a man with a wooden leg, they immediately laid their evidence before the coroner. He agreed that in view of the extraordinary circumstances, Superintendent Hacking should be notified at once. Hacking instructed Inspector Wainwright to begin an immediate investigation of Pell. The results are not yet complete, but Pell seems to have suborned at least three constables, each of whom profited from the crimes in their districts."

"I trust that Sergeant Oliver was not one of them," Bea said.

"No. Pell had sent Tod to approach him. The sergeant misled Tod into believing that he would join them. When Tod realized that the sergeant was gathering evidence to charge them with theft, he and Brock murdered him."

"And P.C. Bradley? Was he involved?"

"Apparently not," Kate said, "although Pell seems to have had his eye upon him as a possible recruit. Nor was Edward Laken." She smiled a little, thinking of Edward. "In fact, it was Edward's reputation for stubborn honesty that persuaded Pell to take him off the investigation. He told the superintendent that he wanted to handle it himself, and Hacking concurred—ignorant, of course, of Pell's real motive."

"And of course by taking the case himself, Pell thought he was ensuring that the sergeant's killers would not be discovered."

"Exactly. That is why he assigned P.C. Bradley to the case, knowing him to be a young officer who would take orders without question."

Bea sat back in her seat and looked out the window. "An amazing series of events," she said reflectively. "Coming to Bishop's Keep, Kate, we both wished for adventure. Have you had your fill of it yet?"

Kate laughed and patted her hand. "Enough to keep Beryl Bardwell occupied for some time. I fear, however, that she may never get her fill—if she intends to go on writing, that is."

"If?" Bea raised her eyebrows. "There is a doubt?"

"Not about writing itself," Kate said, and hesitated. The excitement of authorship, as she had discovered upon the publication of her first story, ran deep in her veins and would not be denied. But the writing of sensational stories, with their fragile, fainting heroines, dastardly villains, and neat moral lessons, was not as easy or appealing as it had once been. Was she running out of enthusiasm or inspiration? Or had her own experience become more complex, so that she could not so readily portray the world in terms of right and wrong?

"I think," she added, "that I should like to try my hand at a different kind of writing."

Bea smiled. "Less lurid and more literary?"

"Something like that," Kate replied. "Having to keep my work secret because I fear that some may be offended by it takes much of the pleasure from writing.'' She thought briefly of Sir Charles, imagining with an apprehensive shiver what *his* response would be if he knew about Beryl Bardwell.

Bea looked directly at her. ''Then don't keep it secret,'' she said. ''Your stories are exciting in their own right, if rather sensational. They are nothing of which you should be ashamed.''

Kate considered. There was merit in Bea's advice. If she were truly an independent woman, or if she truly believed in what she wrote, she would not fear others' reactions. If she did, then perhaps she was not as independent as she thought, or her stories as well worthy as she had believed.

''I myself am certainly aware of the problem,'' Bea went on ruefully, ''although it is not *I* who am concerned. It is Papa who would be sorely distressed at the thought of my writing for publication. It would utterly dismay him to see the Potter name appear on anything so commercial as a book. In his mind, publishers are at the same low level of society as pawn-brokers and policemen. He would be utterly horrified at the idea of my doing business with any of the three.''

Kate smiled. ''Well, then, what of you, Bea? What are *your* writing plans?''

Bea looked down at her hands in her lap with the self-deprecating smile Kate had come to know so well. ''I fear that is too grand a term for my little schemes, Kate. But I have learned from observing the discipline you bring to your craft. I shall set about making a book of my little Peter Rabbit story, and perhaps one about Jemima Puddleduck, and Mr. Tod and Mr. Brock, as well—a fox and a badger, if ever I saw them. You knew, didn't you, that the name Tod means *fox*, and Brock means *badger*?''

''No, I didn't know,'' Kate said, ''but it sounds like a wonderful story, about two very disagreeable men. But how shall you get around your father's difficulty with publishers?''

Bea considered. ''If I had the books printed up myself, Papa could not complain.''

''Of course!'' Kate cried. ''As miniatures, just the right size for children, illustrated with your marvelous drawings!'' She squeezed Bea's hand. "You see? Your trip to Bishop's Keep has not been wasted."

"Wasted?" Bea was half-amused. "You have whetted my appetite for more than the writing life, Kate. You have given me a taste of what it is like to live singly, obliged to no one. I am even more determined now to have my own cottage near Sawry, far from London and Bolton Gardens and Papa and Mama. And you and Beryl Bardwell shall visit me there, and we shall have even more adventures!"

"Agreed," Kate said.

But as she looked out the carriage window, she thought of Sir Charles and weighed her own single life against the feelings that had grown in her for him. She did not feel the kind of wistful, painful longing that the romantic novels associated with love, nor did she wonder frantically whether she had been too eager or too chilly in her demeanour toward him, or too bold or not bold enough. But she did wonder what he felt for her, if he felt anything at all. And she did think with affection about his concern for Agnes and Betsy, and with respect and admiration about the clear, insightful reasoning that had so neatly impaled Chief Constable Pell. And it did occur to her that perhaps she had lived singly almost long enough.

51

At last he rose, and twitch'd his mantle blue;
To-morrow to fresh woods, and pastures new.
—JOHN MILTON
Lycidas

"Well, I am pleased, I must say, Ned."

"I hoped you would be, Charles." Edward loosened the reins to let the horse have its head on the straightaway just outside Chelmsford and glanced at his friend beside him in the gig. "It's thanks to you, old friend."

Charles gave him a querying look. "How so?"

"If it had not been for the scientific evidence you brought Pell's guilt would remain in question. I doubt that he would even be arraigned, given the reluctance of the police bureaucracy to publicly launder its filthy linen."

"You don't think Betsy's testimony would be enough, then?"

"The word of a little girl, against that of a respected officer of the constabulary?" Edward gave a short laugh. "Murderer or no murderer, the man would remain free, to corrupt other young police officers."

Charles's face was sober. "I suppose you're right, although for some reason I had the impression that police corruption was confined to London."

"Hardly. Men are greedy everywhere." Edward spoke with the passion he felt in his heart. "But once Pell is convicted, all will be put on notice that such a thing will not be tolerated.''

Charles gave him a sideways glance. ''The constabulary needs men like you in positions of authority, Ned. I saw you talking with Hacking after the arraignment. Does the superintendent have something in mind for you?''

A cart came toward them and Edward pulled the horse to one side and gave it room to pass in the narrow lane. ''As a matter of fact,'' he said, ''he has begun to shift men about. Wainwright is to be promoted to Pell's position.''

''Bravo!'' Charles exclaimed. ''Now perhaps Wainwright will be able to install that telephone for which he has been chafing these past months.'' He turned to Edward, his face keen with interest. ''And you, Ned? Will you have Wainwright's place?''

Edward felt himself tighten inwardly at the thought. ''That is Hacking's idea,'' he admitted, lifting the reins again. It had not come at him like a bolt out of the blue, of course. Since his several interviews with Hacking and Wainwright about the investigation into Pell's corrupt practices, he had the impression that both of them thought highly of his abilities. Still, it was a considerable jump from constable to inspector, and there were several sergeants who might be expected to look askance at the promotion.

''And you?'' Charles inquired thoughtfully. ''What is *your* idea, Ned?''

Edward sighed. ''I don't know, Charlie. I am an ambitious man. I have long wanted a larger district and more responsibility. And the promotion would mean a substantial increase in income at a time when I shall want more money.'' He paused. ''I intend to wed Agnes, you know. I have asked and she has agreed, although we shall have to wait until the end of her mourning year.''

It seemed like a century away, the end of Agnes's mourning. Edward yearned for it to be over so he could make her his own, as she had been in his imagination so many times before. But he had waited a dozen years; he could wait as many months, with the certainty that in the end he would have her and their life together could begin.

He looked sideways to catch his friend's reaction. "You *did* know, or surmise?"

"I did," Charles said with evident satisfaction. "My heartiest congratulations, old chap. She's a fine woman."

"Yes," Edward said, and laughed a little, feeling like a schoolboy. "I was a fool once, and let Artie make off with her. I don't intend to be a fool again." He sobered. "But she's had a hard time of it these years, living on a constable's wage. It seems almost unconscionable to ask her to continue, if by accepting promotion I can bring her more."

Charles's voice was wry. "But some part of you is not delighted with the idea of moving to Colchester and becoming a police inspector?"

Edward could not help but laugh. "Isn't it queer? For years that was my ambition—to rise in the ranks, to gain in experience and opportunity, to make a name for myself. But now . . ." He shrugged, scarcely knowing what to make of the melee of feelings within. "Now, I'm not sure. Dedham is a fine village, quiet, orderly, a friendly place for children to spend their young years. And Napthen's little farm, or its like—that idea has its charms, too. I have saved enough money to have it, or nearly so."

"Ah-hah," Charles said lightly, smiling. "I thought as much. Agnes in the dairy, Betsy in the market garden, a rosy-cheeked little Edward helping his father herd the cows. An island of pastoral peace and placidity amid the tumultuous sea of modern civilization." He chuckled and fetched up a pair of lines that Edward recognized from his long-ago school days. " 'At last he rose, and twitch'd his mantle blue; to-morrow to fresh woods, and pastures new.' That's it, eh? A twitch of the blue mantle, and you're off to tend the sheep, with Milton under one arm."

Edward laughed again, helplessly. "When you put it like that— But yes, I suppose so. It certainly *is* peaceful. Agnes and I and our children would have a good life."

Charles turned to look at him steadily. "And yet, there is something alluring about the Colchester position, is there not? Aside from any personal ambition, that is."

"There is," Edward said, grateful to his friend for posing both sides of the question so clearly. "I suppose I could make a change in the way police business is done. If I were there, paying attention as attention should be paid, men like Pell might find it more difficult to do their dirty work under cover of the law."

"Suppose, man?" Charles clapped him on the back. "It's not a matter of supposition! A man of your brains, your integrity—you're what the constabulary needs, Ned."

"You're suggesting that I should do it?"

"I'm suggesting that you and Agnes ought to confer and decide together. If both of you honestly prefer the cows and cheeses, then have your farm. I shall gladly visit your rustic retreat and revel in the delights of the country. But if there is a question in your minds, give the Colchester position a go and see what happens. You can always have the farm, can you not?"

"We can," Edward said, feeling much easier. "I will bring it up to her this very evening." He turned to Charles. "And what of you, my friend?"

Charles, who was applying his attention to a blue tit in the hedge, did not answer immediately. "Well?" he replied after a moment. "What of me? Ah, yes, what of me?"

Edward felt his question had been bold, but Charles had, after all, offered him advice. And he had seen the unguarded way his friend looked at the lady when he thought no one was watching. He knew Charles to be a man who placed his affection deliberately, but not one to make speed. Miss Ardleigh appeared to fancy him, Edward thought, from his observations of her behaviour in Agnes's kitchen several days before. But one could not read a lady's heart in her face—especially a lady as independent-minded as Miss Ardleigh. That she had resisted marriage as long as she had was testimony to her commitment to the single life. Still, just a day or two ago, one of the Marsden kitchen servants had let it slip in the butcher shop that Bradford Marsden fancied her, and the Marsden name and title had to be an attractive incentive to any woman. If Charles did not look out, he might find himself left behind, as Edward had been a dozen years before. And that would be a great pity, Edward thought, remembering with a melting in his stomach Agnes's soft, yielding "yes" when she agreed at last to marry him.

"I have told you my intention," he said. "What is yours? With regard to Miss Ardleigh, that is."

Charles continued to consider the blue tit singing merrily in the tangle of sprouts growing out of a pollarded willow. At last he spoke.

"It is not my intention that is in question, my dear Ned. It is Miss Ardleigh's."

52

And what is better than wisedoom? Womman. And what is bettre than a good womman? Nothyng.

—GEOFFREY CHAUCER
The Tale of Melibee

"The business was safely done, was it?" Charles asked. He did not allude directly to the emeralds, but Bradford knew of what he spoke.

"Well and safely done," Bradford replied. "Mama is pleased."

He laid aside the paper he was reading, an engineering description of a new motor car built by John Henry Knight, a three-wheeler propelled by a rear-mounted engine with a single horizontal cylinder, powered by kerosene. He had been to see the car and talk with its developer, who was already soliciting the interest of investors. His face darkened with annoyance. "Mama is not at all pleased, however, with me."

Charles quirked an eyebrow. "No?" he asked, sitting in the leather chair beside the fire. "She does not approve of your interest in motor cars, I take it."

"Worse than that," Bradford said wryly. He opened a drawer, took out a leather cigar case, and carried it to Charles. "She does not approve of my choice of wives."

"I have my pipe, thanks," Charles said absently, shaking

his head to the cigars. "She does not approve of Miss Ardleigh?"

"Unfortunately, no." Bradford took a cigar, lit it, and sat down across from Charles. "It appears that the lady is too modern for Mama—and a little too common."

Charles gave an odd chuckle. "Too common, eh? Your mother has interesting standards."

Bradford pulled on his cigar. "It's very annoying," he said. The conversation with Mama had taken place several days ago, but he was still stinging from its effect. "It seemed to me the perfect answer to a vexing question. A lady of means, whose property adjoins that of the manor, whose person is reasonably attractive, and whose wit—" He waved his cigar. "You understand."

"I do, indeed," Charles said soberly. "Property, proximity, personableness. It would seem that your mother would applaud your choice."

Bradford sighed. "So it would. However, she does not. She has forbidden it."

"Owing to—?"

Bradford stood and paced restlessly to the window, which gave onto the green slope of the west lawn. Eleanor and Patsy, his younger sisters, just returned from Paris, were playing a savage game of croquet.

"Owing to Mama's assessment of the lady's costume and character," he said, feeling petulant. "She wears bloomers and rides a bicycle. And there was apparently some sort of rumour about her and the constable." He went back to the chair and dropped into it, stretching out his legs.

Charles did not respond immediately. When he did, his voice was serious. "And do you intend to respect Lady Henrietta's interdiction?"

Bradford laid his head back against the chair and frowned at the ceiling. "Respect it? Of course I will respect it. I could not marry someone of whom Mama and Papa did not approve. Mama would make life impossible for us both, and Papa would very likely cut off my allowance."

"And what of your heart?" Charles's question was mild.

"My heart?" Bradford gave a short laugh that expressed

only a small part of the bitterness he felt. "Is any man in my station allowed to have a heart? If I am to marry, it will be someone like Hermione Poulett or Madeleine Dyke, neither of whom has the wit of a windlestraw." He pulled on his cigar and blew out a puff of blue smoke. "*If* I marry, which I doubt," he added, staring up into the cloud. "The idea of it puts me in a cursed funk. I cannot abide a witless woman."

Charles stood. "I take it, then, that you did not call on Miss Ardleigh, as you planned?"

Bradford shook his head gloomily, reflecting that he had acted a cad. "Sent her a note saying I'd been called to London. Coward's way, of course." He sighed. "But what could I do?"

"What indeed?" Charles said.

Bradford stirred uncomfortably. "My most immediate problem is how to repay the money you loaned me."

"Not to worry," Charles said. He seemed to study the fire. "I presume that you would not take it amiss if I should call on Miss Ardleigh?"

Bradford stared. "You?" He caught cigar smoke in his windpipe and began to cough. "*You?*"

Charles turned, half-smiling. "Is it strange that I, too, should find Miss Ardleigh attractive?"

Bradford felt suddenly and uneasily envious. "Strange?" He coughed again. "Not strange, old chap. Utterly mystifying." He went to the sideboard, unstoppered the whiskey decanter, and poured two glasses. "I had given you up for a bachelor—and now to find that you fancy the very lady to whom I had yielded my heart!"

Charles's eyes were merry. "If you will pardon me, Marsden, your heart has the constancy of a crocodile—and about as much tenderness. And I have remained a bachelor only until I found a woman worthy of my interest."

Bradford turned, glasses in hand. "Worthy of your interest! Charlie, my dear fellow! She's a peach, as the Americans say. A good woman. A fine woman. The two of you should be damned happy together. If she'll have you, that is." He handed one of the glasses to Charles. "But what of the constable? Are you not concerned about their rumoured connexion?"

"The constable is to marry the widow of the murdered sergeant," Charles said.

"So the way is clear for you." Bradford lifted his glass. "But she still may not have you. She's a deuced independent woman. Worst I've ever met. And too clever by half. But I'll drink to your success, Charlie, my boy."

"Thank you," Charles said, and they drank.

A Note About Beatrix Potter

The much-beloved illustrator and author of many delightful children's stories, Beatrix Potter lived a suffocating early life, much as she describes it in *Death at Gallows Green*. Twenty-nine at the time this fiction takes place, she was still a creature of her Victorian parents and increasingly aware of her isolation. "I wonder why I never seem to know people," she wrote sadly in her journal. "It makes one wonder whether one is presentable." She spent her time avidly pursuing interests in photography, drawing, and mycology, surrounding herself with the animals she loved.

But by the late 1890s, Beatrix began to pursue the publication of *The Tale of Peter Rabbit*, written for the child of her former nursemaid in 1892. After the little book was rejected by six publishers, she decided to publish it herself, selling copies to friends and relatives at one-and-twopence a copy. In 1902, Frederick Warne & Co. offered to publish it, and any other stories she might write. During the next ten years, Beatrix wrote and drew, became engaged to her publisher (who tragically died), and began to spend more time in the Lake District near Sawrey. She eventually used her writing income to buy a little farm there, and finally, at the age of 47, married William Heelis, a local solicitor. For the thirty years of their marriage, she managed their farm, raised sheep, and lived out the fantasies of her early life. But she didn't write any more stories.